SINFUL SACRIFICES

KRISTINE MASON

This book is dedicated to the Cleveland winters. You're horrible. Cold. Gray. Unforgiving. You give me seasonal depression and little joy. Except…you did help inspire this book. I also love watching the snow fall, curling up under a blanket by a warm fire, and eating comfort foods with my family. I suppose I don't hate you, and that you do have a few good qualities. But do you have to stick around for so long?

Acknowledgements

Thank you, Mark (my darling husband), for giving me such fantastic ideas for this book. I know you don't like brainstorming, but you're very good at it! I'd like to thank Jamie Denton for being a fabulous critique partner and friend. I'd also like to thank my editor, Tessa Shapcott, my proofreader, Sherry Fundin, and my talented cover artist, Elle J Rossi of EJR Digital Arts.

1

I remember the time I was kidnapped and
they sent a piece of my finger to my father.
He said he wanted more proof.
—Rodney Dangerfield

Interstate 71, West Salem, Ohio
Friday, January 20ᵗʰ, 7:43 a.m. Eastern Standard Time

A GUST OF wind pushed the school bus to the right. Brennan
Williams glanced up from the game he'd been playing on his
cell phone and toward the window where his best friend, Tyler,
slept. While Imagine Dragons blasted in his ears, the bus barreled
north along the interstate slicing through Ohio. Fat white snowflakes dropped in a steady sheet, blocking out the gray morning
sky and blurring the bare, skeletal trees.

Brennan looked to the front of the bus, where Matt Shultz,
assistant lacrosse coach and one of Newhouse Academy's health
and physical education teachers, rose from the seat behind the
driver. Coach Shultz put on a pair of leather gloves and said
something to the bus driver. He then leaned over the aisle and
spoke to his cousin, Joel Shultz, who didn't work for the boarding
school, but who had come along as one of their chaperones. He

was also a former ski instructor who'd recently moved back to Ohio from Colorado, which made him a great addition to the ski trip. Since Brennan had only hit the slopes twice and had spent most of those times falling, and not all of the guys on the lacrosse team could ski, having an instructor with them was a bonus.

The two men glanced to Wayne Pembroke. The head coach sat in the second row, reading from a tablet. When Coach Shultz caught Brennan staring at him, the corner of the man's mouth slid into a strange smile and his eyes glittered with excitement. Instead of returning the smile, Brennan's skin crawled with unease, which was ridiculous. This was Coach Shultz. Brennan and the other guys on the team liked the twenty-five-year-old. He was cool, good looking, drove a kickass Camaro and had a hot girlfriend. Plus, he always gave out A's in his class.

Brennan yanked out his ear buds and decided hunger had him seeing things. Knowing his mom had packed snacks for him, he reached for the backpack he'd stored beneath his seat and pulled out a granola bar.

When he looked up again, Brennan froze. He locked his gaze onto the gun Coach Shultz pointed at Coach Pembroke's head. A silent scream lodged in his throat. His heart racing, his chest tightening with fear, he nudged Tyler.

"What, dude?" Tyler yawned. "Why'd you wake—?"

Shultz fired. Red mist shot from Coach Pembroke's head as blood and bits of brain and flesh hit the window and the back of the first seat.

Brennan's ears rang from the explosion. Tears blurred his vision. Stunned and scared, he gaped at the dead coach. Ignoring the pandemonium and the terror-filled cries from the others, he concentrated on the blood dripping from Coach's head, and the way it streamed down the rubber tread in the aisle and toward the back of the bus.

Tyler gripped his arm and tugged. "Get down."

Brennan blinked. He leaned forward with Tyler and opened his phone. He quickly closed down his game, then began texting his dad.

"Sit up and raise your arms," Shultz shouted. "And shut the fuck up!"

The bus went silent. Heart pounding, Brennan hit send, straightened and lifted his arms in the air.

Joel also had a gun, but took Shultz's when he passed it to him. Shultz held up a canvas bag. "Listen well and you might survive. I'm going to come around and collect phones. Keep your arms raised until I get to you. If any one of you tries to attack me, Joel will shoot you." He lifted Coach Pembroke by the back of his coat until they could all see his bloody, damaged head, along with the coach's lifeless eyes and the haunting shock they'd permanently hold.

Brennan swallowed back bile and looked away. He squeezed his eyes shut and fought to keep from crying, to stay strong and not look like a pussy in front of the others. He was sixteen, not six. Almost a man, and yet, right now, he wanted his mom. Though he had her by a foot and probably sixty pounds, he needed her arms around him, wanted to inhale her familiar flowery smell and pretend this wasn't happening. That he'd simply fallen asleep and was having a nightmare.

"Give me the fucking phone, Demko," Shultz shouted.

Brennan opened his eyes just as their coach easily hauled Chris Demko, the smallest, skinniest and fastest member of their team, from his seat. "I swear, I left it in my dorm," Chris cried, his pubescent voice cracking. "Please, I swear."

Shultz pounded his meaty fist into Chris's stomach. The kid's knees buckled, but Shultz kept him standing only to backhand him across the face. Blood burst from his teammate's lips and sprayed along Shultz's mouth and nose. The coach spat on the floor, then used his coat sleeve to wipe away the blood. "Last warning," he said.

"He's not lying." Alex McGuire, a senior and their team captain, stood but quickly sat again when Joel trained the gun on him. "Chris was complaining about it to Coach...Pembroke," he said, then cleared his throat. "But Coach wouldn't let him run back to get it."

"Since dead men don't talk, and I don't trust any of you, I'm going to assume you're all liars. Hands up and spread your legs," Shultz said to Chris, then began patting his arms and legs. "Okay, Demko. Looks like you're telling the truth. But you didn't mention the tablet in your bag." He chuckled. "That's right. When Joel and I were going through everyone's gear looking for drugs and alcohol, we took anything you might be able to use to contact the police."

He shoved Chris back into his seat and moved on to the next kid. After he collected their phones, he opened Joel's window. "How're we looking?" he asked the driver.

"Hang tight. A car is passing us." Minutes ticked by. Frigid air and snow whipped in through the window and immediately chilled the bus's interior. "You're good," the driver finally said.

Shultz tossed out the bag. Brennan looked to the window, but between the snow, the speed and height of the bus, he couldn't see where it had landed.

The window closed. "Everybody pay attention." Shultz took one of the guns from Joel. "Obviously, there's been a slight change in plans. We won't be going to New York, there'll be no skiing and Coach Pembroke is no longer in charge." He pressed a gloved thumb to his chest. "I am. If all goes to plan, you'll be home within days." He focused on the team captain, Alex McGuire. "So don't be a hero. Don't try to defy me or my crew. Just do as you're told and no one will get hurt."

The bus slowed and veered right. Through the haze of snow Brennan read the green exit ramp sign: Lodi. Although born and raised in the Columbus area, his dad was a Browns season ticket holder. He'd been to Cleveland more times than he could count and knew Lodi was about an hour outside of the city. Since the trip to the Twin Peaks ski resort in New York was supposed to take about four hours and they were only an hour into the drive, this meant no one would know Shultz and his crew had hijacked the bus until around noon, when they'd miss their scheduled time of arrival. Even then, why would anyone suspect such a thing?

Shultz and Joel continued to face them as they both kneeled in their seats. Shultz lowered his weapon slightly and shifted his gaze out his window as they rolled to a stop at a red light. "Don't be dumb," Shultz said as he looked to the snowplow idling to the left.

Brennan quickly glanced over his shoulder. A tractor trailer and other cars were stopped behind them. He then stared at the gas station to the right, along with the McDonald's next to it. Help wasn't far away, but with two guns aimed at them, they all kept silent. He wouldn't be dumb. He had no intention of dying and wouldn't be the reason someone else was killed.

The light turned green and the bus continued at a slow pace. The inclement weather made visibility bad as snow accumulated on the road. Minutes later, the driver turned right, but Brennan wasn't able to read the street sign. After passing a travel center and truck wash, the landscape turned desolate. For the next few miles, there were no homes or businesses, only bleak fields of snow or thick patches of woods, and nothing but gray skies.

Tyler hit his leg. Brennan looked down at the folded knife his friend had slipped from the pocket of his khaki cargo pants. Fearing what would happen if Shultz saw, he pushed Ty's hand, hoping he'd catch a clue and put it away. Later, hopefully, they'd have the chance to talk and come up with a plan. There were fifteen of them, and only three bad guys. The blade was small, but if used properly, it could incapacitate one of the men and give them an opportunity to grab their gun. If they could use the weapon against Shultz and his guys, they could find a way to escape.

The driver veered the bus to the right. The road narrowed and there wasn't a car in sight, but there were a few homes set back at the end of long driveways, then, once more, nothing but trees or a massive blanket of snow. Tyler hit his leg again and nodded to the left. Brennan looked over the head of Chris Demko, who sniffled and wiped his bloody mouth, just as the bus passed a wooden sign reading, *Village of Fred Glen*. Who the hell named a village after a guy named Fred? The childish question shouldn't be on his mind, not given the situation. But there it was, for whatever reason. Maybe because he wanted to be a kid again, back in his bedroom at home, playing with a Lego set. Or maybe he just wanted to be anywhere else but here.

He shifted his gaze to the dead coach, then to his hand where he fisted the granola bar. His stomach churned. Not with hunger, but utter dread.

"Almost there, boys," Shultz said, facing the front windshield.

Tyler leaned close. "I know where we are," he whispered. "We're totally screwed, man."

"Why?" Brennan asked, concentrating on the men.

Shultz turned back to them and smiled. "Any of you ever hear of Ottawa Lake Park?" When no one answered, he shrugged. "Doesn't surprise me. Your rich parents wouldn't lower their standards and make Medina, Ohio, a vacation destination." Shultz sighed and slid his gaze to the window where the bus passed several small darkened cottages and a closed gas station. When they drove by a country store with a sign stating the place was closed for the season—*see you in May*—Brennan's hope hung by a thread. If this was a summer vacation spot, Ty was right, they were screwed.

"Here's a little history lesson for you," Shultz continued. "Ottawa Lake was created about thirteen thousand years ago when massive sheets of glacial ice melted and left a depression along Ottawa Creek, making it the largest natural lake in the state. Two thirds of the lake is surrounded by forest. We just passed through the Village of Fred Glen and are making our way to the Village of Ottawa Lake. I hate to break it to you, boys, but don't even think about running off and looking for help. You won't find any at this time of the year. Ninety percent of the houses you'll see are unoccupied during the winter months. The other ten percent?" He grinned. "If you do escape, good luck finding them. The temperature is supposed to drop to zero tonight. With the wind chill, it'll feel like nineteen below. Did you know under those circumstances you can develop frostbite within thirty minutes?" He shook his head. "Now, there *is* the lake. If you don't want to risk the woods, you could always go that route. The lake's frozen, but some areas might be a little thin, and if you break the ice and go under, you've got about an hour to survive. That is if you find your way back to the surface and get out of the water." He smiled. "In other words, do like I say and don't be dumb. Stay where we tell you, and you'll eventually get out of this."

"What is *this*?" Alex asked.

Shultz's smile fell as his eyes narrowed. "This is a kidnapping."

"You're gonna use us for ransom," Simon Thorpe, their team goalie, said as he folded his massive arms across his broad chest.

"Yes, genius, that's exactly what we're gonna do. And once we have the money, you can all walk. Until then, we play by my rules."

The bus turned left and lurched along a narrow single lane road. Branches from overgrown trees scraped along the side of the bus. The ride became bumpy, making Brennan wonder if this was even a legit road, or if it was a dirt path when not covered with snow. The thick patches of bushes and trees gave way to an open area. Brennan leaned into the aisle to look out the front window. Ahead, a chain link fence gated off buildings and a...roller coaster. He met Shultz's gaze. The man smiled again.

"Did I mention where we're staying?" he asked as two men, wearing ski masks and dressed in white and gray camouflage snow pants and coats, tried to force open the gate. But the heavy snow allowed them to only move the fence a foot or two. Shultz swore and opened the bus door. "Stand back!" He came back and closed the door. "Ram the gate."

The driver, a skinny guy around Shultz's age, glanced over his shoulder. "You sure you want to do that? What if we can't repair it?"

"He's right," Joel said. "If the cops figure out where we are, they could storm the place."

"They could storm it whether the gate is open or not. But that's not going to happen, because they won't find us." Shultz clapped the driver on the shoulder. "Ram it."

"Okay," the driver said, reversed the bus, then drove forward.

As the gate gave way, so did the last shred of Brennan's hope. Fear filled his stomach and took root in his chest. How would the police know where to find them? They could track their phones and tablets, but would locate the devices buried beneath the snow along I-71. Visibility had been bad. Would any of the drivers they'd passed after exiting the freeway remember seeing a school bus?

The snow churned beneath the bus's tires. One of the two men in camouflage had a rifle slung over his shoulder and stood near what must have once been a ticket booth since there were a few rusted turnstiles still standing. Wanting to take it all in and learn the layout of the area, Brennan looked in the opposite direction. He swallowed hard and stared at an eerily imposing wooden roller coaster. Its hills were tall, but the trees growing through the tracks were even taller. In front of the coaster stood a couple run-down buildings. He glanced away from the coaster to the guys sitting near him. But they were also focusing on their surroundings. Hopefully, they too had the same thing in mind—escape.

Tyler gained his attention and pointed toward the left front window. A shiver ran up Brennan's spine as he stared at an old wooden building. The porch sank. The handrail was rusted and missing in places. Several of the windows were boarded or broken. Against the dreary palette of white and gray, faded blue, yellow and red letters stood out in stark contrast across the front of the building. The F and the S were missing, but he could clearly tell that at one point the building had been labeled *Fun House*. It didn't look fun. It looked like something out of a bad horror movie. Next to the fun house were the remains of another building. Its jagged wooden posts jutted from the snow, and near it was a small car that reminded him of the bumper cars he'd gone on when he was a kid.

When the bus swung right, a large Ferris wheel came into view. Rising through its center was a tree, whose branches reached through the wheel as if Nature was grabbing hold of it to reclaim this land for herself. As they made their way deeper into their prison camp, there were other buildings—all wooden. With the way its walls bowed out and the roof was flattened, one looked as if a giant had stepped on it. Several feet away stood a small stand, a sign reading *Waffles* hung haphazardly on its front. They drove past the remains of a men's room, then metal tracks. Brennan once again imagined that giant picking up a roller coaster, then twisting and bending it.

He used to enjoy watching dystopian and disaster movies, and this place reminded him of what the world might look like if aliens landed and tried to exterminate humans, or if people exterminated one another out of fear, hate and greed. There was nothing good here, nothing that brought joy or peace. The twisted metal, broken glass and decaying buildings were a sad reminder that happiness was fleeting, that in the blink of an eye the world could change and become a bad place.

Despite the chill, his armpits became damp. He'd been afraid before, but nothing like this. Kidnapping. He'd watched enough movies and TV shows to know they were in serious trouble. Although he knew movies and television weren't real life, the reality was Coach Pembroke was dead. That was real. The guns the men carried were real.

The bus came to a stop near a large building which, like all the others, had seen better days. Shultz stood and cleared his throat. "Here's how this is going to work." He pointed the gun at their goalie. "Thorpe, I want you, Williams and Huneck to take Pembroke's body off the bus. Drag him to the Ferris wheel and bury him in the snow. There're coyotes out here. I don't want them sniffing around our camp. If they do and go after Pembroke, that's a wide open area and we'll be able to see them coming."

Logan Huneck dropped his gaze to the coach's dead body. "W-why me?"

"The rest of you will help unload the gear," Shultz continued without answering Logan.

"Can you at least tell us where we are?" Alex asked.

Shultz shrugged. "Ottawa Lake Amusement Park. Back in the day, this place was supposedly the shit. It was shut down almost forty years ago after being in business for one hundred years." He looked to the Ferris wheel and grinned. "Creepy, huh?" He waved the gun. "Okay, let's go. Thorpe, Williams and Huneck, grab your hats and gloves and head out first. The rest of you stay seated until they're off the bus."

"Wait!" Logan stood. "Please, have someone else help with Coach."

"No. I need muscle on this. Don't be a pussy. Just do it."

Simon and Brennan also rose from their seats. While Brennan had no desire to touch a dead body, let alone bury it, he didn't trust Shultz or the other men. Between his folks and what he guessed the other guys' parents were worth, the combined total would likely be a billion dollars or more. These men wanted money. They wouldn't go through all this trouble to walk away with nothing, and he doubted any of them would hesitate to shoot anyone who stood in their way—including a teenage kid.

Simon rested his hand on Logan's shoulder. "Take it easy. I'll take his arms and Brennan will get his legs." He glanced to Brennan. "Okay?"

Brennan nodded and set his backpack on the seat. "You'll bring my bag?" he asked Tyler as he retrieved his hat and gloves.

"Yeah. Be cool, man," Ty whispered. "Those other guys outside look like frickin' mercenaries."

The only mercenary Tyler might have seen was in a movie or on a video game. But Brennan understood what his friend meant: these men would shoot first and not even bother to question it later.

Once he had his coat zipped, and his hat and gloves were on, he approached Coach Pembroke. Logan had already exited the bus and stood outside with one of the men in camouflage. Simon stepped to the front of the bus and nodded to Brennan.

"Ready?" the goalie asked.

Brennan dragged in a deep breath and glanced down at the seat where Coach lay and, avoiding looking at his bloody head, focused on the man's boots. "Ready."

Simon gripped the coach's wrists and pulled him from the seat. Once his boots hit the aisle, Brennan bent and grabbed the man's ankles. Together, they began carrying him. When Brennan reached the opened door, the blast of icy air momentarily took his breath away and he regretted not wearing a scarf or ski mask. His cheeks already prickled and burned from the cold wind, as if the gust carried tiny pointed icicles.

One of the camouflaged men handed Logan a shovel. "Go!"

Brennan's arms, back and legs strained as he and Simon trudged through less than a foot of snow. Logan had taken the lead, and the gunman trailed behind them. Brennan glanced to Simon, whose narrow gaze was on Logan's back. He'd seen that angry, bitter, 'I want to kick your ass' look before, both on and off the field. While Brennan couldn't blame the goalie, he tried to tamp down his resentment toward Logan. None of them had been prepared for anything like this. By the time it was over, he suspected many of his teammates would show sides of themselves he hadn't witnessed before—strength, weakness, cowardliness. He wanted to be one of the strong ones, but he also wanted to survive.

When they were about ten feet from the Ferris wheel, the gunman ordered them to stop and dig. After he and Simon rested Coach's body in the snow, Simon held his hand toward Logan. "Give me the shovel."

While Logan handed it over, Brennan picked up a broken wooden plank sticking out of the snow, then began using it to help Simon clear a shallow grave. As he dug, perspiration dampened his armpits and made his scalp itch.

"Enough," the gunman ordered. "Put him in and cover him."

His breath labored, his face cold and wet from the falling snow, Brennan turned to Logan, who stood with his arms crossed over his chest. He stared at the coach, tears streaming down his blotchy red cheeks.

"Logan," Simon panted. "Help us move him."

Logan shook his head. "I can't believe…" He drifted his gaze to the gun the camouflaged man held, then to the path carved out between an overgrowth of bare bushes and saplings. "I can't be here. I can't."

Though Logan had been with the team since freshman year and he'd had a few classes with the guy, Brennan didn't know him well. Logan kept to himself, never talked much and spent his off time holed up in his private dorm room playing video games. But Logan played great defense with the long pole, and was fast and aggressive on the field, which made him an okay guy. And if he didn't want to hang out and have fun with the team, or join in any of the school's other activities, that was his business. Except right now, Logan had to participate and be a team player. If they were going to survive this, they all needed to stick together and have one another's backs.

"I can't," Logan repeated, his eyes wild with fear.

Worried the guy would freak, try to run for it and get shot, Brennan stepped over to the dead body. "I've got it."

"No," the gunman said, his eyes brightening with amusement. "He can do it."

Brennan tensed, held his breath and stared at Logan, hoping to God he'd man up and do as he was told. But Logan shook his head, took a few steps until he stood a foot away from Brennan. "I-I don't belong here. I…" He ran.

"Hey," the gunman shouted as he raised his rifle and aimed it at Logan's back.

"Don't!" Brennan tackled Logan, who kicked and punched and tried to break free.

"Let me go!"

He rolled Logan until he had him pinned. "Don't be dumb,"

he whispered. "Remember? What you did is dumb. Look where the gun is aimed."

Eyes wide, he looked over Brennan's shoulder.

"Get the fuck off him." The man kicked Brennan in the side, knocking him into the snow. He leaned forward, gripped Logan by the front of his coat and hauled him to his feet as if the six foot, one hundred and seventy five pound kid weighed nothing. "You're going to bury him with your bare hands," he said, dragging him over to the dead body. "Alone." He held him with one hand, cocked back, then sent his fist into Logan's face. "That's for not listening." He hit him again. "That's for making me stand in the cold."

"Stop," Simon shouted when the man raised his fist a third time. "Please, just let him do it."

The man kneed Logan in the stomach and let him go. "Take off your gloves and get to work."

Groaning and clutching his midsection, Logan dropped to his knees. But he made no move to obey.

"Hey!" The other camouflaged man kicked up snow as he rushed over, his rifle raised. When he reached them, he aimed his weapon at Brennan's chest. "This doesn't have to be hard."

Heart racing, Brennan lifted his arms over his head. "No, sir."

"So what's the problem?"

"Crybaby over here don't want to do his share of work," Gunman Number One replied in a slow drawl.

"Doesn't surprise me." He knocked off Logan's hat, then gripped him by the hair. "You rich boys don't understand what it's like to work. To go without. Have you ever gone to bed hungry? Not by choice, but because there was no money to buy food?" He forced Logan to his feet by his hair. "Have you ever worked until your hands bled? Until you were sweaty, bruised and exhausted?" He released Logan's hair and took his hand. After ripping off a glove, he looked at the kid's palms and knuckles. "Soft hands. Do you get manicures?"

Gunman Number One chuckled, revealing crooked, stained

teeth. "All of 'em probably do." He nodded to the snowy grave. "Which is why I was wantin' him to finish the job."

Gunman Number Two rolled his eyes. "Can we teach him life lessons once we're inside? I'm freezing my nuts off out here."

"I thought your ex-wife took your balls when you guys split."

Gunman Number Two laughed and shook his head. "Fuck you, Woody." He shoved Logan toward Coach Pembroke's body. "Get it done. I don't want to be forced to show my buddy over here that I have the balls to shoot you in the fucking head, understand?"

Sniffling and wiping his bloody nose and mouth, Logan nodded. He took off his other glove, then bent down and gripped Coach's wrists. He dragged the man through the accumulating snow until he reached the grave. When Simon went to help him roll the body inside, Woody lifted his weapon.

"Uh-uh," he grunted. "Crybaby's got this."

Logan looked up at Woody, this time not with fear, but hatred. Fortunately, he kept his mouth shut. Brennan wasn't sure about these men. He understood their agenda was money related, but he didn't like the way they were taking pleasure in their misery. Especially Logan's.

After Logan shoved the body into the grave, he used his bare hands to push the snow over the corpse. Within seconds, they turned bright red. "Can I at least use the shovel?"

Woody shook his head. "You seem to be doin' just fine."

Blood from Logan's nose dripped into the snow. He pushed one of the piles Brennan and Simon had shoveled over Coach's head. Minutes passed, how many Brennan wasn't sure, but he guessed about ten. During that time, Logan had managed to cover the dead man's body. Breathless, he stopped and rubbed his wet red hands.

"About damned time," Gunman Number Two said. "Let's get to the ballroom and warm up."

Logan stood and looked down on the grave. Hands trembling, he made the sign of the cross.

"Oh, Christ," Woody said, then walked over and hit Logan in the stomach with the butt of the rifle. When he dropped to the ground, Woody laughed. "Save your prayers for yourself." He lifted the gun to hit him again. Logan coughed and raised his hand to ward off the blow, but Simon dove forward to stop Woody.

In seconds, both men had their rifles pressed against Simon's chest. "Please," Simon began. "He did what you wanted."

"So?" Woody half shrugged. "Shultz needs you boys to know we ain't messin' around. He made it clear he wants an example to be made."

Brennan's stomach dropped. He glanced away from his teammates and the men and over to the bus. The rest of the team stood outside it. Shultz, Joel and the driver were with them, each carrying a gun.

"What are you waiting for?" Shultz shouted, his voice echoing off the buildings and trees.

Woody grinned. "Move out of the way, big guy. I wasn't planning on killing you...today."

Simon shifted his nervous gaze to the rifles and scooted away from Logan. "You don't have to kill anyone."

"I know." Woody cocked his head. "But I really want to," he said, and fired the gun.

2

FBI Cleveland Division, Cleveland, Ohio
Friday, January 20ᵗʰ, 3:43 p.m. Eastern Standard Time

UNEASE WORKED THROUGH Summer Raines. Her boss, Special Agent in Charge Dave Coldwell, sat at the head of the briefing room table, his expression grim and worried.

"In a moment, we're going to have a conference call with Lieutenant Jack Nelson from Ohio State Highway Patrol," Dave said, then asked Special Agent Lauren Adams, who sat next to him, to turn on one of the monitors hanging from the wall.

Instead of looking at the screen, Summer glanced toward the windows of the Lakeside Avenue office. Unfortunately, a whiteout prevented her from seeing Lake Erie or the neighboring buildings. God, she hated Cleveland's weather, and couldn't wait to be on a plane Sunday morning, and, by noon, sitting poolside at her parents' Bradenton, Florida, home. She needed a break, not only from Northeast Ohio's gray skies, and cold and snow, but also her position as Assistant Special Agent in Charge. The long hours—the stress—exhausted her, and she needed a week to refill the well.

"What's this regarding?" Summer asked, refocusing her attention on Dave.

"There's been a kidnapping."

"Adult or child?"

Dave let out a tired sigh. "Could be both. Nelson called our division because he believes the bus was traveling northbound and could possibly be in our jurisdiction."

Bus? Before Summer could ask him to explain, the phone rang. Dave hit a key and the monitor came to life.

A man she placed in his mid-forties, and dressed in a standard gray uniform shirt and black tie worn by Highway Patrol officers, filled the screen. "Special Agent Coldwell?" he asked.

"Yes, Lieutenant. And to my right is Summer Raines, Assistant Special Agent in Charge. Special Agent Lauren Adams is to my left."

"Agents." He nodded and focused on Dave. "Have you told them about the kidnapping?"

"Just that we have one. I thought I'd leave the rest to you. Please, start from the beginning."

The lieutenant leaned forward and folded his hands. "At approximately six-thirty this morning, a bus containing fifteen members of a lacrosse team—ages fifteen to seventeen—and four adults, left Newhouse Academy for a ski trip at the Twin Peaks resort in Clymer, New York. At around one p.m., Ohio State Highway Patrol was contacted by Kevin Williams. His son was on that bus. Mr. Williams said he'd gotten a text from his kid, Brennan, at seven forty-seven that said, *help fun*, and nothing more. He'd thought it was strange but figured autocorrect had something to do with it. When he tried calling Brennan, the call went into voicemail, and his son didn't reply to his texts. He let it go until twelve-thirty when the bus was scheduled to arrive at the ski resort. Brennan was supposed to call once they'd gotten there. After Mr. Williams didn't hear from him, he contacted Jeff Ziss. Ziss not only owns Twin Peaks, but his son, Tyler, was on the bus too. I guess Tyler and Brennan are best friends. Anyway, Ziss was also worried and claimed he couldn't get in touch with his son, either, but assumed the weather had delayed them."

"Which makes sense," Lauren said, opening her laptop.

"Right. Because neither man could get in touch with the boys, Williams contacted the school's headmaster and asked that he get ahold of the chaperones and/or the driver. The headmaster, Dennis Kavel, had no luck. That was when Williams used the Find My Phone app to locate his son's cell. He found it on I-71 northbound between exits 204 and 209, which is about eighty miles outside of Columbus. A trooper went to the area but didn't see a bus. We had Ziss use the app on his son's phone and it traced back to the same exact location."

Lauren's dark brows pulled together as she typed. "Odd. And?"

"Mr. Williams gave the troopers access to the phone app," Lieutenant Nelson continued. "Which helped them not only find his son's cell, but a canvas bag buried in the snow filled with thirteen others, along with four tablets."

Tension worked up Summer's spine. She hated any investigation that had to do with children, and there were fifteen of them in this case. "There were nineteen people altogether on the bus," she said. "If there were four adults, that means either one of the kids didn't have a phone or is involved."

Lauren's eyes held dismay. "Don't go there."

"How can I not? You're just as much of a realist as I am, and you know damned well kids are capable of planning elaborate crimes."

"I do, which is why I don't want to go there." When Lauren faced the monitor again, her long black ponytail fell over her shoulder. "Have you checked the bus's GPS?"

"We did, and found the device in the bushes on the academy's property."

Dave rested his hands on the mahogany table. "Tell them about the ransom text."

The lieutenant lifted a piece of paper. "Mr. Williams received a text approximately thirty minutes ago which read, 'We have your son. Deposit two million dollars into the following account. You have forty-eight hours or your son is dead. No police.' Mr. Ziss got the same text. The headmaster from the academy called us minutes later saying that he'd just gotten calls from other parents saying they'd also received the text, and wanting to know if this was real, or if the kids were pulling a prank."

"What's the account number?" Summer asked. Offshore accounts were traceable. If it were a Swiss bank account, discovering the owner would be difficult. Those accounts were anonymous. But to open a Swiss bank account that was completely secret, the owner would have to not only do it in person, they were required to make an initial deposit of one hundred thousand dollars. Which would tell them they were dealing with someone who had access to cash.

After Nelson rattled off the account number, Lauren moved her hands from the keyboard to tighten her ponytail. "That's a Bitcoin account."

The lieutenant frowned. "And that is?"

Worse than a Swiss bank account. Summer glanced at the dozen empty chairs surrounding the large oval table and suspected this case would have those seats filled with additional agents within the hour. Time and the weather were not on their side and they would need to work quickly to find the bus. "Digital currency," she replied.

"Crypto currency," Lauren added.

"Have you heard of the Dark Web?" Summer asked, referring to a small part of the World Wide Web.

"Yes, it's illegal, right?"

"Not illegal, but there are activities and services dealing with child pornography, human and drug trafficking, and more. With the use of special software, anyone can access the Dark Web. And if you have a Bitcoin account, you can—if you cover your tracks properly—make anonymous transactions." Summer blew out a breath as she considered how difficult it could be to trace the account back to the kidnappers. "We'll look into the owner of the account and hope he or she made a mistake. Meanwhile, we need to focus on who was on the bus. Not just the adults, but the kids, too."

"I agree," Dave said. "Lieutenant, aside from the Williams and Ziss boys, have your people been able to match the phones to their owners?"

"Only three others so far. One of which belonged to Wayne Pembroke, the head coach of the lacrosse team."

Lauren raised a brow. "Then, either they tossed his cell to make it look like he wasn't involved, or he's also been kidnapped. Was a ransom text sent to his family?"

The worry in Nelson's eyes matched Summer's. "Not that I know. The headmaster said Matt Shultz, and his cousin, Joel Shultz, were chaperoning, too. Matt is the lacrosse team's assistant coach and a PE teacher for the academy. I don't know anything about his cousin yet."

"What about the driver?" Summer asked, jotting everything down onto her notepad. Lauren liked to keep notes on her laptop, Summer preferred paper. She wanted to be able to go back and highlight information, add to it, brainstorm ideas about cases, especially those that weren't cut and dried. "Was he employed by the school?"

"No. Headmaster Kavel told us the school rents from Able Bussing Ltd. for field trips. We've contacted the company and they claim their driver, Frank Stokes, has been with them for five years. He has a clean record, so we're wondering if he was forced—maybe at gun point—to go along with the kidnappers' program."

Forced or dead? "We'll need to contact Stokes's family and look at his finances."

Though not all the facts were in front of her, Summer's earlier unease had escalated to fear. Meteorologists had predicted the snow would fall throughout the night, with an accumulation of up to a foot or more. The temperatures were supposed to drop to single digits. Add on the wind chill factor, and those temperatures would dive below zero. A school bus would not be enough to protect the kids or their abductors from the elements.

"It wouldn't be easy to hide a bus," she continued, "let alone fifteen teenagers. There are plenty of rural areas between where the phones were found and Cuyahoga County."

"A barn or abandoned warehouse would be big enough to hold a bus," Lauren suggested.

Dave leaned into his chair. "Have you set up a search radius?"

"We have several designated areas." Nelson rose and, carrying whatever device he was using for the video call, walked over to a large wall map. Red pins created a circle along one area, slightly overlapping blue and green pins that did the same around another, and a yellow pin stuck out between the three. "As Special Agent Raines said, it wouldn't be easy to hide a bus, so we believe they didn't stay on the freeway long." He pointed to the red pins. "This is the Burbank exit, which they would've passed just prior to tossing out the canvas bag. The yellow pin is where we found the bag." He moved his finger to the blue and green pins. "This is the Lodi exit, which most of us believe would be the logical route they'd take."

"Medina's the next exit," Lauren said, staring at the screen. "I know there are quite a few businesses and residential areas there, but there are a few rural pockets, too. Or, they could've back-tracked to the Burbank exit."

"True, but two truckers who'd heard us looking for the bus on their police scanners called in claiming they'd seen a bus leaving the Lodi exit. Both had thought it odd since the schools were closed in that area. Unfortunately, neither remembered the name on the side of the bus. We did call other bus rental companies. Due to the weather, all but one company had cancelled any trips, and that bus wasn't anywhere near the Lodi exit."

"This is good." Summer focused on the map and pins. "Which direction did the truck drivers see the bus heading?"

"West."

Other than the town of Lodi, the map showed a few roads. "There's nothing out there."

"Right, it's mostly farms."

Lauren tapped at the keyboard. "Do you know if Able has buses with roofs painted white?" she asked.

Back in the 90s, a study had showed that painting the roofs white lowered the temperature by ten degrees during the warmer months. A lower temperature meant happier kids.

"Unfortunately, yes," the lieutenant said. "Once we're able to put a chopper in the air, it'll be more difficult to locate it with all this snow."

"If the bus is outside," Lauren countered. "What do you know about this area?"

"It's quiet. Low crime."

"No industrial parkways?" Summer asked, considering Lauren's earlier suggestion. A warehouse or barn would make for a good hiding place.

"I'm not aware of any that have been abandoned. As for barns? That's a possibility."

Lauren squinted at the map. "What lake is that?"

"This one?" Lieutenant Nelson pointed to a large body of water. When Lauren nodded, he answered, "Ottawa Lake. There's nothing much there. A couple of small villages take up one side of the lake, the rest is part of the Medina County park system. There are a few farms nearby, but it's primarily a summer community. Stores, restaurants and gas stations close in November, and reopen in April or May."

Summer spotted the Villages of Fred Glen and Ottawa Lake. "The woods would provide cover for the bus. Lack of residents would allow the kidnappers to break into one of the summer houses."

"It would," Nelson replied, not sounding convinced. "The problem is there's only one road leading to that area." He ran his finger along Elm Road. "I can't see these kidnappers cornering themselves between a lake and a single road. They're going to want multiple escape routes."

Dave drummed his fingers along the table. "They could take a boat across the lake."

"No boats. The lake should be frozen by now."

Dave nodded. "Okay, let's concentrate on abandoned farms. Another thing we should consider is that the kidnappers have taken over a working farm. We could have more than the kids being held hostage."

Fifteen abducted kids were bad enough. She'd hate to see another innocent family involved. "Let's hope that's not the case."

Dave took over, requesting everything Lieutenant Nelson had, and promising him they'd do what they could to help. After the conference call ended, he let out a breath and rubbed his eyes with his thumb and index finger. "What a mess." He dropped his hand. "Summer, have our SWAT team on standby."

"What about HRT and CNU?" Lauren asked.

While the Cleveland Division had an enhanced and highly trained SWAT team, Hostage Rescue Team, or HRT, was basically a Tier-1 Special Forces team deployed when a threat exceeded the capabilities of a field office, and was part of the Tactical Support Branch of the FBI's Critical Incident Response Group (CIRG). These men were agents who did not carry a caseload. Their only job was to train and be ready for any mission at a moment's notice. They also had access to military transportation, which would allow them to fly during poor weather conditions. The Crisis Negotiation Unit, or CNU, which was composed of FBI agents who worked as full-time hostage and crisis negotiators, was also part of CIRG, and were often brought in with HRT.

"It'll depend on the scope of the situation," Dave replied. "If we can't locate the victims, HRT will do us little good. And if the kidnappers stick to text messages, CNU won't be much help, either."

"Do you want me to contact the Medina County Sheriff?" Summer asked.

"Let's wait. If the kidnappers continued west, we could end up in another county. Lauren, see what you can do with that account number. This could be an act of terrorism or an inside job, so let's cover all our bases. Summer, get a couple of agents to help you pull together everything you can about the kids, their families and the chaperones."

"Are we back to speculating a kid could be part of the abduction?" Lauren asked.

"I'm suggesting one of the families could be involved."

Lauren shrugged. "A family falls on hard times, recruits the chaperones, but tells them not to touch their kid...that'd work."

Summer ignored the goose bumps coating her skin. "This is a lacrosse team. These kids have been playing together, live and go to school together. I don't want to consider a parent going to that extreme and putting one of their son's friends in danger—not to mention their own kid. But thirty million is a lot of money."

"It sure is," Dave said, rising. "Nelson should have—"

"Dave." His assistant stepped into the room. "There's a call for you. Line two."

"Take a message."

"It's Senator Patricks."

The popular United States senator had been serving Ohio for nearly fifteen years. Rumor had it that Senator Aaron Patricks, who was the chairman of the U.S. Senate Appropriations Subcommittee on Homeland Security, was considering running for president during the next election.

Dave frowned, slowly sat and took the call. Summer looked to Lauren and jerked her head toward the door. When Lauren didn't get the hint, she cleared her throat, then mouthed, "Let's go."

Dave held up a finger, and neither Summer or Lauren moved.

"Yes, sir," Dave said, sliding his sharp gaze to Summer. "I'm familiar with him and the agency. I have no problem with them helping us, but let's be clear: this is our investigation. He has no authority here." Dave rubbed his eyes again and was silent for a moment. "I understand, sir. We will do everything possible to bring your grandson home."

Grandson? Summer met Lauren's worried gaze. This was a high-profile case. The kidnappers had said, *no police.* Keeping the investigation from the media would be difficult. If the senator's grandson was also on that bus, she predicted a media circus would ensue. Journalists would salivate over this story. They'd want to be the first to break the news, to be on the frontline and give their audience a play-by-play of what law enforcement was doing, or not doing, to save these children. Once the story broke, the kidnappers would know the authorities were involved. And she worried how they'd react.

Dave hung up the phone. He smoothed a hand over his balding head. "Do we have the list of kids?"

Lauren turned her laptop toward him. "This just came in from Lieutenant Nelson."

Leaning forward, Dave studied the small screen. "Senator Patricks' grandson is Dillon Patricks."

"I take it the senator is sending someone to babysit," Summer said, keeping the bitterness from her tone. While she understood why the senator would want to have someone on the ground, he needed to let them do their job, and not have an outside party interfere with the case.

"I wouldn't use the term, *babysit*. More like monitor our progress and report back to him. That being said, I'm not particularly upset about it."

"I am." Lauren frowned. "I don't like that he's using his position to bully his way into our investigation."

"You don't have to like it. You just need to deal with it." Dave glanced to Summer. "Patricks' man will be here in an hour. He's former FBI, had been part of the Crisis Negotiation Unit, and currently works for the private criminal investigation agency, CORE."

Summer stilled. Dread balled in her nervous stomach. She knew only one person who fit that description and she wasn't ready to see him. Not yet, not for at least another four months.

"Who's *the man*?" Lauren asked.

Summer looked to her friend. "My ex."

Lauren's eyes widened. "Chase? But...this." She let out a

breath and shook her head. "This can't be good for him. Not after what happened in Baltimore."

"He'll be fine." Dave pushed the chair back and stood. "He's a good agent."

"Was," Lauren reminded him.

"And an excellent negotiator," Dave continued. "We might need him." He faced Summer. "There won't be any issues, correct?"

"Not on my end."

But maybe on Chase's. Especially once he realized she was five months pregnant.

Ottawa Lake Amusement Park, Village of Ottawa, Ohio
Friday, January 20th, 4:21 p.m. Eastern Standard Time

Everything had gone to plan. His crew wasn't the greatest, but they were efficient and expendable. While he had concerns about Woody's friend, Randy, the man was a former Marine who'd served in the Persian Gulf War. If things went bad and the police found them, he'd be a valuable team player.

Team.

He glanced around the ballroom, which was finally warming up now that Joel had the kerosene heaters going, and stared at Simon, who wore a salty expression and kept jiggling his right earlobe. Woody had shot the rifle into the ground, but the blast had been inches from the goalie's head. The guy's ears were probably still ringing. Maybe next time he'd think twice about playing hero.

The thing was, he didn't mind Simon. He and a few of the others were okay guys. They were also worth more to him alive than dead. By now, their parents should have received the ransom text and might demand to either talk to or see pictures of their sons. He wasn't dumb enough to assume these people wouldn't go to the police. Their kids had been abducted for two million each. The police were likely involved and trying to locate them. Good fucking luck with that. The blizzard would work in their favor. By now, the bus's tire tracks were probably hidden. Even if they somehow discovered their location, it wouldn't matter. He had a backup plan. Killing wasn't his thing, but he had no problem doing it. Especially if someone was in his way.

He didn't get off on deciding who should live or die. Didn't gain some weird sexual gratification by watching a person take his last breath, or the gore as a head exploded. Money was his thing.

And revenge…

FBI Cleveland Division, Cleveland, Ohio
Friday, January 20th, 5:06 p.m. Eastern Standard Time

Chase Sawyer brushed snow from his winter coat and stepped inside the FBI field office. Several armed agents stood near the high-tech security desk. One of the men, Special Agent Anthony D'Angelo, grinned.

"Look who Jack Frost blew into the building. When I heard you were coming, I couldn't believe it. How've you been?" Tony asked as he walked over to him.

Chase shook the agent's hand. "I just flew through a snow storm in a small jet. The turbulence was so bad, I still feel like puking. Don't get me started on the landing." The runway had been a mess, and Cleveland Hopkins International Airport had shut down its runways minutes after they'd arrived. "Other than that, I'm doing fine. How's the family?"

There was no need to tell the agent his stomach had been wrecked prior to stepping onto the jet. The moment Ian Scott, owner of CORE, had informed him that he'd be heading to Cleveland, and the reason why, it had taken everything inside of him to maintain a stoic veneer in front of his boss. He hadn't seen Summer since last August, when he'd come to the area as backup for an investigation. While he'd been in town, he hadn't been able to stop himself from calling her, from going to her house, or keeping his hands to himself and his dick in his pants. Then what had he done? He'd run. Back to the safety of his Chicago condo, to his PI job, to pretending life was good, and that he wasn't a fuck-up.

"Good. Can't complain," Tony said as the other agent stepped from behind the desk with a wand to check Chase for weapons.

"I'm carrying." Chase opened his winter coat, then lifted his arms. "One around my left ankle, the other two on my waist."

The agent went back to the desk and exchanged the wand for a secured case. Chase knew the drill. He was licensed to carry concealed weapons, but not in a federal building. Not any longer.

"What's it like working for a private agency?" Tony asked as Chase removed his weapons and set them in the case.

Easy. Boring. No challenge. "It's been great. No bureaucratic BS, and I'm off on holidays and most weekends. I don't have to deal with being on-call twenty-four-seven either. Plus, the agency I work for has cool perks."

"Like a private jet?" Tony grinned. "It's funny. Today is Friday, the start of the weekend. We find out a busload of kids was abducted, and you fly in just like that to consult with a bureaucratic agency." He snapped his fingers. "Yeah, it sounds like things have changed for you."

"Today's an exception to the norm," Chase said, irritated he'd walked right into that one. Once the other agent had checked his weathered briefcase, he left his overnight bag with the man, then caught up with Tony at the elevators. "Any word from the kidnappers?"

Tony shook his head. "And we're no closer to locating the bus."

They entered the elevator. "Has Dave contacted CIRG?" he asked, thinking about his former counterparts with CNU, and hoping they and HRT would be on the scene should they make contact with the kidnappers. In his former life, he'd spent five years as a crisis negotiator for the FBI. But that wasn't something he was interested in doing. Not now. Not ever again. Negotiators were known for keeping their emotions in check, but two dead bodies had stripped him of that ability. His stomach dropped as the elevator rose. He pushed the memories aside and focused on the present.

"He has. Crisis negotiators are getting in touch with the parents, and we've sent agents to the families' homes to set up recording devices should the kidnappers call. Once we locate the bus, HRT and CNU can be here within ninety minutes. We have our SWAT team on standby, too." Tony faced him. "Is this going to be awkward?"

"What, working with the FBI again? Not at all. CORE works with the bureau all the time, along with other government agencies."

The disappointment in Tony's eyes had Chase looking away to see which floor they were approaching and fighting regret. He and Tony had once been good friends. He'd been to the man's house for barbeques and parties, had gone out for beers with him, or he and Summer would meet Tony and his wife for dinner. When Chase had moved to Chicago, Tony had tried to stay in touch. Like Summer, he'd called, texted and emailed. But Chase had done little to maintain their friendship. Summer, Tony and their continued work with the FBI had served as too much of a reminder that he was no longer cut out to be an agent. That he'd become a failure.

"Yeah, that's exactly what I meant," Tony replied, sarcasm in his tone.

The elevator reached the fourth floor and the doors opened. Chase was tempted to stop Tony in the hallway and apologize, to explain why he'd been a shitty friend, and why he was avoiding the truth. But making amends and dealing with the past weren't the reasons why he was back. He was here to help find and save a U.S. senator's grandson, along with fourteen other kids.

Instead, Chase followed Tony into the briefing room. Monitors lit up the walls with maps, and photographs of adults and teenaged boys. Papers and laptops covered most of the large table, where four agents were seated. He immediately looked to Summer, who was talking with Lauren. Damn, she'd cut her blond hair into one of those styles where the sides were longer than the back. He hated how it was too straight and severe, and missed her long waves. Lauren looked up at him, which drew Summer's attention, and everyone else's.

Every agent went silent.

Chase glanced to Tony. "Remember when you asked if this was going to be awkward?"

"It doesn't have to be," Dave said from behind them.

When Chase faced the Special Agent in Charge, he offered his hand. "Good to see you. Thanks for giving CORE the opportunity to help with your investigation."

"Senator Patricks happens to be close friends with the Director of the FBI. I really wasn't given much choice." Dave shook his hand, the small grin tugging at his mouth softening the slight insult. "That being said, I'm glad to have you here." He turned to the agent Chase didn't recognize. "This is Chase Sawyer. He used to be with the FBI as a crisis negotiator. Hopefully, he'll be able to tell us something about our kidnappers."

"Like you said, I was a negotiator, not a profiler."

"Who's gotten into the minds of kidnappers." Not meeting his gaze, Summer picked up a notebook and stood. "Good to see you, Chase," she said, her tone cool as she turned toward the wall of monitors.

He tamped down his disappointment. How had he expected her to react? Run over and kiss him? Not a chance. The room was filled with her colleagues, and he was an asshole. He'd treated her badly, had showed no respect for what they'd once had between them.

"Before we get started, do you have any questions?" she asked him.

"Has anyone responded to the ransom text?"

"Not yet. Some of the families have said they want to pay and get their boys back, a few want to negotiate the amount, two can't afford the two million, and the rest want to talk with their kids before they make a move. Every parent is concerned that even if they pay, they won't get their sons back."

As they should be. Kidnappers were untrustworthy criminals. For all they knew, those fifteen kids could be dead. "I think the parents need to be unified on whatever decision is made. I also think communication needs to be established, and I'd be interested to know if they'll release the boys as deposits are made, or if they plan on waiting for the full thirty million. If they do release kids as the money comes in, this could give us an opportunity to locate the kidnappers."

She shifted her gaze to the monitor. "We were just about to discuss who we feel is behind the abductions. First, I want to talk about the chaperones and driver. Only the kids' parents have been contacted by the kidnappers, leading us to believe the four men are either involved or dead. Let's start with the head coach," she said, pointing to the screen which showed a photograph of a blond man in his fifties.

Despite her hair, which with the way it framed her face, was actually kind of sexy, she looked fantastic. Her black suit did little to hide her soft curves. If anything, her breasts appeared bigger.

Focus.

"This is Wayne Pembroke," she continued. "He's been coaching Newhouse Academy's varsity lacrosse team for the past six years. Age fifty-eight, married, with two grown kids. Other than a mortgage and a car payment plan for one of their vehicles, the couple has no debt, and Pembroke has a clean record. Lieutenant Nelson from Highway Patrol recently discovered Pembroke's tablet was in the canvas bag. Forensic investigators found traces of blood on the device, along with small fragments of flesh. They're going through his house now to find something they can use for DNA analysis. Since only Pembroke's fingerprints were found on the device, I think we should consider him injured or deceased, and not one of the kidnappers."

She glanced to Lauren. "Please pull up Matt Shultz's photo."

Within seconds, a good-looking man in his twenties appeared

on the screen. He had light brown hair, cut and styled in a contemporary fashion, brown eyes and an athletic build.

"This is Matt Shultz." Summer glanced to her notebook. "He's from the Cincinnati area. He teaches health and phys ed at Newhouse. He's been with the school for two years, coming on board after graduating from Ohio University. He's twenty-five, single, owes eighty grand in student loans and another thirty-five in credit card debt. Two semi-automatic pistols—a Smith & Wesson M&P9 Shield and a Sig Sauer P938—and a kel-Tec SUB-2000 rifle are registered in his name. All three weapons were purchased in October. His record is also clean." She looked up from the notebook. "His cell wasn't in the bag. That being said, the school's headmaster claims he's a great teacher, and that the students love his classes. There's never been a complaint about him from a student or parent."

"The missing cell is very telling," Tony said.

"Indeed. Especially after what we've learned about his cousin, Joel Shultz."

Chase cleared his throat, gaining Summer's attention. Her expression bland and devoid of emotion, she stared at him as if he were a stranger, as if they'd never kissed or made love. Because her reaction—or lack thereof—toward him was his own fault, he ignored the hurt. "Our researcher learned that Matt spent a week under psychiatric care."

Her brows pulled together. "When?"

"He was fourteen," he said, recalling what Rachel Malcolm, CORE's computer forensic analyst and go-to person when it came to research, had sent him while he'd been on the jet. "When he was twelve, he was diagnosed with oppositional defiant disorder, meaning he basically had an issue with authority. Two years later, after he'd killed his elderly neighbor's dog so he could sneak inside their house and steal from them, his parents had him reevaluated."

"He has a juvenile record?" the agent he didn't know asked.

"No. The neighbors didn't press charges. They moved. Anyway, after spending several days with Matt and questioning his family, he was diagnosed a sociopath. And while he was in college, he allegedly beat a student and put him in the hospital. Because of lack of evidence, no charges were brought against him."

"How could you possibly know this?" the agent asked.

Because Rachel was a damned efficient hacker. "Well, Agent…"

"Leary."

"Agent Leary, our researcher has sources available to her that have allowed us access to his juvenile record."

"But the neighbors…"

"That was a matter of finding out who had lived next door during that time period, then making a simple phone call. The couple made it clear they moved because they were terrified of Matt."

Agent Leary frowned. "I pulled together everything I could find on Matt Shultz. You would need a judge to grant you access to his juvenile files, plus there's medical confidentiality."

"Let it go," Dave said with a smirk and a shake of his head. "Chase, do you have any more info on Matt?"

"He and his cousin both got their passports last October twelfth, which shows me that neither Matt or Joel are the master-minds behind the kidnapping." Chase took a seat. "These men had to know they would be identified, and that, even if they were successful and got ahold of the ransom money, they'd never get out of the country using their real names."

"Unless someone promised them safe passage." Summer nod-ded to Lauren, who changed the picture on the monitor to another man. "Here's his cousin. What has your *researcher* found about him?"

With the exception of Joel Shultz's dark shoulder-length hair, he and Matt had similar eyes, bone structure and physique. "Joel and Matt are the same age. Their mothers are sisters and they were essentially raised together. Joel has a juvenile police record for theft. Since turning eighteen, he's been in jail twice for the same reason."

"He's also never been to Colorado," Agent Leary added. "The

school's headmaster said Matt told him Joel was a ski instructor who'd recently moved back to Ohio from Denver. When I asked him how Joel had cleared a background check to chaperone, he told me Matt had assured him Human Resources had taken care of it. After the bus went missing, the headmaster checked with HR to hand over what they had on Joel to the authorities. They had nothing, and said Matt never even approached them about a background check."

"I'm glad to hear safety is important at an upscale private academy filled with rich kids," Summer said with heavy sarcasm. "Moving on… Matt and Joel share an apartment. Highway Patrol searched the place. TVs, DVD players, laptops, anything of value was gone, but there was dust on the entertainment stand which indicated a few of those items had recently been there."

"What about their cell phones?" Chase asked. "I'm assuming Joel's wasn't in the bag. Have you tried tracing them?"

"We're not having any luck. The last place there was a signal from either phone was their apartment, and that was at approximately four-thirty this morning. We believe they destroyed the phones before making their way to the academy, because even turned off we have the software to track them. On to the driver…" A copy of a driver's license, bearing the photo of a heavy-set man in his sixties, filled the screen. "This is Frank Stokes. Rich, you talked to his wife," she said looking to another agent, Rich Cochran.

"Yeah. She said Frank was excited about going to the ski resort, and planned to do nothing but relax in the lodge. He's a retired construction worker who became a bus driver for Able Bussing to earn travel money. He and his wife were supposed to leave for Hawaii next week. Frank picked up the bus from the company garage at six a.m., so we know he was, at one point, driving the bus. We traced his cell to Newhouse Academy. State troopers found it about thirty yards from where the kidnappers had tossed the bus's GPS."

"Did anyone from the school see the bus leave?" Lauren asked.

Rich shook his head. "Not that we've discovered."

"Then it's highly possible Stokes drove to the academy, but never left." Summer stepped over to the next monitor. "Rich, contact Lieutenant Nelson. They need to search the academy grounds for the driver. Have they located Matt's Camaro?"

"It's at the school parking lot," Rich said. "Same with Pembroke's SUV."

"Stokes might be in one of those cars. Matt and Joel could have brought in another man to drive."

"They'd need more than just the two of them to execute the kidnapping," Chase said. "You've got fifteen teenage boys, most of them the size of grown men. They're going to be scared, but some of them are going to be willing to risk finding a way out of their situation."

Summer nodded. "Agreed. We think they're using a barn or warehouse to hide the kids and bus. It's possible there are even more men working with the Shultz cousins, and those men have readied the place they're using."

"Rich," Dave began, "after you talk with Nelson, I want you and Leary to look into the Shultzs' activities since October, when Matt bought the guns and they both got passports. We need to confiscate Matt Shultz's school computer as well." He looked to Lauren. "Any luck with the Bitcoin account?"

"Nothing yet. Whoever set up the account covered their tracks. They used a software program to conceal their identity and, as an added measure, I'm thinking they likely used a public Wi-Fi network and spoofed their computer address."

"Help out those of us who aren't techies," Tony said. "What's *spoofed*?"

"Short version: he created a false IP address. Essentially, he made the account anonymous. I've sent it to Washington. Hopefully some brilliant computer forensic analyst can do something more with it, because I've hit a dead end."

"If they don't have any luck, you should have CORE's analyst take a look," Chase suggested. Chances were Rachel was already on it, though. The woman loved a challenge.

Lauren shrugged. "Sure. Couldn't hurt."

"Okay, good. Let's move on to the students." Summer looked to her notebook. With a slight shake of her head, she sat next to Lauren and opened the laptop in front of her. "You can review the photos later. For now, I want to run through this list."

She spent the next twenty minutes discussing the kids who were on the bus, along with a brief description of what each student's parent did for a living, and their financial status, most of which Chase already knew. After the call from Senator Patricks, Ian had had Jag Stone, CORE's newest agent, help Rachel research everybody on the bus, then send everything over to him. He'd gone through the information during the flight to Cleveland, but, because of limited time, had ended up skimming through some files before the jet had landed. When Summer had mentioned the Connelly family, he'd recalled reading that they were having financial trouble. Wanting to refresh his memory, he pulled out his cell to retrieve the files from Jag and Rachel.

Summer stopped talking.

He looked up and met her irritated gaze. "Sorry, you said Victor Connelly is CFO of National Insurance."

"Yes. And?"

He glanced to his cell. "He has a civil lawsuit filed against him for sexual harassment."

"I was about to bring that up."

"Sorry," he said. Which was something he'd been saying for over a year... *Sorry I'm a fuck-up. Sorry I left you. Sorry I killed a kid and my partner.*

"Right. Connelly is looking at a lawsuit that could potentially bankrupt him. We've also discovered that Hunter Perry's parents are getting a divorce. Between alimony and child support, his father will lose more than half of his assets." Summer looked to Tony. "I'll need you to dig deeper into these two families. Thirty million dollars would make their financial issues go away."

"What about the Everett family?" Tony asked. "Both parents

work and have a combined income of one hundred and fifty thousand a year."

"The cost to attend Newhouse Academy is approximately forty thousand a year," she replied. "They're able to send their son, Chad, because his grandfather, who'd attended the academy, placed money into a trust account so his grandson could be educated at his alma mater. Other than a mortgage and car payments, their debt is minimal. We haven't found anything that would raise our suspicions."

"We're waiting on a few warrants to come through," Lauren said. "But the agents who are going to the families' homes to set up recording devices will also be confiscating computers and checking cell phones."

"What about the academy?" Chase asked. "I think we'd be foolish to not look into these boys' recent online activities. I guarantee a high school kid knows more about the Dark Web and crypto currency than their parents."

Summer tucked a lock of hair behind her ear. "We currently have agents from the Columbus resident agency getting warrants to search the academy dorm rooms. They'll also grab Matt's school computer."

"Since laptops are mobile, and the account owner has been able to maintain anonymity, we're especially interested in those devices," Lauren added. "Like I said, you need special software to create a Bitcoin wallet, so we're also looking for that. The software can be installed onto a cell phone, too, which is why we're having agents search through the parents' phones."

"I'm not suggesting it's impossible that a student or parent is involved, but our primary focus will be on the Shultz cousins." Dave stared at the monitor displaying a map marked with three circles. "Chase, if you were running this investigation as a crisis negotiator, how would you proceed?"

Chase shifted his gaze to Summer, who watched him with curiosity. He didn't know why, or what the look in her eyes meant, but he cared. Damn it. He still loved her, and he wanted to make her proud. Was that possible? Maybe this investigation was his chance to not necessarily win her back—he'd made too many mistakes and had changed too much for that to happen—but she could come to respect him again. But what if he was wrong? What if he made a suggestion that ended up getting a kid killed?

Again.

Haunting memories surfaced. With his heart racing and his fingers growing numb, he knew if he didn't rein in his emotions and stop thinking about the past, he'd make an ass of himself by having a panic attack. Something he hadn't been able to shake since the night his life had changed with the pull of a trigger. "I would…" he began, his own voice sounding tinny. He drew in several deep breaths and did as his psychologist had suggested—cleared his mind and went to his happy place, which was the moment when he'd first met Summer Raines.

He pictured her smiling at him, the sun shining behind her making it look as if she were an angel. Her blond hair moved with the breeze. Her blue eyes held interest…desire.

Calmer, his heart rate slowly dropping, he focused on what he knew, and on the job he'd done for five years. "Hostage takers are unpredictable. They're often fueled by emotion. What I don't like about what's happening here is that emotion isn't likely to come into play unless the kidnappers are cornered. The cousins, and whomever they're working with or for, want money. Period. They won't care about the kids. They'll care about walking away with thirty million. My gut is telling me both Pembroke and Stokes are dead, and that these men won't hesitate to harm the boys."

"But what would you do?" Agent Leary asked.

"Choose one parent to be the spokesperson and make contact. I'd have that parent demand to speak with the kidnapper, no more texting."

"Chances are they're using burner phones," Tony said.

"Doesn't matter. Engaging in conversation with one or more of the kidnappers would allow us to get into their minds, maybe find their weaknesses. And you'd be surprised by what you can hear in the background. It could help us with their location."

Dave rose. "I'll call CNU." He glanced at his watch. "The text arrived around three, which means we now have forty-five hours to resolve this."

Another agent entered the room. "Sir, Lieutenant Nelson is on line one."

Dave picked up the phone. "Coldwell," he said, listened for a moment, then nodded. "I would advise you not to engage. Keep me posted." He ended the call and placed the phone on the receiver. With excitement brightening his eyes, he turned to Summer. "Ready SWAT. Nelson thinks they found them."

3

Ottawa Lake Amusement Park, Village of Ottawa, Ohio
Friday, January 20ᵗʰ, 5:51 p.m. Eastern Standard Time

BRENNAN'S STOMACH GROWLED. He looked to the high ceiling of the ballroom. With the exception of the wall he leaned against, two rows of windows lined the massive room. The top row was mostly broken. Snow and wind gusted inside, howled and blew hard enough that the walls occasionally shook. Darkness had swallowed the park about thirty minutes ago, and he assumed it was close to six. As his stomach continued to grumble, he looked to the lower windows, which were now partially boarded with plywood, leaving two cracks. One was large enough to see through, the other could fit the tip of a rifle. Shultz and his cousin had proven this earlier, and he figured they'd done this in case the building came under attack.

Fear outweighed his hunger. He tried to ignore both and instead thought about his family. Had Shultz given them the ransom conditions? Did his mom and dad have the money to free him? He'd heard Shultz mention thirty million to Joel. Thirty divided by fifteen was two. His mom and dad owned twenty-five Happy Jax restaurant franchises throughout Ohio and Pennsylvania. They lived in a huge house, drove a Mercedes and a Denali, took family trips to Hawaii, the Caribbean and were planning on going to Europe this summer. He understood that they had money, more than most families, but still. Did they have enough? If they did, and they paid these guys, would he be released?

"I'm starving," Tyler whispered.

Brennan shook his head, hoping his friend would understand he didn't want to talk, didn't want to draw attention to himself. He didn't want to die.

After the deal with Woody firing a round into the snow, Brennan wanted to do nothing but obey. He'd also overheard the driver, whose name was Clay, tell Woody and the other gunman, who went by the name of Randy, that he'd killed the real bus driver, and had put him in the back of Coach Pembroke's SUV. They'd killed two men, and, with thirty million dollars on the line, there was no doubt in Brennan's mind that they'd shoot any one of them if necessary.

Alex leaned away from the kerosene heater and sat next to Tyler. "I have to piss."

When they'd first entered the park's ballroom, their captors had had them line up against the wall, then sit until the heaters were running. Afterward, they had been split into groups of five and allowed to warm themselves. They'd also been given permission to go through their gear, which had been left near the rotting stage, and gather extra clothes to help keep them from freezing. If he moved too far from the heaters, his frosty breath hung on the air. But he hadn't complained. No one had. The five men were always armed, and three were always inside the building. The other two stood watch outside, which was currently Randy and Clay's duty.

"You'd think they'd give us a bathroom break and something to eat and drink," Tyler said.

"I don't care about food." Simon kept his voice low and his gaze locked on Joel, who stood by one of the boarded windows across the room. Brennan measured distance by the yards on a lacrosse field, and figured Joel was about twenty away. "I want to know what they're planning."

"It's a fucking kidnapping. How do you think it'll work?" Nick Janson, one of their midfielders, also stared at Joel. "They're gonna get their money, then kill us. We gotta fight."

"We need one of their guns," Tyler suggested.

Brennan had expected Nick to push to fight the men, not Tyler. Last year, Nick had been suspended for kicking a kid's ass, and rumor had it that he held Newhouse Academy's record for the most detentions for arguing with teachers and being an overall asshole. Tyler wasn't a fighter. On the field, he was aggressive and had no problem taking down an opponent who'd gotten in his way. Off the field, he would rather talk his way out of a situation that could lead to punches being thrown.

"Remember, don't be dumb," Brennan reminded them.

"So we just sit here and wait for them to kill us?" Nick leaned against the wall. "*That's* dumb. I didn't realize you were such a pussy."

And the prick wondered why the guys called him Nick the Dick. "I'm not saying we do nothing," Brennan insisted. "But I say we wait. The cops could be on their way."

Tyler also rested against the wall. "What if they're not? What if they have no idea where we are?"

Brennan had worried about the same thing. "I say we hold off until morning. It's dark, freezing and still snowing."

"Duh, if I get a gun, I'm not walking out of here, I'm taking the bus," Nick said.

"*That's* stupid." Brennan shifted his gaze to Shultz, who was also across the room and looking at his cell phone. "Even if you get a gun, they still have more. Do you even know which one of them has the keys to the bus?"

"I saw Clay put them in his coat pocket," Alex said. "And he's outside with Randy. We could ask to go to the bathroom and, if there's an opportunity, we can try for their guns."

Brennan looked to Simon for help. The goalie had come close to being shot by Woody after the gunman had busted up Logan's face, and knew firsthand the man had no problem inflicting pain or fear. With the way the light from the battery-powered lanterns revealed the hatred and excitement in Simon's eyes, Brennan suspected the goalie didn't care. The guy wanted revenge. He did, too. He also didn't want to rush into anything and get them killed.

"I don't have a good feeling about this," Brennan said. "I think it's too soon."

"It's not." Tyler patted the pocket of his pants. "Don't forget I've got a knife."

Nick, Alex and Simon didn't look at Tyler, but their eyes widened slightly. Alex's mouth curved into a small grin. "Me, Simon and Nick will go outside to pee. We can start something with Clay and Randy. Even if we don't get the guns, Joel, Shultz and Woody are going to be distracted."

"Right." Nick nodded. "As soon as they turn their backs, Tyler can use the knife and go for one of their guns." He looked to Brennan. "Unless you're still too much of a puss, you can help by yelling for the rest of the guys to rush these dicks."

Brennan's empty stomach soured with dread. "This won't work. Someone could get killed."

"If I get a gun, those dudes are gonna be the ones who get killed," Nick said. "It'll be fucking epic."

"Come on, Brennan." Tyler nudged him. "Go along with it. There're more of us than them. We've got this."

"Who gave you permission to talk?" Shultz shouted. He pocketed his phone and, carrying a pistol, approached them. "What are you boys talking about? Coming up with an escape plan?"

Alex shook his head. "We're hungry and thirsty, and some of us have to go to the bathroom."

Shultz stared at him with disbelief, then rolled his eyes. He looked over his shoulder at Woody, then Joel.

Joel adjusted his knit hat. "Told you we should've had them go out before it got dark."

"They ain't goin' anywhere," Woody said. "If they do,

fuck 'em. Let 'em freeze to death. Just one less kid we gotta babysit."

"Okay, assholes," Shultz began, "whether you have to go or not, this is a bathroom break, and the last time I'm letting you out of this room until morning. You'll go in groups of three. Williams, Janson and McGuire, you go first."

Brennan's heart sped. Shit. He didn't want to be part of Alex and Nick's plan to go for a gun. But he couldn't let the others down, not when this could be their opportunity to rescue themselves. Clay and Randy were about his size, and he had speed and agility on his side. Same with Alex. Nick wasn't as big as them, but craved confrontation and loved a good fight. Yeah, they could do this. They could overpower the two men and get the hell out of here.

As Brennan rose, Shultz waved the pistol at them. "Lose the coats, hats and gloves. Be glad I'm letting you keep your boots." He chuckled and glanced to Woody. "They won't go anywhere now."

Woody held his rifle in both hands and grinned. "But I'd love to see them try."

Brennan didn't doubt the man. Earlier, Woody had made it clear he was in a killing mood. Brennan could picture him at the boarded window, the tip of the rifle through one of the cracks, picking them off one by one as they ran across the open area outside.

With reluctance, Brennan removed his coat, hat and gloves, and was grateful for the thermal underwear he'd put on under his pants and heavy sweatshirt. Despite the heaters, a chill instantly rushed through him. He followed Nick and Alex to the double doors. One side had been boarded shut, while the other door had been rigged with a modern, shiny metal bar latch that in no way could've been original to the building.

"Joel, you go with them." Shultz lifted the latch. "Your shift is coming up anyway."

"Screw that. You haven't been out there yet. You're up, cuz."

When Shultz looked to Woody, the older man shook his head. "I still got an hour before it's my turn to freeze my ass. I'm staying right here. You might want to do the same. Joel's got it right...you *will* take the next shift."

Brennan had been under the impression that Shultz was in charge. The way Woody bossed him around had him rethinking this, until Shultz narrowed his eyes at the man.

"Watch how you talk to me. I don't want to have to cut your throat during the night." While Woody laughed, Shultz opened the door. Snowflakes blew inside with a gust of wind. "Bathroom break," he shouted to the men outside.

Brennan couldn't see Clay or Randy yet, and although he hadn't wanted to go to the bathroom before, cold and fear cut through him, giving him the urge to pee. Hugging himself to keep warm, he winced when he stepped through the doorway. The icy air had his penis and nuts shrinking into his body. The snow came down as if it were a white sheet of rain and immediately dampened his face and hair. He glanced around them. The dim light from the ballroom did little against the darkness, but did touch along the sloped landing and steps which led toward the main grounds.

He jerked when a light came on beside him. Randy laughed.

"You're a jumpy one," the gunman said, holding the lantern high. He turned to the partially opened door. "How many are you sending out here?"

"Three at a time," Shultz said, frowning. "Where's Clay?"

Another lantern brightened the landing, this time from the left. "Right here."

"Have them go by the trees next to the landing. When they're done, bang on the door," he said, sealing himself inside the ballroom.

"You heard him," Randy said, motioning for them to head down the steps.

Brennan's teeth chattered, and the tip of his nose was already numb. The only thing warming him was hope and a small amount of confidence. He didn't want to try to overpower these men, but now that he was out in the cold, he wondered if they did have an actual advantage. Randy and Clay had been outside for about thirty minutes. Even with heavy coats, pants and gloves, these men had to be cold. Maybe they were a little stiff and moving slower than usual. Or maybe he was just trying to keep from wimping out on Alex and Nick.

Once they trudged through the snow and reached the area Shultz had told them to use, Randy and Clay flanked the three of them. As he and the other guys unzipped their flies, then took care of business, Clay rested his rifle against a large tree, the lantern in the snow, and slipped off his glove.

"What the hell, man?" Randy held the lantern toward the driver.

Clay had what looked like a cigarette between his lips and was cupping his hand over the flame from a lighter. Within seconds, the strong smell of weed floated toward them.

"Seriously?" Randy asked as Clay blew out a stream of smoke.

Brennan looked to Alex who stood next to him. The team captain gave him a slight nod and zipped his fly.

"It's not like I can smoke dope inside," Clay said, taking another hit.

"You shouldn't be doing it all. Now's not the time. If Matt—"

"Fuck him." Clay took another drag, then snuffed out the joint. "And fuck you. I saw you drinking from the flask you've got in your pocket, so don't threaten me."

Randy swore and raised the lantern toward them. "Finish it."

"It's total bullshit that we get stuck with bathroom duty," Clay continued, and now tried lighting a cigarette. The wind shifted directions, blowing out the flame and soaking the cigarette with snow. "Damn it." He tossed it and reached inside his coat.

"I'll take one of those smokes," Randy said, then turned to them again. "Christ, aren't you done yet?"

Brennan and Nick zipped their pants. Nick and Alex started toward the ballroom, while Brennan brought up the rear. Filled with both relief and disappointment, he shoved his hands in his pockets. If they'd gotten hold of a gun, they could be home tonight. If they'd made a wrong move, they could have ended up being buried beneath the Ferris wheel.

"I saw you bum one off Woody," Clay responded, lighting another cigarette. "You know how much a pack runs? Screw that. Go buy your own. I can't stand—"

Alex lurched right, dove and tackled Clay. The man fell into the snow, and immediately reached for his rifle. Alex stopped him with a punch to the face. Wanting to help Alex get Clay's weapon, Brennan took a step toward them, but froze when the cold tip of the rifle pressed against his cheek.

"Don't think about it," Randy said, then yelled out when Nick jumped on his back.

"Get his gun," Nick shouted as he tried to drag Randy to the ground.

Randy dropped the lantern into the snow, put his finger on the weapon's trigger, and fired. Brennan fell to his knees as the round hit the tree to the right of him. But Nick never let go. He clutched Clay by the throat and wrapped his legs around the man's waist.

Worried Randy might accidentally shoot him during the struggle, and that Shultz and the other men would run out any second and start firing, Brennan stood but hesitated, waiting for the right moment to rush toward Randy and Nick. A gunshot echoed around them. Brennan lurched back. Froze. Stared toward the landing where Shultz stood, his weapon aimed toward Clay and Alex.

Dread wrapped around Brennan's chest and squeezed. He slowly slid his gaze to the trees, then sucked in a breath. "No," he whispered. Alex lay face down in the snow. He didn't move. Didn't make a sound.

"Little fucker," Randy shouted.

Brennan looked away from Alex, just as Randy flipped Nick to the ground. He immediately pointed the rifle at Nick's face. Breathing hard, Randy took a couple steps back, but never lowered his weapon. "Did you think you could take me? Huh, mother-fucker?"

Shultz jumped from the landing and into the snow bank below. "What the hell happened?"

Clay lifted his rifle from the snow. "Kid surprised me. Knocked me off my feet."

Shultz crouched, and flipped Alex onto his back. "Damn it!" He stood. "How could he attack if you had your gun on him?" He turned toward Randy. "*Did* he have his gun on him?"

"I wasn't paying attention. I was too busy watching them."

Shultz picked up Clay's lantern and knocked the snow from it. He scanned the ground, then shook his head. "Come closer," he said to Clay.

Clay wiped his face with his bare hand and approached Shultz. "Where's your glove?"

"Must've dropped it in the snow."

"Why was it off?"

"Had an itch."

Shultz leaned closer. "I can smell weed on you. There're two cigarettes on top of the snow. Wanna try again?"

"Sorry, Matt. I—"

"Save it." He turned away and started toward Randy, then came to an abrupt halt. "Do you realize how much money is on the line?"

"I said I'm sorry."

A wry grin crossed Shultz's mouth. "Sorry." He faced Clay again. "You should be," he said, then shot Clay in the head.

As the driver dropped to the ground, bile rose from Brennan's throat. He bent over and puked. Fought to catch his breath. He hated Clay, hated all these men, but to watch a man's head explode...he didn't have that kind of hatred in him.

"Williams, get it together. You and Janson carry McGuire inside."

"The kid's still alive?" Randy asked.

"For now." He eyed Randy with suspicion. "Do I have to

worry about you drinking or doping? The ransom cut just got larger for all of us. I have no problem making it even bigger."

"No way. Ask Woody," Randy said, his gaze drifting to Clay's body. "What do you want to do with Clay?"

Shultz looked over his shoulder to where the dead man lay in the snow. "Leave him for now. I want all these little pricks to see what'll happen if they try to pull another dumb move. Tomorrow, they can bury him with Pembroke."

"You heard him," Randy said when Shultz headed back to the ballroom. "Get McGuire into the building."

The snow came up to Brennan's knees as he made his way toward Alex. Nick leapt through the high drifts as if he were a rabbit. When they reached Alex's body, it was too dark to tell where his friend had been shot.

"Careful," Alex whispered, springing hope in Brennan's chest.

"You're conscious. That's good. Where're you hit?"

"Stomach. It hurts so bad," he said, his voice cracking.

"We gotta get you inside, man." Nick went to Alex's feet. "It's not going to be easy."

"Touched the rifle. Almost did it," Alex said, as Brennan hooked his arms under the team captain's armpits. "Nick, get the keys."

Nick shifted his gaze to Randy. Since Shultz had taken Clay's lantern, chances were the gunman couldn't see what they were doing.

"Hurry," Brennan quietly urged him.

"Got 'em." Nick slipped the keys into his boot, then grabbed Alex by the ankles. "Ready?"

Together they lumbered through the snow, which had drifted to three or more feet in some areas along the way. When they reached the steps, Randy made no move to help them. The light from his lantern exposed the worry on his face, and Brennan wondered what kind of effect Clay's murder would have on the other men. Would they be even more trigger-happy? Or would they eventually turn against Shultz?

The door swung open. His eyes narrowed, his mouth twisting in anger, Shultz held the door while they carried Alex inside the building. The room filled with commotion, his teammates panicked, called out to them, questioning what had happened. Simon started to rise, but Shultz pointed the pistol at him. "Stay." Once Brennan and Nick had carefully lowered Alex near the heater they'd been using, Shultz glanced around the room. "Shut up! I want you all to listen carefully. I gave your parents forty-eight hours to pay for your release. Two days isn't a long time, but it'll feel like it if you boys don't play by my rules. McGuire's been shot in the stomach and Clay is dead. That's what happens when you don't obey. Now, this isn't a vacation. You will not be given food or water. We will not provide you with blankets and pillows. What you see around you is all you're going to get, so I don't want to hear any bitching about needing something to eat or drink. If you're thirsty, eat some snow."

"Just make sure it ain't yellow," Woody said with a chuckle.

While Joel also laughed, Brennan ignored his outrage and looked to Alex's wound. Blood coated his gray sweatshirt, and, on the lower right side of the boy's stomach, there was a hole in the material. His hands trembling from the cold and fear, Brennan lifted the sweatshirt by the hem. With each breath Alex took, blood seeped from the wound. He looked to Alex's ashen face, then met his gaze. The pain in his friend's eyes had him swallowing back the urge to cry. Now wasn't the time for that. He didn't know much about the human body, but knew Alex needed to get to the hospital. If only he had the nerve to say something to Shultz about it.

"Coach." Nick also stared at the wound. "Alex needs a doctor."

"Since I can't pull one out of my ass, he's going to have to suffer."

"What if he dies?" Simon asked. "What if his parents want proof he's still alive?"

Woody cocked a brow. "Kid has a point."

"There's a medical kit on the bus." Evan Barry, a senior who played attack with Brennan, stood. He'd been sitting around the heater next to theirs with Logan, Chad, Chris and Dillon. "I'm an Eagle Scout and have my merit badge in first aid."

Shultz ordered Joel to retrieve the kit from the bus. Once the kit was next to Alex, along with a bottle of water to clean the wound, Shultz had Evan go to work. Brennan stayed by his side, lifted Alex's sweatshirt again and, per Evan's instructions, poured water along the wound. "Do you know what you're doing?" he asked, the watery blood and the tear in Alex's flesh causing his empty stomach to churn with nausea.

"On paper, but it's better than just letting him bleed to death." Evan had Brennan help him roll Alex slightly to check if there was an exit wound. Once they discovered there wasn't, they rested him on the cold floor. Evan touched Alex's face with the back of his hand, then checked his pulse. "Face is clammy, pulse is weak. Alex, do you know where you are?"

He slowly nodded. "Hell."

Evan turned to Shultz. "We need to get him warm. We can't let him go into shock."

"I don't have blankets." Shultz thumbed toward the stage where they'd been forced to leave their gear. "Use what's in the bags," he said, then had a few of the guys grab clothes and coats to wrap around Alex.

While that was happening, Evan placed a gauze compress over the wound. The white material instantly turned red. "The kit only has a few of these."

"Just use them," Brennan said, worried Alex would bleed to death before they were released.

Evan placed the other two gauze compresses along Alex's stomach, then used tape to keep them in place. Once clothes and coats were brought over, Nick helped them do what they could to make sure Alex stayed warm, then they moved him closer to the heater. By the time they were finished, Alex had closed his eyes and was unresponsive.

"He's gonna die." Nick shifted his angry gaze to Shultz. "Alex is gonna die," he shouted.

"Shut it, Janson," Shultz warned him. "McGuire shouldn't have tried to take Clay's gun. It's his own fault if he dies. As it is, you're lucky I didn't shoot you, too." He turned to Joel. "Let's relieve Randy."

When he opened the door, snow blew inside. Shultz and Joel left. Moments later, Randy entered the room, brushing snow from his coat and hat. As he talked quietly to Woody, Nick leaned toward them. "Why didn't you guys try to take them out?"

"Couldn't," Simon said. "When we heard the first gunshot, Shultz told Joel and Woody to watch us. They had their guns on us. There was no way we could do anything." He looked to Brennan. "What happened out there?"

Nick answered for him, explaining what had gone down outside. "If Brennan had manned up, Alex wouldn't be dying on the fucking floor."

"How is this my fault? I told you guys this was a bad idea."

"But it wasn't. Alex had that gun, and if you would've helped me, we coulda had Randy's, too." Nick eyed him with disgust. "Typical Brennan Williams move."

"What's that supposed to mean?"

"Just like on the field…you get the ball and hesitate, or pass it to someone else and let them score. Why can't you just do something without overthinking? 'Cause that's what you did. You just stood there and let Alex get shot."

"You were on Randy's back, not facing his rifle." Brennan's cheeks grew hot as guilt and embarrassment rushed through him. "I didn't hesitate, I was afraid I'd get hit if I tried to grab the gun from him."

"Whatever, dude," Nick said glancing to Alex. Then he scooted away from them to sit on the other side of the heater.

Angry with himself and Nick, Brennan moved away from the heater to sit against the wall. In his mind, he replayed what had happened. Could he have handled the situation differently? Had there been an opportunity to take Randy's gun?

Yes, and yes.

Tyler joined him. "Don't listen to Nick," Ty said. "He's a dick. You scored more goals than him last season. I don't know what he's talking about. You don't hesitate or pass off the ball."

Brennan knew what Nick had said was the absolute truth. He did overthink. He preferred to analyze a situation rather than jump in and hope for the best. Ever since he was a little kid, he'd been that way. He liked winning, liked pleasing people and being praised for doing a good job. Making mistakes wasn't an option. He never wanted to be the guy who cost them a win because he'd reacted rather than taken his time to make the right shot. But they weren't on a lacrosse field. This wasn't a game. People were dead or dying.

"I was scared," he admitted. "Randy had his finger on the trigger and was trying to shake Nick off his back. I was afraid he'd fire again and hit me." He blew out a breath and rested his head against the cold wood. "Nick's right. I could've done something instead of just standing there. Now Alex..." His throat tightened. "If he doesn't make it, I have to live with that."

"It not your fault he was shot. It's also easy to say what you should've done when you look back. You were the one who didn't want to go along with the plan, and you were right."

"I don't want to be right, I want out of here." Anger warmed his body. "Shultz needs payback." He rolled his head and faced Tyler. "Nick has the keys to the bus."

Tyler's eyes brightened with excitement. "Seriously?"

He nodded. "I don't think we should've taken them. I can't see how we're going to get all of us on the bus and drive out of here. So much snow has fallen the bus might get stuck. Then what?"

"Yeah, but if a couple of us manage to get to the bus and we're able to drive it, we can get help."

"Or get shot."

"You think they'd shoot at the bus?"

"They're not going to care what happens to it. Think about it...Randy and Woody were already here, so they've got to have a car or truck somewhere at the park."

Tyler frowned. "I didn't think about that. You're right. Nick shouldn't have taken the keys. If Shultz finds out, he's going to be pissed."

Brennan settled his gaze on Alex. They had transportation sitting right outside, and he knew there was a hospital in Medina. They could have Alex there in thirty or forty minutes. But it would be a huge risk, one he wasn't prepared to take.

Why can't you just do something without overthinking?

Because he didn't want to be a hero. He wanted to survive this and go home to his family.

Except...Alex had been in the process of looking at colleges for next year. Now he might not make it to the morning. Tension and guilt crawled up his back. Alex was wealthy, good looking, super-smart and athletic, but he was also the kind of guy who stood up for the weak, to bullies, and ran the academy's annual charity drive. Damn it, *Alex* was the hero. He was supposed to lead them out of this mess.

"Do you think Nick will try to take the bus?" Tyler asked.

Nick was as bad as Shultz. He didn't think. He acted. Which was why he was constantly in trouble at school or in the penalty box during a game. "He'd be stupid to do it."

Tyler shrugged. "Maybe not. Only one person needs to escape and get help." He sighed. "I want you to know that I was scared, too. You know, about using the knife."

"Thanks."

"You saw Shultz shoot Alex and Clay?"

Images of Clay's head partially exploding filled his mind. "Yeah."

"Are you okay?"

The door burst open and Shultz rushed into the room, leaving a trail of snow behind him. He walked over to Randy and Woody, said something Brennan couldn't hear, then turned his attention on the team. "Janson and Williams, get up and come over here."

Oh, shit. The keys. Why else would Shultz single out him and Nick?

Brennan tried to make eye contact with his teammate, but Nick's gaze was on the floor. When they both reached Shultz, the man smiled, then slammed his fist into Brennan's stomach. Pain shot through his core as he doubled over. Before he could catch his breath, Shultz delivered another blow, slamming his fist against Brennan's head. Swaying and seeing stars, he staggered and fought to remain standing. He rubbed his head, and tried to bring Shultz into focus.

"What'd I do?" he managed.

"The bus keys are missing."

Randy rammed the butt of his rifle into Nick's gut. "I bet this little asshole did it," he said as Nick fell to his knees clutching his midsection.

"One of you took them." Shultz looked across the room to where they'd left Alex. "Unless McGuire somehow managed to get them."

"I'll check," Woody said.

Moments passed. Brennan wanted to turn around and make sure the man wasn't causing more injury to Alex, but didn't dare make a move. The coldness, the 'I will fuck you up' look in Shultz's eyes, kept him frozen with fear.

"Nothing," Woody called.

"Okay, that settles it. One of you two took my keys. I want them back." Shultz forced Nick to his feet. "If you give them to me now, I won't punish you."

Brennan didn't believe him. Not after witnessing two executions and Alex's shooting.

"I don't know where the keys are," Brennan lied.

Nick rubbed his stomach. "Me, either."

Shultz looked to the ceiling and released a frustrated breath. "Fine. Fuck it. Strip down. Everything off. Now."

Brennan's body shuddered with an involuntary shiver. He was

no longer scared for himself, but for Nick, and didn't want to consider what Shultz would do to him once he discovered the keys in his boots.

"I don't have them," Brennan insisted as he pulled his sweatshirt over his head.

"I've been coaching you for two years. Never once have you shown any balls. But, who knows? Maybe you finally grew a pair." Shultz nodded to Brennan's pants. "Lose them," he said, then turned to Nick. "Come on, Janson. If I have to force you out of your clothes, you won't get them back."

That last threat had Nick moving. In less than a minute, the two of them stood naked. Goose bumps immediately coated Brennan's skin as the icy air blew over his body. Never in his life had he been this cold or vulnerable. He didn't care that he was nude, that his teammates and the other men were likely looking at him. Freezing trumped humiliation. The only thing warming him was knowing Nick didn't have the keys on him because he'd stripped, too. Where he'd put them, Brennan couldn't be sure. He was just glad Nick had been smart enough to do something with the keys before now. He didn't want to consider the punishment Shultz would've given him.

"Are you gonna give them a cavity search?" Woody asked with a chuckle. "I saw those keys. If one of those boys managed to shove them up their—"

"Shut up." Shultz looked over Nick, then him. A smile tugged at his mouth. "What do you know? Looks like you have a small pair of balls after all." He chuckled. "You even have hair on them. Get dressed before I puke."

Brennan's entire body burned with hatred. Forcing them to strip wasn't just about finding the keys. Shultz was trying to demoralize him and the entire group. The stupid prick probably didn't even know what the word meant, but that was exactly what he was attempting. Proving he was in charge hadn't been enough. He wanted to crush their spirit, discourage them from having even the smallest amount of hope.

As he dressed, he thought back to what had happened outside. Shooting Alex hadn't been necessary. Alex had barely touched the rifle when Shultz fired. He knew their team captain. The kid had never held a gun in his life. A warning shot would've had him dropping the weapon. But putting a bullet into Alex's stomach had sent a message.

Obey or die.

He finished zipping his fly, then pulled his sweatshirt back over his head. He'd obeyed. Because he was cautious, because he did overthink things, he had tried to discourage the others from trying to get a gun and the bus keys. What had it gotten him? Not a fucking thing.

After slipping back into his coat, then putting on his hat, he stared at Shultz. The man didn't think he had balls. Fine. He was good with that. It meant the piece of shit wouldn't look at him as a threat.

"Got something to say?" Shultz asked him.

He had plenty, but shook his head.

Shultz snorted. "Doesn't surprise me." He stepped closer. So close, Brennan could see the man's pores. "You know what, bud?" he asked, his tone quiet, thoughtful. "You're a big kid, have great grades, you're good looking, your family has money…you got it all. But you're missing one key thing. Wanna know what it is?"

He didn't. At one time, he'd respected Coach Shultz, had looked up to him, had wanted to drive his Camaro, have a hot girlfriend like him. Now he wanted the man to be like Clay.

Dead.

"Guts." Shultz shoved him. "Both of you go back to your place," he said, then added, "It's still early, and we've got a long night ahead of us. Take a look at McGuire. Don't make it painful for yourselves. Just go to sleep. Unless your parents hate you, tomorrow morning this should all be over. Let's finish this bathroom break."

After ordering three more of the guys to head outside, cold air swirled through the room when Shultz opened the door. Brennan sat back in his spot next to Tyler. Nick also went back to where he'd been sitting. As far as he knew, only he, Nick and Tyler knew about the keys.

"That sucked," Ty said, offering him a couple of sweatshirts to keep warm.

Brennan pushed them away. "I'm not cold. I'm pissed."

"Don't blame you. Shultz is fucking crazy."

And right. Shultz and Nick didn't think he had any guts. Before he left this park, he'd prove them wrong.

He met Nick's gaze over the kerosene heater. Off the field, he and Nick didn't get along. During a game, the two worked in sync. They all did, and would need to act as a team to get through this.

Wind and snow rushed into the room as Shultz and Joel herded the guys back inside the ballroom. "Kill the lights," Shultz shouted, and turned to the team. "Not a fucking word!"

"What's happening?" Randy asked, shutting off the last lantern. Other than the soft glow from the heaters, the room was plunged into darkness, and the kidnappers went to the boarded windows.

Shultz exchanged his pistol for a rifle, then placed the muzzle in between one of the cracks of the plywood. "We might have company."

4

FBI Cleveland Division, Cleveland, Ohio
Friday, January 20th, 6:48 p.m. Eastern Standard Time

DISAPPOINTMENT CUT THROUGH Summer. She looked away from Dave, who'd just informed them that the Medina County deputies and Highway Patrol hadn't located the kidnappers and kids. A snowplow driver who'd heard about the missing bus on his police scanner had contacted the authorities after driving by a house near Ottawa Lake. He knew the owners of the house, which was for sale, and also knew they'd moved to South Carolina last November, leaving their realtor and son to look after the house until it sold. The plow driver had become concerned when he'd noticed lights coming from the barn and home. Since the bus was allegedly last seen heading west from the Lodi exit, and the barn would provide ample cover, she'd had SWAT en route to surround the property, hopefully bringing the situation to a peaceful resolution. Instead, SWAT had discovered that the homeowner's son had decided to bring his family to the home after losing power at his own house.

"The weather has gotten worse," Dave continued. "A state trooper is currently in the hospital with severe injuries after getting into an accident while helping with the search. Lieutenant Nelson and I do not want to risk the lives of any of our people, so we're calling it off for the night. Tomorrow morning, with the help of Medina, Ashland and Lorain County Sheriff's departments, along with Highway Patrol, we'll resume the search."

"The media is going to hear about this," Tony said. "Too many agencies are involved to keep this quiet."

Dave let out a tired sigh. "Local reporters already contacted our offices and Highway Patrol. Nelson and I agreed to tell them nothing for now. We've also asked the families to not discuss the kidnapping outside of law enforcement. But you're right. Too many people are involved and word about the kidnapping will likely surface soon. I'm hoping we find the bus before they do. This will make national headlines, and I don't want the kidnappers panicking and doing something to those kids."

"I don't disagree," Summer began, "but making the public aware could help us locate the bus. I'd rather we feed the media the information we *want* to give them, than have reporters possibly impede our investigation."

"I don't want to put those kids' lives at risk," Dave countered. "Nelson also informed me that they found the body of Frank Stokes in the back of Wayne Pembroke's SUV. Stokes had been shot in the head." He rubbed his eyes. "DNA gathered from Pembroke's tablet matched the coach's. Investigators said they not only found his blood on the tablet, but traces of brain, leading them to conclude the man is likely dead, too. If the Shultz cousins are the kidnappers, which we've all agreed is the obvious assumption, they're extremely dangerous. Whoever murdered two people in order to pull off this kidnapping is not going to have a problem killing anyone else who might stand in their way. Even juveniles."

"Have you talked with CNU?" Chase asked. "We need to make contact with the kidnappers."

Summer fought to keep from looking at her ex. Guilt over her pregnancy had anxiety twisting her stomach. She had no idea how he'd react once he learned she was carrying his child.

When they'd first started dating eight years ago, Chase had

made it clear he hadn't wanted children. He'd admitted that, at one time, he had pictured himself with a couple of kids, but after his years with the FBI, especially his time as a crisis negotiator, he had changed his mind. Witnessing violence against children had warped his perception of fatherhood, and he hadn't wanted to bring a child into a world filled with monsters who wouldn't think twice about hurting, sexually abusing, or killing a kid.

While she had understood his logic, she'd had her own selfish reasons for not wanting babies. Her career had been her top priority, and becoming pregnant would slow her rise within the FBI. When she'd first discovered she was expecting, she'd been devastated. She had been promoted to Assistant Special Agent in Charge of the Cleveland Division about eighteen months ago, and had hoped to continue to prove to her superiors she deserved to run her own field office. Hopefully, in a warmer, sunnier state.

But the moment she'd heard her baby's heartbeat, she'd fallen in love. No matter how defunct her relationship was with Chase, she still loved him and honestly believed he loved her. The child she carried had been created out of love, was a part of the man she still wanted but couldn't have because he didn't know how to deal with his emotions or forgive himself.

"Kevin Williams volunteered to be the spokesperson for the other parents," Dave replied. "Not all the parents were happy with this, but looking into his background and personality, we explained that he has the right temperament for the job. The rest of the parents bought it and backed off. The two crisis negotiators working the case replied to the text on his behalf."

"And that was?" Chase asked.

"They asked for proof of life, and stated that they wanted to talk, not text." Dave glanced to his watch. "That was twenty minutes ago."

Chase rubbed a hand under his chin, drawing Summer's attention to his mouth. Which only reminded her of how much she missed kissing him. But now wasn't the time to think about that, or about running her hands through his dark hair. Or over his wide chest…rubbing his arousal…

She cleared her throat. "Is there a typical response time?" she asked, forcing herself to stay focused. Except that she'd been up since five a.m., had been at the office since seven, was concerned about the victims, about Chase and how this case might bring back painful memories, and therefore extremely exhausted.

He half-shrugged and shifted his hazel eyes to her. "I can write a book about the cases I've worked, and each one would be different. They could be taking pictures of the boys as we speak, or discussing their next move, or giving us a big FU. It's possible they won't engage at all." He looked back to Dave, but before he did, she swore his eyes held regret and apology. If that were the case, she didn't want him regretting or apologizing. She wanted the man she'd fallen in love with back. Not only because having a baby on her own scared the hell out of her, but because she missed him. Missed *them*.

"If you don't hear from the kidnappers by morning, I think you need to bring in the media." He held up a hand before Dave could counter. "I get that will mean you'll have to deal with reporters and news vans, but as we've discussed, a bus would be hard to hide. Someone has to have seen something. If we could find where the kids are being held, we'll be in the game."

"Meaning?" Lauren asked.

"We've been forced to play by their rules. If we're able to surprise them, surround their location, that'd be a game changer. They'd still have the upper hand because they have fifteen hostages, but once they're aware there's no way to leave unless they're in a body bag or the back of a squad car, we might be able to end this before someone else is murdered."

Lauren leaned back in her chair. "Or things could escalate and they might decide to kill all the hostages, then themselves."

"This kidnapping isn't about a cause, it's about money. If there are three or more men holding these kids hostage—like we think—I have a difficult time believing they've made a *do or die* pact." Chase looked past Lauren to the wall behind her, his expression growing thoughtful, his eyes seeing but unseeing. As if he were remembering another time. He blinked, then looked directly at Lauren. "We won't be able to dissect their state of mind until we make contact."

Summer wanted to ask him where he'd just gone, what he'd been thinking about, but refrained. She'd save that for later. With the exception of Agent Greg Leary, the rest of the team knew Chase's history. What they didn't know was how many nights he'd woken, incoherent, inconsolable, shaking and drenched in sweat. Though this kidnapping wasn't like the one which had driven him into a dark place, and had ultimately led to the end of his career with the FBI and their relationship, there was one thing both situations had in common...the age of the victims.

Before images of the dead teen forced their way into her head, she pushed them back into the deep recesses of her mind. "If we locate the hostages, and HRT isn't here yet, as you know, our SWAT team is equipped with snipers."

"I know," he said, not looking at her. "I hope there's no need to use them. But if a sniper takes out one of the kidnappers, the others might be willing to surrender."

Dave pushed back his chair and rose. "Summer, update the agents coming in about the situation. When you're finished, head home. Everyone else, do the same. Let's hope the meteorologists are right and the weather is clear tomorrow." He glanced around the room at each agent. "Let's hope we find those boys. Dismissed."

As the team rose to leave, Summer was torn between catching up with Chase or her boss. Since she was the Assistant Special Agent in Charge, she went to her boss first. "I can stick around. If the kidnappers make contact, we might need to act fast."

Dave ushered her into his office, then closed the door. When he met her gaze, his eyes held worry and...defeat. "I don't predict a good end to this."

She stared at Dave, her own worry escalating. Dave was one of the most levelheaded people she knew. He wasn't an alarmist. He assessed a situation and became a doer, got the job accomplished without making it personal. But he also had two sons, ages seventeen and fifteen. Plus, Senator Patricks had forced Chase onto them, and her ex's last case with CNU had resulted in the death of his partner and a fifteen-year-old boy.

"If you're concerned about Chase…"

He shook his head and slumped into the chair behind his desk. "He was a good agent and great negotiator. The decision he made that day was the right one. No one could've predicted the end result. It's not knowing where the hostages are that's bothering me. Badly. These guys have us by the throat right now, and I don't like it. There're no perfect crimes. A detail is always missed. We need to find it."

"We need to find the kids."

"Right. But Chase's theory about the Shultz cousins not being the masterminds…that's been bothering me, too. Who is then? So far the parents have all checked out and none of them are suspects."

"What about friends of one of the families? Or someone else who works for the academy? I can have the agents coming in for the night dig deeper into the school's faculty and also have them look into people with financial issues who are associated with one of the boys' parents."

He nodded. "Do that. Then ask Chase to have his people do the same."

Surprised, she stared at him. "We're the FBI. Our resources—"

"Just do it. Chase had details about the Shultz cousins we didn't. Which leads me to believe whoever was feeding him that information wasn't going through legal channels."

"Are you suggesting someone from CORE hacked into various institutions?"

"I'm not suggesting it, I firmly believe it. We'd need a court order to obtain juvenile records, and yet he had them within an hour of finding out about the kidnappings?" He shook his head. "I don't care how they got the intel, I care about getting these kids home. By any means necessary."

She did, too. While she wasn't sure CORE had gotten their information through hacking, she saw no reason to not use every resource available to end this situation. "I'll talk to the team coming on, and to Chase." Since Dave wanted to use CORE to help with research, she worried who else he might be willing to use. She gripped the doorknob. "If we find the bus, and the kidnappers want to negotiate before CNU arrives, will you ask Chase?"

Dave looked away. "Let's hope it doesn't come to that."

Her stomach twisted with anxiety. She released the knob and went to the desk. "Chase can't be involved." Research was one thing, but actual hostage negotiating was another. He had yet to heal from the last negotiation, couldn't grapple with or accept that what had happened wasn't his fault. "Ask the Cuyahoga County Sheriff or Cleveland PD to put one of their negotiators on loan."

He lifted his brows. "You know as well as I do that those people don't have the experience Chase does." He held up a hand. "Don't worry about that for now. We need to find the hostages first. Go home and get some rest."

She wanted to protect Chase from himself, but knew Dave was right. At one time, Chase had been one of the best crisis negotiators CNU had, and on the path to run the unit. Still, if he were to work with the kidnappers and things went bad, she worried she'd lose him altogether. When she'd been with him back in August, they'd come together physically and emotionally. He hadn't said anything about his move to Chicago, or wanting to try to revive their relationship, but he'd had a hard time keeping his hands off her, and an even harder time leaving. He'd flat out told her this. Which had made her angry, yet had also given her a frayed string of hope. She wanted to go back to where they'd been before he'd pulled the trigger. Or did she? With Dave looking at her expectantly, now wasn't the time to take a swim in that dark hole.

"Call me if you hear anything. Otherwise, I'll see you in the morning." She left Dave's office, and ran into Tony in the hallway. "Is everyone here?"

"Ready and waiting."

"Chase?"

"I just saw him get in the elevator."

Damn it. "Call security. Stall him until I get downstairs. I need to talk to him."

After Tony walked off, she went back into the briefing room. Lauren and Rich had remained behind and helped her bring the new team up to speed. Thirty minutes later, she was bundled up in her winter coat and headed for the elevator. When she reached the lower level, Chase wasn't there. "Where's Chase Sawyer?" she asked the agent working security.

"He left before Tony told me to keep him here."

Of course he did. After saying goodnight, she prepared herself for the bitter cold, then went to her car. His leaving without saying a word was a jerk move which shouldn't surprise her. Yes, she was certain he still cared, but also realized it might be time to stop avoiding the dark hole and dive into murky waters she hadn't wanted to penetrate. Maybe it was time to stop coddling him. It had been nearly two years since the shooting, and a year since he'd left her so he could hide from his emotions, from what had happened and to make a fresh start. Except she didn't believe he'd made a fresh start, but that his demons had followed him to Chicago.

As she slowly drove through the snowy streets to her small ranch in Fairview Park, a suburb on the west side of Cleveland, anger began to build inside her. Not only toward Chase, but herself. She'd been a fool to want a man who'd left her. Who hadn't been able to communicate his emotions, trust her enough to share his pain. He'd had no problem calling her once in a while, or hopping in her bed last August, but ask him how he was doing, how he was feeling and he would shut down completely, then run or end the phone call.

Perhaps his being here now was a sign, and it was time she was honest with herself and faced the harsh truth: they were over and had been for a long time. At this point, she didn't even know why she'd hung onto her love for him. Looking back to how their relationship had been prior to the fateful shooting, Chase would frustrate her. As a crisis negotiator, he'd been trained to keep emotion at bay, to stifle his feelings when dealing with a hostage taker. Unfortunately, his training had bled into *their* relationship.

He'd been taught to alter a person's behavior, to lessen negative emotions and to help those people think rationally. If she and Chase argued, as most couples did, he'd shrink into his negotiator shell, become unemotional and use his skills to manipulate. When she'd first realized he had been doing this, it had irritated the hell out of her. She hadn't been holding anyone hostage, or threatening to jump off a building, she'd been trying to communicate whatever it had been that had her upset. And while he'd become less and less emotional, the passion had remained once they'd gone into the bedroom. But just because he still turned her on, she needed to stop hanging onto the man he used to be, and become more rational. She had her career, her life in Cleveland, and a baby on the way. She needed to be as selfish as he'd been and put herself and her unborn child first.

Which was easier said than done because she did still love him, and couldn't stop remembering how good they'd been together. Chase was a strong, proud man. Unlike her, he'd come from nothing and had been given no opportunity to succeed. He'd been the youngest of three boys, had grown up poor and living in a tiny two-bedroom house outside Detroit, Michigan. His determination to escape poverty and make a life for himself had taken him away from a lifestyle that could've led him down the opposite road to law enforcement. His father had been an alcoholic and had issues with the law. His older brothers had spent their juvenile and adult lives in and out of jail and rehab. If Chase had followed their influence, he would've ended up like them. Instead, he'd worked three jobs, earned scholarships which had helped him attend college, and worked hard to earn his way into the FBI. And he was a good man. A solid guy she used to be able to depend on, turn to for support and advice. He had a dry sense of humor and a kind heart.

Her eyes misted with tears. She missed his smile and hated the constant stress etched on his face. If only he could let go of the past, realize living with regret was destroying him, and that it was okay to show his emotions. That it was okay to love himself again.

When she reached her driveway, relief eased the tension in her shoulders. One of her neighbors, likely Carl, who was a landscaper in the summer and ran a plow business during the winter, had cleared her driveway. A couple of inches of fresh powder remained, but that was better than trying to drive her sedan through a foot of snow. After she parked in the garage, she went inside. Instead of wondering where Chase had gone for the night, and why he'd chosen a hotel over her place, she thought about how she could repay Carl. Maybe she'd invite him and his wife over for dinner once she was back from Florida. Since they planned to look after her house while she was gone, a gift certificate to a nice restaurant might be the better way to go.

As she tried to decide which restaurant her neighbors might like, and she changed out of her suit and into flannel pajamas, the doorbell rang. Her stomach immediately tightened with anticipation and the hope Chase had chosen to come over after all. Which was stupid. Hadn't she just told herself she couldn't continue holding onto a relationship that was no longer there, to a man who couldn't trust her with his emotions? Who couldn't love her enough to put the past to rest and be with her?

Except she had to face an extremely important fact: she was carrying his child. That hope and anticipation soured to dread. She owed it to him to confess about the baby, but hadn't been prepared to tell him today, or anytime soon.

Exhausted from a long, stressful day, and tired of the two-year emotional roller coaster he'd had her riding, she refused to deal with informing him about the pregnancy tonight. He had a right to know about the baby, and she'd tell him once he returned to

Chicago. Call her a coward, but she didn't want to see the disappointment in his eyes, not when she was already in love with her unborn child. Not when she—no matter how much she fought it—was still in love with Chase.

Chase stood beneath the small porch and ignored the cold. As if he were a stalker, he'd spent over an hour sitting in his car, either waiting for Summer to leave the office building, or following her home. Rachel had secured him a hotel room in downtown Cleveland, not far from the FBI's Cleveland Division, but he had yet to check into his room. Not because he'd hoped Summer would let him stay with her, but because the roads were bad, visibility was still terrible and he'd wanted to make sure she made it home safely.

Then why are you ringing her doorbell?

He'd asked himself that question as he'd exited the rental car, again while walking to the door, then for the third time as he'd pressed the doorbell. The answer had been simple and selfish: he missed her.

But as he waited for her to answer the door, he had the sudden urge to rush back to the rental. Everything he'd done over the past two years had been one colossal mistake after another. The last had been when he'd been on assignment in Cleveland. He should have never called her, touched her, made love to her. Being with Summer during those few days had only reminded him of the future he'd thrown away. Even if he'd told her then that he still loved her, and that he still wanted to be with her, he hadn't been sure if she would accept him for the man he'd become. His therapist had told him showing his emotions wouldn't make him less of a man, but that hadn't been how he was raised. Men didn't cry. Despite being an alcoholic and having a record, his dad had taught him to be strong, confident, and show no signs of weakness. While he hadn't wept since his mom had died when he was ten, he'd become emotionally and mentally weak, and that wasn't acceptable. Summer deserved a man she could depend on, and who could shoulder any and all problems they might face.

In the last two years, roles had been reversed. Yes, Summer had always been a strong woman, a badass agent who had proven herself to their superiors and fellow agents time and again. But there were times when he'd sensed she was the one shouldering their problems, babying him. He'd practically raised himself, had gone through life depending on no one but himself. Even when he'd been living with Summer, he hadn't needed her, he'd wanted her. Until two years ago, he hadn't realized there was a difference. Now he didn't know what to do with any of that, with his feelings, with her.

Leave before she opens the door.

Yes, he could play the role of coward quite easily. Where Summer and his career were concerned, he'd become quite adept at running. But he was tired of fleeing from the memories and mistakes that kept him awake every night.

The porch light went on, and he stiffened. Seeing her in the briefing room surrounded by other agents hadn't been easy, but it'd been safe. Nervous energy whipped through him like the cold wind gusting against his back. It would just be the two of them now. Weakened by exhaustion, by regret and guilt, he would have to dig deep to maintain a strong front, to make her think he was still the guy she'd once loved…maybe still loved.

The door opened and he sucked in a deep breath. The soft glow from the light coming from the living room haloed her, made her look as if she were an angel. Her blond hair was no longer poker straight, but wavy and damp, likely from the snow, and had him longing to grip it, bring her mouth close to his.

"Hi," she said, opening the door wider and motioning for him to come inside. She grinned when he stepped onto the rug in front of the door. "You look like the abominable snowman." She brushed her hand along his sleeve, knocking away the snow. "How long were you out there before you rang the doorbell?"

"Just long enough for you to answer," he lied. She didn't need to know that he'd probably stood outside her door for about ten minutes before gathering the courage to ring the bell. He ran a hand through his wet hair. "It's amazing how it's still coming down out there."

"I'll get you a towel." She turned toward the living room, pink flannel pajamas unfortunately hiding her curvy body. "You can hang your coat on the hook by the door."

"No towel. I'm good. I won't be staying long. I need to check into my room."

She stopped and faced him. Her big blue eyes held uncertainty and disappointment, something he'd become accustomed to over the years, and something that made him ache inside. He didn't want her looking at him like that, and missed the love that used to brighten her eyes.

"You don't want to stay here? You know I have a spare bedroom."

"You didn't offer me that room the last time I was in town." She hadn't exactly offered her bed, either. Being the selfish bastard he was, he'd seduced her. He knew her body as well as his own, kissed her and touched her the way she liked until they fell into her king-sized bed. When irritation flashed in her eyes, he added, "That didn't come out right."

"No, it came out exactly how you meant. I admit it, I was an easy lay."

Guilt kicked him in the ass. "Don't say that."

"What, the truth? I was lonely. All I do is work, and I don't have time to date. When you rolled into town, having sex with you was a no-brainer. You're familiar, know how to get me there, and I didn't have to worry about relationship junk," she said with an eye roll. "That's not something I cared to deal with then, or right now."

A new ache blossomed in his chest. Maybe he'd finally accomplished what he'd set out to do when he'd left Cleveland a year ago. Maybe she no longer had feelings for him. The thought should please him. He'd wanted her to move on and forget about him, not because he no longer cared, but because he hadn't wanted her to watch him battle depression. He hadn't wanted to show her he'd become vulnerable, weak.

When his throat tightened, he cleared it. "I...you don't have to worry about any relationship *junk* with me."

Her smile didn't reach her eyes. "Oh, I know. You've made that clear. You fucked me for a few days, then didn't bother calling me until two months later."

"You didn't call me, either."

She crossed her arms over her full breasts. "What did you say to me before you went back to Chicago? That's right...this doesn't change anything. So you've gotta ask yourself, why would I bother to call you? To see how you're doing? How you're coping?" She shook her head, knocking her bangs from her forehead. "You wouldn't let me in before you rushed off to join CORE, so I saw no reason to make the effort."

"I'm sorry," he said, welcoming the guilt. Because she was absolutely right. He deserved her anger, deserved it if she shoved him completely out of her life.

"I know. You've told me dozens of times. Instead of constantly apologizing, why not do something to change?"

"Change what? Time?" Anger flirted with guilt. "If I could go back two years ago and make a different decision that wouldn't result in killing a kid, I would."

She dropped her arms. "God, you still can't say his name. Come on, Chase. You know damned well if you hadn't pulled the trigger we wouldn't be having this conversation. I'd still be grieving over *your* death."

He would never know. As for saying Brody Wakefield's name aloud...yeah, that was tough. When he did, he saw Brody's face, the shock in his eyes when the bullet had pierced his chest.

"I didn't come here to talk about the past, or for an *easy lay*," he said with bitterness more targeted at himself than her. He couldn't blame Summer for being defensive or accusatory, but every time they talked about Brody's death, and how it had led his partner, Larry Olsen, to an early grave, anger and guilt always surfaced.

"Then why are you here?"

I miss you. I love you. I'm struggling through life without you.

"The roads are bad. I wanted to make sure you got home."

"You could've saved yourself a trip and called." Her eyes held hope and challenge. "Try again."

"The case—"

"Don't. If you can't, for once, be honest with me or yourself, then leave. What you're doing to me isn't fair. Chase, you need to let me go." Her eyes glistened with tears and her hand trembled as she tucked a lock of hair behind her ear. "*You* need to go. Before you do, Dave wants your people at CORE to help research academy employees and anyone experiencing financial difficulties who are associated with the boys' parents."

When she turned away, he grabbed her arm. As if he had the right, he pulled her close enough her breasts touched his chest, and her breath fanned along his chin and throat. "I'm sorry," he repeated, not interested in talking about the case right now.

She gripped the front of his shirt. "Stop saying that."

"It's the truth." Unable to resist, he ran his hands along her upper arms. "I don't know why I came here."

"Liar."

He drifted his gaze from the hurt in her eyes to her lips. "I missed you," he admitted, then quickly added, "But I'm not here hoping to share your bed. There are so many unsaid things between us. I know I can't tell you everything on my mind...all I know is I needed to see you away from the office."

"You could never truly talk to me, could you?"

The realization dawning in her eyes gave him pause. "What do you mean? We talked. I've never been closer to anyone else."

She loosened her grip on his shirt to touch his cheek. "I know, but it wasn't until recently when I realized how much of yourself you've kept hidden from me. You'd open the door to what's going on in here," she said, running her hand through his wet hair. "But you never really invited me inside. Does that make sense?"

"If it was true. Are you doubting that I didn't love you? Because I did." *And still do.* "Just because I didn't always say or do the right thing didn't mean I loved you any less."

"It's not that I doubt you loved me. After…the shooting, you never let me in, you only let me see what you wanted."

Frustrated, angry with himself and her flowery scent for driving him crazy, inundating him with memories of waking up smelling her on his skin, he released her and stepped back. "You had enough going on during that time. Your dad's heart attack, the upcoming promotion, and I was doing okay."

She stepped forward, bringing their bodies together again. "Right. Withdrawal, weight loss and insomnia are signs of a healthy person. Why couldn't you have saved being rational and unemotional for your job, and kept it out of our relationship? Why can't you smile anymore?"

"Certain emotions are a sign of weakness," he said, unable to resist touching her cheek. Her skin was so soft, so smooth.

"When you saw me cry, did you think I was weak?"

"Of course not."

"But you're not a woman, right?"

He stopped caressing her skin. "I have total respect for women. But I wasn't raised to wear my emotions on my sleeve."

"No, you were raised by an alcoholic who didn't care about you or your brothers, and who beat the emotion right out of you." She gripped a fistful of his hair when he tried to move. "There's nothing wrong with admitting the truth about who you are, and how you were raised. Honestly, I'm learning something new about you."

"I already have a therapist and don't need you analyzing me. I just wanted to see you. Clearly it was a mistake coming here."

The moment she let go of his hair and moved back, he started for the door.

"What you see as a sign of weakness," she continued anyway,

"is, to me, a sign of strength."

Angry she couldn't let it go, he faced her. "If I started bawling over killing a kid, that'd make me a strong man? Cleanse my soul, my guilt? Bullshit."

"I never said that. Ever. But you couldn't, not once, talk to me about that night, or how you were coping." A tear slipped down her cheek. "Do you have any idea how much it hurt me to lie next to you, knowing you were awake, probably reliving the shooting and dealing with how it made you feel? That not once did you roll over and hold me."

"I held you all the time."

"But you wouldn't let me comfort you. You wouldn't let me take on some of the burden so we could deal with what had happened together." She wiped her face and straightened her shoulders. "You were always there for me. Did it ever occur to you that I wanted to be there for you? That I wanted to know our relationship was a partnership, a give and take, that *you* needed me just as much as *I* needed you? Or didn't you think I was strong enough?"

He'd forgotten how damned perceptive Summer could be when it came to him. If he told her the truth, that he hadn't realized he'd needed her until it was too late and he'd already run, it would hurt her. And he'd done enough of that.

Leaving his coat on the hook, he went to her. "You're one of the strongest people I know." He caressed her cheek. "I admire that you're comfortable with yourself and have no problem expressing how you feel. There've been times when I wished I could be more like you. But I don't know how to be that way. I don't know how to let go of so many things." He cupped her face. "Including you."

She rubbed her eyes, which knocked his hands away and smeared the little makeup she still wore. "I'm too tired to deal with you right now. I can't even digest what you just said."

He drew her into his arms and hugged her. "I'm sorry."

She embraced him, tightened her grip around his back. "Stop

apologizing and just hold me."

Loving having her back in his arms, he kept his mouth shut and enjoyed this special moment. Tomorrow, he'd wake in his hotel room alone, then face her across the briefing room table. It'd be back to business, and nothing would likely change because he didn't know if he ever could. For now, he'd soak up this time with her. Brand it onto his memory for the sleepless nights.

As he held her, she rubbed his back, nuzzled close to his neck. Needing just one kiss before he left, he turned slightly and sought her mouth. Kissed her softly, leisurely. When she parted her lips, he pushed his hand through her hair and deepened the kiss. Their tongues met. She released a tiny moan that had his balls tightening. Knowing he should stop, that this was a mistake and unhealthy for both of them, he ignored his conscience and ran his hands along her sides, until he gripped her hips, urging her against his arousal.

Her breasts were fuller than he'd remembered, her stomach harder and slightly swollen, but she hadn't looked as if she'd gained weight anywhere else...

He froze. His mind raced. Back to the end of August, to when they'd had a sex marathon. No. Couldn't be. He'd used a condom every time, except when they'd had sex in the shower. But he'd pulled out then. Or had he?

Breathing hard, he inched his mouth from hers and met her gaze. The uncertainty in her eyes had returned, and now he suspected why it'd been there from the start. Trying to keep his hand steady, he reached between them and pressed his hand along her stomach. Summer had always had an hourglass figure and flat abs. This curve to her belly, the roundness...

"I was going to tell you," she said, fresh tears filling her eyes.

Arousal no longer gripped him by the balls, but fear did. "Don't say it." He pulled his hand away, jerked back as if he'd been scorched by fire. Shoved his fingers through his hair and gripped the base of his neck.

She was going to tell me?

"When?" he asked, trying to desperately reel in his shock, the terror of bringing a child into the world. "After the baby was born?"

She looked to the hardwood floor. "I...I wasn't sure. But don't worry. I'm not expecting anything from you."

Hurt that she thought so little of him, that he wouldn't take care of her or the child they'd created, even if he hadn't wanted one, he took another step back and began to pace. "Didn't expect anything from me?"

"You made it very clear you didn't want kids."

"So?"

"So, after the baby's born, you can just sign off your rights. I make enough money and don't need you to pay child support."

Summer was an independent woman, a quality he loved. Raising a child on her own, though, was completely different. She had a few friends in the area, but her family was out of state, leaving her with little support from them. Yes, she made decent money, but the cost of childcare, diapers, formula and all the other things that went with having a baby would be expensive. And how could he, in good conscience, sign away his rights to his child? What kind of an asshole did she take him for?

Before he'd killed Brody, Summer had been hinting at marriage. Instead of following his gut and heart, he'd justified to her, and himself, how they already lived together, loved each other and didn't need a piece of paper to acknowledge they were a couple.

What he hadn't told her was that he'd worried once they were married, she'd change her mind about wanting children. At the time, her sister had been pregnant with her second child, Summer's friends were also marrying and starting families. When he'd visited those people with her, and watched her holding their babies, her eyes had brightened with awe and love. That had made him uncomfortable. Kids were cute if they belonged to someone else. He hadn't wanted to be responsible for his own, for what could possibly happen to them or face the devastating loss of a child.

He hadn't always felt that way, but before becoming a crisis negotiator, he'd been part of a manhunt for a serial killer and a missing twenty-year-old girl. The girl, Tara Miller, had been later found strangled, her body dumped under a bridge. He'd had the unfortunate job of informing her father of her murder. The man's response had been, "I wish you could have known her. She was an angel." Chase hadn't been able to shake off the man's words, or forget the pain and misery in his eyes. All he'd known was he never wanted to be in Tara's father's place.

Now he was going to be a dad. He knew nothing about babies, probably couldn't change a diaper without watching an instructional video on the Internet. He was a fast learner and would figure it out, but there'd be more for them to do. The house would need to be baby-proofed, he would have to increase Summer's security system, and buy her a better vehicle—preferable something that would rival a small tank. A college fund was important, too. When he returned to Chicago, he'd set one up immediately. What about a GPS chip? CORE's other branch, DecaLab, had been fine-tuning the use of a chip on humans. If he could talk Summer into having one surgically implanted in their child, he'd probably sleep better—when he actually slept.

"Chase," she said, "would you please say something instead of wearing away my floor? I know this is a shock. I took two tests because I couldn't believe it. But, again, I don't expect you to be responsible for this baby."

He stopped pacing. "No."

"No, what?"

"No, I'm not signing away my rights." He pictured a little girl with Summer's blond hair and blue eyes. Rather than experiencing that gut-clenching fear, warmth spread throughout him. "I'll want custody, too," he said, his own words shocking him. How could they share custody if he remained in Chicago? Ian Scott was a fair and good boss, but he doubted the man would let him use the company jet to fly his child back and forth between Chicago and Cleveland.

"Are you hearing yourself?"

"Loud and clear. What's the problem?"

She let out an exasperated breath. "You live six hours away."

"I'll move."

"That's ridiculous. Look, go to the hotel and let this sink in before you make any rash decisions."

"I don't make rash decisions."

She cocked a brow. "I'm fully aware. Spontaneous is not part of your vocabulary." She folded her arms across her chest. "And have you considered your...health?"

He stared at her with disbelief and disappointment. He didn't know what shocked him more, the pregnancy, or that she'd question his mental health, and whether he was capable of taking care of their child. "I'm not a nut job."

Her eyes filled with sympathy. "I never said you were. It's just...you have to admit these past two years haven't been the best for you. Not to sound like a bitch, but I don't know if I'll be comfortable letting our baby stay with you."

His disappointment transformed to anger. "You didn't just sound like one." He took his coat off the hook. "I know I've made plenty of mistakes when it comes to you, but it really pisses me off that you can't recognize your own. The moment you found out you were pregnant, you should have told me." He shrugged into his coat. "Like it or not, I *will* be part of our baby's life. You can make it easy on both of us, or expect a fight. Your choice," he said, then left without another word.

Snow soaked his face as he made his way to the rental car, then proceeded to clean the windshield. He welcomed the cold and the bitterness. He loved Summer, had from the moment he'd met her, and probably always would, no matter what direction their lives took. Was he thinking rationally? Hell, no. Did the idea of being a father scare the shit out of him? Abso-freaking-lutely. But years of therapy had taught him one thing: life was unpredictable, and sometimes you couldn't rationalize why things happened.

As he drove through the snowy streets toward the downtown hotel, his temper cooled. Knowing his thoughts on kids, he understood why Summer had waited to tell him. Maybe she was right. Maybe he wasn't father material. But he was tired of living with regrets. Tired of being alone and unhappy. Yet, for the first time in years, knowing a part of him, a part of them, grew within her womb, made the future look a little brighter, and had him looking forward to tomorrow.

Tomorrow... He wiped a hand down his face. His future might have brightened, but what about that of the fifteen missing kids?

Why couldn't she keep her mouth shut?

Summer finished washing her face and brushing her teeth. She toweled off, only to unravel a handful of toilet paper to dry her eyes again, then blow her nose. Until recently, she'd never been much of a crier. But now, with her hormones going crazy, everything made her weepy and she could probably cry on command. Just yesterday, she'd cried over a diaper commercial. Who did that?

She tossed the used tissue into the toilet and drew in a ragged breath. Tonight's tears were different. She hurt and ached inside. What a cosmic joke. A cruel twist of fate. The man she loved, who'd never wanted kids, now planned to be part of their baby's life. Which meant he'd remain part of hers. She would have to spend the next eighteen years periodically seeing him without actually being with him.

She left the bathroom to sit on her bed, where she'd left her laptop. She opened it and began researching *Rights of Unmarried Fathers in Ohio*. Her mind should be on the missing kids, instead she could only think of her own. Despite what she'd said about his health—which she completely regretted—she trusted Chase. Not necessarily with her heart, but she knew him well enough to firmly believe he would never harm their child.

Then why had she become defensive, brought out the claws to cut him? By not allowing him visitation or partial custody, she would be doing a terrible disservice to their child. She'd grown up in a stable home, had the love and perspectives of both her mom and dad, and couldn't imagine not having had a male role model. Her baby deserved the same.

Their baby, she amended.

And what was she supposed to do with what he'd admitted to her? He'd said he couldn't let her go, not that he loved her and wanted to get back together. Ten minutes later, he'd threatened to fight for custody of a child he had never wanted. Maybe this sudden change in attitude was an excuse to continue to stay connected to her, not with the baby.

She spent the next thirty minutes going through websites which discussed both her and Chase's rights, and discovered he would have none to their child until a court order was set in place. To obtain the court order, a paternity test would have to be taken. From there, another would be needed to give him visitation or custody. Would the court look into his past? Chase had suffered a mini breakdown shortly after Brody Wakefield's death, requiring him to seek therapy and take antidepressants. Last she'd heard, he no longer needed the drugs, but was still meeting with a counselor. No matter what, she didn't want him to go under the microscope, or force either of them to suffer through the court process.

She closed the laptop. Whatever Chase's motivation, they were going to have to sit down and discuss how they'd play out the next twenty-two weeks. Was he now planning on coming to doctor's appointments, ultrasounds? Would he want to help decide a name…step in and take over as he'd done in the past? Because of his position as a negotiator, Chase had been comfortable directing those who worked for or supported his position during a hostage situation. When they'd lived together, deciding paint colors and furniture had usually been her thing, but when it had come to money and large purchases, he'd been a little…domineering. Since she tended to be a spender, she hadn't minded the way he'd kept her feet on the ground, and them out of debt. Still. She'd been living on her own for a year, and didn't want him thinking he could suddenly interfere with the way she went about her business.

Or maybe she was worrying over nothing. Tomorrow morning, he could wake up and come to his senses, realize they couldn't continue nursing an unhealthy relationship, but needed to cut ties and move on before they ended up hating and resenting each other. If not, she'd focus on the kidnapping, her upcoming vacation, and deal with him when her head had cleared.

But after she'd put away her laptop and turned off the lights, all she could think about was Chase and the kiss he'd given her before discovering she was pregnant. Deep down, she'd foolishly fantasized he'd be there through the pregnancy and birth of their baby, and pictured him living back in the ranch they'd originally rented together. Considering all that had been said and unsaid, it would likely remain a fantasy until Chase learned to forgive himself. Even then, after a year apart, she wasn't sure if they could find common ground other than sex and the baby.

That last thought had tears filling her eyes. She curled on her side and prayed for sleep. As she drifted off, the images of the missing boys filled her mind. Like Dave, she didn't predict a good end to the kidnapping. Something—she couldn't put her finger on what it was—about the situation unsettled her, had unease knotting the muscles in her shoulders and back. Maybe it was Chase's presence, her worry that he'd be on the line when a kid close to Brody's age was killed. Or maybe it was her whacked hormones. No matter the cause, she needed to keep her personal life out of the investigation.

Her cell phone chimed, indicating she had a text. That unease intensified and she worried Dave was contacting her. She snatched the phone from the nightstand and looked at the screen. Not Dave, but Chase…wanting the name and number of her obstetrician.

Damn. So much for him coming to his senses…

5

Ottawa Lake Amusement Park, Village of Ottawa, Ohio
Friday, January 20ᵗʰ, 10:44 p.m. Eastern Standard Time

BRENNAN DIDN'T FLINCH when the door opened, sending in more cold air. He remained curled on the floor against the wall, watching as Shultz and Joel shook off the snow covering their hats, coats and boots. Without moving his head, he glanced to the guys near him. They were either pretending to sleep or had somehow managed to rest. Not him. Not with Alex dying a few feet away, or with the prospect that help might be on the way.

"Well, what'd you find?" Woody asked Shultz.

Earlier, Shultz had burst into the building saying they had company, and that there were vehicles driving along the main road outside the park. Equipped with guns and binoculars, he'd then left with Joel, and had been gone for what had seemed like hours.

"Four armored SUVs and three squad cars." Shultz pulled off his gloves to hold his hands over the heater. "We saw them heading south, then west, likely to the other side of the lake. So we crossed the lake at its narrowest point, and entered the woods there."

Joel also began warming his hands by the heater. "Yeah, there was a faint light coming from that direction. We almost didn't see them because of the way the snow was falling."

Randy frowned. "See what?"

"Farmhouse and barn," Shultz said. "The three squad cars were in the driveway. Since we didn't see the SUVs, we waited in the woods until the cops left. We're only maybe a half mile—if that—from the farm, and I wanted to make sure the place wasn't getting raided or something. It'd be my fucking luck."

Joel chuckled. "No shit. But we don't think anything was happening at the house. As soon as the cops left, the headlights from the SUVs lit up from the side of the road. Then they all left in the opposite direction they'd come."

"Could you see lettering on the SUVs?" Woody asked, his tone darker than usual.

"Hell, it was so damned snowy, we couldn't even see the trucks until they turned on their lights."

Shultz nodded. "It's true. But two of the squad cars had *Sheriff* on them. We're in Medina County so..." He stepped away from the heater to pick up a Thermos. "I'm tempted to go back to the house and see who's there. If we need to vacate this place, we won't be able to use the bus. The problem is, it'll be hard to cover up the tracks in the snow."

"Don't go back to the house," Woody said. "Focus on finding the bus keys. We need to move it first thing in the morning. 'Cause once the snow stops falling, you can bet your ass the cops or Feds are gonna use a chopper to look for that bus."

"If the parents went to the police," Joel countered.

"Come on, boy. Don't be an idiot. Of course they went to the police. So, if we don't find those keys, we gotta figure out a way to camouflage the bus."

Shultz set down the Thermos. "Woody's right. We need those keys. First light, we search Clay's clothes again, and the area where we left him. They could've fallen out of his pocket when he was fighting the kid."

Randy snorted and turned his back.

"Got something to say?" Shultz asked.

The other man glanced over his shoulder to Woody, who shook his head. "Nope," Randy replied. "I'm good. We're going to need to fill the heaters with kerosene, too."

Shultz narrowed his eyes and looked first to Woody, then at Randy's back. "And bury Clay's body." He slipped on his gloves again, then picked up the Thermos. "I'm jacked up from the cold and cops, so I'll stay up for a while and keep watch. The rest of you get some sleep."

As the other three men settled themselves near the heater they'd been using, Brennan closed his eyes. He hadn't thought about them needing to move the bus, and was now glad Alex had told Nick to take the keys. If Woody was right, and the police used helicopters to search for them, this whole ordeal could be over tomorrow. Except...if the police showed up here, would Shultz and his men give up or fight? They were murderers and kidnappers. He didn't know much about the law, but figured they'd go to prison for life for what they'd done. Maybe they'd even get the death penalty.

His skin crawled with dread. Shultz and the others had to know what they faced if caught, which had him considering the house across the lake. Since he couldn't see Shultz giving up, but instead pictured him killing them all, they needed to find a way to contact the police before they found them by helicopter or whatever. If they caged Shultz in, he might start shooting. But if Shultz had no idea the police had surrounded the park, a sneak attack would end this before anyone else was hurt.

Brennan tried to recall what the park had looked like when they'd first arrived. He saw the snowy path leading to the lake. Had Shultz and Joel used that to cross the lake, or had they walked farther down and cut through the woods first? Shultz had told Woody and Randy that the police cars and SUVs had been heading south, then west, so Brennan knew what direction to go in. What he didn't know was how far the two men had walked once they'd crossed the lake. Getting lost in the woods was not an option, not with the current temperatures. But he'd rather face hypothermia than a gun, and if they didn't do something proactive, Alex could die.

They all could...

He looked over the heater and around the ballroom. The farmhouse added an interesting twist. He believed the cops were at the house for one reason only: they were looking for the bus. Which meant they were close. Too close. He'd expected the cops to eventually find them, just not this soon. He wasn't ready to put an end to the kidnapping. There was still work to do.

And people to kill.

Woody was going to have to go. The old man talked like a dumb hillbilly, but was definitely no idiot. He was too sharp, too fucking bossy. Yeah, Woody was going to die in the morning. Randy would follow. That prick hadn't been happy about Clay dying. Honestly, Clay's death had surprised even him. He hadn't been ready to kill him off, but supposed it didn't matter. Like the others, he'd served his purpose.

As for McGuire...Alex was a problem, too. He'd figured there'd be casualties from the team. Maybe a few bloody noses or a broken bone, but hadn't planned on any of them dying. He figured if any of them had to die, Alex was the best choice. The team captain was a born leader, and *he* preferred to stay in charge.

He relaxed by the heater and fought from smiling. None of these people had a clue who they were dealing with, or what was coming at them. Not the team, his crew or the police. He'd orchestrated the perfect crime. Had successfully devised an elaborate kidnapping without much of a hitch. When it was all over, he would be free to do whatever he wanted.

And they'd never catch him.

Brennan woke. His eyes burned with exhaustion. His head pounded from lack of food and sleep. He squinted toward the broken second-story windows. The wind had stopped gusting sometime during the night, and snow no longer blew into the building. He'd hoped the morning sun would chase away the cold temperature, but it remained hidden behind dark-gray clouds, leaving the interior of the ballroom unbearably freezing.

He glanced to Tyler, who'd covered himself with every article of clothing he'd had in his bag and slept against the wall. With the exception of a few of the guys, most of the team were also asleep, same with Joel and Randy. Woody was awake and drinking from a Thermos. Since Shultz wasn't in the room, Brennan assumed he'd gone outside and was probably looking for the bus keys. If he were in Shultz's position, he wouldn't have the guys from the team looking for them. How could Shultz trust that if one of them found the keys they'd turn them over to the man who'd kidnapped them? Not that it mattered at this point. He just hoped Shultz didn't discover Nick had taken them. He wasn't a fan of the kid, but also didn't want to see him end up like Alex.

He looked over to the team captain. Alex's face had become alarmingly pale. Because clothes had been piled on top of him, Brennan couldn't tell how much blood he had lost during the night, or if his chest was rising or falling. Worried Alex had died, he inched away from the wall and quietly scooted toward him. When he reached Alex's side, he touched the kid's neck and searched for a pulse.

"Is he...dead?" Nick whispered.

"No. I found a pulse." Brennan looked to Alex's face. The team captain's lips had taken on a bluish hue and dark circles underscored his closed eyes. "He doesn't look good."

Simon moved away from the heater to sit near them. "Should we check his wound?"

Brennan shrugged. "No clue. But if we mess with it, he might start bleeding again."

"*If* the bleeding stopped," Nick countered.

"If he bled all night, he probably wouldn't be alive." Simon looked at the heater when it clicked, then stopped running. "Not good. We've got to keep him warm."

As the rest of the heaters turned off, a few of the other guys groaned. Woody woke up Randy and Joel. "Heat's out. Watch them. I'll go tell Matt."

After Woody left, Randy told them to shut up, then he and Joel began talking and sipping from their Thermoses. Brennan knocked Tyler's boot to wake him, then motioned for him, Simon and Nick to move closer. "I think the police might be looking for us," he began, then quickly told them what he'd overheard last night.

"If any of us try to escape, all they have to do is follow our tracks," Tyler said. "We need to get one of their phones."

"Like we did with their guns?" Brennan shook his head. "Too risky."

"For once, I agree with Brennan." Nick moved closer. "I've been thinking...something isn't right about any of this."

Simon rolled his eyes. "No shit."

"Dude, just let me finish. Don't you think it's weird they chose this place? If the cops come, they'll be cornered. They've got a lake, woods and one road out of here. If they try to run, the police can track them in the snow. And *all* of us can ID them."

Brennan shifted his gaze to Joel and Randy. "And have any of you seen Shultz use his phone? All I've watched him do is check the screen, not talk or text."

"Maybe he's doing that when he goes outside," Simon suggested. "It'd be quiet on the bus."

"Right. Makes sense."

"No, it doesn't," Nick argued. "If Shultz is in contact with our parents or the cops, he'd be on the phone constantly." He also looked toward the gunmen. "Plus, none of these guys has said a word about the ransom, or asked Shultz if they've gotten any money yet."

Tyler wrapped his arms around his knees and drew them to

his chest. "They probably don't want us hearing about that."

"Or maybe a ransom demand hasn't even been made."

Brennan stared at Nick. "Then what'd be the point of kidnapping us? To teach rich, spoiled kids and their parents a lesson? No way. It's got to be about the money. Do you really think Woody or Randy care about teaching anyone a lesson?"

Tyler shook his head. "Those guys are like mercenaries."

"That's what I'm thinking," Simon agreed. "They got to be in it for the money."

"But they haven't taken any pictures or video of us," Brennan said. "In every movie I've seen about kidnappings, the cops always demand to talk to the hostage or see a picture of them."

"See?" Nick scooted closer. "Told you something isn't right. It's like I said last night, we gotta fight our way out of here before we all end up like Alex." He glanced at their team captain. "I'll try for the house."

"I'll go with you," Brennan said, determined to do what he could to get them out of this mess. Nick had him also wondering why their kidnappers had chosen the abandoned park. It made zero sense. Why pick a location without an easy escape route? Or maybe they had a backup plan. Maybe they had snowmobiles stored on the property. They could race across the lake, across one of the many open fields he'd seen during the drive here, to where a car could be waiting for them.

The ballroom door opened before Nick could respond. Woody entered first, followed by Shultz, whose breath hung on the air as he looked from his men to the team. "Good morning, assholes. Time to get to work. Thorpe, Barry and Ziss, you'll go with Woody. I want you three to move Clay's body to the Ferris wheel and bury him in the snow with Pembroke." He pointed to Brennan. "Williams, Janson, Demko and Huneck, you're going with Randy and bringing back kerosene for the heaters. Patricks, Everett and Connelly, you're with me. You get to search for the bus keys. Joel, you're in charge of the rest. Have them shovel around the bus, so we don't have trouble moving it."

As Brennan put on an extra pair of gloves, he avoided making eye contact with Nick. He had no idea where the kerosene was located, but this could be his and Nick's chance to make a break for it and try for the house.

"Actually," Shultz began, eying Zach Strauss, Riley Gallagher, Kyle Dodson and Hunter Perry, who were all going to be shoveling with Joel, "let's change it up. I want Janson switching places with Perry."

Shit. The bus was just outside of the building, where Shultz would be overseeing the search for the keys. There was no way Nick could risk running for the lake. He'd have to cross the open area between the ballroom and Ferris wheel, leaving him a target for any of the gunmen. Which meant that if Brennan had the opportunity to run, he'd have to do it alone.

Once everyone had finished adding extra layers of clothing, and gone to their designated gunmen, Shultz looked to Alex. "Anyone check on McGuire?"

"He's alive," Brennan said. "But he doesn't look good."

"Well, let me know when he's dead. I don't know about you boys, but I'm not down with hanging out with a rotting corpse." He opened the door. "Be sure to take a look at McGuire before you walk outside. If you pull any shit with us, that can and will be you. Remember, don't be dumb."

After Shultz finished his *inspiring* speech, they were ushered from the building. The cold air didn't take Brennan's breath away like it had yesterday. Either it was a little warmer, or his lungs had grown used to the low temperatures. Even without snow and the wind whipping, the park still gave off an eerie vibe. Nothing moved. Other than his own breath and that of those around him, nothing made a sound. Although he wasn't exactly sure how far they were from the freeway, he'd hoped to hear traffic, maybe see a plane overhead, anything to take away the sense of isolation surrounding this place.

Except for boot prints to the bus, which he assumed Shultz and Woody had made, there were no tracks in the snow. Looking toward the Ferris wheel, he could no longer say with certainty where they'd buried Coach Pembroke.

Over a foot of snow sat on top of the bus roof and hood, and had slid down the windshield. As he followed Randy, passed the bus and went toward what he assumed was a road or wide path—based on what was left of the structures and rides on either side of it—he wondered how Shultz planned to move the vehicle. Even if he had the keys, it would take a snowplow to clear the area and make it drivable. He glanced over his shoulder. Joel handed Zach and Nick shovels, then pointed to a massive snowdrift covering the bus's front tires and left bumper. Yeah, there wasn't a chance in hell any of them could use it.

Randy slowed. "Keep walking. We're heading for the hotel," he said, pointing to a rotting structure that still had walls and a roof.

He had Brennan and the other three guys walk ahead of him. Brennan couldn't blame Randy for being cautious, not after how Nick had attacked him last night.

"This sucks," Chris said, coming up alongside him. "That building is at least one hundred yards away."

Logan and Hunter caught up with them, flanking Brennan from the opposite side. "More like seventy-five." Logan panted hard. "I think my nose is busted. It hurts and I can't breath."

Brennan turned his head. Logan's profile had changed. His mouth and nose were swollen and the skin beneath his eyes was bruised.

"My face hurts, too." Chris rubbed the back of his glove along the purple and black marks covering his puffy jaw and mouth. "But I don't think anything is broken."

"I'd take a broken bone over a bullet to the stomach," Hunter said. "Did you see Shultz shoot Alex?"

Logan let out a huff of breath. "Jesus, why don't you talk a little louder?"

"I've got an idea," Randy said, his breath labored. "Why don't you all shut the fuck up?"

They walked in silence for a few minutes, then Chris looked back at the man. "The douche can't keep up with us," he whispered after he'd faced forward. "What were you guys trying to do last night?"

Brennan didn't want to talk about how it was his fault Alex had taken a bullet to the gut. If Alex died, he had the rest of his life to deal with the guilt.

"Isn't it obvious?" Hunter asked, keeping his voice low this time. "They were going for their guns. That's what I wanted to do. I tried to talk Dillon and Evan into making a plan, but those two pussies were too scared. I wish I'd been sitting by your heater. I'd have been all over that shit."

Brennan was thankful Hunter had been at a different heater. The kid was a lot like Nick. They both played the same position and they both liked trouble. Hunter's type of trouble wasn't fistfights. He was the guy who snuck alcohol into the dorms, and somehow scored weed. Brennan wasn't into either, so he tried to avoid Hunter when they weren't on the lacrosse field. Which wasn't easy to do, since less than three hundred students attended the academy.

Brennan kept his gaze locked on the old hotel. "You saw how that worked out for us."

"So did you see Alex get shot?"

"Geez, dude," Logan said. "Why would you even ask that?"

"Like you're not curious about what happened?" Hunter sniffed. "Forget I said that. After how you got all freaked about moving Pembroke's body, forget I asked."

"Fuck you."

"Whatever."

"Both of you need to shut it," Brennan said, trying to maintain his cool and not let Randy know they were still talking. "Let's get our job done. Alex needs the heater on him."

They continued on in silence. If Randy hadn't had a rifle aimed at their backs, Brennan might've enjoyed the walk. Although the old park was creepy, there was something beautiful about the way the snow coated the trees, old coaster tracks and buildings. Especially when the morning sun occasionally peeked through the clouds, causing any of the snow it touched to sparkle as if loaded with diamonds.

"Turn the corner," Randy shouted. "Use the double doors to the left."

Brennan studied what was left of the hotel and tried to imagine what this place had looked like back in the day. Half of the building had surrendered to the elements. Large and small trees, bare of any leaves, had taken over the collapsed portion. His mind repaired the building, coated the exterior with bright white paint, replaced the rows of broken windows, and fixed the damaged columns. As he rounded the corner, the double doors came into sight, along with another snowy path carved out between rows of naked trees. The path sloped downward, and without leaves blocking his view, Brennan realized this was another route to the lake. He quickly glanced to the snow around him before the others trampled it, and searched for any indication that Shultz and Joel had gone this way last night.

"What are you looking for?" Hunter asked.

"The snow is blocking the doors," he said, not willing to risk Randy overhearing him tell Hunter or the others that he and Nick wanted to make an attempt to reach the farmhouse. "We need something to help us shovel it out of the way."

"Or help us knock out Randy and take his gun," Hunter whispered.

Liking that idea more than trying to escape to the farmhouse, Brennan nodded. Chris and Logan agreed. As he and the others searched for large pieces of wood, Randy came up behind them, holding the rifle in both hands. "What are you assholes doing?" he asked, and looked from the broken two by four Hunter now held to the door. "Drop it. Use your hands. There's not that much snow there."

Hunter dropped the wood, and the four of them went to work clearing the snow. After last night's attack, Brennan understood

Randy's paranoia. Shultz had proven he wasn't loyal to his men, and had no problem killing them. But, man, it would be awesome if they could take out Randy. They could use his rifle and...what? Kill Shultz, Joel and Woody? Could he do that? He hated those guys, but could he live with the guilt and responsibility of taking another persons life?

"That's enough," Randy said. "Try the doors now."

When Logan gave the handle a hard tug, the hinges creaked and the door swung open, revealing a dirt floor and the front bumper of a vehicle. Chris opened the other door. The light behind them exposed a rusted old SUV, which Brennan assumed Randy and Woody had used to drive here. He once again thought about how these men would escape should the police discover their location. He hadn't been driving for long, and never in more than a couple inches of snow, so he was no expert. But could the SUV plow through two feet of the stuff?

Randy pulled a flashlight from his coat pocket. "One of you take this. Grab only the blue cans. Those are kerosene."

Hunter took the flashlight, and entered the building. "Where are they?" he asked, slipping behind the SUV.

"Right where you are."

Brennan stepped inside to get one of the cans, but jumped back when a stack of wooden planks fell against the SUV and floor.

"Sorry," Hunter shouted. "My bad. Hang on a sec. I dropped the flashlight."

"Christ," Randy mumbled, then let out an impatient breath. "Just get the fucking cans and don't touch anything else." He nodded to Brennan. "Help him."

Brennan went back inside and made his way toward the back of the SUV. The beam from the flashlight darted around the dark room, which had other stacks of wood leaning against its walls, along with a few empty, rusted shelving units. How easy would it be for him to take one of those wood planks and knock Randy over the head with it? He looked toward the opened double doors, and after meeting the gunman's narrowed gaze he got his answer: not easy at all.

"Here," Hunter said, emerging from the darkness with a blue can.

After Brennan took it, then handed it to Logan, he went back to retrieve two more. Hunter followed him out with the last can. Once they'd closed the doors, they made their way back to the ballroom.

"God, this weighs a ton," Chris complained, and adjusted the can in his arms.

"Technically, it weighs forty pounds," Hunter corrected him.

"How do you know?"

"A pint's a pound, dumbass, and there are four pints in a gallon. We're carrying five-gallon cans. Do the math."

Chris's face reddened from either the cold or embarrassment. "Whatever."

"Reuse the tracks we made going to the hotel," Brennan suggested. Forty pounds wasn't all that heavy, but trudging through deep snow made it awkward to carry. By the time they reached the bus, Brennan was exhausted and out of breath. Which was ridiculous considering he worked out regularly. He needed food, water and a warm bed to renew his strength, and hoped to God he'd have those things soon.

"Look," Logan said, jerking his head toward the Ferris wheel.

Woody stood there holding his rifle, Clay's dead body at his feet. Meanwhile Simon, Tyler and Evan dug a snowy grave. Brennan glanced away from them and to the bus. The snow had been cleared from around the front tire and bumper, but even if they had the keys, he still believed they'd need a plow to move the bus. If he were in Shultz's place, he wouldn't have cleared the snow. Instead, he'd have had the guys build up snow around the bus to conceal its bright yellow exterior.

"They find the keys?" Randy asked Joel as they continued toward the ballroom.

Joel shook his head. "If they don't find them, I'm going to try to hotwire the bus."

"That's what you're going to have to do." Shultz stood on the landing outside of the ballroom, the same location he'd been in when he'd shot Alex. "I'm going to have these guys call it quits on looking for the keys, and have them help clear the way for the bus instead. Randy, after your guys are finished, send them out to do the same. We need to keep the room warm."

"You got it," Randy said, motioning for them to carry the cans inside.

Brennan brought his over to the heater he'd been using, and where Alex still lay. The team captain hadn't moved. His skin was now paler and the dark smudges under his eyes were more prominent. His breath hung on the cold air and his body trembled. Anxious to warm his friend, Brennan knelt in front of the heater. "Do I just pour the kerosene in here?" he asked, pointing to the screw cap at the base of the heater.

"Yeah, I'm not sure what to do, either," Chris said from behind the heater next to Brennan's.

After the others admitted the same, Randy chuckled. "You boys are useless. Can you at least change a frickin' light bulb?" He sighed. "Everyone, unscrew the caps on the bottom, then pour in the kerosene." Minutes later, after they'd done as instructed, he said, "Replace the cap. Do you see the *to ignite push* switch? Press on that and we've got ourselves heat."

Brennan pressed the switch and the heater came to life. He glanced over and saw Chris had done the same.

"Got mine running," Hunter called from the heater the gunmen had been using.

"What's your problem?" Randy asked Logan.

"It won't turn on."

"Batteries might be dead." Randy pulled a lighter from his pocket, dropped to one knee, and set the rifle on the floor. "When that happens, you open this little door and manually light the wick." He flicked the lighter and created a flame. "It's so simple," he said, placing the lighter inside the small opening. "Even you morons could—"

The heater exploded, throwing Randy across the room. Huge flames shot out and up, and punched a large hole in the wall. Randy screamed, and writhed on the floor and gripped his face as flames engulfed his hat and coat.

"He's on fire!" Hunter ran for the door. "Randy's on fire!"

Brennan rushed to Alex and grabbed him by the shoulders. "Help me," he shouted to Chris. "Hurry!"

The fire quickly spread to the walls, eating up the old wooden planks as if it were a hungry beast. Together, he and Chris carried Alex from the building, while Shultz rushed inside. Over the ringing in his ears, he could hear Shultz yelling to his teammates and men, ordering them to get the remaining heaters and gear from the building before they were destroyed.

"Put him in the bus for now," Chris suggested.

They rushed to the opened bus, and gently placed Alex on the floor. "Stay with him," Brennan said. "I'm going to help."

Brennan climbed out of the bus, started for the burning building, and made a sharp left. He ran to the side of the ballroom, then into the woods behind it. The snow wasn't as deep, allowing him to move fast. He dodged trees, snow-covered debris and logs. When he wasn't far from the hotel, he stopped and caught his breath.

If the explosion didn't alert the police, he would. His stomach fluttered with excitement as he peered around one of the trees. The hotel and path to the lake were about thirty or so yards away. Because the snow outside of the woods was deep, he wouldn't be able to run as quickly. And once he left the woods, he'd have no cover.

Branches snapped behind him. Brennan held his breath and slowly turned. Relieved, he exhaled. "You scared the shit out of me. What are you doing here?"

"Same as you." His teammate approached. "Going for help. How do you want to do this?" he asked until they stood only inches apart.

Happy he wouldn't be on his own, Brennan pointed toward the hotel. "I say we take that path. We can run along the shore until we reach the narrow part of the lake, then cross. We—"

His head bounced off the tree, shooting pain through his skull and betrayal through his heart. His vision blurred with stars and tears as he turned. "Why?" he asked as another explosion blasted in the distance.

"I'm not ready for us to be rescued." He held Brennan's face with both hands tightly. "Nothing personal, dude," he said, then slammed his head into the tree again and again, until blackness swallowed Brennan whole.

Summer's House, Fairview Park, Ohio
Saturday, January 21ˢᵗ, 8:34 a.m. Eastern Standard Time

Summer finished straightening her hair, then pulled eye shadow and eyeliner from her makeup bag. What was she thinking? She dropped both items back in the bag. She never wore either to the office. Chase knew this about her, and would assume she was trying to make herself pretty for him. Which had been the intent. But to what end? Being in his arms last night had been both blissful and painful. She'd missed the way he held her, touched and kissed her. More than that, she'd missed being able to pick up the phone and talk with him, complain about her day, or share important news. She missed those lazy days when they'd lain around and done absolutely nothing but watch mindless movies, snuggle and make love.

Last night, even before he'd arrived, she had tried to convince herself that they weren't good for each other. That pining after him was a waste of time. He'd changed since they had first met. Being a hostage negotiator had made him, at times, remote, cold, had hardened him in a way she couldn't understand. Accidentally killing Brody Wakefield had changed him once more. There'd been times afterward where he had reminded her of someone who'd just woken from a long coma. As if he'd opened his eyes to the world for the first time in years, and now had to grapple with what had happened while he'd slept, along with unfamiliar emotions. Only he hadn't been sleeping. Instead, she believed he had been living life on autopilot. Going through the motions with his job...with her.

She had never doubted he loved her, but toward the end of their relationship, she had questioned the direction in which he planned to take in life, and if she'd be included. Prior to Brody's death, she'd worried Chase would burn out because of the job, or if he was already on that path. He'd smiled less and less, laughter had been a rarity, and sleep had been his escape. She had once asked him if he was unhappy working for the FBI. He'd admitted to sometimes wishing he had taken another career route. What that would've been, he'd had no clue. Which explained why he had joined CORE after leaving the FBI.

When he'd told her he planned to leave the Bureau, she had encouraged him to take some time and consider a job outside of criminal investigation. But, like her, law enforcement was all he knew. Honestly, what would she do if she were no longer a federal agent? She would soon be a single mom and had to consider her safety. If something were to happen to her on the job, who would care for her child? Chase?

She trusted him, knew in her heart he would never let anything happen to their baby. But if she were to die prematurely, it would make sense to have one of her sisters raise her child. They could offer a strong, stable family environment.

After she finished applying a light layer of mascara, she cleaned the bathroom counter. God, talk about premature. Rather than deal with these depressing thoughts, she shifted focus. While she would love to leave for vacation tomorrow, she doubted that would happen, and had already texted her mom about flying down later in the week. The kidnapping case was too high profile for her to up and go during the middle of it. Plus, she didn't like the idea of leaving Chase. He hadn't worked as a crisis negotiator in more than two years. If he had to take part in a hostage situation, she wanted to be there to support him.

Her stomach growled at the same time as she stifled a yawn, signaling it was time for coffee and breakfast. When she opened the bathroom door, the aroma of bacon, sausage and hazelnut coffee had her mouth immediately watering. Except, she didn't own any bacon or sausage.

Chase.

When she'd been promoted, and Chase had agreed to move with her to Cleveland, they'd chosen to rent, rather than buy. Neither had been familiar with the area, and had wanted to hold off purchasing a home until they'd explored the suburbs. After Chase had moved out, she'd decided to stay in the house they'd rented together. Not for sentimental reasons, but because moving was a pain in the butt, and she liked her neighbors and the location.

But she'd never changed the locks after he had moved, or asked for his set of keys. Without saying the words, she had wanted Chase to know he would always have a home with her. Looking back, that hadn't been a healthy decision. By hanging onto a dying relationship, she'd avoided moving forward, meeting new people and dating. The only man she'd had sex with in the past year had been Chase. While she really hadn't been interested in or had the time for dating, if she had, maybe she wouldn't have slept with Chase in August. Maybe she wouldn't be pregnant.

Yet, carrying this baby, imagining the birth, and holding her child after, brought her more joy than she'd ever expected. She carried a part of Chase, and the love she couldn't deny. Before she started crying and ruined her mascara, she slipped into a pair of sensible black boots, yanked her suit coat from the hanger, then walked to the doorway. She stopped, trying to decide what tone she should use with him.

She should be angry that he'd let himself into her house uninvited and was cooking in her kitchen. Last night, he'd threatened to fight her for custody over a child she thought he hadn't wanted, then he'd later demanded to know who was her doctor. If he thought to control her during and after the pregnancy, she'd give him a reason to think differently. She wouldn't fight him. He had the right to be part of their child's life. But he had to understand that, after being gone a year, he couldn't—as he'd done many times in the past—stroll in and take control.

After drawing in a deep breath, she left the room and headed down the short hallway. When she reached the kitchen, the delicious aromas had her mouth watering and her stomach growling again. But she foolishly hungered for Chase. He'd removed his suit coat and stood in front of the stove, his broad back to her, his shirtsleeves rolled up exposing his forearms. He'd put on weight since she'd last seen him, which he'd needed to, and, with the way the material stretched across his back and biceps, it seemed he had also put on muscle.

When he'd held her last night, the moment had been so quick, she hadn't had the chance to explore his body. Now she wanted to…badly. Since becoming pregnant, she could not only cry on command, but she also had sex on the brain. She'd been dreaming about making love with Chase, would fall asleep while fantasizing about the two of them in positions that in reality they hadn't even tried. Even now, she could imagine him setting the frying pan aside, shoving down her pants, and bending her over the kitchen counter.

"Morning," he said, glancing over his shoulder. "I hope scrambled eggs work for you."

She snapped out of the fantasy. "Morning. The eggs work. You making yourself at home without calling me first doesn't." Drawn to the strong sent of hazelnut, she went to the coffee maker and picked up the bag of grounds sitting in front of it. Decaf. Ugh. "This isn't mine."

"I know. I brought it."

It's starting already. "I don't drink decaf."

He set the pan aside and turned off the burner. "I read drinking caffeine during pregnancy isn't good for the baby."

"Which is why I limit myself to one cup."

"Why have any at all?"

"Why drink coffee if I'm not getting anything out of it?"

"For the taste."

When he reached over her shoulder to open the cabinet, his clean, masculine scent surrounded her and once again had her thoughts drifting to him bending her over the sink. She cleared her throat and ducked out of his way to stand by the kitchen table. "I don't drink coffee for the taste, and I'm going to be in a bad mood if I don't get my daily dose of caffeine."

After setting the plates on the counter, he pulled out the tray of bacon and sausage from the oven. "If you wake up thinking you're going to have a bad day, then you will."

"Actually, I woke up thinking about you and last night."

A sexy smile played along his lips, but he kept his concentration on plating their food. "You were thinking about me? Were we naked?"

She turned away to hide her grin. "Hardly."

"It's okay to admit it. I confess, I think about your naked body all the time." He set the plates on the table, then filled a mug with the decaf coffee. "I think about a lot of other things, too. Remember the day you insisted on going to the Metroparks for a picnic?"

It had been their first spring in Cleveland. The moment the temperature had hit the mid-seventies, she'd had the itch to head outdoors and soak up the sun. Chase had wanted to stay home, claiming he'd have an allergy attack if he joined her. But she had dragged him out anyway. Within an hour, she'd wished she had left him at home. All Chase had done was complain until they'd gotten into a huge fight and she had burst into tears. While she didn't remember what the argument had been about, she did remember the hurt and disappointment.

He sat down and lifted his fork. "I was a dick, and I regret that." When he looked up at her, his eyes held acceptance, not guilt. "Your eggs are going to get cold. I didn't make toast because I know you watch how much bread you eat. But if you want some…"

She shook her head and sank into the chair. "Why did you bring up that day?"

"And not the many others I've ruined?"

"You weren't like that," she said, picking up the coffee mug. She would trick her body into believing it was getting caffeine, just as she'd trick her mind into believing her own words. Purposefully or not, Chase's unpredictable mood swings had ruined many days.

"Yes, I was. You were fun and bubbly. I was angry and hurting. I don't know…maybe a part of me wanted you to hurt, too. What I regret the most about that day was making you cry. You never cry."

He was right about that. What he didn't know was that after Brody and Larry's deaths, when she was alone, she'd cried plenty. She'd ached for him, for all that he'd gone through and for how he had continued to punish himself.

Shooting the boy had been a tragic accident, the bullet meant for the kid's father, Rudolf Wakefield. Neither Chase, nor his partner, Larry Olsen, had known that Brody had been brainwashed by Rudolf. The two crisis negotiators, along with HRT, had believed Rudolf—whose wife had recently divorced him—was holding his ex and kids hostage. Unfortunately, the gullible teenager had trusted his dad, and had been a willing participant in the kidnapping of his mother and younger sisters.

"You're not eating," he said. "Should I add ruining your breakfast to the long list of other shitty things I've done?"

"Stop it." She stabbed a forkful of scrambled eggs. "I told you last night that I was tired of listening to you apologize."

"I didn't apologize. I'm pointing out what I've done."

"The bad things. Why focus on that and not the good?" she asked, going back for more eggs, which were the best she'd had in a long time.

"Other than making a baby with you, I haven't done anything good for over two years."

"How did you make these? They're delicious." she said, her

throat tightening with the threat of tears. What he'd said was depressing. How could the baby be the *only* good thing?

"I added cream cheese so you could get a little dairy in your diet." He stared at her, his expression guarded. "No comment?"

Her vision blurred with tears anyway. "About the cream cheese? I wouldn't have thought to put that in eggs." She picked up a piece of bacon, then tossed it back down. "And I do believe this baby is a good thing. The *best* thing," she said, tears streaming down her face. "Damn it." She wiped her cheeks, then looked at the mascara on her palms. "I can't do this right now."

"Why are you crying?" His expressionless mask slipped. Concern creased his brow, filled his eyes, as he leaned forward. "I didn't mean to make you cry."

"It's my hormones." She picked up the napkin and wiped her nose. "If I'm not crying, I'm nostalgic, quick tempered or horny."

His face hardened. "There's someone else?" He held up his hands. "It's been a while, so I get it. But if you think I'll allow any asshole to be around *our* baby, think again."

"Are you hearing yourself? Do you always have to be in control?" She pushed back the chair and stood. "I never said there was anyone else, all I was trying to do was explain why I'm having a hard time controlling my emotions. You know what those are, right?" She brought the plate to the counter. "Before I totally lose my temper, I want to know if you're here this morning because I'm pregnant."

"I'm here to make you breakfast."

"Bullshit."

He leaned back in the chair. "If you weren't pregnant, I'd still be here making you breakfast."

Not caring that she was using her fingers, she snagged the piece of bacon. "Explain."

"Last night, I would have pulled out all my best moves and seduced my way into your bed. Spent the night and *then* made you breakfast." He shrugged. "Either way, I'd still have filled your belly."

She pretended her body wasn't responding to his words, shoved images of them naked, him filling her and driving her to orgasm, to the back of her mind. After she finished the bacon, she went for the piece of sausage. "Charming."

"I have my moments."

"Like when you texted last night wanting the name and number of my OB?"

He nodded. "You never sent it to me."

"Because it was late, and I don't understand why you think you need to know."

He rose and brought over his plate. "Would you rather I not care?" he asked, rinsing both of their plates. "Be one of those guys who walks away and pretends a part of him doesn't exist?"

"Of course not."

"Then why fight me?" He toweled off his hands and faced her. The worry and uncertainty in his eyes tugged at her heart and provoked guilt. "From the moment when Brody and Larry died, I haven't cared about the future or looked forward to anything. Last night, you gave me the greatest gift…hope. I don't know how to be a good dad, since I never had a good example. But I'll do everything possible to try." He moved closer, brushed his fingers along her cheek and captured a tear. "I lost you, and you were the best thing that'd ever happened to me. I don't plan on making the same mistake with our child."

His sincerity and his gentle touch had her ready to fall into his arms. She wanted to tell him he hadn't lost her, that she'd been here holding out, waiting for him to come back to her. But then what? When they'd still been together, she hadn't just been living with him, but also with his guilt. She couldn't do that again. The stress, the worry, and constantly tiptoeing around his erratic mood swings, had been suffocating. Their house had become dark and depressing, and she would stay late at the office just to avoid coming home. Based on everything he'd said last night and this morning, she believed he hadn't let go of the past. If she invited him back into her life, she would also be inviting that dark cloud which still hung over his head.

"I won't fight you," she said. "But you also can't control every aspect of this pregnancy, or take it upon yourself to map out our baby's future."

"Where is this *control* thing coming from? I'm not controlling. I like to have a plan."

She half-laughed. "Same difference," she said as her cell phone rang. She pulled it from her jacket pocket and glanced at the screen. "It's Dave."

Chase inched closer. "Let's hope he has good news."

Praying for the same, Summer answered the call. "Is Chase with you?" Dave asked after greeting her.

Her cheeks heated. She cleared her throat. "I…ah…"

"Good. Don't come to the office. An explosion has been reported near Ottawa Lake."

She put the phone on speaker so Chase could hear. "That's where SWAT went last night."

"It was, and the family occupying the farmhouse were the ones who reported the explosion. The Media County Sheriff's deputies and fire department are heading over to investigate. In case this is the kidnappers, I have SWAT assembling now. If this is it, I want you and Chase to meet me there. Once I have confirmation, I'll call with the exact location." He let out a tired sigh. "The blizzard we had is currently hitting the east coast, and they're getting it worse than we did. If our crisis negotiators can't make it here, we're going to need Chase on this."

When the call ended, she looked to Chase. His face had become stony and grim, but the insecurity in his eyes gave away his fear. She gripped his arm. "It might not be them."

"And if it is?"

"You'll get those boys out of there," she said, hoping to God she was right. The lives of those fifteen kids depended on it.

6

Ottawa Lake Amusement Park, Village of Ottawa, Ohio
Saturday, January 21ˢᵗ, 9:07 a.m. Eastern Standard Time

COUGHING, CHOKING ON the smoke billowing from the burning building, Matt Shultz knelt in the snow. Rage consumed him, making it difficult to see or think straight. How in the fuck had the ballroom exploded? Gas was the only thing that made sense, but he'd watched the boys carry *blue* cans inside, indicating they were using kerosene, *not* gas. Unless someone had switched the two fuels. But who and why?

"Are you okay?" Joel asked, crouching beside him.

He wiped spit from his mouth. The roar of the fire, Randy's agonizing moans and the panicked cries of the team finally penetrated his brain. He blinked his watery eyes, lifted his head and glanced around. Randy lay in the snow. Behind Matt, a few of the kids were coughing and trying to catch their breath. Woody was rounding up the rest and had them carrying the gear they'd salvaged from the ballroom toward the bus.

He pushed to his feet. "I'm fine."

Joel jerked his head toward Randy. "What are we going to do with him?"

Welcoming the rage, Matt pulled his pistol from his pocket

and walked over to Randy. The man looked like a melted wax figure. His hair and eyebrows were gone, and his skin was red and raw. His nose and half of his teeth were missing, and his jaw hung loosely, leading Matt to believe he'd had his face near the heater when it had exploded. Dumbass. He raised the gun and fired. The bullet pierced the middle of what was left of Randy's forehead, and he stopped his moaning.

"Jesus," Joel whispered.

"What the fuck?" Woody rushed over and stood next to Randy's body. "What the fuck?" he repeated. Narrowing his eyes, he glared at Matt. "Are you going to put a bullet in me, too?"

"Would you rather I let your buddy suffer?"

"I..." Woody glanced back to Randy's body and shook his head. "What could've happened?"

"Some idiot put gas in a kerosene heater."

"Impossible. I stored those kerosene cans at the hotel. And I know for a fact they had kerosene in them, 'cause I'm the one who bought 'em." Woody shifted his suspicious gaze to Joel, then back to him. "You're the one who told us what to bring and where to store them. Maybe you two came out here early and switched the cans."

"That's bullshit." Joel stepped forward. "Why would we do that?"

"Since last night, the ransom split has gone from six ways to four. If you get rid of me, you'll walk with ten million each." He held his rifle with both hands. "Was that your idea, or your boss's?"

Killing off the men who would help him make millions hadn't been Matt's intention. When he and Joel had decided to ask their longtime buddy, Clay, if he'd wanted in on the kidnapping, they'd questioned if it was a smart move. Clay was a pothead. But even though he liked his weed, and spent most of his days stoned, he'd always been reliable. He'd never called off work after partying too hard the night before, and had also never been in trouble with the law. After he'd agreed to take part in the kidnapping, Matt had told Clay no one was allowed to have alcohol or dope until they were home free. Clay had broken that agreement. Because Clay had chosen to get high, McGuire had almost taken his gun, which had given Janson the opportunity to attack Randy. Now the fucking bus keys were missing.

"We've already been over this. Clay couldn't be trusted to do the right thing. And if Randy's injuries weren't so bad, he'd still be alive." Matt slipped the pistol back into his pocket. "I'm not going to kill you. Very soon, this place is going to be crawling with cops. The shit just got real. We can do one of two things: get the fuck out of here, or continue on with the plan. Either way, I'm going to need both of you to get out of here."

Joel looked at the bus, where the boys were standing. "The kids know us."

"We'd have to kill 'em," Woody added.

"Do you guys really want to off fifteen kids?" Matt asked, not too upset by the idea. Newhouse Academy's annual tuition fees were more than what he earned in a year. For that reason, he'd hated these boys from the start. They were entitled, rich pricks who had no idea how things worked in the real world. They didn't know what it was like to be broke and in debt. All they knew was how to ask their mommies and daddies for something, anything, and they'd get it. Yeah, he wouldn't have a problem getting rid of them. He'd already killed four people. For that, he'd go away for life or face execution. Not killing the boys wouldn't change either outcome.

Woody grinned. "For seven point five million, I'd kill my granny."

Joel paled and stepped closer. "So we're going to murder fifteen boys?" he asked, keeping his voice quiet. "I'm not down with that. At all. Matt, I told you I wouldn't kill anybody. And you said it wouldn't be a problem. I mean, come on. Look at them. You really want to waste a bunch of kids?"

Woody stared toward the bus. "Wouldn't we have to anyway? Like Joel said, they know us."

"And like I told you all from the start, it doesn't matter. We've got a guy on the inside who's going to help us get out of the country."

"I don't trust dirty cops," Woody said.

"He's a federal agent," Matt corrected him.

"Same difference."

Not really, but he wasn't going to argue with the man. "I don't trust him, either. But Graves said he's got something on the guy. He's literally our ticket out of the country."

"So we don't need to kill the kids," Joel said, relief clear on his face.

"Not unless any of them do something dumb." Matt turned to the boys. "I need Thorpe, Williams, Patricks and Strauss." Three out of the four stepped forward. "Where's Williams? Demko, I saw you two take McGuire out of the building. Where'd he go?"

The kid shrugged. "I was making sure Alex was okay, so I didn't see. I thought he went back inside."

Once the heater had exploded, chaos had ensued. Everyone was running and shouting, and smoke and flames were shooting out in all directions. Was it possible Williams had gone into the building, but never made it out? Or had the shithead escaped?

"Want me to look for him?" Woody asked.

Hell, no. He no longer trusted Woody. The Army vet had admitted to being the one who'd bought and stored the kerosene, and could have switched the fuels. Woody could say Randy had done it, but if that had been the case, why would the man stupidly blow off his own face? No. Woody had to be behind the switch. But why? He had just as much to gain and lose, depending how this ended.

He would consider his suspicions later. Right now, they needed to prepare for the shit storm about to hit them. "It doesn't matter if he escapes. The cops and Feds will have us surrounded within an hour, maybe less. Forget about Randy's body. Get the kids and gear into the fun house."

Woody didn't move. "What about Mr. Graves?"

Mr. Graves. The moneyman. The one who'd set up the kidnapping. "What about him?"

The older man's eyes flashed with irritation. "Has any money been deposited?"

"You'll know when I do."

"Have you talked to him?"

"Just move the kids."

"That ain't no answer," Woody said. "And I'm gonna expect one." After he turned to the kids, then ordered them to head for the fun house, Matt glanced around the park, and weighed their options.

"*Have* you talked to Graves?" Joel asked.

Matt stared at Woody's back. "No. He hasn't returned my texts. I'm starting to get a bad feeling about this."

"Then let's fucking bail. Come on, man. You know me. You know I go where you go."

He did. Joel was more a brother than a cousin, and probably the only person he actually liked. But they were already in deep, and there was a lot of money on the line. "We can't. Graves said if we don't stick with the plan, his inside guy won't help us."

"But you haven't heard from Graves. What if something happened to him? What if he's dead or in prison?"

Joel wasn't book-smart. Sometimes he wasn't exactly street-smart, either. Yet his cousin had a valid point. When Mr. Graves had first contacted him, Matt had been mildly interested in the idea of kidnapping, then holding the team for ransom. Money was a big problem for him. He didn't have any. He'd tried to stay legit, and, unlike Joel, had—for the most part—managed to avoid trouble with the law. Between student loans, credit card debt and his measly salary, Graves's offer had been tempting. Tempting, but scary.

From the start, he'd known that if they were caught, his view of the world would be through metal bars. He'd expressed this to Graves during the one time they'd spoken, and the man or woman—he couldn't be sure since Graves had used a device to disguise his voice—had assured him the plan was foolproof. Graves would provide the funds needed to set up the kidnapping, and would supply them with detailed instructions on how to go about it. Meanwhile, Matt had to find the crew, then execute the plan. Graves would also handle contact with the parents and, if necessary, the cops or Feds, along with providing them with a way out via his inside guy.

The last time he'd heard from Graves had been prior to arriving at Newhouse Academy with Joel and Clay. That had been around six a.m. yesterday morning. Matt had texted Graves several times, expecting a response. Maybe letting him know that two of their crew were dead, and that they'd blown up the ballroom would get his attention. Or maybe Joel was right, and the police had busted Graves.

"Graves said he might not be able to communicate with us right away," Matt said. "I've been thinking…it could be *he's* the inside guy. But if he is out of the picture, whether we stay or go, we're screwed. It's no secret we volunteered to chaperone, and the cops will probably assume we're the kidnappers. If we run now, that's what we'll be doing for the rest of our lives."

"If the kidnapping works, we'll always be on the run."

"Yeah, but we'll be doing it with lots of money and new identities." He rested a hand on Joel's shoulder and gave him a reassuring squeeze. "We both knew the risks. Just keep thinking about the reward. Come on, man. I can't do this without you. Are you with me?"

Joel let out a long breath. "We're gonna live on an island in the Caribbean?"

Relieved he'd coaxed his cousin into staying, Matt grinned. "I don't ever need to see snow again."

"Same here. So what do you need me to do?"

"I want you to switch places with Woody," he said, knowing he couldn't count on Joel to kill anyone who tried to infiltrate the park. He looked to Randy's dead body. "We really need one more guy with us. I want to go to the hotel and see if there're any other surprises, but I'll need to help Woody when the cops arrive."

"I dunno, man. Why would Woody or Randy do something to get us caught? It doesn't make sense."

No, it didn't. "Then who else could've changed the fuels?"

Joel shrugged. "Who picked this place?"

Graves.

"We get his money, and he finds a way to have us killed or arrested," Joel continued.

Betrayal overrode his rage. He was nobody's fucking *patsy*. And if it turned out Joel was right, he'd do everything in his power to make Graves pay. "We need to get ready for the cops," he said, not wanting to discuss this any further. He needed time to think and consider their options should Graves fail them. "Head over to the fun house. Tell Woody to meet me by the gate." When Joel started to walk away, Matt stopped him. "I know you don't want to kill anyone, but if you see a gun aimed at me…"

His cousin's eyes widened slightly, before he nodded and looked to the ground. "You know I've got your back," Joel said, then made his way to the fun house.

Five minutes later, Matt stood with Woody at the gate. From here, they had a full view of the parkway leading to the entrance, and a partial one of the main road.

"What's the plan?" Woody asked. "If we start killin' cops, they'll be gunnin' for us. And I don't think they'll shoot to wound."

Of that, he had no doubt. "We'll fire warning shots to start with." His cell phone vibrated in his pocket. Since the burner phone had come from Graves, and Joel and Woody were the only ones who knew his number, relief momentarily loosened his tense muscles. He pulled out the phone and quickly read the text:

No money has been deposited yet. Heard from one parent. Haven't responded.

Disappointed that this was far from over, Matt replied: *Two crew are dead. One kid shot. He's alive. Ballroom exploded. Expecting cops.*

Seconds later, Graves responded: *Talk to them. Stall them. I want the ransom money. If deposits aren't made by noon, hurt a kid. I will text when I see a deposit.*

Damn it, Matt hated texting and just wanted to talk to the man. The police or Feds would bring in a hostage negotiator. With his temper, he could predict that any conversation with a negotiator would not go well. He texted: *Can you talk?*

No. Too many eyes around. Trust me. Do as I say and I will get you out of there. I'll text when I can.

Matt looked up from the phone and met Woody's curious gaze. "Your boss?" the older man asked.

He nodded. "I think I know why he might've sent us here. We must be in his jurisdiction."

"I don't care about that. What'd he say?"

Woody was a dick, and Matt hadn't liked him from the start. If Joel hadn't vouched for the bossy, condescending douche, or if Woody hadn't *supposedly* had a badass military background, he wouldn't have brought him in on the kidnapping. "You should care. He could be the inside guy who's going to help us escape." He slipped the phone back in his pocket, then told Woody what Graves had texted.

"Hell, this just went from shitty to shittier." Woody looked over Matt's shoulder and toward the road. "Looks like the shittiest is about to come."

Matt turned, just as a Medina County Sheriff's cruiser rolled to a stop, a red fire truck behind it. His heart rate sped up when two deputies, guns raised, began walking down the parkway toward them. Instead of seeing them, he saw prison bars.

Fuck that.

"Let's give them a reason to stay away," he said, aiming his rifle.

Two gunshots echoed around the park and in through the broken windows. Everyone in the fun house jumped and started talking, while he hid a smile.

"Shut up!" Joel faced them. "Just sit down and keep your mouths shut."

While Joel leaned out the door, he looked around to make sure no one was watching. He then took the phone—one of several he'd had planted around the park prior to the kidnapping—and quickly tucked it inside the torn lining of his coat.

He hadn't had this much fun since the day he'd hazed his sister so badly, she'd tried to commit suicide. If she'd gone through with it, if his bitch of a mother hadn't run from him, none of them would be freezing their asses off in this old park. Thinking about his mom had him wondering if she would offer the ransom money or let him be killed. He'd guarantee his death would come as a relief to her. What kind of mother moved, but didn't tell their kid? A scared and pathetic one.

He'd find out where she and his sister were soon. Before that happened, he needed to drag out this kidnapping just a little longer, long enough to hopefully have a few million deposited into his Bitcoin account, and to kill off Joel, Woody and Shultz. He also wanted to make sure Brennan was dead. After he'd slammed the kid's head into the tree a couple times, he'd lost his balance and accidentally rolled Brennan down the hill. Since he'd used Brennan's snow tracks to follow him into the woods, he hadn't wanted to create additional ones in case Shultz or the others decided to look for Brennan. Shultz believed in Mr. Graves, and he needed to keep it that way, not have his asshole coach suspect a kid he'd abducted was the mastermind.

Damn, he couldn't wait to see the look on Shultz's face once he realized he'd been set up by a sixteen-year-old. Even more, he looked forward to the fear in his mother and sister's eyes, and hoped their terror was the same as his father's had been...just before he'd killed him.

Interstate 71, Middleburg Heights, Ohio
Saturday, January 21ˢᵗ, 9:42 a.m. Eastern Standard Time

Summer adjusted the temperature of the sedan's seat warmer, then the seat itself. The moment Dave had called, informing them shots had been fired outside Ottawa Lake Amusement Park, and that one deputy was injured, she and Chase had rushed out the door. Chase had insisted they take her car, since she had a trunk filled with investigative equipment, and that he should drive. She didn't mind that he drove, but not being behind the wheel gave her nothing to do except think—about them, the baby, the fifteen kids being held hostage.

"Do you know anything about lacrosse," she asked Chase, while opening up an Internet browser on her cell phone. "Not that I'm complaining, but I thought there'd be more kids on the team."

"I knew a couple of players in college. After I went to a few games and started to understand the sport, I'd go as often as I could. It's fun to watch. To me, it's a cross between hockey, soccer, football, baseball and even basketball."

She looked up *lacrosse*, then clicked on IMAGES. "They pass a small ball around with a stick that has a little net at the top."

"It's not easy to do. I tried it a few times. Learning to pass, throw and run without dropping the ball takes practice. Then there's shooting the ball into the goal." He used the windshield wipers to clear the spray of water being kicked up by the truck in front of them. "As for the number of kids on the team, Rachel—"

"Your person from CORE."

"Correct. She found out that there were six players who weren't able to go on the ski weekend."

"Lucky kids," she said, typing *ottawa lake amusement park*. Eerie images filled her phone's screen. "This is nuts."

"What's that?"

"The amusement park. It's creepy," she said, viewing the photo of the Ferris wheel with a tree running straight through it.

"When Lieutenant Nelson first called and showed us the map of where they were targeting, I asked about this area. But he said they didn't think the kidnappers would go there because there's only one road in, woods on one side and the lake on the other." She checked out an aerial view of the park. "I agreed. I *still* agree. Why would they corner themselves?"

"Why would they think they could get away with kidnapping a bus and make thirty million in the process?"

Summer pulled up information about the park. "They're either stupid, or know something we don't." She glanced at his strong jawline and cheekbones. Chase had very few pictures of himself from when he was little. His mom had died young, and his dad had cared more about booze than making memories. The few he did have were grainy and adorable. If they had a son, would he have Chase's dark hair, hazel eyes and dimpled smile? Or maybe he'd inherit her blue eyes. Or maybe they'd have a girl.

Or maybe she should focus...

"Why don't you think the Shultz cousins are the masterminds behind the kidnapping?" she asked while searching for more information about the park.

He sighed. "Now that I know where they're holding the kids, I think my assumption was too premature."

"You've always gone with your gut. Stick with it and tell me why."

"I did during the briefing."

"I know. I also know you. I think you were holding back."

He glanced at her, then faced the road. "Because?"

"You tell me?"

"I'm not FBI anymore. CORE is an excellent agency, and I have the utmost respect for Ian Scott. He's created a topnotch company."

"But?"

"He took a chance on me, and I don't want to be the person who makes him or the agency look bad."

She understood. After Brody Wakefield died, the media storm

that followed was a nightmare. Reporters hadn't liked how FBI officials explained Brody's death as unfortunate and accidental, or that Chase was allowed to keep his job. They aired interviews with Brody's mother who, along with his two sisters, had been held captive by Brody and her husband. Anita Wakefield—even though her own son had used a gun to force her and his sisters to remain in the house—accused Chase of murder.

Because no criminal charges were made, Anita filed a wrongful death suit against Chase. Before proceedings began, both her daughters gave the judge a detailed account of the shooting and made it clear their father—just as Chase fired—had quickly pulled Brody in front of him. While using his own son as a human shield, he'd then shot Larry. Anita's attorney suggested she drop the suit. Thankfully, she took his advice, and within a week, Chase became old news.

"I get it," she said. "But you can't do your job properly if you're constantly worried about screwing up, right?"

"Which is why I keep wondering if I shouldn't just get out and do something else."

"Like what?" she asked, curious. Even after the Wakefield shooting, Chase had never expressed an interest in anything but criminal investigation.

He half shrugged. "I don't know. I've been taking online cooking classes. Maybe I'll go work in a restaurant."

"You're going to trade your gun for a spatula? I can't picture it."

He grinned. "Yeah, I can't either. Plus, restaurant hours aren't exactly nine to five. Whatever job I have, I need to make sure I'm around for our kid. I don't want to be one of those absent dads."

"This is interesting," she said, redirecting the conversation. She loved Chase, and she wanted him to be part of her and their child's lives. But her love hadn't been enough to keep them together. She resented that, resented Chase for rejecting her love, for being selfish and unable to move forward. "Ottawa Lake Amusement Park first opened in 1878. It closed one hundred years later."

"Smooth subject change." He switched lanes. "If the place has been closed for nearly forty years, there can't be many buildings still standing."

"Dave said he sent a helicopter to fly over the area and give us an aerial view. The man who owns the property is also meeting us out there. He knows the layout better than anyone. But I'm going through a website created by a guy who blogs about abandoned places in Ohio, and he was there just last year. Based on the pictures he posted, it looks like the old ballroom and fun house are still standing, along with a portion of the hotel. There are a few smaller structures, nothing that would hold a large group of people, though." She came across a photo of one of the roller coasters which had been overrun by trees. At its base was a rusted car that had once been used to ride the coaster. "Seriously creepy." She went back to the pictures of the buildings. "Again, why this place?"

"Like you said, maybe they know something we don't."

"A hidden tunnel beneath the lake?" She set the phone on her lap. "Dirty cop? Or maybe they're just not that smart."

"Without communicating with them, it's hard to say. Rachel sent me everything she could find on the Shultz cousins. Before bed, I read more about them to get a better handle on who we're dealing with, and to try to gauge their personalities. I think Joel is more of a follower than leader. Every time he was arrested, he was working with someone else. And that someone was always the person who'd set up the burglary, or who'd had the plan."

"So, you think Matthew Shultz came up with the kidnapping scheme, and Joel came along for the ride?"

"It's hard to say. The thing about Matt is, he's never really been in any trouble with the law."

"He killed his neighbor's dog and also put a man in the hospital," she reminded him. "Based on those two incidents, and that he's been diagnosed a sociopath, I'd put money down that he's done other illegal things. He just hasn't been caught."

"Possibly. Newhouse Academy did an extensive background check on him, and there wasn't a single red flag. You also know that not all sociopaths are criminals."

Confused, she stared at his profile again. "What are you suggesting? That the Shultz cousins are victims?"

"Not at all. If Joel's a follower and Matthew hasn't engaged in criminal activity, it's odd to me that the two of them sat down one day and said, 'Hey, we could use thirty million, so let's kidnap a bus load of kids.'" He shook his head. "What *does* make sense to me is the involvement of a third party. Someone who has the funds to supply them with weapons and whatever they'd need while at the park, who's smart enough to know the bus has a GPS, to get rid of the cellphones and set up the Bitcoin account."

"Except the location wasn't a smart choice."

"Agreed. But we don't know what they have there. Is the place rigged with explosives? Or maybe they have snowmobiles or some other vehicle that can take them quickly over the snow."

"Like a team of Huskies, or a tank with a flame thrower?"

"Smartass," he said, a smile tugging at this mouth. "Whatever the case, you'll need to make sure the park is surrounded by cops, and that there's no chance of escape. My other concern is the number of kidnappers. This is a big job, and thirty million is a lot of cash. There could be a dozen guys taking part in this."

She'd considered this, and feared a lengthy standoff that could lead to children being injured or killed. With the weather on the East Coast delaying HRT and the crisis negotiators, it would be up to the Cleveland Division SWAT team, local cops, highway patrol and…Chase to bring this situation to a peaceful end.

"How are you feeling about possibly running negotiations?" she asked as he veered toward the Lodi exit. Nervousness had her stomach twisting. From the exit, they only had a short ten-minute drive before they reached the park.

"You sound like my therapist." He slowed the car as they approached a red light. "When will you find out the sex of the baby?"

"Smooth subject change." She stared out the passenger window. "I was supposed to have an ultrasound last week, but I had to cancel. I'm scheduled to go Friday, after I get back from Florida."

"You're going to Florida? When?"

"Tomorrow. But I've cancelled my flight. The kidnapping is more important than my vacation."

He turned right. "You shouldn't fly anyway."

"Because?"

"What if the plane crashes?"

Thank God they lived in different states. Chase was not only controlling, but had developed a chronic case of anxiety. "What if I get hit by a bus? Don't be ridiculous."

"I'm not sorry for worrying about your health, or for caring about you and the baby."

"I appreciate that you care, but pregnant women can function just fine."

"I think you should stay in the SWAT vehicle, since it's bulletproof."

"Oh, my God. Chase, stop. I have a vest and plan to wear it. Besides, Dave would question why I was in the SWAT truck."

He glanced at her. "He doesn't know you're pregnant?"

"The only people who know are you, my family and my doctor. I'm hardly showing, but planned to tell Dave soon."

"You're embarrassed," he said, his voice laced with disappointment. "Lauren's your closest friend, and you haven't even told her."

Shame made her face grow hot. Lauren was her good friend, and would be upset and probably accuse Summer of not trusting her. "I'm *not* embarrassed. I haven't told Dave because I'm worried he might lighten my caseload."

"Just admit it. You don't want people knowing you got knocked up by your crazy ex." When he looked at her again, there was hurt in his eyes. "Or maybe you planned on not telling anyone I'm the father. You certainly waited long enough to tell me."

"Fine." She crossed her arms over her chest. "I didn't want to deal with you rejecting the baby, or my coworkers' questions. Because you know at least one of them would ask about the *baby daddy*." Angry with herself for worrying about what people would think, and with Chase for forcing her to confess something she hadn't wanted to admit to herself, she faced the windshield. Up ahead, two Medina County Sheriff's cruisers blocked the road. Behind them were two SWAT trucks, a fire truck and several other police cars, a haze of dark smoke surrounding them. "How dare you blow me crap about any of this. *You* walked out on *me*. What really ticks me off is that you planned on seducing me last night."

"I never said that."

"You certainly did. Right after you took away my caffeine and made sure I reached my dairy ration." She drew in a steadying breath. "I don't want to talk about this. What's done is done. We need to focus on the investigation, not our fucked-up personal life."

"I'm focused," he said, slowing the car and rolling down his window. After Summer had flashed her badge, and the deputies had moved their cars to allow them access to the road, Chase parked next to the fire truck. "You really shouldn't swear like that. I've read that babies can hear sounds outside the womb."

Yes, it was a very good thing Chase lived out of state. Otherwise she might have this baby in prison. "And you really shouldn't—" A flutter in her belly had her catching her breath.

"What's wrong?" he asked, quickly turning to her.

"I...I'm not sure." The flutter happened again and she grinned. "I think I just felt the baby move," she said, unzipping her coat.

Chase had his hand on her stomach the same time she did. "Is it still happening?"

She waited a few seconds, met his gaze, then quickly looked away. The excitement in his eyes was too much. She was just as excited, but also knew there would be disappointment. He lived far away. As the baby grew and became stronger, he wouldn't be lying on the couch next to her, touching her belly as he was now, connecting with their baby, with her. "I don't think so," she said, covering his hand with hers. "I also think it's too early for you to feel the baby move this way."

When she pushed his hand away, he curled his fingers through hers. "Thank you."

With reluctance, she looked at him again. "For what?"

"Telling me."

Confused, she tightened her hold on his hand. "Why wouldn't I?"

"You weren't going to tell me you were pregnant. Why would you share something so special with me?"

Because she was scared and didn't want to have this baby on her own. "It took me by surprise," she said instead.

Before Brody's death, Chase had been predictable. After, she'd never known how he'd handle a situation. If she told him the truth, that she still loved him, that she'd been waiting for him to come back to her, she didn't know how he would react. He could think she was pathetic for hanging onto him, or he could decide to quit his job, move to Cleveland and insinuate himself back into her life. She didn't know if that would be a good or bad thing. Prior to the shooting their relationship hadn't been going great. She'd wanted marriage, and to purchase a house. Chase hadn't been ready for either, which had made her wonder if he'd had commitment issues. Did he still have those same issues? Would he blow back into her life all gung-ho about being a dad, only to blow back out if things became tough?

"It's a nice surprise." He gave her hand a gentle squeeze. "Promise you'll put on your vest?"

"Promise not to hover over me?"

After agreeing, she quickly donned the bulletproof vest, her coat, gloves and a knit hat. Chase did the same, then met her at the front of the car. She tasted and smelled the smoke as they approached Dave, who was surrounded by several agents from the Cleveland Division, along with Commander Kipp Taggart, who led their SWAT team. An elderly man wearing an ear-flap hat also stood there, flanked by Medina County Sheriff's deputies.

Dave introduced the man as Eugene Ambrose, the owner of the abandoned park. Eugene's wrinkles deepened with worry as he scanned the road leading to it. "This is no good," he said, his voice gravelly. When he met Chase's gaze, she noticed one of his eyes was filmy, likely from cataracts. "We get trespassers here all the time. Kids, mostly. I guarantee my father's rolling in his grave right now."

"Sir, can you confirm the number of buildings on the property?" she asked.

He looked to the trees, where the fire burned behind them. "The ballroom, fun house and a portion of the hotel." Eugene shook his head. "You shoulda seen this place in its heyday." His gaze took on a faraway look. "Packed with families, musicians and carnies. We'd get tourists from all over Ohio, but we couldn't compete with Cedar Point and Geauga Lake. Those amusement parks had bigger rides and a better location. Eventually we had to close." His eyes misted. "For nearly forty years, this place has sat here. If Mother Nature isn't taking her land back, trespassers are sneaking in, trying to steal a bit of history. Now this."

"Mr. Ambrose," Summer began, keeping her voice gentle when she wanted to smack a sense of urgency into the man. "Can you tell us the ways in and out of the park?"

"Cars can only get through on this road." The man pulled a weathered map from his pocket, then laid it on the hood of one of the nearby cars. "There are paths leading to the lake, but most of them are overgrown. Other than that, through the woods."

She studied the map, which depicted the park before it had been abandoned. "How many people could the ballroom hold?"

"Hundreds. Same with the hotel."

"And the fun house?"

"Maybe thirty."

Dave ran his finger along the map. "How was the structure of the ballroom?"

"Windows were gone, but she was still standing last time I saw her," Eugene said with pride.

"And the fun house?"

"Same. But the roof was in bad shape. I had a big hotel chain interested in buying the property and putting in a spa resort. But they backed out of the deal. I was hoping it'd go through. I don't have the money to demolish any of the other structures on the property, and I worry about those trespassers I mentioned." His eyes grew watery again. "You say a deputy was shot?"

"In the shoulder," Dave said. "He'll be okay. Thank you for your time. Why don't you keep warm in one of the deputies' cruisers?" After a deputy helped Eugene to his car, Dave's attention went to the SWAT commander. "Ambrose helped confirm that the ballroom is what's on fire. Aerial view from the chopper showed the bus and plenty of tracks in the snow, but no kids. I think it's safe to say they're in the fun house. We need to make sure no one shoots at that building."

"I'll let my people know," Kipp said. "I'm going to have them set up a perimeter around the park, but I'll need more bodies."

Dave pulled off his gloves and retrieved his cell phone from his coat. "I'll contact Highway Patrol and the Medina County Sheriff and have them send people."

"Should we tell the parents?" Summer asked Chase.

"No," he said, walking backward. "Taggart, have your guys cover me."

Fear gripped her. "What are you doing?" she asked, knowing exactly what he was about to attempt. She knew him, had listened to him detail the various crisis situations he'd dealt with while working for the FBI. But he hadn't been a negotiator for over two years. He also hadn't been able to let go of how badly that negotiation had ended, and she didn't know if he was emotionally capable of handling this one.

Instead of looking at her, his gaze was focused on Dave. "We're good?"

Dave nodded. "Absolutely."

While Kipp ordered his team to watch the gate, Chase turned his back on them, raised his arms, then headed down the road leading to the park. "Hello," he shouted. "I'm unarmed. I just want to talk."

"Are *you* good?" Dave asked her.

"Yes," she lied, not good at all with the possibility of the father of her child being killed.

7

CHASE'S INSIDES TWISTED with dread. One deputy had been shot, a building had exploded and he had no idea how many men had their guns aimed at him. His heart beat hard, thumped in his head, and his skin prickled with unease. As he drew closer, breathing became difficult and he grew dizzy. He wanted to stop or kneel to right his equilibrium, but didn't dare. The kidnappers might think he was reaching for a gun, and they'd already proven they had no problem shooting a cop.

Pushing through his panic attack, he continued forward, following the bloody drag marks the deputy had left in the snow. Other than the crackle from the fire, and the occasional creak of a gently swaying tree, the area was eerily quiet. His breath grew labored, not from fear, but from trudging through the deep snow. His irritation also surfaced. He should have thought this through, and anticipated the depth of the drifts. If these guys started firing, he couldn't run and had little cover. The trees on either side of the road were tall and too thin to use as a shield. Even if they were wide, he'd likely be shot trying to reach one.

Keep it in check, he told himself. *You've done this dozens of times and can do it again.*

Except now he was walking into a negotiation with more than hostages on his mind. He had a child to consider. He'd abandoned

Summer once, and while there was a good possibility he didn't stand a chance in Hell of getting back together with her, he didn't want to leave her with a baby to raise on her own. Then again, he was worth more dead than alive, and he'd never removed Summer as the benefactor of his life insurance policy. If he died today, she would inherit three hundred thousand dollars, and would be able to raise their child without worrying about money.

When he spotted the bent and broken gate, which led him to believe they'd used the bus to ram their way into the park, his morbid thoughts fled. To his right, and through the bare trees, a few rusted turnstiles stood near what had once been a ticket booth. Inside the park was a small structure that reminded him of an old hamburger stand. He glanced to the ground. The bloody tracks from the wounded deputy began here. He looked back at the burger stand, which was not only a perfect place for the kidnappers to hide, but it gave them an advantage over anyone attempting to enter the park via the gate.

"Hello," he called again, and raised his hands higher. He took a few steps. "My name is Chase Sawyer. I want to give you my phone number, so we can talk this over."

The muzzle of a rifle slid out the corner of the stand's window. "That's far enough!"

Chase froze. Familiar anticipation hummed through his body, and he'd forgotten how much he had enjoyed being a crisis negotiator. Taking control, getting inside the head of a hostage taker and bending their thoughts in his direction. The cat-and-mouse game, where he played the friendly cat ready to pounce on his trusting prey.

"Matt?" Chase asked, knowing he was taking a risk. He didn't want Shultz to panic because they knew his name, but he needed to establish a rapport with the man if they were going to resolve this situation. "Take my number and call me. We've received your ransom text and need to discuss some of the terms."

"What terms?"

"Timing, ransom amount, how the boys are doing and if

they're being treated well."

"They're fine, and we're not changing the amount or timeframe. Make the fucking deposit, or we'll start hurting kids."

Chase kept his arms in the air. "Matt, do you realize we have the entire park surrounded?"

"Do you realize I don't give a shit?"

"I need you to care. I need you to think about what you're doing. Thirty million is a lot of money. Hell, I wish I made one percent of that. But I've spoken with the parents of these boys. Not all of them can afford the two million dollar ransom, and some need time to pull that kind of money together. Other parents aren't willing to do anything until they see that their sons are unharmed. Work with me, Matt. I don't want you or those boys to get hurt."

Laughter came from the burger stand. "No, you want to see me in prison. Not happening. So why don't you turn around, head back to your car and after you drive away, go fuck yourself?"

Anger had Chase's vision blurring. He wanted to head back to the SWAT team and tell them to light up the stand and take out Matt Shultz. He blinked a few times instead and tried to rein in his temper. He had dealt with stubborn hostage takers in the past, but back then he'd had patience, and had been able to keep his emotions from tainting a negotiation. Knowing he was no longer qualified to handle a crisis negotiation, he should tell Dave to wait for HRT and the negotiators they would bring with them. Except Dave couldn't confirm when they would arrive. He also wouldn't be able to live with himself if something were to happen to these kids because he'd done nothing to help them. And how would Summer look at him if he chose to take the coward's way by hiding behind his past?

"Why are you still standing there?" Matt asked.

"Sorry, I thought that was a rhetorical question. Unfortunately, I can't leave just yet, and I'm in no mood to fuck myself. I'm also freezing my ass off out here. If you and the boys are planning to keep warm by sitting around the ballroom you set on fire, I'll send in marshmallows. If not, and you need supplies, I can get that for you."

More laughter echoed from the stand. "You've got balls. Okay, what's your number?"

Once he'd rattled off his cell number, the phone immediately rang. Keeping one arm raised and assuring Matt he was reaching for his cell, he answered the call.

"Hello, Agent," Matt began. Unsure whether the man would cease dialogue if he were to find out he didn't work for the FBI, Chase didn't deny or confirm his title. "We could use a few things. How about sending us strip steaks, shrimp, potatoes... We could also use something for breakfast. Lattes would be nice, omelets and home fries, too."

"Should the food come cooked, or do you plan on using the fire to make everything?"

"You're a funny guy," Matt said, no amusement in his voice. "I'll tell you what...forget about the food and lattes. What I want is our money. I also want you to warn your people that my men will shoot anyone who enters this property. Understand?"

"I will tell them. Anything else?"

"When will deposits be made?"

"I've already explained that we need more time. I also need to be able to prove to the boys' parents that their sons are okay. Give me photos, video, or, better yet, let us talk to each boy."

Matt was silent for a moment. "I'm sure we can arrange this. But I'm going to expect something in return. If, after I prove the boys are fine, and a deposit isn't made within the hour, one boy *won't* be fine. After two hours, another kid will be made...uncomfortable. Do you see where I'm going with this, Chase?"

"I do."

"Good." The man sighed. "How come you haven't asked me about Coach Pembroke?"

Chase stared at the muzzle still aimed at him and debated how to respond. "We found his DNA on one of the tablets in the bag tossed on the highway," he said, hoping his honest answer would help establish trust between them. "We're assuming he's dead."

"What else have you found?"

"The driver, Frank Stokes, in the back of Pembroke's SUV, and the bus's GPS unit." Wanting to keep the trust thing going, Chase turned and began walking back toward the cars and trucks. "We also know your cousin, Joel, was on the bus with you."

"Sounds like you know quite a bit. Did you know I could order my men to put a bullet in your back right now?"

Chase kept his shoulders squared as he continued through the snow. "I'm fully aware, but I don't think you will. You could have killed the deputy, but wounded him instead. Listen," he began, going with another tactic, "we've done our research and know you have no history of violence and have never been in trouble with the law. But you do have plenty of debt. Joel? His prison record concerns us. It's a fact that a large percentage of inmates leave prison only to commit more illegal and violent offenses. I wouldn't be surprised if Joel murdered Pembroke and Stokes. Or maybe Joel brought in a few guys he met while incarcerated." Except for the last line, the rest Chase had fabricated. Joel Shultz had been a model prisoner, who hadn't showed any sign of violence. But pitting the cousins against each other could give them an advantage.

"I have to go," Matt said. "Warn your people."

Before Chase could stall and keep him on the line, the call ended. When he reached Summer and the others, Dave asked about their conversation. Chase gave him the details, then turned to Taggart. "I couldn't see inside the park, and only one gun was pointed at me. I know Matt Shultz was in the burger stand, but I can't say for certain whether he was alone."

"We need to know the number of kidnappers," the SWAT commander said. "During the helicopter flyby, officers said the burned body outside the ballroom was dressed in white and gray camo, so we're thinking he was one of the abductors. There were also track marks in the snow leading to the fun house and Ferris wheel. At that location, the snow has been moved and piled into two mounds."

"Graves?" Summer asked.

"Hard to say, but if that's what those mounds are, did they bury *their* guys, or are we going to find hostages? They did leave one of their men in the snow."

"Probably because they didn't have time to move him," Chase said. "Aside from the bus, what about other tracks or vehicles?"

"They noted what looked like five sets of boot prints traveling from the ballroom to the hotel. But there were only two sets on the return, and one of them stopped midway."

"Maybe when they were on their way back they used their original tracks," Summer suggested.

Taggart nodded. "That was my first thought, too. But what were they doing, and whose prints are they? The kids' or the kidnappers'?"

"Do you have the photos from the helicopter?" Chase asked, interested in seeing, rather than hearing about it.

Taggart had one of his men bring him a tablet. After he touched the screen a few times, he handed it to Chase. Summer moved closer and pointed at the bus, which was parked about thirty feet from the ballroom.

"The snow's been trampled between the bus and the building," she said. "It looks like they were trying to dig the bus out of the snow." She took off her gloves, then used her fingers to enlarge the photo. "There's more trampling here, next to the side of the ballroom. Odd. I expected to see more footprints throughout the park. You'd think the kidnappers would be patrolling the area."

"You'd think there would be more kidnappers," Taggart said. "Talking with my team, we don't feel there are more than four or five men. If you swipe to the next photo, there are two sets of tracks heading to the burger stand. That's not to say there aren't six men in there. We got more than a foot of snow during the night. The fresh powder and wind gusts would've covered any prints made yesterday."

Chase's heart rate slowed to normal and his adrenaline burst subsided, leaving him chilled to the bone. "If that were the case, when the ballroom caught on fire, those men would've rushed out of the stand or any of the other small buildings. I think you're right. There might only be a handful of kidnappers, if that."

"Let's hope," Taggart said. "If you can't negotiate the hostages' release, I suggest storming the place during the night."

"That would put the boys at risk," Summer said before Chase had the chance. "We can't allow them to be caught in the crossfire."

Dave shook his head. "It'd be a PR nightmare."

Chase understood where Dave was coming from, even if the comment was insensitive. Though he didn't want to misrepresent CORE, he was more concerned with being responsible for any loss of life than the media. That included the kidnappers. He considered it a personal triumph if he were able to resolve a hostage situation without a single casualty. His job was to bring a close to those circumstances, not to decide the fate of the people involved.

"I agree with Summer," Chase said. "I also think going in at night will be our best option, should it come to that. My biggest concern right now is the welfare of the boys. Shultz expects a deposit."

Summer tugged her hat over her ears. "What if we make one? Lauren and I were talking about this yesterday after she did more research on Bitcoin. With Bitcoin, users have a 'wallet', which is similar to a bank account, and allows them to send, receive and store Bitcoins. Now, we might not be able to identify the owner of the Bitcoin wallet, but any transaction he makes will become public knowledge. We could follow these transactions, and possibly link the wallet to a name."

"We have a name," Taggart said. "Make a deposit, then once we have Shultz, get the money back to the parents."

"We're not one hundred percent sure Shultz is in charge," Summer said. "If he is, and he owns the Bitcoin wallet, your suggestion should work. If not, and Shultz ends up dead or refuses to reveal who he's working for, the money and person leading the kidnapping could disappear."

Taggart's brows furrowed. "But you just said you can follow transactions and link the wallet to a name."

"I said *possibly* link. If the Bitcoin user knows what he's doing, he could make those transactions anonymous by creating new wallet addresses and running the coins through a 'coin mixer', which is equivalent to laundering money."

Chase thought the use of crypto currency and the effort made to create and run these accounts—anonymously or not—sounded like a convoluted pain in the ass. "How hard is it to do all these things with Bitcoins?"

"If you do your research, it's not hard at all."

"I'll call Kevin Williams," Dave said. "He's Brennan's dad, and volunteered to be the spokesperson for all the families. He made it clear that he would pay to get his son back. Chase, what are your thoughts?"

While Chase wasn't a fan of giving into kidnappers' demands, Shultz was a sociopath who had probably murdered the bus driver and coach. This had him worried Shultz would make good on his threat and begin harming the boys if he didn't receive the ransom money. "Have Williams make the deposit *after* Shultz shows us the boys unharmed. Not the entire two million. If he can swing five hundred thousand, have him do that. It might anger Shultz, but it could also make him more communicative."

"Five hundred thousand?" Taggart let out a low whistle. "We're gambling a lot of money."

Chase shifted his gaze to the park. "And a lot of lives."

Matt Shultz stared at the phone's screen, waiting for a reply from Mr. Graves. He wanted the man to know he'd made contact with the FBI, and that the Feds were expecting evidence that the boys were okay. McGuire was probably going to die from the gunshot wound, and Williams was missing, so Matt wasn't sure how to handle those two. To string law enforcement along, he could send them a couple pictures or videos every hour, and save McGuire and Williams for last. He also wanted to suggest to Graves that he set up their escape once they'd received twenty million dollars. Yes, thirty would be better, but he couldn't enjoy the money from prison. The Feds and cops might not expect them to leave before the full amount had been deposited, which could give them an opportunity to put distance between them and the park.

"The park's too big," Woody said as he continued to stare out the burger stand window. "There're only three of us, and over thirty-five acres of land to cover. Plenty of hiding spots, too. The helicopter that flew over us? You know damned well that was police."

Matt nodded. "They know there's only one building left that could hold the team. Maybe we should split up the kids. Take four or five to the hotel, bring the same amount here, and leave the rest in the fun house."

"I don't know if I like it. They're going to find a way to watch us. If they see us moving kids around, they'll figure out there're only three of us."

He didn't like the old fucker, but Woody was right. "Then you stay here. Shoot anyone who tries to get in this way."

"What about the Fed you talked to on the phone?"

"Only if he's armed and gets too close. But don't kill him." Matt thought back to the phone conversation he'd had with Chase. "He never asked me how many men we have, or how we plan on leaving. That makes me wonder if Chase is our inside guy."

Woody shook his head. "Don't know about that. It could be he was saving those questions for later, or he don't think we've got a chance in Hell of getting out of here. I'm really startin' to wonder about Graves. Why not tell us who the inside guy is so we don't shoot him?"

Woody's concerns mirrored his own. If they accidentally

killed their ticket to freedom, they'd be screwed.

"Or," Woody continued, "what if Graves texts you and says, give yourselves up because the inside guy works for the county jail or whatever? And what if there's *no* inside guy? We go down for kidnapping and murder, while Graves keeps the ransom money. If there is any."

"If you think this, why did you join us?" he asked, angry with Woody for pointing out worries that had been needling him too, and angry with himself for letting dollar signs cloud his judgment.

The older man shrugged. "I'm pushin' sixty. I'm an ex-con, been dishonorably discharged from the Army, I have no job and no money. If Randy didn't let me crash on his couch, I'd be homeless." He narrowed his eyes at him. "I guess I *am* homeless now."

Matt refused to get into why he'd shot Randy. He'd explained himself once, and that was enough. He needed to stay focused on the situation, and because Graves could betray them, he also had to come up with a possible escape plan. The farmhouse, and whoever resided there, tempted him. If someone was there, he could steal his ID, his money and vehicle, then be long gone before the Feds knew it.

His cell vibrated and he quickly read the text from Graves. "Boss says to give them pictures of some of the kids."

"Ask if his guy is one of the cops outside the park."

He texted the question. Seconds later, Graves responded. "Yes," Matt said after reading the message. "Graves says we'll know his guy because he's wearing a black coat with a gray patch sewn on the sleeve."

"The agent you talked to had his arms raised most of the time. I don't remember seeing a patch."

"I don't, either. I still don't want you to kill him yet." Matt pulled his rifle from the window. "I'm going to head to the fun house. I'll text you later."

"Phone's gone," Woody said as he aimed his rifle out the window.

Fuck. Now they couldn't quickly communicate. Rage blinded him, had him fisting his hands and envisioning Woody's face bruised and bloodied. "How?"

"Not sure. It must've fallen out of my pocket when I was pullin' out a pack of smokes. Could be buried in the snow, or maybe it fell out when I was in the ballroom."

"What about the two-way radios?" Matt asked. Beating the shit out of Woody wasn't an option. At least not right now. He needed the man. After this was over, he'd take pleasure in making him suffer.

Woody's eyes brightened. "I forgot about those. I think Randy left them in the car."

Which meant he would have to walk across the park to the hotel, then back to the stand. He'd have no cover and, because the snow was deep, he wouldn't be able to run. "I'll figure out a way to get one to you."

"Well, if you hear gunfire coming from this direction, consider that a text message," Woody said with a chuckle.

Not amused, Matt left without saying another word. Because of Woody, and their need to be able to communicate, he had to risk his own ass by going to the hotel. Or did he? He could force a kid or two to go with him and use them as his shield. Otherwise, he'd have to use the trees and brush along the lake, and at the edge of the park, as camouflage. He didn't want to do that. Both Woody and Randy had warned him one section was loaded with sharp, twisted metal from one of the old coasters and other hazardous debris. Of course, that section was one he'd be forced to pass through if he stuck to the trees.

Worried about taking a bullet in the back, and using a few trees and small, rotting structures for cover, Matt panted hard as he rushed toward the fun house. When he reached the building, he pulled Joel outside, but left the door open in order to see some of the kids.

"What's happening?" his cousin asked, panic in his voice. "Who was shot? Why didn't you answer my call?"

"I didn't want to tie up the phone in case Graves called. And our phones only have eight hours of talk time. Just shut up and listen," Matt said quietly, then told his cousin what had occurred. "I'm going to take pictures and send them to the agent. Then I'm going to have a couple of kids go with me to the hotel so I can get the radios. Fucking Woody is a pain in my ass."

"We need him."

"Yeah, I know. I don't need the reminder."

Joel looked inside the fun house. "I don't like being responsible for all these kids," he whispered. "It's thirteen to one in there. If they rush me, I don't know that I'll be able to shoot anybody. Even if I did, I could miss and they'd get my gun."

Which was one reason why Matt had suggested splitting the team into smaller groups. "Did the duct tape and rope make it out of the ballroom? They were in the blue bag."

"I don't think so."

He tried to maintain his patience. "Either it did or didn't." Matt stepped inside the fun house. If any of these kids had the balls, they could probably punch a hole through the rotting walls which were coated with a mixture of modern graffiti and the original—now faded—drawings of clowns. Snow had piled on the floor below each broken window, forcing the boys to remain on the opposite wall. "Demko and Ziss," he said, his breath hanging on the air. "Go through the gear and see if my dark blue bag is in the pile. He shifted his gaze to Patricks, who was a senator's grandson, then Barry, whose father was an investment banker and worth a ton of cash. "Patricks and Barry, come here and say cheese."

After he took the boys' pictures, he sent them to Chase, adding that he expected a deposit within the hour, or both of these boys would be punished. Meanwhile, Demko and Ziss hadn't found his bag. Because both boys posed no threat to him, he ordered them to come with him to the hotel. As they were about to leave, Chase texted him:

Thanks. Boys look good. Want to see others. I will call when money is deposited.

Matt replied: *More pics when I see deposit.*

After pocketing the phone, he, Demko and Ziss began their trip to the hotel. Anticipating an ambush, he constantly shifted his gaze to the woods, the lake, the smaller rotting structures and rides. As they made their way, he also considered what Chase had said earlier about Joel. They thought Joel was the violent criminal, not him. Dumbasses. Joel felt guilty for stepping on an ant. The Feds didn't know this. If they were busted, for a lesser sentence or to avoid the death penalty, he could blame Joel for Pembroke and Stokes murders. Clay and Randy would be difficult to explain. There had been too many witnesses, and Joel wasn't outside when Clay was killed.

Thinking about what he'd do if they were caught was a waste of time. He had no intention of going to prison, and would rather die while escaping. What the hell else did he have to live for? Spending his days working at a school catering to rich kids was bullshit, and not something he was willing to do for the rest of his life. He wanted the lifestyle of the rich and famous. To walk into an exclusive club and have women falling all over him. He had the looks, but without the cash, he was nothing. And he was tired of being nothing. Fuck those people who said he needed to pay his dues, that he was only twenty-five and had time to build for his retirement.

Blah, blah, blah.

He had no interest in credit scores, saving for a home, equity loans and whatever else. Why not enjoy life now, rather than when he was dragging around an oxygen tank?

When they reached the hotel, he glanced toward the path leading to the lake. This had been the route he and Joel had taken last night when they'd discovered the farmhouse. He could send the kids back to the fun house and leave. Better yet, once he and Joel tied up the team, they could run for it and let Woody deal with the FBI. Screw Graves. Woody might be right about the guy. This whole thing could be a setup. But what if it wasn't and they were successful?

Damn, he wanted the money. He also didn't want to die. In-decision weighed heavily on him. For now, he'd move forward with his original plan: retrieve the radios, and search for the rope and duct tape. If there was no deposit made by the time he'd given Chase, then he'd talk to Joel about getting the hell out of here.

"Ziss, get in the car and look for two-way radios." He turned his attention on Demko. "Search around and look for rope and duct tape. It's probably in a duffle bag."

While the boys did as instructed, he also searched for supplies. As he moved pieces of wood aside, and brushed away dead grass and leaves, he came across a hunting knife covered with a leather sheath. The handle and leather looked brand new, leading him to assume the blade hadn't been left behind by past trespassers, but belonged to Randy or Woody. They must have dropped it at some point while unloading supplies. He pocketed the knife, then continued to look for the tape and rope.

"I found the radios," Ziss said, climbing out of the SUV.

Matt took them from him. "Help Demko." With a nod, Ziss went to the back of the room.

"I can't see anything back here," Demko said. "Do you have a flashlight?"

"Yeah, why don't you go into the burning building and get it for me?"

Ziss cleared his throat. "We could open the car doors. Chris is right. It's pitch black and we can't see a thing."

Since Matt doubted they'd use the SUV, he wasn't worried about running down the battery. "Whatever." He opened the back passenger door. "Let's just get this done." While the boys contin-ued searching, he went to the opened double doors and stared at the path again. He'd prefer to wait until dark to make an attempt for the farmhouse, but a lot could happen between now and then. They could be free and wealthy, arrested or dead.

He rubbed his head where the insulated hat was making his scalp sweaty and itchy. *When the going gets tough, the tough get going* was an expression that had never applied to him. He'd spent his life lying, cheating, using threats or violence to make difficult situations go his way. He could do that now, except the police weren't going to simply disappear and let him walk. They would hunt him for the rest of his life. And what about Graves? If the man had a dirty agent on his payroll, how much power did he have? If he betrayed Graves, would he come after him? Fuck, he had no answers. His gut told him to bail, while his head said it wouldn't matter and that he was screwed, no matter what he attempted.

He stared at the lake again. Still. Running could buy him more time. He could—

Ziss knocked him into the snow. Matt gripped his rifle and quickly flipped onto his back…just as Ziss sliced a knife through the air.

Horizon Pointe Estates, Avon, Ohio
*Saturday, January 21*st*, 11:27 a.m. Eastern Standard Time*

The Fox 8 News anchor announced they had a breaking story. Patsy glanced up from her laptop and stared at the flat screen television hanging on her office wall. The anchor was replaced by a bird's eye view of Ottawa Lake Amusement Park. Orange flames and black smoke stood out against the white snow. Along the road outside the park were police vehicles, fire trucks and ambulances. The shot panned out, revealing roadblocks created by police cruisers which prevented news vans from moving closer to the park.

"We can't see any activity, or locate the hostages," the reporter in the helicopter said. "But as you can see, a building is on fire, and there is a victim in the snow. The FBI and the other law enforcement agencies involved have refused to comment."

When pots clanked together, Patsy used the remote to lower the volume, then rose and closed the office door. Her daughter was in the kitchen, likely making herself a late breakfast, and Patsy didn't want her to hear the news. Emma had become a fragile shell of the young woman she'd once been, and Patsy wasn't sure how her daughter would react to her brother's kidnapping. They'd already been through so much.

Seven years ago, her eight-month-old baby boy, Shawn, had died of SIDs. Four years later, Tim, her loving husband, best friend, business partner and father of her children had accidentally drowned during a fishing trip. Tragedy had struck again this past summer when Emma had attempted suicide. And now her son had been kidnapped and was being held hostage. Even though she'd made millions as a motivational speaker, written bestselling books that dealt with overcoming adversity, and had helped hundreds of thousands of people rebuild their lives, she was no longer sure if she could practice what she preached. She wasn't sure how many more life shattering blows she could take.

After the view from the helicopter had switched back to the news studio, she moved closer to the TV. "The FBI just asked us and other news stations *not* to fly helicopters over Ottawa Lake Amusement Park and the general vicinity," the anchor said. "The kidnappers are armed and dangerous, and law enforcement is concerned aircraft will draw fire or impede the hostage situation. For those of you just joining us… A bus, carrying fifteen boys—ages fifteen to seventeen—three chaperones and one driver, has gone missing. They left Newhouse Academy, located in Dublin, Ohio, early yesterday morning, and were reported missing later that day when the bus didn't arrive at its final destination. The blizzard made locating the vehicle difficult for authorities, but an early morning explosion alerted Medina County deputies and fire to the scene, where one deputy was shot. We have no word on the condition of the children or chaperones."

Patsy turned off the television. Worry ate at her, made her stomach twist with unease, and guilt. She picked up a picture frame containing a baby photo of her missing son. He'd had it rough from the start. When she'd been pregnant with him, she'd had difficulty carrying him, had always been sick and had eventually been put on bed rest. His birth hadn't been easy, either. She skimmed her finger along the picture. He'd been breech and she'd been forced to have a C-section. After he was born, he'd been colicky and a terrible sleeper. As he grew older, he'd had his sweet moments, but had been prone to horrible temper tantrums. He'd hated Shawn, never got along with Emma or even the dog.

There'd been times when she'd wondered if he had hated her and Tim, too. The way he had looked at them...with condescension, as if he'd known something they hadn't.

The guilt grew. She and Tim hadn't ignored their son or daughter, but they'd grieved over Shawn. Then they'd taken that grief, turned it into something positive and had started helping others. Within a year of publishing their first book, they were traveling across the country, filling auditoriums, then eventually convention centers with people who were fighting to move past their losses or failures, and looking to her and Tim to help them turn their lives around. Life had been good. They'd been earning millions of dollars and, in the process, helping each other deal with the loss of Shawn.

Then Tim had drowned. She'd wanted to curl up and die, but her children had needed her. Their following had needed her, too. And she'd been forced to put everything she and Tim had preached to the test, prove to herself, and every person who believed in them, that she would and could overcome yet another horrible loss.

She set the frame back on the bookshelf. Except that, in trying to keep the business running, she'd left her children in the care of therapists and nannies. Emma had been fourteen, her son, twelve. Instead of writing and traveling across the country for speaking engagements, she should have been home, caring for her kids.

She should have been there for Emma. A tear slipped down Patsy's cheek. She couldn't turn back the clock, or change the past, but she could right her mistakes. Could she possibly help the FBI save those poor boys? The problem was, she might be wrong. Her son was smart, secretive and devious. Was he smart enough to design such a complex kidnapping?

God, what kind of mother was she? Her son had been created out of love, and looked just like his father. Yet she disliked and feared him so much she'd sent him off to boarding school, then moved without telling him.

She sat behind the desk and ran her fingers through her hair. Maybe the problem wasn't him, but her. Since Tim's death, dark gray clouds of depression had constantly followed her. Each time she gave a motivational speech, it drained her. Although she'd put on a happy face and wow the crowd, she had begun to question her own spiel. She would tell people that the positive thinker saw what no one else could, and achieved the impossible. However, lately, her thoughts hadn't been positive but laced with suspicion.

Her son had been the last to see Tim alive. He'd also been the last person to be with Emma before she'd attempted suicide, and had threatened Patsy numerous times when she'd refused to place more money into his account. Which had been why she had chosen to sell the house in Bath and move to Avon. He was greedy, self-entitled, selfish and disrespectful. But did that make him a killer or kidnapper? No, it made him unlikable and some-one she didn't want in her life. And what if she went to the FBI with her suspicions and was wrong, not only about the kidnap-ping, but everything else? She couldn't prove her twelve-year-old had had anything to do with her husband's accidental drowning, and Emma refused to talk about her brother or what had hap-pened prior to her suicide attempt.

Patsy focused on the laptop. The idea that he could kidnap his teammates was ridiculous anyway. Yes, he was smart and devious, but how would a sixteen-year-old boy be able to convince grown men to help him, or supply them with weapons? No, for once, her son was a victim. Maybe fear would change his behavior and personality. Maybe being held captive and at gunpoint would give him time to reflect on life, and he'd come to realize he hadn't been a kind, loving person. Or maybe he would die at the hand of one of the kidnappers. Another tear slipped down her cheek as she glanced to his baby picture. She'd already lost Shawn and Tim. She might not like her son, but she didn't want him dead.

Even if it would make her and Emma's lives easier...

8

Ottawa Lake Amusement Park, Village of Ottawa, Ohio
Saturday, January 21ˢᵗ, 12:09 p.m. Eastern Standard Time

"WE HAVE LESS than ten minutes to make the deposit."
Chase paced at the front end of Summer's car. "What is
taking so long?"

Shultz had sent them pictures of Dillon Patricks and Evan
Barry fifty minutes ago. After Kevin Williams found out his son
wasn't in one of those photos, he'd refused to put up the five
hundred thousand they'd planned to deposit in the Bitcoin
account. While Summer understood why the man hadn't been
willing, he'd cost them time they couldn't afford. Evan's father
and Dillon's parents said they would gladly pay the ransom, but
transferring the money from their banks would take more than a
half an hour. Fortunately, Senator Patricks had stepped in with a
donation. That had been ten minutes ago.

"Be patient. Lauren knows what she's doing." Summer
stepped in his path. "Are you okay?" This was the first time they'd
been alone since Chase had walked down the parkway to talk to
the kidnapper, and she worried how he was dealing with being
shoved into the middle of a crisis negotiation.

When he stopped in front of her, excitement brightened his

eyes. "Honestly, this is the best I've felt in a long time. I can't explain it. At first, I thought I was going to have a panic attack, then I got back into the groove and, damn, the adrenaline rush was sweet."

"Really? That's...great," she said, forcing a smile. Though relieved he'd handled the situation well, emotionally and as a negotiator, she wondered what this meant. Would he want to work in crisis negotiation again? If so, would he return to the way he'd been before Brody's death?

"That sounded positive. What's the matter?"

I like the emotional Chase more than the cold, distant one. "Nothing." Over his shoulder, she spotted Dave waving, then pointing toward the trees. Seconds later, several EMTs emerged from the woods and onto the road carrying a gurney. Some of the SWAT team were behind them, their weapons ready, and their gazes on the woods they'd just left. "Oh, my God. They've got someone."

She and Chase reached the ambulance just as the EMTs were loading an unconscious boy inside. Summer immediately recognized Brennan Williams. Although thrilled he'd made it out alive, the blood coating his head alarmed her.

As the EMTs worked on Brennan, Dave walked over, holding his cell phone to his ear. When he reached them, he ended the call. "Lauren said the deposit has been made." He looked to the boy. "Brennan Williams?"

Summer nodded. "I believe so."

"Where'd you find him?" he asked one of the SWAT agents.

"When we were tracking Shultz and two kids, we found him in a frozen creek. Looks as if he fell or was tossed down the hill."

"Did he speak to you at all?"

"No, sir. But the location where we believe he was before rolling down the hill isn't far from the old hotel."

"Outside the hotel there's a path leading to the lake," Summer said, remembering the map of the park. "Brennan could've escaped when the ballroom blew and run in that direction."

"Except one of the kidnappers got to him first," Dave added.

"I went up the hill," the SWAT agent began, "and found only one set of boot prints. We're thinking he slipped, lost his balance, then cracked his head during the fall."

"Gotta go," an EMT said with urgency.

"Tony." Dave turned to the agent. "Follow them and let the father know where they're taking the boy."

"I suggest keeping this from the media," Chase said. "If Shultz is watching the news, we don't want him to know we found one of the kids. We don't want him panicking and doing something that could cause injury to the remaining boys. Plus, if Brennan wakes up, he can tell us how many men are there, and maybe even where they're located."

Once everyone had agreed and the ambulance had left, Dave motioned for her and Chase to follow him. Along the way, he snagged the SWAT commander. "Chase, you're up," Dave said, opening his car door. "Everyone inside. I want you to call Shultz, but put it on speaker so we can all hear."

Summer and Chase slid onto the backseat, while Dave and Kipp sat at the front. As Chase placed the call, she thought about Brennan and how he'd ended up at the bottom of the hill. The kid's forehead had been bloody and swollen, and there'd also been blood staining the sheet beneath his head. She'd noticed two oval bruises on each cheek that mirrored each other as well. Was it possible the bruises and head trauma occurred as he fell down the hill? Absolutely. Or was it possible someone had gripped his face and slammed his head against a tree or rock? Maybe, except SWAT had found only one set of boot prints. But hadn't Chase followed his own tracks in the snow when he'd returned from talking to Shultz?

Chase hung up the phone. "He's not answering. I'm going to text him."

After he'd sent the text, Summer told them her thoughts about Brennan, and the possibility the bruises were someone's thumbs. "I get why Shultz wouldn't want us to know Brennan isn't with the other kids. What I don't understand is, why dispose of him the way they did? Why let him live?"

"I thought those marks were dirt or soot from the fire." Chase frowned. "If you're right, it could be the kidnapper who did this hadn't meant for Brennan to fall down the hill. After it happened, they didn't want to waste time finding him to finish him."

"Especially if there are only a few kidnappers," Kipp added. "They'd need every available man to keep an eye on the kids and the park's perimeters, which we've fully secured. I also have deputies parked within the pockets of summer homes, and officers stationed in the woods across the lake." His mouth twisted into a smug smile. "There is no escape."

Matt's right ass cheek hurt like a motherfucker. If he didn't have to take a picture of Ziss and send it to Chase, he would have used the pocketknife he'd pulled from his butt cheek and sliced the son of a bitch's face. He would've been happy, too, using his fists to bust up the kid's mouth and nose, but he'd refrained. Instead, he'd taken his anger out on Ziss's body. Based on the pain crossing the kid's face, he wouldn't be surprised if he'd cracked a rib or two.

The fun house loomed ahead. Unfortunately, he wouldn't be able to rest just yet. After he dropped Ziss and Demko there, he had to make his way to the burger stand and give Woody a radio.

Minutes later, they arrived at the fun house. Joel let the boys inside, then stood in the open doorway. "No tape or rope?"

Matt shook his head. "All I got were the radios and a knife in the ass," he said, then told his cousin what had happened. "Ziss is lucky I didn't kill him."

"For sure. Look, I told you I don't like being the only one with all these kids."

Joel's whining grated on his nerves. He leaned in close. "Just hang tight. I heard from the Feds. They made a deposit."

Joel's eyes widened before a big grin split his face. "No shit?"

"I texted Mr. Graves to confirm it. I'm waiting to hear back from him. So, like I said, just hang tight. We might walk out of here millionaires after all."

Matt left the fun house, then headed for the burger stand. When he was almost there, he received a reply from Graves:

Deposit was only 500k! Hurt a kid.

"No problem," Matt muttered, and decided Ziss would be the one.

"Took you long enough," Woody said, once Matt entered the stand.

"Fuck off. I wouldn't have had to go all the way to the hotel if you hadn't lost your phone." He handed Woody a radio, then pulled the knife from his pocket. "Here. I found this at the hotel."

"What do you want me to do with it?" Woody asked, not taking the sheathed blade.

"It's not yours?"

"Nope. Ain't Randy's, either. He hated knives."

Unease weighed heavy on Matt's chest as he shifted his gaze back to the knife. First the switched fuel, now this. "It's not mine or Joel's."

"Finders keepers," Woody said as if discovering a knife—a brand new knife—in a one hundred-year-old abandoned room was nothing odd. "There's been some activity on the road."

"What kind?"

"I saw an ambulance leave."

Ambulance? Damn it. Fucking Brennan Williams. Had to be.

"I'm thinking they found the kid that went missing," Woody continued. "That ain't good. Now the Feds know there're only three of us left. Did you notice the news choppers stopped flying overhead? I wonder if the Feds thought we'd shoot them down. Or maybe they're gearing up to attack and don't want it filmed."

Matt's head and right glute throbbed. The kidnapping had been going to plan until the explosion. Now everything was fucked up and he didn't know how to regain control. "Graves said he received a ransom deposit for five hundred thousand."

With a sigh, Woody glanced at him. "Said or texted?"

"Texted. He wants me to hurt a kid."

The older man winced. "That right? Don't you think it's strange that you didn't hear from Graves until *after* the ballroom fire? If I were the money man in charge, I'd want to know how my commodities were doing, wouldn't you? I'd have called the moment I found out the bus made it to the park."

"Graves explained he had too many eyes around him. Which was also why he couldn't talk, only text."

"You don't honestly believe that. I know you ain't no dummy. Graves had all night to respond and he didn't. Again, he waited until *after* the fire. It's almost as if he knew."

A chill swept over him. "Are you saying you think Graves is *here*?"

Woody shook his head. "Before the blizzard hit, me and Randy searched the park. There was no sign of anyone having been here, except for us."

Matt would not allow Woody's paranoia to infect him. "Then what are you saying?"

"Not really sure." Woody shrugged. "But who switched the fuels and left behind that knife? Me and Randy dropped off everything on Thursday, then got a hotel. It snowed four inches that night. Who's to say Graves didn't come in while we were gone? He could've switched the cans and planted the knife, and the snow covered his tracks."

"That makes no sense. Why would he sabotage the kidnapping after spending months and thousands of dollars planning for it?" Matt shoved the blade back into his pocket. "The Ziss kid stabbed me in the ass with a pocket knife when we were at the hotel." He rolled his eyes and waited for Woody to stop laughing, then said, "We didn't check the kids for weapons. I'm wondering if one of them who brought the kerosene back from the hotel had a knife on them, and left it there."

"Why leave it when they coulda used it on one of us?"

"I don't fucking know," Matt snapped. "But I'm going to frisk the fuckers when I get back to the fun house."

Woody's smile fell. "While you're doing that, think about something else…it'll start getting dark around five thirty, maybe sooner because of how gray it is today. I guarantee your agent buddy is stringing us along, and they plan on coming in once it's dark. I can pick off a few from here, but if they come in from the woods and lake, they'll have us surrounded in a heartbeat."

"Then before dark, come to the fun house. If they surround us, they're not going to shoot up the place and risk killing a kid."

"And hope your Mr. Graves and his inside guy come through?" Woody rubbed the gray scruff along his jaw. "We shoulda run right after the ballroom exploded."

No shit. "We knew staying was a risk."

"Now our share isn't even half a percent of the thirty mil." Woody sighed again. "I'll head to the fun house before dark."

Angry, concerned and, thanks to Woody, paranoid, Matt left the burger stand. Woody wasn't right in the head, and Matt didn't buy into his theory that Graves had come in during the night to sabotage the kidnapping. That was just dumb.

But it did bother him that Graves had waited so long to contact him. The fuel and knife bothered him, too. While there could be a logical explanation for those things, he couldn't think of one.

He leaned against the snow piled up behind a rotting structure, pulled the phone from his pocket, then dialed Chase's number. The agent answered after the first ring.

"Matt, did you get the deposit?"

"I did, but it's missing some zeroes. I gave you pictures of two kids and expected at least four million."

"I know, and I did the best I could. You have to understand it's not easy to move that kind of money."

"Bullshit. I bet if I sent you a video of me holding a gun to one of the kids' heads you'd have the money. Because you didn't hold up your end of our deal, I have to make good on my threat."

"You don't. *Not* at all. More money is on the way."

Matt punched the snow. "I don't believe you."

"Believe me. I'm doing everything I can to get those boys out of there. I just need more time."

"Time to wait until dark so you can raid this place? Try it and we won't just hurt these kids, we'll start killing them."

"Matt," Chase said, his placating tone scratching at his nerves. "There's no need for that."

"Who was in the ambulance?" he asked, not interested in going round and round with Chase's lines of bullshit.

"We found Brennan Williams unconscious. What happened to him?"

"Unconscious? You're a fucking liar."

"No, it's true," Chase said, his tone sincere. "He's uncommunicative. Trust me, if he was awake and able to tell us what was going on in there, we might not be talking. We'd be acting. Do you understand what I'm saying?"

He did. If the FBI realized he didn't have an army of men at his disposal, they would storm the place. Which had him thinking back to what Woody had said about the news helicopters no longer flying over the area. "To prove I won't be fucked with, I'm still going to hurt a kid. I'll send you the video for your entertainment. And if I don't see more money in the account, I'll do it again."

"Matt, violence isn't you. That sounds more like your cousin." Chase let out a breath. "I'm not going to bullshit you. You're going to do hard time for this. You could even get the death penalty if jurors believe you killed Pembroke and Stokes. If you work with me, I'll testify on your behalf. You might end up doing twenty years for your part in the kidnapping, maybe less. You're only twenty-five. You could still have a shot at a good life."

Except a bunch of kids had watched him kill Clay and Randy. Unless Graves came through, he was fucked.

"Even if we get the families to make the full deposits," Chase continued, "what happens next? We have the park and lake surrounded. There's no way to escape."

"Then I guess I have nothing to lose." Matt ended the call,

then pressed his head back against the snow. He looked up at the gray sky, and imagined himself away from this place. On a beach, listening to music through his ear buds, drinking a beer and watching the girls in their bikinis. Chase was right, there was no way out unless Graves' guy helped them. Woody...he could be on to something, too. The old man hadn't come out and claimed this kidnapping scheme was a setup, but his paranoia had said as much.

A motor revved to the right of him. He quickly pushed off the snow bank, then fell to the ground. He looked toward the burger stand, just as Woody shot out from behind it on a snowmobile.

That motherfucker. Rage tearing through him, Matt rushed toward the back of the stand. The old man sped from the open field and onto the frozen lake. Wanting the man dead, he raised his rifle and aimed it.

A gunshot echoed from the lake and through the park. Matt flinched, watched blood spray from the top of Woody's head with both horror and satisfaction. The old man fell from the snowmobile, which continued forward until it puttered to a stop. Stunned, Matt staggered back and fell into the snow.

Now there were only two of them. And Chase hadn't been lying. They were surrounded. There was no chance of escape. The only leverage they had were the kids.

And their only hope was Graves.

The cell phone vibrated. Matt quickly pulled it from his pocket and looked at the screen. He immediately recognized Chase's number, but didn't answer. He didn't want to talk to the agent. The only person he needed to speak to was Graves.

Chase gripped the phone. With anger burning through him, he rushed toward the SWAT commander. "What the fuck, Taggart? Your men weren't supposed to shoot to kill unless a kid was in danger."

"Back off, Sawyer. Fourteen kids *are* in danger, and we've just eliminated one of the reasons why."

He'd worked with Kipp Taggart when he'd been with the Cleveland Division. The man was smart but extremely aggressive. "I understand that, but we could've questioned him, found out how many kidnappers we're up against and their agenda."

"We know their agenda. They want the ransom money."

No shit, asshole. "And how are they going to get out of the park once they have the money?"

Taggart shrugged. "Doesn't matter. They're not leaving this place." The commander walked off, radioing his people to cover the SWAT agents who were heading to the lake to retrieve the body.

Not leaving this place? Screw that. Chase met up with Summer and Dave, who were viewing the lake from near Dave's car. "Did you order Taggart to shoot to kill?" he asked Dave, and didn't bother to mask his frustration. The man's death was unnecessary and would set a new, shitty tone in his negotiation with Shultz.

"No. But now we know how they planned to escape."

"There is no escape. Taggart made that clear. He also claims the kidnappers aren't leaving this place."

Summer's eyes widened. "What?" She looked to Dave. "Killing suspects is not how we do things. We need them alive."

"To beat or murder those boys?" Dave's face reddened. "Don't tell me how we do things. I know the law. My top priority is getting those kids out of there by any means necessary. In a perfect world, the kidnappers would walk out with their hands raised. But you and I know there's nothing perfect about our world. I don't necessarily disagree with Taggart's call to shoot the man. The remaining suspects are going to start to panic. They're going to become desperate and make mistakes."

Chase shook his head. "Or want to get even. Have you thought about that? Tit for tat. First we stiffed them on the ransom money, then killed one of their men."

"The ransom money was your idea," Dave reminded him.

"Meant to build trust and open the line of communication."

"Have you tried calling Shultz?" Summer asked, worry in her eyes.

"He's not answering." He looked to the lake. Agents and deputies came out from the woods along the opposite side to remove the snowmobile, while the other agents hauled the dead man's body to the snowy shore. "I'm hoping Shultz wasn't on that snowmobile. Otherwise, we can probably kiss any further negotiations goodbye."

His phone rang and he quickly looked at the screen. "Wasn't Shultz," he said, relieved, and answered. "Matt—"

"So this is how it's going to be?" Shultz asked, his breathing labored.

Wind whipped over the line, giving Chase the impression the man was on the move. "I'm not the one in charge. Shooting that man wasn't my call. Who was he?"

"An asshole."

Interesting. "Because he defected?"

"Yeah, you could say that."

"I warned you. I told you we had this place surrounded. If you attempt to escape, you could end up dead, too. I don't want that. Matt, believe me. I'm doing what I can to help bring this situation to a peaceful close."

"Peaceful, my ass! Blood shot up and out of his head like a fucking sprinkler," Matt shouted. The wind stopped whipping. "How's that for peaceful?"

Gunfire rang out from the center of the park. Everyone on the road ducked. Chase rushed to Summer's side, took her by the elbow and hurried them toward her car. "Matt! What are you doing?" he asked, as panicked male voices came over the line. His stomach twisted with dread. "Talk to me, Matt. Please tell me you didn't shoot anyone."

"Not now. But don't doubt that I will," he said, the wind returning and making the male voices inaudible.

"I don't doubt you at all."

"Then you better tell your men not to enter this park. I'm sure it'd be tempting to hit us once it's dark, but that would be a very bad idea. I have over a dozen men with me and we have this place rigged with explosives. Unless you want this place to turn into a war zone, you'll be smart and stay the fuck away." He drew in a shaky breath. "I promised I'd hurt a kid if you didn't make the deposit. Because you shortchanged us, you've forced me to keep that promise. What happens next is on you."

Shultz ended the call. Chase slid the phone from his ear and into his pocket, and stared at the dozens of agents and deputies scrambling along the road. Commander Taggart and Dave were shouting orders, but all Chase heard were Shultz's parting words...

What happens next is on you.

Summer tugged at his arm. "Chase? What is it?" she asked pulling him harder.

He glanced down at her. It'd been so long since he'd truly stared into her eyes, he'd forgotten how expressive they were, how their shade of blue was darker than denim and hinted at violet. He touched her cheek with his gloved hand and wished he could caress her bare skin. He wished they were anywhere but here. "Shultz is going to do something very bad."

He sat in the corner of the fun house, pretending to fear for his life. He supposed he should be somewhat nervous. After all, he'd told Shultz to hurt a kid and the man could choose him. But he'd said *hurt*, not kill. A few punches would be worth the look on his mother's face when he returned home. Wherever the hell that was now.

"Ziss!" Shultz stood at the opened door. "Get over here."

Joel grabbed Shultz's arm. "What the hell is happening? I heard a motor, then gunshots and—"

Shultz shook off his cousin and faced the team. "Listen up! Since we're all in this together, I'm going to tell you what's happening. The park is surrounded by agents. They found Williams dead. And Woody just tried to escape on a snowmobile. They shot him in the head."

Brennan was dead? Nice. He relaxed against the wall. He'd hated leaving the kid without finishing him off, but now he no longer had to worry about him. Woody's death was an unexpected and pleasant surprise. He hadn't been sure how to kill the old man. Thanks to the FBI, he didn't have to concern himself with a plan, and only had the Shultz cousins to kill now.

"Your cheap-ass parents must not give a shit about you boys. So far, we've gotten next to nothing from them." Matt took Ziss's pocketknife from his coat. "I warned them that if they didn't pay up, someone was going to get hurt." He grinned. "Ziss, it's your lucky day."

Tyler Ziss didn't move.

He still couldn't believe Tyler had stabbed Shultz in the rear. He'd wanted to laugh about it, but had managed to refrain. He'd privately gloat later, after the Shultz cousins were dead and the FBI thought the kidnapping was over.

"Joel, help Ziss up and bring him to me."

Joel paled as he shifted his gaze from Tyler to the knife. "What are you going to do to him?"

Shultz stared at Tyler. The hatred blazing in his eyes matched the fire still burning across the park. "Do you really care?"

Joel walked over to Tyler, who was seated next to Alex's dying body. The man swallowed hard. "Get up," he said, his gaze imploring.

Tyler finally stood, then went to Shultz, who turned the kid to face the team. Shultz handed Joel his burner phone. "Record this, but keep my face out of the shot," he said, and, once Joel was ready, Shultz sliced Tyler across the cheek.

The kid cried out and pressed a hand to the side of his face. Blood immediately seeped between his fingers. His knees buckled. Shultz shoved him against the wall before he could drop to the floor and raised the knife again.

Joel lowered the phone. "Stop! You proved your point."

Breathing hard, Shultz wiped the blade along Tyler's coat. "Drop your hand."

With tears filling his eyes, Tyler obeyed and revealed a bloody, vertical slice that ran from just beneath his right eye down to near his jawline. Holy shit, he hadn't seen that coming, and didn't want to end up like Tyler. Next time he texted Shultz, he'd have to make it clear: no playing with knives.

"Everyone take a good look. If you haven't figured it out by now, I'm not fucking around. If Ziss hadn't stabbed me, his face wouldn't be bleeding. So don't be mad at me or feel sorry for him. He got what he deserved."

Matt grabbed Tyler by the coat and pushed him back toward the team. After taking his phone from Joel, he pulled his cousin aside. While some of the guys tried to console Tyler, he kept his gaze locked on Shultz. Matt pulled a knife from his pocket, said something he couldn't hear, then showed it to Joel, who shook his head.

He fought from smiling. Shultz had to be freaking. He had to be wondering who the knife belonged to, and how they'd ended up with gas in a kerosene can. Shultz would soon know the truth.

Unfortunately, it would die with him.

"You need to eat something." Chase handed Summer a granola bar and bottled water. "And keep hydrated."

"Thanks." She took the water. "I'm not hungry." Ever since viewing the brief video of Tyler Ziss having his face cut, her stomach had been upset.

"You haven't eaten in almost eight hours. That's not good for you or the baby."

She lowered the heat, then rested her head against the headrest of the car's passenger seat. "According to my doctor, I only need to eat an extra three hundred and fifty calories per day during my second trimester."

"That can't be right."

"It is, and you know I don't eat that much anyway."

"True. What about the third trimester? How many calories then?"

"Four hundred and fifty." She rolled her head against the headrest to look at him. "What's going to happen?" she asked, her mind on the kids and their abductors. "It's going to be dark soon, and I'm scared for those boys."

"I am, too. I don't like that Shultz has gone radio silence on us."

Shortly after the shooting of one of the kidnappers, who'd later been identified as Woodrow "Woody" Bakanowsky, Shultz had sent the video. After, he'd refused to text or return Chase's calls.

"I do think we can assume the Shultz cousins are the only kidnappers left," Chase continued. "SWAT hasn't spotted anyone but those two since we've been here."

"I know that's a good thing, but one person with one gun can do plenty of damage. Plus, there are the explosives."

"Unless Shultz was lying about those. It's possible they're what caused the ballroom to catch fire." He turned in his seat to face her. "Taggart asked me to go into the park with them."

Alarmed, she straightened. "No way."

"I'll be armed and wearing SWAT gear." He took her hand and caressed her knuckles with his thumb. "If Shultz is willing to talk, do you really want Taggart to be the one who tries to negotiate with him?"

"God, no. He's extremely arrogant and a little too quick tempered."

"Which is why I'm going. And why I want you to head home."

She pulled her hand away. "Excuse me?"

"Don't get upset," he said, earnestness in his eyes and voice. "I just want you safe. If the Shultz cousins manage to escape, I don't want you in danger."

"I'm surrounded by agents and officers, and I carry two guns. I'll be fine." She leaned forward. "I would never leave you."

Disappointment clouded his eyes. "Like I left you."

"I didn't say that." She hadn't meant for him to misunderstand or be hurt by the honest admission, but maybe it was a good thing. Sometimes she wondered if Chase had a clue as to how badly he'd hurt her, or had he been too selfishly wrapped up in his self-inflicted guilt to notice? "You know I wouldn't walk off the job if any of our agents were about to enter a possible firefight. I'd join them." She held up a hand before he could speak. "Don't worry. I'm not suggesting that I go into the park. But I'm not leaving. I...need to make sure you, ah, that you're fine." She glanced out the window. "Crap, it's starting to snow," she said to change the subject.

"You still like me," he said, drawing her attention.

"I never said I disliked you. We have history and are going to have a baby."

He leaned closer. A boyish smile tugged at his mouth. "Admit it. You still care about me."

Her cheeks heated. Of course she still cared. Damn it, she foolishly still loved him. But she had to be cautious with Chase and what she said to him. He had a track record of either shutting down or running when things became tough or too complex. She refused to live with a man who constantly kept her on a yo-yo string. "Look," she began, but her phone rang, saving her from having to continue. She quickly answered.

"We have movement," Dave said.

She glanced out the windshield toward where Dave and Kipp stood, aiming binoculars at the park's gate. After ending the call and telling Chase what Dave had said, she donned her hat and gloves, then exited the car.

As the day had faded into the evening hours, the air had grown colder, the wind blustery. Meteorologists had predicted there was an eighty percent chance of snow throughout the night, and unfortunately it appeared they were right. Blizzard-like conditions could make a rescue attempt more harrowing than usual, and she worried about Chase going into the park with SWAT because it had been years since he'd been in the field.

"What's happening?" she asked when they reached Dave and Kipp.

Dave passed her the binoculars. "Two individuals are dragging a body."

She looked through the lenses. Between the falling snow and zero light coming from the park, she could barely make out the figures. "Has any of your men ID'd them?" she asked Kipp.

"We know Matthew Shultz is one of them. We're not sure about the other two." Kipp turned to Chase. "Call him. They could be setting a trap."

"Or delivering an injured boy," Summer countered.

"Taggart is right." Chase turned away from the wind to use his phone. "Shultz is desperate. If they do have explosives, he could've strapped them to whoever they're dragging, then planned to detonate once our people have him."

The image he described horrified her, and she preferred her idea over his.

"Matt," Chase said. "It looks like you're making a delivery." He paused. "I see." After sliding the phone into his pocket, he faced the park again. "The boy they're dragging is what he's calling a *human message*, and motivation to keep the deposits coming. He said for me and only one other agent to go to the gate."

Fear ran up Summer's spine. The snow was falling harder, and she swore it had grown darker since they'd exited the car. This most definitely could be a setup, and Chase would be walking right into it.

Kipp instructed one of his men to bring Chase SWAT gear to wear, which included body armor, a protective helmet and eyewear. Once he was dressed, and this time armed, he walked over to her, then pulled her away from the other agents.

"Are you sure you don't care about me?" he asked, the worry

in his eyes belying his teasing tone.

"Considering what you're about to do, how am I supposed to respond to that loaded question?"

Snow had already begun to cling to his helmet and clothes. He glanced toward where he would be heading before meeting her gaze again. "With the truth."

She stepped closer. "I never stopped caring."

His face relaxed. "Thank you."

"For what?"

"Giving me permission to ask you on a date."

"What? Chase—"

"Can I take you to dinner?"

The old Chase wouldn't have said a word to her before going off to deal with an armed suspect. "Instead of asking me out, shouldn't you and Kipp be discussing your plan of action?"

"Of course. So you better hurry up and give me an answer."

"Chase," the SWAT commander called. "Let's go."

Chase focused on her. "I'm not going without an answer."

"Fine," she said, anxious, yet dreading what would happen once they reached the gate. "I'll have dinner with you."

He gave her a small grin. "That's what I wanted to hear. See you soon."

As he walked off with Kipp and she lost sight of him in the darkness and snow, she hugged herself and whispered, "I hope so."

Ottawa Lake Amusement Park, Village of Ottawa, Ohio
Saturday, January 21ˢᵗ, 5:36 p.m. Eastern Standard Time

O NE LANTERN HAD survived the ballroom explosion, and
Joel was in possession of it. He stood outside and out of
sight, the dim light glowing through a couple of broken windows.
The wind gusted, blowing snow inside the fun house. No one
from the team made a move or talked. The slice and dice Shultz
had done on Tyler's face had scared the shit out of them.

Well, not *all* of them.

Joel and Shultz didn't scare him. Any idiot could see Joel was
just as afraid as the guys on the team. But he was surrounded by
idiots who hadn't paid attention to the way Joel's hands trembled,
how he never held the rifle properly, how he'd showed sympathy
for some of the guys who'd been injured.

Joel would be an easy kill. Shultz? He had no clue what Shultz
had planned for Alex and Simon, but was glad he hadn't been
chosen to haul their team captain's body from the fun house. He
was ready to go to his *new* home, and for a family reunion with his
sister and mom.

They had plenty of catching up to do.

He wished he could pull out his cell and check the time, but worried the bright light would draw attention to him. The moment they had been forced inside the fun house, he'd commandeered a corner of the large, narrow room, where the outside walls butted up against overgrown trees and brush. What no one knew, and never would, was that when he'd come to the park Thursday evening, he'd removed several nails along the lower portion of the wall so that he could slide the old wood planks to either side. He'd also used a saw to cut out a portion of the floor. Not wanting anyone to see the freshly cut wood, he'd sacrificed warmth by sitting over the opening. An opening he'd tested several times and would use to escape.

Excitement filled his stomach. This would be it. An end to what he believed would become one of the nation's most famous kidnappings. Though he wouldn't get any credit, knowing he had fooled everyone would be all the satisfaction he'd need. But he had to complete his mission before he could pat himself on the back.

Shultz had been gone for what he guessed to be about fifteen minutes. Had the douche left before darkness had engulfed the park, he would've already been outside. The threat of being caught, of Simon possibly discovering his secret, had kept him staying put. His teammate might not suspect he'd been part of the kidnapping, but if the kid caught him with a bloody knife in his hands, then told the police, suspicion might fall on him.

He darted his gaze around the darkened room, and keeping on his hat and gloves, he slipped out of his heavy coat. After moving the wood planks aside, he quietly slid through the opening. Once he put the planks back into place, he crept around the building with the intention of sneaking up on Joel from behind. Along the way, he brushed off a pile of snow that had accumulated on top of the box he'd also left there on Thursday, then pulled out a replica of the knife Shultz had found in the hotel and now possessed.

When he'd first realized Shultz had the knife, he hadn't cared. His prints weren't on any of the burner phones and knives he'd left throughout the park. Now he was pumped that the other man had the knife. The FBI probably believed Shultz had set up the kidnapping and had brought the knives to the park. He'd watched plenty of cop shows. Detectives always liked to say there was no such thing as a perfect crime. If it hadn't recently occurred to him that Joel and Shultz's deaths could be questionable, those detectives could've been right. Except he *had* realized his mistake, and was about to prove there *was* such a thing as a perfect crime.

Now to execute it.

He drew in a breath, and thought about how to attract Joel's attention. The snow called to him. He quickly made a snowball, then unsheathed the knife.

He edged around the corner of the building. Part of the landing outside the fun house had rotted away, leaving a four-foot drop six feet from the entrance, where the stairs were on the other side. The lantern was now hung on a protruding nail outside the door, snow blowing around it. Joel had his back to him, his concentration toward the park's entrance. Two beams of light, likely from flashlights, danced in the distance. Since their equipment had been burned in the fire, those had to belong to the FBI.

Had Shultz turned Alex over to the agents? Why would he do that?

Whatever. It didn't matter. All that did was to make sure Joel and Shultz didn't survive. No one could know about Mr. Graves.

With nervous energy bursting from his gut, he tossed the snowball at Joel, then quickly pressed himself against the wall.

"Hello?" Joel whispered, seconds later. "Matt?"

Instead of jumping off the landing, Joel must have used the steps. Otherwise, one of the guys inside the building would've seen him on the move.

"Here," he whispered back.

Joel came toward him, then froze. The glow from the lantern revealed the shock in his eyes. "How—"

He slit Joel's throat, forever silencing him.

Joel dropped the rifle and gripped his neck. As blood sputtered from between the man's lips, he left the bloodied knife in the snow, then edged around the corner of the building again. The beams from the FBI agents' flashlights were moving toward the road. Which meant it was time for him to head back to his section of the fun house.

He entered the building as silently as he'd left it, slid the planks back into place and put on his coat. Shivering from the cold, from the rush of killing a man, he pulled his knees to his chest and glanced around the room. If only they knew. If only they had a clue. They'd hate him. They'd come after him. He could make it so he looked like the hero, but that wasn't part of his agenda. He had one end goal: getting home to Mom and Emma.

Needing for one of these dumbasses to take notice that Joel wasn't doing much...of anything, he scooted toward Dillon and the friggin' Eagle Scout, Evan. "Why would Joel leave us alone?"

Evan shrugged and looked to Dillon. "Don't know," Evan whispered. "Why would Shultz take Alex to the cops now?"

Dillon leaned forward. "Maybe he's worried about getting the death penalty."

Evan shook his head. "He's going to get that, no matter what. We all saw him kill Coach Pembroke and Randy. He killed Clay and shot Alex. Shultz is screwed."

In so many ways. "Maybe Joel went with Shultz," he suggested, hoping Evan or Dillon would play into his plan. "The lantern hasn't moved since he hung it outside."

"Maybe," Evan said. Staying seated, he inched his way across the floor toward the window by the door. He looked through it, then motioned for them, and the others to come over to him. "He's not out there."

Dillon proved he was bolder than Evan by popping his head out the window. He turned to them, excitement in his eyes. "Evan's right. He's not out there. Shultz said we're surrounded by the cops. If we run for it, we can be rescued."

One by one, members of the team rose and whispered amongst themselves. When Dillon opened the door, they all froze.

"Anything?" Evan asked.

Dillon shook his head. "Nothing."

They all slowly eased from the fun house. Blood-orange embers—all that remained of the ballroom—glowed against the blackness. Snow whipped around them, making it difficult to see. He looked to the right, expecting Shultz to surprise them and start firing.

"Where are Shultz and Simon?" one of the guys asked.

"I don't know," he said, then looked to the lantern. "It's so dark, he's going to be able to see us under this light. We should leave the lantern and hide behind the fun house."

"Why would we do that?" Tyler asked. "I want out of here."

"Ambush him," Evan said with a nod. "We don't know where he is, and I don't want to leave Simon behind. Shultz might kill him when he sees we've escaped."

Damn, Evan had played into his plan perfectly. "Agreed," he said, anxious for one of the guys to discover Joel and trample over the tracks he'd made in the snow. "Don't use the steps. We'll leave footprints in the snow."

"Good call." Zach led them off the landing. When he jumped off, he quickly staggered back and fell against the snow. "Oh my God, oh my God," he said, panting.

Tyler pushed his way to the front of the pack, then jumped off the landing. "What is it?"

He hurried over and joined the others in the snow. "Holy shit." He pretended to be shocked. "Why would Shultz kill his cousin?" he asked, hoping to plant that kernel of bullshit in their minds.

"He shot Clay and Randy," Tyler said. "Woody's dead. Maybe he's running and took Simon as a hostage."

"Maybe," Chris said, picking up the bloody knife.

"Dude, what are you doing?" Zach asked.

"Arming myself in case he comes back." Chris wiped the knife across Joel's coat. "I don't know how to shoot a rifle."

"I'm not shooting anyone," Evan said, holding up his hands.

"Not even if you have a clean shot and Shultz is holding a gun to Simon's head?" Tyler picked up the rifle. "Screw that. We're on our own until the FBI raids the park. Shultz could be anywhere. He could be watching us right now."

Several of the guys looked into the darkness. The thing was, Tyler was right. Shultz could be anywhere. He could've also decided to leave Joel behind and use Simon as his ticket out of here. But he didn't believe that. Shultz was depending on Mr. Graves and his inside guy.

"Down," Dillon whispered with vehemence. "He's coming."

They all either ducked below the landing or crouched next to the fun house. "What do you see?" he asked Chris, who was next to him and near the corner where the building met the landing.

Chris moved his head slightly, then pressed himself against the wall. "Shultz is walking behind Simon. It doesn't look like Alex is with them." Chris bent down, then crawled to Tyler. He motioned for the rest of them to gather around. "Wait until Simon is inside, then shoot Shultz."

Tyler shuddered. "I hate him, but I don't think I can kill him."

"You don't have to," he said, when he really wanted to encourage Tyler to put a bullet in Shultz's head. "Hit him in the shoulder or something. Once he goes down, we can attack him."

"Beat the shit out of him," Chris added.

Evan nodded. "Exactly."

No one moved or said another word. Minutes passed. As he knelt in the snow near Joel's body, he realized he'd made one more mistake. *The burner phone.* The fucking thing was still on him, hidden in the lining of his coat. He glanced to the ballroom. The bus now blocked his view, but he'd seen the embers. Before they left the park, he needed to dispose of the phone.

"Get inside," Shultz said as his heavy footfall pounded on the landing's steps. The pounding stopped. The door creaked, then clicked shut.

Chris tapped Tyler's shoulder. The kid gingerly touched the cut along his face, then, narrowing his eyes, held the rifle in both hands. With a cry, he jumped up and fired three times.

"Motherfucker," Shultz shouted, and fell to the landing with a thud. "You fuckers!" He fired several rounds. "First I'm going to kill Thorpe, then, one by one, I'm going to kill each of you. Come out here, Thorpe!"

"Don't do it, Simon." Tyler ducked. "I hit him," he said, breathing hard. "I...I'm not sure where. Leg and maybe stomach. I don't know. What are we going to do? Shit. Simon. We've got to get him out of there."

So much for a bullet to the head. He needed Shultz to die, damn it. He grabbed Chris's arm. "Let's go around the back and surprise him from behind."

"Good idea," Chris said, encouraging Evan, Dillon and Zach to join them.

As they quietly made their way to the steps, Shultz continued to swear and demand Simon leave the fun house. If Simon were smart, he'd stay hidden in the dark room until this was over.

When they reached the steps, he peeked around the corner, then pulled the others in for a huddle. "He's sitting up and his back is to us. He has the gun pointed in the other direction."

"I say we just go for it." Chris clutched the handle of the knife. "It's a risk, but if he's hurt, do you think he could turn quick enough to shoot at us?"

"No clue," he said. "But he knows he's screwed."

"He has nothing to lose," Evan added.

Zach nodded. "Which makes him dangerous."

"Are we going for it?" Dillon asked.

Chris tapped the blade against his gloved palm, and grinned. "Fuckin' A."

They broke from the huddle. He moved alongside Chris. Because only two people could walk up the steps at the same time, the others followed behind.

When they reached the steps, Chris glanced at him, then mouthed, "Go."

He and Chris rushed up the steps and lunged, knocking

Shultz forward. The man yelled and fired several more rounds. Evan, Dillon and Zach hurried over, while Tyler and the others jumped onto the landing. Someone knocked Shultz's gun from the landing, and they all took their turns kicking and punching their former coach. Even Simon had come out from hiding to join them.

After what seemed like an eternity, but was probably seconds, he stepped away from Shultz. Most of the guys did, except for a few who gave Shultz several more kicks.

"Is he dead?" Tyler asked, and he noticed the kid no longer carried the rifle.

Evan the Eagle Scout rolled Shultz onto his back. The man groaned and muttered something.

Rage contorted Chris's face. He kicked Shultz in the side. "How can he not be dead?"

Several of them took a backward step. Chris's eyes were wild as he frantically continued to kick Shultz. "Why won't you fucking die?" he asked, his voice manic. "Because of you, Coach is dead." He delivered another kick, this time to the head. "Brennan is dead." Tears streamed down the kid's face. "And Alex…" He dropped to his knees. "I hate you!"

Before anyone could react, Chris buried the knife in Matt Shultz's chest. His breath labored, he wiped his nose with his coat sleeve. "Oh, my God. I just killed Shultz. They're gonna know," he said, panicked. "They're gonna arrest me and—"

"They won't," he said, before Chris lost his shit, and he lost his patience. "You didn't kill him. Look, he's still breathing." He stared at the slow rise and fall of Shultz's coat, and also wondered why the man wouldn't fucking die. Though tempted to pull the knife out of Shultz's chest and stab him again himself, he had to remain cool. The burner phone needed to be tossed. He'd prefer the fire, but wasn't sure what excuse he could use to walk over to what remained of the building.

"Screw Shultz." Tyler hopped off the landing. "If he dies, and I hope he does, none of us should feel guilty."

"Yeah." Dillon joined Tyler in the snow. "It was him or us."

Simon took the lantern off a nail, then headed down the steps. "Let's get out of here."

As his teammates left the landing and began walking, he realized he had made yet another error. Taking advantage of the darkness, he checked Shultz's pocket. The man released a gurgled groan. He looked at Shultz's face and, even in the darkness, saw the blood oozing from his mouth and the white slits of his eyes.

"Hey, are you finally going to die?" he whispered, and took Shultz's burner phone from his pocket. He checked it, noticed there were two missed calls—probably the negotiator, since they were made minutes ago—turned off the phone, then slipped it inside the lining of his coat. He leaned close to Shultz's face, where snow began to gather. "Mr. Graves thinks you're an asshole. I should know, since *I* am Graves."

Shultz's eyes opened slightly before returning to small slits. The gurgling worsened as he wheezed.

Satisfied the man would die knowing a kid had played him, he hurried off to catch up with the others. Now that the fun at the park had come to an end, it was time for the second part of his plan to begin. It was time for a family reunion...

Still dressed in the loaned SWAT uniform, Chase joined the other agents as they made their way along the parkway. Even with the use of night vision goggles, the falling snow made for bad visibility. Although Shultz had told them not to enter the park, and had left the wounded boy, Alex McGuire, at the gate earlier as a message—he would continue to harm the boys if deposits weren't made—they needed to investigate the gunfire. And Shultz wasn't answering his cell.

Because of the heavy snowfall and increase in the wind's speed, agents who had been in the trees were forced to take to the ground, and no one could see the interior of the park. He didn't want to believe that Shultz had decided to start shooting kids, but during their last phone conversation, he'd heard the desperation and fear in the man's voice. Still. Why release a dying boy, only to hurt another? Or maybe the shooting had been between Shultz and his own men.

"Over here!"

Shouts floated on the gusting wind. Taggart came over the radio, saying he'd spotted people heading for the gate.

"How many?" Chase asked.

"Eight…no, thirteen!"

Thank God.

As the shouting grew closer, along with the grainy glow of a lantern, Taggart radioed for medics to be ready. Less than a minute later, they reached the gate the same time the boys did. The agents flashed lights on them. Chase searched the crowd.

"Where's Shultz?" he asked.

Tyler Ziss, who he recognized by the cut along his cheek, stepped forward. "Fun house."

"Is he armed?" Taggart asked.

Simon Thorpe, who had helped Shultz deliver Alex to the gate earlier, shook his head. "He might be dead."

"Are there any other kidnappers in the park?"

"No," the boy said. "You guys killed Woody, Shultz killed Joel and we…made it so Shultz can't hurt anyone again." He glanced around to his teammates. "Right?"

The kids stood unified and proud as they yelled out in agreement. Chase stared at them, not with shock, but concern. What had happened would forever change these boys, and he hoped their parents put their wealth toward hiring top-notch therapists for their sons. There shouldn't be any pride over taking a man's life, even if that man had kidnapped and tortured them.

Taggart ordered half of his men to go with the boys, and the other half to head into the park. "The fun house is about one hundred yards away on the left."

Chase glanced around him as he moved through the thick

snow. To his right, the ballroom still smoldered. In front of it was the school bus which was surrounded by drifts of snow. Up ahead, the green glow from the night vision goggles made the Ferris wheel more eerie than usual. As they neared the fun house, Taggart warned them to be ready in case the kids were wrong and Shultz was alive and armed. But as they approached, a body lay supine on the snow-covered landing outside the building, the handle of a knife protruding from the chest.

Gun raised, Taggart went to the body first. While he checked for a pulse, the other agents searched around the building.

The commander lowered his weapon. "He's dead."

"Found Joel Shultz," an agent shouted. "His throat's been cut."

Taggart turned to Chase. "Why would Shultz kill his cousin? You'd think he would keep him alive to help watch over the boys."

Chase considered the same. "It doesn't make sense." He removed the night vision goggles, then produced a flashlight. "Shultz just turned over Alex's body, and gave me the impression he was in for the long haul. But it could be Joel got scared, wanted to give up, and Shultz wasn't having it."

He stepped closer to the landing and stared at Shultz. More than an inch of snow coated the man's clothes, hair and part of his face, which was bloodied and swollen. Blood also marred the snow around his stomach and right thigh. He imagined what had transpired. Fueled by hatred and fear, he pictured the kids succumbing to a mob mentality, and beating then stabbing Shultz.

While he walked over to where Joel's body had been discovered, Taggart called Dave, and asked how he wanted to handle the scene. Because of how much snow had fallen in the last few days, they wouldn't be able to drive into the park to remove the bodies. But they had Woody's snowmobile and also planned to bring in a snowplow to clear the area. The issue he had was with forensics. Because of the weather, discovering—scientifically—what had happened here would prove difficult. They had thirteen witnesses, fifteen if Brennan and Alex recovered, but eyewitness accounts weren't always accurate, especially if the witness had been through a traumatic experience.

A motor hummed from behind him. He turned as a snowmobile neared the building. When it came to a stop, Summer let go of the driver and hopped into the snow. Why, at five months pregnant, would she think zooming around on the back of a snowmobile was an okay thing to do?

Taggart and Summer joined him by Joel's body. "What do you think?" Taggart asked. "The kids found Joel and the knife, then used it on Shultz?"

Summer slipped off her backpack. She pulled out a flashlight, then aimed it at Joel. "My God. His throat's been slit."

Chase told her the boys claimed Shultz had killed his cousin, and they'd taken care of him. "I noticed Shultz has wounds on his stomach and leg. We heard, what, about a dozen gunshots? One of the boys could've used Joel's rifle to shoot Shultz. But how did they get ahold of the rifle and knife?"

Summer frowned and glanced to the dead man on the landing. "Shultz could've killed Joel before bringing Alex's body to the gate."

"And leave twelve kids free to not only escape, but to arm themselves?" Chase asked, not buying it.

Taggart shook his head. "Doesn't add up, does it?"

"No. We need to talk to those boys." Chase shined the flashlight toward the body, then the snowy ground near the building. "We have to photograph as much as we can before the snow covers these tracks."

"I have a camera." Summer handed Taggart the backpack. "And more agents are on their way."

"Good, but…" The SWAT commander let out a deep sigh. "Look, let's say the kids killed Joel, then ambushed Shultz. What then? Would you want to see them prosecuted for that? And who would you go after? You saw how they acted when we found them."

Chase nodded. "Proud and unified."

"Exactly. Are they going to rat out each other?"

Summer stared at Chase, disbelief in her eyes. "Are you suggesting one of those boys is capable of slitting a man's throat?"

"I'm suggesting that something about what happened here isn't right," Chase said.

"There's nothing right about fifteen kids being kidnapped." She looked to Taggart. "Have your men tape off the area in front of the Ferris wheel. One of the kids said that was where Wayne Pembroke was buried, along with the man who drove the bus. The kids said Shultz shot them both, and Randy. Randy's the victim lying in front of the ballroom." She faced Chase. "We're going to start interviewing them, if you want to join me."

"Separately, I hope."

She cocked a brow. "Of course. With the exception of two boys, none of them said they needed medical assistance, and every one of them just wants to go home. We're contacting their parents now. Since you're the only one who talked to Shultz, I thought you'd want to hear what the kids had to say."

"Absolutely," he said. He wanted to sit in on as many interviews as possible. Unless there was an additional kidnapper the kids hadn't known about, they were lying. Shultz wasn't a genius, but he also wasn't stupid enough to arm twelve kids, then let them ambush him.

Twenty minutes later, after he'd used the snowmobile to take Summer back to the road, he sat in the back of an ambulance with Summer and Tyler Ziss. The medic had just finished cleaning and dressing the cut along Tyler's face, saying the kid would want to see his doctor, but that he didn't believe the cut was deep enough for stitches.

"Are my mom and dad here?" Tyler asked Summer.

"They're on the way. We're going to transport you to the hotel they've booked." She offered the kid a gentle smile. "Can you tell us what happened?"

Tyler started with Wayne Pembroke's murder. When he came to the part where Shultz killed Clay and shot Alex, he admitted to not seeing the shootings first hand, but told them who had. When he mentioned Brennan's name, his eyes filled with tears. "I can't believe he's gone."

Summer's brows pulled together. "Gone?"

"Shultz said Brennan was dead."

That would have been likely to crush the boys' spirits. "He's alive, but unconscious," Chase said. "He was found at the bottom of a hill. Did you see him or any of the kidnappers run from the ballroom after the fire?"

"No. I was trying to help get the gear before it burned."

"What about the kidnappers? Were they all present when the building was on fire?"

He nodded. "Randy was..." He licked his lips, then swallowed. "He was screaming and rolling in the snow. Chris, Logan and Hunter were in the ballroom when the explosion happened. They said Randy had his face by the kerosene heater and was trying to get it going with a lighter. Then...boom."

Summer held up a hand. "Take us back to this morning, before the explosion."

"Okay." He cracked his knuckles. "Shultz gave us jobs. Nick stole the bus keys the night before. Because Shultz thought they might've fallen out of Clay's pocket, he made some kids search in the snow next to where Clay died. Some had to bury Clay's body by the Ferris Wheel, four went with Randy to the hotel to get kerosene to refill the heaters, and the rest tried shoveling around the bus. I don't know if Nick still has the keys."

"Doesn't matter, but we'll ask him," Summer said. "Go ahead and continue."

"That's pretty much it. Randy had his group take the fuel inside. Next thing I know, there's this huge blast. Randy was covered in flames as he ran out of the building. Then I saw Brennan and Chris carrying out Alex. Shultz yelled to the rest of us to grab what we could. I didn't realize Brennan was gone until after Shultz did."

The boy went on to tell them about Randy's murder and how

he had stabbed Shultz with the pocketknife. But Chase was more interested in what had happened near the end.

"Tell us how you escaped," he suggested.

He puffed his cheeks, looked away and let out a breath. "Shultz made Simon help him take Alex's body out of the fun house. He didn't say why, he just left. Joel was acting all nervous-like. He told us to stay where we were and keep quiet. Then he took the lantern with him and went outside. There were only a couple of windows near the door of the fun house. They didn't have glass and there was snow all around them inside the building, so none of us sat near them. But we could see the light." He tried cracking his knuckles again. "My face hurt, but I fell asleep, then woke up when I heard a couple of the guys talking. Dillon was saying Joel wasn't outside. That's when we all started talking about what we should do."

"So Joel was alive when Shultz left?" Chase asked, and now wished he was sitting in on the interview with Simon. If Simon had left with Shultz, and the two had never parted ways, then there was no way Shultz could have killed Joel.

Tyler scrunched his brows together. "I guess." He sighed. "I don't know."

"Just go on with your story," Summer said, sending Chase a look that said to back down.

"Okay, so we all agreed to take our chances and try to escape. But when we got outside and didn't see Joel, we were worried about Simon. Shultz had him. We didn't know if he was going to keep Simon hostage so he could escape or what. Since we didn't want to leave Simon behind, and we were worried Shultz would come back, find us gone and do something bad to him, we decided to wait."

"Your plan was to ambush Shultz," Chase said, and ignored the death stare from Summer. He'd known the moment he had looked at the scene outside the fun house that something wasn't right. And this kid was backing his theories.

Tyler pushed a hand through his dark hair. "I don't know. We just wanted to get Simon away from him, you know?" He met Chase's gaze, and he couldn't dismiss the sincerity in the boy's eyes. "I kept thinking about what Shultz did to me, to Alex and Brennan. How he killed Coach Pembroke, Clay and Randy. I didn't want that to happen to Simon. None of us did. So, yeah, we decided to hide out and wait for him. But then we found Joel." Tears filled the kid's eyes. "I've never seen a dead body before, and my first had his throat slit."

Summer took Tyler's hand. "I know this is hard. But we're trying to make sense of what happened."

"Sense?" Tyler gripped her hand. "Why do adults say crap like that? Shultz and his guys wanted money. That's it. He made it clear the moment he killed Coach and splattered his brains all over the bus seat. Do you have any idea how scared we were?"

She rubbed his shoulder. "I know and I'm sorry. We're just trying to piece together what happened."

Tyler pulled his hand away. "I...I don't want to get in trouble."

"You won't."

The boy looked away. "We jumped off the landing with the plan to attack Shultz and get Simon away from him. Shultz told us the park was surround by FBI agents, but we didn't know if you guys could see what was happening or what. We found Joel with his throat cut." He shook his head as if trying to shake away the image. "Chris picked up the knife and I took the rifle. Then we waited."

"And?" Chase prompted him.

"Dillon saw him first. We ducked and waited some more." He voluntarily took Summer's hand, reminding Chase that he and the other boys were young, not mature adults. "I heard him come up the steps and I was so scared." Tears streamed down his face. "He told Simon to get inside, then I heard his boots hit the wood landing. I...ah...I jumped up and fired three times. I didn't know if I'd hit him until Shultz started shooting and yelling at us." His face hardened. "I was freaking out, but saw a bunch of guys go around the building. The ones who stayed behind kept whispering about waiting to shoot again." He looked first at Summer, then to Chase, his gaze filled with terror and remorse. "I don't know how long it was, but then I heard fighting. Me and the guys hiding below the landing jumped up, saw that the others were beating Shultz and..." He looked away. "We joined them."

"It's okay." Summer covered Tyler's hand. "It's okay," she repeated.

"After what he did to us," he said on a sob, "after all the killing..." He used his shoulder to clean his tears. "We kept kicking and punching him."

"Who put the knife in him?" Chase asked. "Chris?"

Tyler leveled him with an eat-shit glare. "Does it matter?"

Chase supposed it didn't. If he'd been in their situation, he would've probably reacted as they had. Still. It bothered the hell out of him that Tyler wasn't sure if Joel had been alive when Shultz had left. Because if he had been, that could only mean someone else had killed Joel.

"No, it doesn't matter." Summer patted his hand. "Come on, let's get you to your parents."

After Tyler left in a police cruiser, Chase sat in on two more interviews. Each account was the same, and not one kids' recall of what had happened with Shultz and Joel made sense. As for Simon Thorpe, he claimed he hadn't seen Joel when he left the fun house and figured the guy was on the side of the building going to the bathroom. He said he'd been too busy worrying about not causing further injury to Alex and the gun Shultz had on him to care about Joel.

When the last kid had been transported to their parents', and the kidnappers' bodies sent to the Cuyahoga County Medical Examiner's, Dave walked over to them. The snow had finally stopped falling, and the wind had also died down. "Hell of a day." He shook Chase's hand. "Thanks for filling in today."

"I'm sorry we weren't able to bring in the kidnappers, but it's always a good day when the hostages go home." Chase released his hand. "Are forensics investigators still processing the scene?"

He nodded. "We're worried about additional snowfall, so they're trying to gather as much evidence as possible. When the weather worsens, they'll call it a night and come back in the morning."

"Do you know if they recovered Shultz's cell phone?" Chase asked, still not one hundred percent convinced Shultz had arranged the kidnapping or killed Joel.

"That I don't know."

"Fire investigators should take a look at the ballroom," Chase said. "Based on the interviews we did, it sounds as if gas, rather than kerosene, was used in one of the heaters."

"Interesting." Dave rubbed his chin with the back of his gloved knuckles. "They're coming out in the morning. I'll be sure to mention this to them."

"Do you mind if I come into the office tomorrow to hear what forensics uncovered?" Chase asked, wanting to know every detail. Since joining CORE, he'd had a couple of interesting cases, but because he'd been the new guy, none of them had given him the adrenaline rush, or that drive to have answers. Instead, he'd been earning a paycheck. Going through the motions. Seeing a therapist and trying to convince himself he'd done Summer a favor when he'd left her.

"Of course." Dave grinned. "You're on CORE's dime, not mine." He glanced toward the park. "The kids are safe, the media is praising our efforts...definitely a good day." Dave looked back at them. "I'm sticking around for a while. You two can head out of here."

Before Summer could argue, Chase took her by the arm and led her to the car. "I wasn't planning on staying," she said once they were inside. "I'm sick of being cold and I'm exhausted."

"You should be hungry, too. I can stop and pick up take-out on the way home."

"It's too late for something heavy. I'll make toast or a peanut butter sandwich." She cranked up the heat. "Does Senator Patricks still want you to take part in this investigation?"

He drove past the remaining news vans and headed for the highway. "Now that his grandson is safe, he'd like his money back."

"Lauren and a few other agents will be monitoring the Bitcoin account. In the meantime, she's going to try to find a way to recover the deposit. Five hundred thousand dollars will be of little use to a dead man."

"Unless Shultz was working for someone."

"You're not going to let this go, are you?"

He knew he should. They had the kids, and the bad guys were dead. But... "The kids who went with Randy to get the kerosene came back carrying blue cans."

"And?"

"Blue is for kerosene, red is for gas and yellow is for diesel. How did gas get into the blue can? And isn't it coincidental that Randy was the one who filled the heater with gas?"

She turned down the heat. "Randy didn't fill the heater, Chris Demko did, then he couldn't get it to start. That's when Randy lit the wick."

"Chris, who'd had the knife and used it on Shultz?"

"Allegedly."

"Right." He turned on the windshield wipers when the snow began to fall again. "We need Brennan to regain consciousness. I'd like to hear what he has to say. He was one of the kids who brought in the kerosene, then he ends up being left for dead."

She released an impatient sigh. "The fuel could've been a deadly mistake. Brennan could've looked at the ballroom explosion as his only chance to escape, and accidentally fell."

"You were the one who noticed the marks on his cheeks," he reminded her.

"I know, but after talking to the kids, I think those were made during the fall down the hill."

Which made sense, since the boys claimed the kidnappers had stayed with them and weren't aware Brennan had left. "You're right. Maybe I'm reaching for something that isn't there," he said, exiting the highway. "My gut instinct has been wrong in the past."

"I don't know about that, and I'm not saying that I don't think it's weird about the fuel."

"It is weird, but then that would mean one of Shultz's crew was trying to sabotage the kidnapping." He shook his head as self-doubt crept up on him. "That doesn't make sense."

"You know, maybe it does. Shultz killed Clay, then threatened Randy. Maybe Randy wanted out, but hadn't planned on blowing himself up in the process."

He turned down Summer's street. "Maybe."

"You'd rather stick with the phantom kidnapper theory?" she asked, amusement in her voice. "Fair enough. I won't discount your theory until we have all the evidence."

"Most of which is probably buried under three feet of snow."

He pulled into her driveway, then parked the car. After he helped her to the door and handed her the keys, he stepped off the front porch.

"Did you want to come in for a bite to eat?" she asked, opening the door.

Because he wanted to continue discussing the kidnapping, he'd rather go to his hotel. Though she said she wouldn't discount his theories, he was sure Summer wasn't buying what he was trying to sell. He had also promised himself not to push her. He might be exhausted, but he was never too tired to seduce his way into her bed. He wanted to take it slow and date her, show her he was worth a second chance. Plus, he wanted to call Ian. If his boss thought he should drop the investigation, then he would. If not, CORE had the resources to continue a private investigation.

"I need to head to the hotel," he said with reluctance. "I want to start on my report while everything is fresh in my mind."

The porch light revealed the disappointment in her eyes, which she masked with a smile. "You're just as dedicated as ever. So I'll see you at the office in the morning?"

He stepped forward. "And for dinner tomorrow evening."

She opened the door. "Chase—"

"Summer." He took her hand. "You agreed to dinner."

"You really didn't give me much choice."

"There's always a choice."

Her gaze held curiosity. "What choice will you make if we become involved again, then hit a rocky patch?"

The guilt over how he'd handled their relationship, and himself, sharpened. "I'm sorry I left you."

"That's not an answer." She pulled her hand away. "Goodnight, Chase. I'll see you in the morning at the office, *not* my kitchen," she said, then closed the door.

She knew him too well. He'd had every intention of making her breakfast in the morning. Breakfast was the most important meal of the day. Since she'd eaten so little today, he wanted to fill her belly with a nutritious meal.

With a sigh, he went to his rental car. As he drove to the hotel, he realized that convincing Summer to give him another chance was going to be a challenge. He'd easily seduced her last August, but had been a dick since then. And while he'd love to have sex with her—every single day—he didn't want a purely physical relationship. Now that they were going to be parents, he hoped to show her he was committed to her, to them and to being a father. But how should he go about proving himself?

Dinner was a start, he supposed. He could date her, join her for doctor's appointments, help ready the nursery, shop for baby stuff. Except he lived six hours away.

He had yet to use any of his vacation days. But would spending a couple of weeks in Cleveland be enough time to prove anything to her?

There was only one way to find out…

10

Summer's House, Fairview Park, Ohio
Sunday, January 22ⁿᵈ, 7:23 a.m. Eastern Standard Time

SUMMER SLAMMED THE coffee pot on the counter, then swore when the glass cracked. She immediately blamed Chase for the broken pot. She wouldn't have lost her temper if he hadn't done something with her regular coffee. All she could find was the stupid decaf. She also blamed him for why she'd woken in such a foul mood, but refused to keep wondering why he hadn't come inside last night. Was it because she hadn't completely agreed with the phantom kidnapper theory? Or maybe he figured sex wasn't likely going to happen, so why bother?

He was the one who'd asked her on a date and had acted as if he'd wanted to get to know her all over again. That had been why she'd invited him inside. After everything that had happened at the park, she hadn't been ready to be alone with her thoughts, and had wanted to spend time with him away from work.

She let out a huff and tossed the pot into the trash. And, yes, she'd also wanted him to hold her. Just for a little bit. When he'd donned the SWAT tactical gear and had gone to meet with Shultz, she'd been terrified. Before he'd become a crisis negotiator, Chase had been a special agent, and had also volunteered for the Baltimore Division's SWAT team. That had been eight years ago, and the last time—as far as she knew—he'd fired a weapon in the line of duty had been the day he had shot Brody Wakefield.

She opened the fridge and glared at the groceries Chase had brought yesterday. How could she be mad at him when he'd stocked her refrigerator with her favorite fruits and veggies? When she checked the lunchmeat drawer, her mouth watered. He'd even picked up goose liver. Chase thought braunschweiger was disgusting, but knew she loved the spread, especially on crackers. After checking out the other items he'd brought, she realized she wasn't mad at him, but maybe a little at herself.

She'd dropped a bomb on him when she'd confirmed the pregnancy, and should be happy he acted genuinely excited about becoming a father. This dating thing bothered her, though. Chase's charm, sense of humor and good looks made it easy for her to fall in love with him all over again. After he'd joined the Crisis Negotiation Unit, the change in him had been slow, so slow she hadn't realized how unemotional and controlling he had become until he'd killed Brody Wakefield.

The boy's death had had such a reverse effect on Chase, she'd finally been able to recognize that she had ignored many important aspects of their relationship. Not out of desperation, or because she had worried about a ticking biological clock—she hadn't wanted kids anyway. She supposed that, subconsciously, she'd clung to the old Chase, remembered the good and ignored the bad. Bottom line: she'd loved and adored him and had wanted to make their relationship work. She'd wanted marriage, to buy a house and plan the future with him. Could they do that now?

Deciding on goose liver, onion crackers and grapefruit juice for breakfast, she sat at the kitchen table, opened her smart phone and cruised the news headlines. As she'd expected, the kidnapping had made national news. The kids' names had been kept from the media, along with the medical conditions of Alex and Brennan. Wayne Pembroke and Frank Stokes' murders had been noted, and the only kidnappers listed were the Shultz cousins. She'd like to think no one from their offices had leaked these names, and assumed that the information came from either the academy, or one of the many law enforcement agencies involved with the investigation, not that it mattered at this point. Dave had informed her in a late-night text that he planned to hold a press conference this afternoon.

She finished what most people would consider a strange breakfast, then went to her room to finish getting ready. As she mentally planned her morning at the office, her thoughts drifted back to Chase. The case was over. He'd been sent to Cleveland on the behalf of CORE and Senator Patricks. Other than hearing the findings from the ME, forensics and fire investigators, there was no reason—business-wise—for him to remain in town. A part of her hoped he'd stay for a few days, so they could talk and navigate the pregnancy and future. The other part wanted to see him go. If he stayed, and things went well, her hopes would probably be high. Except Chase was noncommittal and selfish. She did not want him to plant hopeful dreams in her head, only to have them destroyed because he suddenly changed his mind about them or fatherhood.

Maybe she should stop thinking about how he might or might not act, and give him a chance. And while she was giving him that chance, maybe she should try to be more like him: hide her emotions.

She adjusted the waistband extender she'd bought to avoid wearing maternity clothes, then hid it beneath her suit coat. Chase was right, she should have at least told Lauren about the baby. They were good friends and if the situation was reversed, she would be hurt. As for Dave, she was one of three Assistant Special Agents in Charge, was directly responsible for twelve agents, worked with their local FBI Resident Agencies, and was currently assisting with a number of active criminal cases. While on maternity leave, Dave would need to have another agent step in as acting ASAC. Her due date wasn't until May twenty-sixth, which gave her boss plenty of time to find her replacement. Still, she had to tell him soon. She also had to research and visit daycare centers, pick items for the baby gift registry before her mom and sisters nagged the crap out of her, and set up the nursery.

The amount of work and planning was overwhelming, and she could use Chase's help. As she drove to the office, she pictured Chase flying or driving in for a long weekend, them choosing paint colors and names, and him putting together the crib. She also envisioned them cooking together, going on dates, curling next to him on the couch and making love.

She hadn't had sex since last August. Prior to that, it had been nearly a year, and just before Chase had shocked her by quitting the FBI and taking a position with CORE in Chicago. That last thought should have her wondering if she was nuts and desperate to want anything to do with Chase. *He'd left her.* There had been no discussion about him quitting or moving, he'd simply informed her of his decision, then packed up his things and left. Yes, she'd do well to remember how devastated she'd been, how hurt and sad, along with the lonely nights, weekends and holidays, and how he had shattered her dreams of having a life with him.

During her drive downtown, she shoved Chase from her thoughts and made several phone calls. She contacted the Medical Examiner's office first, then Lauren and Tony, and had them start gathering information for Dave to use for the press conference. Once she'd parked and entered the building, she headed for her office. Chase stood outside her door looking super-sexy, holding two cups of coffee and a paper bag from Donut Factory.

"Morning," he said with a smile.

She loved his smile and dimples. The way his muscles filled out his button-down shirt was also rather nice, along with how his jeans rode low on his hips. "Morning. How'd you sleep?" she asked, noticing the exhaustion in his eyes.

"Good." He followed her inside the office and set one of the coffees on her desk. "I had them make yours half decaf/half caffeine."

She hadn't had any caffeine in nearly forty-eight hours. Chase was becoming impossibly sexier. "Thank you," she said, slipping out of her coat.

"Aren't you curious why I had them add caffeine?"

"I figured you were being thoughtful and paying attention to what we'd discussed about my being allowed one cup of caffeinated coffee."

"Exactly right." He placed the donut bag next to the coffee. "Yep, that's me. Thoughtful, good listener…"

"Don't forget generous. I didn't notice all the groceries you bought until this morning. Thank you. That was very sweet."

He cocked his head. "Generous and sweet…I'm a quadruple threat guy. You should keep me around."

She opened the bag and spied chocolate cake donut holes and a chocolate éclair. Thank God he hadn't also bought her a chocolate, cream-filled, powdered donut, or she might rip off his clothes. They were pure sin, and so was the look in his eyes.

Look away. Don't give in to temptation.

She snagged a donut hole before closing the bag. "If I do, I won't be able to fit through the front door, especially if you keep feeding me chocolate. Didn't you get anything for yourself?"

"I had a jelly donut on the drive here."

"I can see that." She placed her index finger on the middle of his chest. "You've got a little jelly on you."

When he looked down, she lightly tapped his nose. "I can't believe you fell for that."

Grinning, he grabbed her wrist. "I must be rusty. It's been years since you've gotten me." He leaned in close. "Now I have to figure out your payback. Kissing?" His gaze dropped to her lips. "Full body massage? Or a hot f—"

"My office door is open." She tugged her arm free. "And what happened to *just a date?*"

"I don't know where your mind was heading, but I was going to say hot fudge sundae."

She could not stop grinning. "You're so full of it. I don't want to talk about food or paybacks. I need to see Dave. He's having a press conference later." She called her team and asked them to meet in the briefing room in fifteen minutes.

"What time is the press conference?" he asked as they left her office.

"I'm not sure yet. I'm not even sure what info he plans to pass along." When they reached Dave's office, he was hanging up the phone. "Good morning," she said.

Her boss smiled. "It is a good morning." He rose, then rounded the desk. "Get your team together. I want everything we have so far, then I'll need to decide what information I'm going to use during the press conference."

"They'll be ready in fifteen. Are forensics going to the park again today?"

"They're already there. They worked until about eleven last night, then had to stop because of the weather. Al Collins promised to stay in the lab for a few hours and have his people begin sorting through and processing what they'd found. That includes photographs."

Al was not only their lead forensics investigator, but a workaholic who admitted to doing anything to avoid his wife and nine cats. "Excellent. I talked to Lee Polowski on my way here."

"The deputy medical examiner?"

"Right. He said they'd already started Matthew and Joel Shultzs' autopsies, and thinks they should be able to work on the others between this afternoon and tomorrow. He should have the preliminary results for all of them by Tuesday morning."

Dave folded his arms across his chest and rested his rear against the desk. "I wish they would've started with our murder victim."

"They couldn't. Wayne Pembroke's body was still slightly frozen. Have we heard how Alex and Brennan are doing?" she asked, wanting to change the subject from murder to hope.

"Both boys were transferred to the Cleveland Clinic, and are in ICU. Brennan is in a coma, and doctors aren't sure if and when he'll recover. Alex is still in critical condition. The bullet missed vital organs, but he lost a lot of blood and they're concerned about infection. He also hasn't regained consciousness. Both families asked that we not reveal any information about their sons."

"I'm assuming we won't be releasing any of the boys' names," she said. Because the kids were minors, they would need parental consent to reveal their names. She couldn't image any of those parents wanting to give it. The kids had been through a horrific experience and needed privacy. If reporters knew who the boys were, the press would hound them.

"Correct." Dave nodded. "We're not releasing victims' names. Just the kidnappers'." When his phone rang again, he sighed. "Head to the briefing room. I'll be there in a few."

Ten minutes later, everyone, including Dave, was seated and ready to discuss yesterday. Summer opened her notebook. "Who has lab results?"

Agent Rich Cochran held up a pen. "I do." He passed around copies of an itemized list, broken down by crime scene and victim. "We have three locations where a murder took place: the bus, outside the ballroom and the fun house. We also have the area in front of the Ferris wheel where two bodies were buried, along with the burger stand and hotel. Except for a two-way radio, a red gas can and a white and gray camouflage tarp, there wasn't anything else at the stand. But the hotel had a few more items."

"Eight blue kerosene cans." Chase studied the paper. "Do you know if they were checked for gas? We think someone poured the wrong fuel into one of the kerosene heaters, which caused the ballroom to explode."

"The fire investigator will determine that," Dave said. "But let's make sure someone at least does a sniff test on those cans." He glanced at the paper. "We've got what I'm presuming is their getaway car."

Rich nodded. "That, and the bus, are still there. Once we remove the snow, we'll bring both vehicles to the lab."

Summer scanned the list. "Investigators found a phone at the hotel, but not on Matthew Shultz or Woodrow Bakanowsky. Was the phone at the hotel one of theirs?"

"It'd never been used, and there wasn't one on or near Shultz. The metal detector helped locate one buried in the snow by the Ferris wheel. Fingerprints found on it belonged to Bakanowsky. We did find the other two-way radio in Shultz's pocket though."

"Impossible." Chase stared at Rich with disbelief. "I talked to Shultz about twenty minutes before we heard gunfire. His phone *has* to be there."

Irritation crossed Rich's face as he stabbed his finger at the paper. "This is what we currently have, but we might get more later today."

"I'm not giving you a hard time," Chase said, softening his tone. "I'm sorry. I know you were working with CSI, and the weather made it tough on you guys."

Rich blinked a few times. Tony and Lauren's brows rose, while she hid a smile and imagined the agents hadn't a clue what to make of Chase. During the six months he had been with the Cleveland Division, he hadn't been the friendliest of coworkers. He'd been demanding, cranky and sometimes an all-around jerk.

"Yeah." Rich cleared his throat and refocused on the report. He talked a little more about the evidence found, then added, "The knife Matthew Shultz carried didn't look as if it had been used, but it was the same brand and model as the one that'd been in his chest. We should have DNA results on both knives within a day or two."

After Rich had finished, it was Tony's turn to tell them about the kidnappers who'd helped the Shultz cousins. "Woodrow 'Woody' Bakanowsky," he began, bringing up the man's mug shot on one of the screens. "He was fifty-nine, served three years in the Army before being sent to prison for assaulting an officer. After his release, he was dishonorably discharged from the Army, then he drifted across the country and accumulated a rap sheet, mostly for robbery or assault. Not too surprisingly, he was in Belmont Correctional Institution in Clairsville, Ohio, during the same time period as Joel Shultz."

Another mug shot replaced Woody's. "Randy Hickman was forty-one. He'd served in the Marines, and had left after four years. Other than a DUI, his record is clean. He was an avid hunter and worked for a tractor company outside of Marietta, Ohio, for the past ten years. Turns out, Woody had also worked for the same company, until he was fired for stealing. Randy was in serious debt, divorced and the SUV still at the hotel was about to be repossessed."

"A portion of thirty million would've been a life-changer for him," Lauren said. "For all of them." She asked Tony to post Clay's picture. "Meet Clay Jacobs. He was twenty-six, a high school dropout, had no record, and worked as a cook. Clay grew up with the Shultz cousins, so there's that connection."

"Okay," Dave began, "so Matt Shultz knows the kids are going on a ski trip, and knows their families have money. He comes up with a kidnapping scheme, and gets his cousin and buddy involved, but knows he needs more men. Joel remembers Woody, who brings Randy along."

"And Matt murders all of them."

Tony shrugged. "Five hundred grand is a far cry from thirty million, but if Shultz had managed to walk away with it, that money could've helped him disappear for a while. Maybe get out of the country."

"Which is why I still think Matt is the owner of the Bitcoin account," Lauren said.

"Will you be able to recover the money?" Chase asked.

Lauren shook her head. "Unfortunately Bitcoin transactions can't be reversed."

"But you can still monitor Shultz's account."

"I can." She glanced first to Dave, then Summer. "Is this something we want to check daily? Not to point out the obvious, but the kidnappers are deceased."

"Yes, daily," Chase answered, then rubbed the back of his neck when Dave chuckled. "Sorry. I'm supposed to just be an observer."

"You're fine," Dave said. "And I do think we should monitor the account, at least until we've closed the investigation."

Summer agreed with her boss. Even if she doubted Chase's phantom kidnapper theory, there was nothing wrong with being cautious or thorough. Besides, checking the account took little time.

"Tony and Lauren," Dave continued, "email me and Summer the kidnappers' photos and info. I'd like to use that for the press conference, which is now scheduled for noon." He pushed back his chair, then stood. "As we discussed, the kids' names stay out, so let's give the media a timeline of events. Keep it PG and make no mention of how the kids escaped." He turned to Summer. "When will you have that ready for me?"

Summer glanced to the clock. If she wasn't interrupted she could have a speech written for Dave by ten, work on her own reports afterward, then leave once the press conference was over. "Ten," she said, hiding her irritation. She should be on a plane flying to Florida, not dealing with a press conference, reports and Chase.

When the meeting ended, she headed to her office. Chase followed her inside, then sat in the chair in front of her desk. After she took a seat, she opened her laptop and met his expectant gaze. "Are you staying?"

"It's better than hanging out at the hotel. And I can help you. Remember, I was there, too."

She let out a breath. Yes, she wanted to spend time with him, but he was a distraction. He had her mind drifting to the past, to the future… She glanced at his chest. To her bed.

"I appreciate the offer," she said, blocking out the memories of the last time he'd been in town, and all the wicked things he had done to her body. "But I can get this finished faster if I work on it alone. I want to leave after the press conference and get ready for dinner." She smiled, hoping that reminding him of their date would motivate him to leave.

He gave her a slow, easy grin. "You're anxious to go out with me."

"*Anxious* is a strong word. I'm looking forward to having a nice dinner."

"With me," he added, his eyes teasing.

"Yes," she said, unable to stop smiling.

"Because you like me."

"Oh, my God." She rolled her eyes. "You're unbelievable. Go." She pointed toward the door.

With a sigh, he rose. "That's fine. Stay in denial."

"Chase."

"Summer." He cocked a brow, then grew serious. "I'm looking forward to spending time with you."

Before she melted, before she let herself become caught up in the fantasy of them being a happy little family, she focused on what had helped her get through the pain of losing him—work. "What time should I be ready?" she asked, staring at her laptop.

"Five?"

She opened her email. "That works. I'll see you then."

After he said goodbye and left, she finally looked up from the computer screen to the empty doorway. She hoped she hadn't come off as bitchy, but he had her worried, confused and way too hopeful. Being with him scared her. The way he'd been acting was similar to the Chase she'd fallen for years ago, and she was afraid to fall for him again, only to have him leave. And yet, while she'd planned to care for their baby on her own, she wanted to raise their child in the same kind of family environment she'd had. She wanted a husband, a father for her child.

But could Chase be that man?

Horizon Pointe Estates, Avon, Ohio
Sunday, January 22ⁿᵈ, 9:17 a.m. Eastern Standard Time

As her son demolished his eggs, bacon and toast, Patsy sat across from him at the kitchen table, guilt coiling through her. He looked more like his father than ever, had grown taller, leaner and his face was more masculine than boyish. He'd changed since she had last seen him, which had been in September when he had left for the academy. She'd used her travel schedule as an excuse to avoid him during Thanksgiving and Christmas. All of it a lie. She hadn't been working, but had spent the holidays at the new house with Emma. Sure, she'd sent him gifts and had kept his bank account stocked with a monthly allowance, but had limited communication to an occasional phone call and text.

God, she was a horrible mother. How could she have abandoned him? How could she have moved without telling him? How could she have ever believed her son had been involved with Tim's death and Emma's suicide attempt?

Last night, when an FBI agent had called to inform her that the boys had escaped the park, she'd had mixed emotions. She'd been relieved, and yet dread had filled her core. Her first instinct had been to send Emma to a friend's house or a hotel. Her daughter was terrified of her brother. Why, she still didn't know. But how would it have looked if she'd sent Emma away? After all, her son had just escaped a deadly ordeal. Her second instinct had been to dump him at a hotel. Yet, when she'd reached the park and seen him sitting in the back of a police car, she hadn't wanted to run from him. She'd had the urge to hold him. He had looked so young, vulnerable and innocent. He'd looked like the boy she had once adored. And when he'd climbed out of the car and embraced her, she had forgotten about the hotel and held him tight. Thanked God that he'd made it out safely.

"Would you like more bacon, Buddy?" she asked, using the nickname Tim had given him.

He wiped his mouth with his napkin, then grinned. "Yes, please. This breakfast is awesome."

"That's only because you haven't eaten for two days." She rose and went to the counter where she'd left the bacon. "Are you sure you don't want to go to the doctor?"

"Mom, I'm fine. I'm more tired than anything." He picked up one of the strips of bacon she'd set on his plate. "And hungry," he added with a grin.

She pushed a lock of his dark hair from his forehead. "You need a haircut."

"You think? I kinda like it longer."

"Then how about just a trim?"

After he agreed, she said, "The FBI is giving a press conference about what happened. It'll be on at noon if you want to watch it."

He shook his head. "I don't need to. I was there."

"Obviously, but…honey, you haven't said a word about what those men did. Do you want to talk about it?" she asked, worried how the kidnapping and murders would affect his mental health.

Her son pushed aside his empty plate, then leaned back in his chair. The bright glow from the kitchen light emphasized the dark circles under his eyes and the concern in his gaze. "I'd rather know how Brennan and Alex are doing."

"I haven't heard. I'll see what I can find out for you." She reached toward him and took his hand. "If you don't want to talk to me about what happened, then maybe you'll talk with a therapist, or one of the academy's guidance counselors?" Since Tim's death, she'd tried taking her son to several therapists, but each time had ended in failure. He had refused to cooperate or communicate, and would berate and threaten her. Still, she wanted to at least try to help him.

He shook his head. "You know how I feel about therapy. The guidance counselors… Mom, I can't go back to school."

When he looked at her, the pain and fear in his gaze broke her heart. Her son might be taller than her, but he was still a boy. And his young mind needed to find a way to process so much heartache and loss. "You don't have to go right away. I'll contact the headmaster and ask that your teachers email me your assignments. We can see how you're feeling after a week or so."

He held her hand. "Mom, I can't go back to the academy. Especially if Brennan and Alex don't… I just can't deal. Coach Pembroke…we saw Shultz kill him. Shot him right in the head." His voice cracked and he cleared his throat. "I just can't," he repeated.

Her throat tightened, and her eyes filled with tears. Summer Raines, one of the FBI agents who had been in contact with her, had said they'd been worried the coach had been injured and hadn't thought him to be part of the kidnapping. But Patsy hadn't realized the man had been killed in front of the boys. "Oh, honey, I'm so sorry. I didn't know. Did you see him hurt Brennan and Alex, too?"

His eyes misted. He let go of her hand and stood. "I can't talk about this right now," he said, walking toward the counter. "If I have to finish out the school year at the academy, then whatever. But I don't think I'll play lacrosse anymore. I mean, both my coaches are dead and two of my teammates are in the hospital."

She followed him to the sink, where he rinsed his dish. "Honey, I want what's best for you. If being home and starting at a new school is what you need to work through what happened, then that's what we're going to do for you." She hadn't considered how he would deal with returning to Newhouse Academy in the aftermath of the kidnapping. No, she'd been too busy running from her son to consider his feelings about almost everything. "And you love lacrosse. Don't let Shultz take that away from you."

"He murdered my coach and maybe my friends," he said with bitterness, and rested the dish in the sink. "When he killed his own guys, I don't know, it was like he took something from me, and part of me died in that park, too." A tear slipped down his cheek. "There was nothing to do there but sleep, be cold and think. I kept thinking about Dad, about Emma, and I... Mom, I don't want to die. I was so scared I would."

Patsy hugged her son and rubbed his back. She cried with him, for him.

"I kept thinking about you and Dad," he said on a sob, and clung to her as he'd done when he was a toddler. "I was so mean. When I was fishing with Dad, he kept trying to get me to talk and joke around, and I kept thinking this is stupid and boring. Then he drowned and I couldn't help him. I can't ever talk to him again and say I'm sorry."

As his body trembled with grief, she continued to soothe him the best she could. "Ssh. It's okay, honey."

He pulled back and wiped his eyes. "It's *not* okay. I was mean to him and to you." He looked to the floor. "Why'd you move without telling me?"

Unsure how to answer, she swiped at her cheeks.

"It's because I kept bugging you for more money, right?" he asked.

"Let's not talk about this right now. You've been through enough."

"Answer me, Mom," he demanded, his gaze not accusatory, but riddled with guilt. "You moved because of me."

She nodded. "I'm sorry," she said, her voice shaky. "I should have told you, but you were honestly scaring me."

His face fell. "I was?" He stepped away, turned his back on her and hung his head. "Is that why you didn't want me around for Thanksgiving and Christmas?"

Oh, my God. She would burn in hell for how she'd treated her own flesh and blood. "I didn't know what else to do."

He staggered to the table, then slumped in a chair. "I know I was a jerk to you and Emma, but I didn't know I scared you." Holding his head in both hands, he rested his elbows on the table. "I'm no better than Shultz."

"God, no." She quickly went to the table and sat next to him. "Look at me," she said, taking him by his forearm. "I love you, but I didn't like the person you were becoming. I shouldn't have moved without telling you. I shouldn't have done a lot of things. But you're here with us now. Can we start fresh?" Tears streamed down her cheeks. "Can we be a family again?"

"Why hasn't Emma come out of her room?" he asked instead.

How did she explain that his sister was terrified of him? He'd already been through enough, and she didn't want to drive the knife deeper. "Emma hasn't been the same since…the suicide attempt. She's very fragile."

"Then maybe it's not a good idea if I live here."

She didn't know what to think. All she wanted was to have her family back. Tim and Shawn would never return to her, but she had her remaining children and, for years, had dreamed of a day when her home would once again be filled with love and laughter. Maybe she wasn't the greatest mom for shoving her son in a boarding school then ignoring him, but based on the way he was acting, she wondered if tough love had changed him. *I'm sorry* had never been a part of his vocabulary. Yet he'd owned up to his mistakes. If she wanted to salvage her relationship with him, it was time for them to put the past to rest and look toward the future.

"Don't say that." She gripped his arm. "We have all had so much pain and misery. First Shawn, then Dad, Emma…now the kidnapping. Don't you think we deserve happiness? Just because two people we love are no longer with us doesn't mean we can't still be a family. Take vacations and celebrate holidays together." She smoothed her hand over his hair. "I miss having dinner with my kids, or just hanging out and watching a movie."

"I do, too."

"I'm sorry," she said again. "For the house, and for sometimes putting work before you and Emma. When your dad died, I had a rough time coping."

"It's okay, Mom." He smothered a yawn, then apologized. "I need to go back to bed."

"We can talk more later," she said. After she embraced him again, she watched him head toward the stairs leading to the second level, then she sat back in the chair. She couldn't recall the last time she'd held her son. Maybe after Tim's funeral? Had it been that long? How sad was it that she couldn't remember?

She dragged in a breath to ward off the tears, then flinched when a hand pressed against her shoulder. Patsy quickly looked up and met Emma's fear-stricken gaze.

"Em—"

Her daughter shook her head. "I don't want him to know I'm awake," she whispered, and sat in the seat he had vacated moments ago. "I heard everything. If he moves home, I'm leaving."

Last August, Emma had been preparing to go to Ohio State University to begin her freshman year. After she'd tried to kill herself, Patsy had suggested she wait until the following year to go to school so she could monitor Emma's progress and ensure herself that her daughter was not going to attempt to hurt herself again. She didn't believe Emma was ready to move out on her own yet. While her daughter was taking a couple of online college courses and held a part-time job at a coffee shop, she preferred to be in the safety and comfort of their new home.

"Don't be ridiculous," Patsy said, keeping her tone hushed. "You're being selfish. Do you have any idea what your brother has been through?"

Emma's forehead furrowed. Her movements jerky, angry, she tugged a hairband from her wrist, then pulled her long, auburn hair into a ponytail. While her son favored Tim's dark looks, Emma had inherited her red hair, pale complexion and freckles. "I don't care," Emma said. "I wish he'd died."

Patsy gasped. "Emma. How can you say such a thing?"

Her daughter looked away, but there'd been no guilt in her eyes before she did. "I hate him. And I don't know why you don't, too." She faced Patsy again, her face stony, grim. "He wasn't just *mean*, he was abusive."

"Verbally, yes. Look, sweetie, I'm in a very rough position. I love you, and I love your brother. If you were listening to our conversation—which was rude—then you heard how he watched people die."

Emma crossed her arms over her chest. "Still don't care."

What the hell was wrong with Emma? Didn't she have an ounce of empathy? God, where had she gone wrong with her children? "Well, you should." Her eyes filled with tears again. "I have been struggling for four *long* years. When your dad died, my world wasn't just shaken, it was destroyed. I have tried my best to be a good mom, and in the process I've made plenty of mistakes. Remember what I like to tell my clients: mistakes are meant for learning."

"I'm *not* a client."

"Emma, stop and listen to me," Patsy began, emotionally exhausted and wishing she too could go back to bed. She needed to think, to digest her conversation with her son. "I know who you are, but you need to understand that I'm human and I'm *trying.*"

"To ruin our lives, because that's what will happen if you let him move in with us." Emma gripped the edge of the table. "I'm not kidding. I *will* move."

"With what money?" Patsy asked, not to be cruel, but to talk common sense into her daughter.

"I'll use my trust fund."

"You can't access it until you're twenty-one. And I won't allow you to use the money we saved for college. That's strictly for school."

"Then I'll live on the street," Emma threatened, her face growing red, her eyes shimmering with tears. "I heard everything he said and I don't buy any of his *feeling sorry for being mean* bullshit. And I can't believe you're stupid enough to fall for it."

Furious that her daughter would treat her so disrespectfully, Patsy slammed her fist on the table. "Not another word," she said, her voice shaking with anger. "For the past six months I've done nothing but cater to you. I've moved. I've cut ties with my own son. I'm trying to run a business and meet deadlines. What do you do? Nothing. You don't help me, don't ask how my day is or how I'm doing. Because it's all about you."

"I'm not listening to this," Emma said, rising.

Patsy grabbed her arm, halting her daughter. "I feel as if my world is crumbling down around me and I don't know how to put it back together." She touched Emma's damp cheek. "I'm hurting and confused. Please. I've been there for you, please be there for me. Help me."

"Help you bring a monster into our house?" Emma tore her arm away. "I didn't mean to call you stupid. I'm sorry. And I love you more than any person alive. But I can't be under the same roof as him."

God, she was a stubborn girl. "Damn it, Emma, why? I know he can be nasty and unlikable, but I don't understand why you won't give him a chance. There's a change in him. I see and feel it. I think the kidnapping and being away from us for five months has shocked him into reality and maturity. Please, just give our family a chance to be whole again."

Emma shook her head. "No way. You want to know why I hate him?" She shoved the sleeves of her sweatshirt up her arms, exposing the scars along her wrists. "Because he did this to me."

11

Summer's House, Fairview Park, Ohio
Sunday, January 22ⁿᵈ, 11:11 a.m. Eastern Standard Time

C HASE LET HIMSELF inside Summer's house, set the grocery bags on the counter, then went back to the rental car for the rest of the items he'd bought. They weren't expecting any snow tonight, but with the wind chill, the temperature was supposed to drop below zero. He couldn't have his pregnant ex-girlfriend out in the cold, so he'd decided to test his culinary skills and make her pecan-crusted chicken with a bourbon sauce, mashed potatoes and roasted asparagus. For dessert, he planned to wow her with raspberry cheesecake chocolate cupcakes.

She'd probably be mad he'd come into her house without permission again, but he didn't care. He wanted to talk about something other than the kidnapping, and remind her why they were good together. Hell, at one time they'd been *great*. If he hadn't been assigned the Wakefield case, they'd probably still be great.

Thinking now about Brody Wakefield didn't bring him down like it usually did, or make his chest burn as if someone had poured acid down his throat. Instead, he thought about the boy, about the choices the kid had made, along with how Brody's father had placed his own family in a dangerous situation. Chase's hands were still stained with the boy's blood, but the outcome hadn't been his fault.

Closing the front door behind him, he wondered if he'd be able to do the same with his past. Finally put it behind him.

As he stowed away the groceries, he took himself back to two days ago when Ian had first assigned him to the kidnapping. He'd dreaded returning to Cleveland and seeing Summer. He loved her, but whenever he was near her the guilt that constantly followed him always worsened. She hadn't deserved the way he'd treated her. Because he hadn't been able to grapple with the unfamiliar emotions brought on by the shooting—emotions that had messed with his head, his sleep, appetite and every other facet of his life— he'd chosen to alienate Summer when he should have been turning to her for help.

Two years of therapy had been a waste. It had taken finding out he was going to be a father and jumping back into a crisis situation to make him reconsider the self-destructive path he'd been taking. If he had any hope of being with Summer again, of being a good dad, he had to work on himself. His mom had died when he was only ten, and his dad had been a useless, selfish, drunken son of a bitch. He never wanted his child to look back on life and say the same about him. Until yesterday at the park, he'd felt useless, and he knew damned well, when it came to Summer, he'd been a selfish ass. Why hadn't she kicked him out or left him years ago? Why did she let him back into her bed last August? They weren't married, hadn't owned a house together. It would've been easy for her to walk away. Had she loved him that much? Needed him in her life?

The guilt that had momentarily disappeared, returned. *Need versus want.* When they'd first met, he had been immediately attracted to her smile, eyes and curves, and had wanted her in his bed. They'd clicked and being with her had been easy. Dating, sex, living together…all easy, all wants. After the Wakefield case, everything had become hard. He'd suddenly needed her, and that had made him angry with himself. Never in his life, not even when he was a kid, had he *needed* anyone, and there wasn't a person on the planet he had loved more than Summer. That crushing realization had scared the hell out of him, had him shutting her out of his life, then running. He never wanted to love someone so much that he'd die a slow, torturous death if he lost them. Yet, that had been, and was, how much he loved Summer.

Instead of thinking about this, he should tell her. Even about the need/want thing. Not to hurt her, but to help her understand some of the reasons why he'd left, and to admit that he had been somewhat of a coward when it had come to his emotions.

He looked around the kitchen and decided to work on the other projects he'd had planned for the afternoon before starting dinner. The press conference wasn't for another thirty minutes. He wasn't sure what time she would be home, and was anxious to surprise her with the meal.

More than that, he was anxious to tell her the old Chase was back.

Horizon Pointe Estates, Avon, Ohio
Sunday, January 22nd, 11:36 a.m. Eastern Standard Time

He fell onto his bed, tucked his hands behind his head and grinned at the stilled ceiling fan. Emma had freaked, yet Mom believed *him*. His sister had thought she was so stealthy, sneaking into the dining room off the kitchen to listen to their conversation. Too bad the stupid bitch hadn't known her reflection could be seen from the glass along the front of the antique hutch. Maybe, after they were dead, he should head out to Los Angeles and start his acting career, because he would've received an Oscar for the role he'd played at breakfast.

Tears weren't easy to come by, and not something he could remember shedding. Well, except when Dad died. Since he had drowned him, and Mom and Emma had been all weepy and devastated, he'd had to play the part right along with them. The hours he'd spent practicing grief prior to killing Dad had been well worth the effort. It had taught him—at the funeral—how easily he could manipulate people.

Which was exactly what he'd done during breakfast. Mom wanted her family back, and he wanted it obliterated. Between her business, publishing contracts, investments and his dad's life insurance policy, she was worth over twenty million. He and Emma each had a trust fund worth three hundred thousand dollars, and would receive those funds once they turned twenty-one. If Emma had slit her wrists a little deeper and bled out, her money, along with the cash in her college account, would have gone to him and he wouldn't have planned the kidnapping. With Emma dead, his mom would have doted on her only living child. She would have given anything and everything to keep her son happy and to maintain a relationship with him, and he wouldn't have had to worry about needing an early inheritance. And when Mom eventually died, he wouldn't have to share her estate with anyone. The plan had been perfect. Except the bitch hadn't died, and his mom hadn't doted on him—she'd ignored and abandoned him.

After he'd gone off to Newhouse in early September, she'd stopped calling him. The only reason he knew she still existed was because of the allowance she placed in his bank account. But it hadn't been enough money, so, on a Friday at the end of September, he'd driven to their home in Bath, which was thirty minutes northeast of Ottawa Lake Amusement Park. When he'd arrived, there had been a real estate sign in the front yard with *Sold* hanging from it. Confused, he had gone to the door of the million-dollar mansion and tried to get inside. His key hadn't worked. A man he hadn't recognized had come to the door and explained he and his family had just bought and moved into the house.

Once he'd realized what she'd done, he had tried calling her but didn't tell her he knew about the house. He'd wanted her to admit that she had abandoned her son. But she wouldn't answer.

Instead, she'd sent him a text saying she was busy traveling and that she would contact him soon. In other words, *go fuck yourself.*

Until the big moment when Emma had told their mom he had caused her to take a knife to her wrists, he'd assumed Mom had kept the move a secret because she feared for Emma, and maybe herself. But Mom hadn't known and Emma's accusations had shocked and angered her.

He grinned again. His mom was so desperate to save her family she had refused to believe her son could *force* Emma to commit suicide. Emma had gotten so pissed, she'd left the room without telling their mom how he *had* coerced her into cutting herself. But he was confident that even if Emma had told her what he'd done, Mom wouldn't have believed it. Emma had no evidence against him, nothing that could tie him back to that night when his sister should have died.

Evidence...shit.

Last night, he had hidden the two burner phones in the closet of his new bedroom. They needed to be destroyed immediately. Brennan hadn't died like he'd hoped. Since the Feds hadn't asked him why he had beat Brennan's head against a tree, the kid must either be afraid to talk, or unconscious. If Brennan was in a coma or something, then suddenly woke and told the authorities what had happened, the FBI would search his dorm room and his mother's house, which was why he needed to take a trip back to Newhouse Academy. The laptop he'd bought for the kidnapping was tucked away inside his mattress. It, too, needed destroying, since it had his Bitcoin account information, along with the special software he'd downloaded to set up the account and keep it anonymous. Before he got rid of the laptop, though, he would need to access his Bitcoin wallet and transfer the five hundred thousand dollars to another bank account. He couldn't use his mom or sister's computers. Neither of them had the proper software to make the transfer. While he had an app on his burner phone that allowed him access to the Bitcoin account, it lagged and made the process a pain in the ass. The only thing the app had been good for was viewing whether or not the ransom money had been paid while he was at the park.

Yeah, his mom had to take him to the academy tomorrow. His car and clothes were also there, and he needed wheels in order to get rid of the phones and laptop. Mom had moved closer to Lake Erie, which would make a great place to dump the evidence, if he could find a spot that wasn't frozen. He also hoped she would agree to pulling him out of the academy, but supposed it didn't matter. She and Emma would be dead soon, and since he was only sixteen, he would be sent to live with his grandma who lived in Savannah, Georgia. His dad's mom was their only living relative, and because he looked just like his dad, she adored him. Staying with the seventy-five-year-old pushover would be easy, and he'd only have to do it until he was eighteen.

Before he started planning funerals and moving to Georgia, he needed to cover his ass. Brennan was the X factor, and he hoped if the kid didn't die, he would at least end up on life support. Fuck, he needed to know about Brennan's condition. If Brennan was still out of it, maybe he could visit his teammate at the hospital and get rid of him.

He sat up and poised himself at the edge of the bed. Brennan and the evidence were screwing with his plan. Agitated, he stood and went to the window. He couldn't wait until tomorrow to retrieve the laptop. It needed to happen today.

He left his room and went looking for his mom. When he found her in the office, she looked up and smiled at him.

"I thought you were sleeping," she said.

"I'm tired, but I can't keep my eyes closed. I'd like to go for a drive, but my car is at school."

"You can borrow mine. We can get your car later this week."

Normally, he would've blown her shit, argued, threatened, anything to get his way. "Can we go today?"

"Honey, you just got home. Relax. After what you've been through you need to take it easy."

"This isn't my home, and I'm not sleeping in my room," he

said, hoping guilt would motivate her to drive him. "I might as well be living in a stranger's house."

She blinked a few times, then cleared her throat. "I'm sorry. I don't want you to be uncomfortable. I tried to decorate your room similar to how you'd had the one at our old house."

"When?"

"When we moved here," she said, looking away.

His mother couldn't tell a lie worth shit. "Are you sure you didn't do it after you found out I was kidnapped? You know, in case I survived and would need a place to sleep before you sent me away again."

Frowning, her eyes filling with tears, she stood and walked over to him. "You make it sound as if I sent you to prison." She gave him a watery smile and rested her hands on his shoulders. "I'm sorry you're not comfortable here, but I want you to be, especially now that you're moving back. Decorate the room any way you like. It's yours."

He'd noticed she hadn't answered his original question. If he'd cared, he would've pushed for an answer. "Thanks, I'll do that," he said instead, then sighed. "I'd really like my car and clothes. Most of the clothes in the closet don't fit." He took a backward step and pointed to his ankles where the hem of his sweatpants had become three inches too short. "I've grown since September."

The guilt he'd been waiting for finally dulled her eyes. "You sure have," she said, sadness in her voice. "If you really want to get your car and things, I can take you."

Yes! "You will?" He grinned. "Thanks, Mom. When will you be ready?"

"Give me fifteen minutes and we'll go. It's supposed to snow again tomorrow and Tuesday, so it's probably a good idea to take care of this today, anyway."

He started for the stairs. "Okay, I'll go see if I can find something else to wear."

"Oh," she began, stopping him. "Headmaster Kavel called to

find out how you are doing. I asked him if he knew anything about Brennan and Alex."

He leaned against the doorjamb. "And?"

"Both are in ICU. Brennan is in a coma. Alex's surgery went well, but he's still in critical condition and is also not conscious. I'm sorry, honey."

"A coma? From what? How long before Brennan wakes?"

"Head trauma, I guess. I'm not exactly sure. Mr. Kavel said the doctors can't be certain if or when Brennan will regain consciousness. Could be days or weeks."

He'd prefer Brennan to be a vegetable, but would take coma. If Brennan snapped out of it, he might not remember how he'd hurt his head. Even if Brennan did, and accused him of knocking him against the tree, it would be Brennan's word against his. And wouldn't the FBI wonder what the point had been for the beating? They could think he'd been part of the kidnapping, but without evidence, without any of his crew alive to say there had been a Mr. Graves who'd put the abduction together, the Feds had nothing. Their only witness would be a kid who'd suffered a major head injury.

"Do you think it'd be okay to visit them at the hospital?" he asked.

"Once they're out of ICU." She studied him with concern. "Are you okay?"

He nodded. "I'm going to get ready."

When he reached the upstairs hallway, Emma's door opened. Her eyes widened with fear and she quickly shut the door. Good, she should be afraid of him. He wanted her dead. But he'd think about that later. He needed to focus on getting rid of the evidence first, and hoped to hell Brennan remained unconscious until the deed was done.

Summer's House, Fairview Park, Ohio
Sunday, January 22nd, 4:18 p.m. Eastern Standard Time

Summer pulled into her driveway and parked alongside Chase's rental car. She should be irritated he'd used his key again, but couldn't care less. For her, a normal Sunday was spent fighting boredom. Unless there was an important investigation she was running, Saturdays were her cleaning, shopping and laundry day to allow her to enjoy chore-free Sundays. When the weather was nice, she'd take advantage of those free days to head outside and bike, run, walk around downtown or visit the zoo. But during the winter months, there was nothing worth doing that motivated her to deal with the cold and snow.

The kidnapping had thrown off her chore schedule. Dave, the press conference and the reports she'd had to write had thrown off her Sunday plans. Even though she had laundry and cleaning to do, she'd rather decompress and relax, and hopefully enjoy Chase's company.

His *you like me* and *you care about me* teases had been cute and sweet. Chase hadn't been, or done, anything cute or sweet since the first year they'd started dating, and that had been eight years ago.

She closed the car door, then stepped along the snow and ice-free walkway leading to the porch. Eight years. That was a long time to know and date someone—it was a long time to wait for a man to come to his senses. Or maybe she was the one who needed to smarten up and move on with life. When she opened the front door, all thoughts fled her mind except one: chocolate. Her mouth watered as she followed the aroma from the foyer and into the kitchen.

Chase stood at the kitchen table wearing one of her grandma's old handmade flowery aprons, drizzling chocolate over cupcakes covered in pink icing. The only way he could look any sexier was if he were naked.

"Hi," he said, keeping his concentration on the cupcakes.

"You're later than I expected. I'm surprised you didn't call and let me know you were on the way home."

She slipped out of her coat. "I'm surprised you're *in* my home."

Chuckling, he finished the last cupcake. "No, you're not. You know me better than anyone. Did you really think I was going to sit in the hotel room and do nothing?"

"During the last year of our relationship you had no problem doing nothing."

"Was that a shot?" he asked, placing the bakery items in a plastic container. "After I made you cupcakes, too."

"Nope. It's the truth." When she walked over to the fridge, another heavenly aroma, this one coming from the oven, had her stomach growling. "Did you make dinner?" She opened the oven to peek inside, but Chase stopped her by pressing his hip against the oven door.

"You can see what I made in about thirty minutes," he said, his hands filled with a bowl and icing dispenser. "I'd like to take a quick shower before we eat."

She used her index finger to capture a smudge of pink frosting from his cheek, then licked it. "Mmm. Raspberry."

He stared at her mouth, his eyes hungry. "Wait until you taste what else I have for you."

Before her thoughts drifted to sex, she opened the fridge and snagged a bottle of water. "I thought we were going out to dinner."

"It's going to be too cold," he said, washing the bowl.

She twisted the cap of the bottle. "Thanks for cleaning off the walkway."

"I didn't want you to slip." He glanced over his shoulder as he dried off the bowl. "Am I being too *controlling*?" he asked, his teasing tone belying the intensity in his eyes.

"Not at all. You were, once again, being thoughtful. I'm going to change," she said, unsure of what to do with him, and needing a moment to herself.

"Okay. Don't open the oven while I'm in the shower. I want dinner to be a surprise."

She left the kitchen curious and confused. As she passed the hall bathroom, she saw an overnight bag on the floor. It should have made her uneasy, but it didn't. This new Chase did. Not necessarily in a bad way, she just didn't know how to react to him. During the last two years of their relationship, she'd never known what to expect. There'd been the quiet, sulking Chase, the lazy, lethargic Chase, the woe-is-me Chase, or the ill-tempered, looking-to-fight Chase—her personal favorite. She'd never liked fighting with him, but at least on those days he would talk to her and show some passion.

After closing her bedroom door behind her, she kicked off her boots and sat on her bed. There had also been those rare days when he would hold her, kiss her and love her body. Those days had kept her from leaving him. They'd given her hope, shown her that deep down, beneath Chase's many layers of tainted moods, resided the man she loved.

So, now the question was how to react to him. Most women would be thrilled with a man as considerate as him. Not that he was her man. Nope, he was the baby daddy. His new role had to be the reason for the change in him. Even before the shooting, he wouldn't have gone out of his way to pick up groceries or make dinner. He'd been a workaholic who would volunteer for one assignment after another, which had forced her to become the handyman around the house. God, the picture she'd painted of him wasn't a pretty one, making her wonder again why she'd stayed. Because he could make her come multiple times? She had a vibrator to make that happen.

Irritated with herself, she slipped into a pair of black stretchy leggings, then pulled on a sweater long enough to cover her slight belly bump and widening ass. When she went into the bathroom, she caught her angry expression in the mirror then gave herself the finger. "You are a dumbass," she told her reflection as she pulled her hair back into a short ponytail. "You're thirty-four, pregnant and your crazy ex is in your shower."

He probably looked hot, too. Wet and soapy. Naked.

Damn her hormones.

"Okay, stop," she whispered to herself. "Think. Maybe he *has* changed. I haven't been around him in five months. He's my baby's father. He said he can't let me go." She turned away from the mirror to lean against the counter. Instead of questioning the change in him or his motivations, maybe she should enjoy the moment and see what happened. Except she swore she wouldn't let him hurt her again.

He might not hurt you this time, her inner voice countered.

No, he might hurt both her and their baby when he left again. She didn't know what to do or how to feel, but she was certain of one thing: she wanted one of those cupcakes.

Deciding to remain cautious and guarded, but to also allow herself to enjoy the evening and her time with Chase, she left the room. Steam streamed into the hallway from the opened bathroom door.

Her body immediately responded as she imagined him toweling off his body. She cleared her throat and dirty thoughts. "Chase?"

"In here," he called from the guest room she'd planned to use for the nursery. He opened the door, then finished tugging down his black long-sleeved thermal shirt. "Did you sneak a peek while I was in the shower?"

She glanced to the bathroom. "No, I wouldn't invade your privacy."

"I meant, did you look inside the oven?" he asked, amused. "And, for the record, if I had the chance to sneak a peek of you in the shower, I would." He zipped and buttoned his jeans. "Just being honest."

"Well, I appreciate your honesty. Now I know to lock my bathroom door."

He chuckled. "I can pick the lock."

"I'll hear you and cover myself with a towel."

"You're no fun," he said, reaching down to grab a pair of socks from his bag. "Are you hungry?"

"Starved." When he bent, she noticed a stack of magazines on the dresser. "What are those?" she asked, walking around the bed.

"I grabbed a couple of parenting magazines when I was at the grocery store."

A couple? He had six, along with a small booklet of paint swatches. "You stopped at the paint store, too?"

"Don't think I'm trying to take over," he said. "but I thought if you picked out the color for the nursery, I could paint the room this week."

She set down the samples and faced him. "You're staying here? All week?" Was she ready for that? Did she want to play house, allow herself to be sucked into the family fantasy, only to have him leave and possibly not return?

His dark brows drew together. "Don't sound too excited about it."

"I'm sorry, it's just...don't you have to go back to work?"

"I have plenty of vacation time." He finished putting on his socks, then headed for the door. "It's time to eat," he said, disappointment in his tone as he left the room.

Summer hugged herself and ignored the guilt nagging her. She had every right to be cautious and concerned. She'd allowed Chase to hurt her too many times, and had herself and her unborn baby to consider. Still, would it hurt to give him a chance?

Possibly.

With a sigh, she dropped her arms and went to the kitchen. He had wine glasses on the table and was setting out napkins and utensils. "Can I help?"

He put on an oven mitt. "You can pour the wine. Don't worry, it's non-alcoholic. Unless you'd rather have something else to drink."

"No, that's fine," she said, unscrewing the cap of the bottle. "I'm sorry for how I reacted about you staying the week. I didn't mean to hurt your feelings."

"You didn't." He placed a glass baking dish on the stovetop. "I deserve pretty much any negative thing you might say to me."

Guilt nudged her again. "That's not true." After she finished pouring the wine, she walked over to the stove where he had a couple of lidded pots on burners. "Smells delicious. Are you going to let me see what you made, or do you plan on making me wear a blindfold while I eat?"

He grinned. "Do you still have that blindfold we used to use?"

Her face heated and her mind rushed back to the time he'd tied the cloth over her eyes, then kissed every part of her body. Every. Single. Part. "I don't know what happened to it," she lied, and told herself not to think about sex.

Thanks to her whacked-out hormones she could easily see them naked and in bed—not sleeping. As much as she wanted that, she knew herself too well. When he'd been in town last summer, and they had spent the weekend making love, she'd wanted him to stay, had wanted to tell him so many things. That she'd missed him, still loved him, wished he would give himself a break and them a chance. Not ready for another rejection, she'd refrained. After he'd left, she had been down, depressed and an emotional basket case because that weekend had reminded her of how good they could be together.

"It's just as well," he said, placing mashed potatoes on the plates.

"Because?"

"If we ever have sex again, I want to be able to see your eyes when you come."

She stared at his profile. His words, the roughness in his voice, the need, had her nipples hardening and her sex throbbing. "Did you catch the press conference?" she asked. Her body might know how to respond to what he'd said, but she hadn't a clue.

He half-laughed and set a breaded piece of what she assumed was chicken onto the plate, leaning it against the mashed potatoes. "I listened to it while I was working in the kitchen. I thought you did a good job."

"You mean Dave."

"I mean you. You wrote his speech," he said, as he poured a light brown sauce onto the plate until it surrounded the chicken and potatoes. After he'd sprinkled chopped chives over the food, he took the plates to the table.

"This looks so fancy." She sat in front of one of the plates. "What is it?"

Chase pulled a baking sheet from the oven, then used tongs to place asparagus into a bowl. "Bourbon pecan chicken. But don't worry about the bourbon. The alcohol burned off as it cooked."

Pecans? She loved almost every nut out there, but hated pecans. "Sounds delicious."

"I've never made it before, so I hope it's good." He finally sat, then served her some asparagus. After helping himself, he lifted his wine glass. "Toast?"

"Sure." She held her glass close to his. "To saving those boys and a job well done." When disappointment momentarily flashed in his eyes, she asked, "No?"

"It was a job well done, but I had something else in mind. Maybe I should skip it. I don't want dinner to get cold."

"Say it," she encouraged him out of curiosity.

"Nope. I'll save it for our next dinner date."

"Chicken," she murmured, then sipped the wine.

"Did you call me chicken?"

"No. I was referring to what's on my plate." She feigned innocence as she cut into the meat. "I'm anxious to try it."

"Right." He sighed. "I don't have to stay in Cleveland, and I wasn't expecting to sleep here. I can come back in a week or two. Aren't you flying out on Friday?"

"I planned on it, but haven't secured a flight. How many days of vacation do you get?" she asked, then took a bite of the chicken. While he talked, she tried to keep from cringing. The chicken was tough and bland, while the sauce had a mustardy, cough syrup flavor to it. She hated mustard just as much as she hated pecans. Did the man know anything about her? She swallowed, then drank wine to wash the taste from her mouth.

"Well, what do you think?" he asked after taking a bite.

"It's very good. What's in the sauce?"

"Dijon mustard, brown sugar, bourbon, soy sauce, Worcestershire and butter." He set his fork down in exchange for his glass. "And you're a liar. It's gross."

"No, it's not," she said, slicing another piece to keep up the ruse. Chase had gone through a lot of work to prepare the meal and she didn't want to be rude or disappoint him.

"Seriously, don't eat it." He reached over and took her plate. "I'll make something else."

She stopped him. "Chase, it's fine. Let me at least try the asparagus."

"Don't bother, because I did. It's stringy and bland," he said, wearing his crabby face. "I wouldn't feed any of this to my dog."

She let him take the plate. "You have a dog?"

"No, I'm just saying…" He rose from the table, then dumped the meal into the trash. "Grilled cheese and fried bologna sandwiches?"

She followed him over to the sink and rested a hand on his forearm. "Thanks for trying. I really appreciate the thoughtfulness."

After setting down the dishes, he turned and leaned against the counter. "I was excited about this evening, and was trying to make it special."

"I was excited, too."

He perked up a bit. "Yeah?"

"Yeah." She stepped closer. "It's been a long time since we've really talked."

Regret hardened his face. "That's my fault." He sighed. "And I'm sorry for so many things. When I got on the jet to come here, I was dreading it. Seeing you reminds me of the mistakes I've made, and how I let them ruin our relationship." He pushed off the counter and gently gripped her arms. "I told you I couldn't let you go, but I didn't tell you why."

Her heart raced. Fearing his words would hurt her, she wasn't sure she wanted to know.

"After I moved to Chicago, life didn't get any better, it was worse. I couldn't sleep, eat or concentrate. All I could think about was you, Brody and my failed career."

"You didn't fail."

"I did. I couldn't get over the shooting. Even though I knew it wasn't my fault, I still took a gullible kid's life. I've got to live with that. But this weekend I realized I don't have to let it *rule* my life. Finding out I'm going to be a dad has changed something in me. It's given me hope, a second chance at being happy again. I want *us* to be happy again." He skimmed his fingers along her jaw. "Summer, I left you because I needed you too much, yet I can't let you go this time for the same reason."

Confused, she blinked a couple times. "I don't understand."

"Don't take this the wrong way, but before the shooting I didn't need you."

She tensed. "How am I supposed to take that?"

"I wanted you in my life."

"But you didn't *need* me to be there." His admission cut deep, because she had given him everything she could, and he hadn't felt the same. Nodding, she stepped away and folded her arms over her chest. "Nice to know. So after the shooting, after six years of being in a committed relationship—five of which we were living together—you suddenly decided you needed me around."

"Yes, exactly. Although you make it sound worse than it is."

"Because it is bad and hurtful and…" She dropped her arms and fisted her hands. "I gave you everything. Everything! I loved you with all my heart and planned on spending the rest of my life with you."

With hope in his eyes, he moved closer. "We still can."

"Why? Because you need me now? Give me a fucking break," she said, and took several backward steps. "Leave the mess. I'll clean it. And on your way out, leave your set of keys on the counter."

Before she could turn and walk away, he gripped her again, and pulled her close. "Give *me* a fucking break and listen," he said, his gaze intense, pleading. "Killing Brody changed something in me. I had all these feelings I didn't know what to do with or how to handle them. Do you realize you're the only person I've ever loved? I'm sure I loved my mom, but I don't really remember her. My dad and brothers...I've got nothing for them, and they couldn't care less about me. But you." He gave her a slight shake. "You taught me to love and, yeah, I wanted you in my life. But it wasn't until after Brody that I realized I'd been blind to my own emotions. Until you, I'd never needed or depended on anyone. I took care of me and I didn't want to need you so much that if I lost you, it would kill me."

He swore under his breath and released her. When he turned away, she stared at his back, stunned by his admission. "You left me because you needed me too much? Bullshit."

"What?" He faced her, shock and anger darkening his eyes. "I open up, and you call it bullshit?"

"I am. Your excuse doesn't make sense to me. Why would you walk away when you were hurting the most? It wasn't because you were afraid to love and needed me too much. It was because the roles had changed. You went from being this tough, over-confident, hardcore, unemotional negotiator to a sensitive man with actual *feelings*. Instead of letting me in, allowing me to be your partner in every sense of the word, you shut me out, then you ran."

He pushed both hands through his hair. "I was a coward. It was easier to leave than to stay and...try."

Her throat tightened. Though she was glad to finally discuss why their relationship hadn't lasted, the truth hurt. Badly. He'd given up on them because it was easy, and that sucked. She'd fought hard to keep them together, to be there for him during his time of need. Would he have done the same for her? Would he be there for their child?

"You're not saying anything, so I'm going to assume you agree with the coward comment."

She stared at him, at his clenched jaw, the challenge in his eyes and stance. "A coward wouldn't admit his mistakes. I do wonder, though... If I wasn't pregnant, would we be having this conversation?"

"No."

Tears welled in her eyes. "I see, and I do think you should go."

"Because I'm being honest?" He took her fist and smoothed it out to hold her hand. "I think about you every single day. Nothing's been fine since I left you. I can't sleep without having your head next to mine, without listening to you breathe or feeling your skin. I asked a coworker out hoping to get you out of my mind. When she turned me down I was relieved. I didn't want to be with her, and don't want anyone else."

She ignored the stab of jealousy and let anger consume her. "I don't want to hear any of this. It took this pregnancy for you to open your mouth and say something. Do you not understand why that hurts me?" She wiped her cheek. "And I'm tired of hurting." She motioned between them. "I can't keep doing this."

His grip around her hand tightened. "Hearing *we're* having a baby... I'm telling you, fireworks went off in my head and zapped something in my brain. For the first time since the shooting, my thoughts are crystal clear. I recognized the emotional coward I've been and immediately wanted to change. I want my child to be proud of me, not think I'm pathetic. Damn it, Summer, I want *you* to be proud of me."

"Who said I'm not or ever wasn't?"

"How could you be when I was such an asshole?"

"Because you were my asshole and I loved you," she said, then burst into laughter when he did. "That did *not* come out right."

He released her hand and cupped her cheeks. "I want to be your asshole again."

Grinning, she wrapped her arms around his waist. "I don't know if I'm ready."

"Maybe this will help… Yesterday, you asked how I was doing after my first meeting with Shultz. Being back in the field was probably the best form of therapy for me. I missed negotiating and I want to get back in it."

Her smile fell as she tensed. "The FBI won't take you back."

"No, but with letters of recommendation from my former CNU supervisors, CORE and Dave, I bet I could get hired by the Cleveland PD or the Cuyahoga County Sheriff's Department."

She bet he could, too. The idea scared her. She didn't want to live with a crisis negotiator ever again. Been there, done that, and it had ended terribly.

"I don't know, Chase. I think you should discuss this with your therapist."

He slid his hands from her face to her shoulders. "I don't need him. I need to be with family—meaning you and the baby—and to be back on the job." Excitement shined in his eyes as he smiled. "I think I'm back. The old Chase is back and ready for the future." His smile wavered. "Why don't you seem happy about it?"

Fresh tears slipped down her cheeks. God, they were making progress and she was beginning to finally understand where his head had been for the past two years. She didn't want to pop his balloon, but this was her life, and she needed to consider her and their baby's future.

"The old Chase made me sad and miserable." She let out a shaky breath. "I'm sorry, but I don't want him back. Ever."

12

C HASE SLOWLY EASED away from Summer. "You don't want me back." He blew out a breath to control his anger. "What the hell does that mean?"

"I said I don't want the *old* Chase."

He would never understand women. He'd finally told her what had been going on in his mind, got all mushy and emotional, and it still wasn't enough for her. "Why the hell not?"

"Because he wasn't always pleasant to be around," she said, not meeting his gaze.

"Right. And I just spent how long explaining to you that I haven't been thinking clearly?"

She shook her head. "I'm talking about *before* the shooting."

"There was something wrong with me even *before* the Wakefield case?" Confused, he tried to wrap his brain around what she was saying. "What the hell are you talking about?"

"How many times are you going to use hell in a phrase?"

"However the hell many times I want," he shouted. "What was wrong with me?"

"You, ah, sometimes talked to me as if you were in a crisis negotiation."

A lock of hair escaped her ponytail. When she went to fix it, he stopped her and pulled the hairband free. "I like it down."

Her cheeks turned a pretty shade of pink as a fire lit in her eyes. "How about straightened? You haven't commented on the new haircut."

She was going to blow. He'd known her for too many years not to read the signs. "It looks nice," he said, certain if he were honest she'd slug him. "Back to how you *think* I talked to you..."

"Tell me the truth about my hair," she demanded. "I know you always preferred my hair longer."

"I didn't mean to upset you. You're beautiful to me, no matter which way you wear your hair."

Her face softened. "Thank you."

He nodded. "But wasn't your hair easier to manage when you had more length?"

The fire in her eyes returned. "*This* is what I'm talking about."

"How does commenting on your hair compare to talking to you as if you're a hostage taker?"

"It wasn't just how you talked to me, it was also your actions, reactions, lack of emotion."

"Whoa, whoa, whoa." He held up his hands. "Before Wakefield we were doing great. We went on vacations, went on dates, spent time together, so I don't know where this is coming from."

She cocked a brow. "Okay, when we were still in Baltimore, do you remember when I wanted to buy new furniture for the living room?"

Smelling a trap, he eyed her with caution. "Yes, we went to the store and picked out a nice set. I noticed it's no longer in the living room."

"I sold it after you left."

"Why? It was in mint condition."

"I hated it. Hated the color and style, and it wasn't comfortable."

"Then why'd we buy it?"

"Because you wouldn't let up about what a great deal it was, how it was a sensible purchase, blah, blah, blah. You did that kind of thing to me all the time. Talked and talked until I was too tired to argue with you anymore."

Had he? Maybe. The furniture *had* been a sensible purchase.

"Once you became a negotiator, something in you changed," she continued. "You kept going deep within yourself. There were no more heated arguments with hot make-up sex. You laughed less, worked more, and you know what I realized? You had issues with commitment."

"Now *that's* bullshit. I was committed to you."

"Then why wouldn't you marry me or buy a house?"

He ran a hand through his hair again. Fuck, she had him pegged right on this one. "I was worried if we got married, you'd change your mind and push to have kids."

"Now you have a knocked-up ex. Worked out well, wouldn't you say?"

"Summer—"

"Stop. I can't go back to the way we were before Wakefield. I love you. I miss you. But I want the man in front of me. I want you to be comfortable showing me your emotions. Shout, laugh, cry…give it all to me." Tears streamed down her cheeks as she pressed her fingers against her chest. "You're so driven and such a workaholic, I'm worried if you go back to negotiating, your work will bleed into our personal life. I don't want an emotionless robot."

Stunned by how she saw him, he wandered into the living room, then sat on the couch, which was much more comfortable than their old one. Had he been that bad? She made him sound like an awful human being.

"Chase, I'm sorry if I hurt your feelings," she said, and sat next to him.

"Don't talk to me as if I'm a child."

"I'm not."

"You are."

He stood. He didn't want to smell her perfume or have her body brush against his. Part of him wanted to leave, head back to Chicago and pretend this conversation had never happened. The other part wanted to have a shouting match. Summer wasn't perfect. There were many things she did that drove him nuts. He couldn't think of any at the moment, but he was sure there had to be a few, or at least one.

"If I was such a dick, why didn't you leave me?" he asked, deciding he'd go for the shouting match. He was tired of running and wanted to fight—for her, for them. His life hadn't been the same since he left her, and he'd been miserable without her.

"Because you weren't always controlling and distant. We had plenty of good days, and it was those days that kept me with you."

"Here we go again with that fucking word. I am *not* controlling."

"Really? Since you found out I was pregnant you've taken away my coffee, bugged me about what I eat or don't, commented on my language, about which, by the way, you have no room to talk. I'm surprised you haven't already baby-proofed the house and bought the crib."

Shit, he'd have to call the baby store and cancel the furniture he'd ordered for the nursery. "What you described isn't controlling. It's efficiency and thoughtfulness."

"Sure it is. Would you like for me to tell you what to eat or how to act?" She pushed herself off the couch and approached him. "You're a smart, sensible guy and I've always appreciated and valued your opinion. But you also need to listen and respect mine." She ran her palm along his arm before taking his hand. "I get you. You practically raised yourself and didn't have anyone to rely on or turn to when you needed help. It's always been you. Your plan, your path."

"There's nothing wrong with having a plan," he countered, the fight in him abating as memories of his childhood and teen years rushed through his mind. "When I was eleven, while my brothers and friends were already getting in trouble, I was doing odd jobs for the guy who owned a small manufacturing company down the street from us. I'd cut grass, clean, run errands. Even at eleven I had a plan, and that was to not end up like my father." If only his brothers had gone along with his plan instead of following in their dad's footsteps and becoming broke addicts with prison records. But they'd been easily influenced by the bad kids in their neighborhood, and with a role model like their dad, they hadn't carried with them what Chase had—hope and determination.

"I know about your childhood." She gave him a small smile that didn't reach her eyes. "And you're right. It's always good to have plans and set goals. But have you ever considered mine?"

"I've always supported you. Hell, I moved to Cleveland when you were promoted."

"Would you have if the shooting hadn't happened?"

Before Wakefield, he had been working his ass off, hoping to eventually run the Crisis Negotiation Unit. Because CNU was based on the East Coast, if he'd followed her, he would have lost that opportunity and had to leave the unit.

"You don't need to answer because it doesn't matter," she continued.

"I wouldn't have moved," he said anyway. If he had a shot at being with Summer again, he needed to be completely honest with her and himself. "Cleveland wasn't part of my plan."

"Then I guess I wasn't, either." Tears slipped down her cheeks as she let go of him. "And I know the baby definitely wasn't."

Fearing he'd lose her, he snagged her arm and hauled her close. "I'm selfish, fucked in the head and, as you've pointed out, a control freak. I haven't had a plan in two years. Before that, I always saw you in my future."

The disbelief and hurt in her eyes was killing him. "And after?" she asked.

"Until I found out about the baby, I couldn't see past the next day, let alone think about the future." He ran a hand through her silky hair and cupped the back of her head. "I told you I think about you all the time. I've wanted to call or come see you."

She gripped the front of his shirt. "Then why didn't you?"

"Because I'm weak." His chest tightened with the admission. He'd always prided himself on being a badass. Being strong. Being the guy who took no shit and made things happen. "When I lived here, I hated the pity in your eyes, hated that you were the strong one and I was nothing but a broken, insecure loser who no longer had a future."

"I never thought those things about you," she said with vehemence. "Ever. That was in *your* head. I wanted you here with me. Why do you think I never changed the locks? I needed you to know I was here for you."

God, he loved her. He'd been an idiot to allow his grief and self-doubt to rule his judgment, heart and head. "In the kitchen you said you love and miss me—present tense. Will you give me another chance? I'm not suggesting I move in, but I'd like to move back here to see if we can make us work."

She touched his jaw. "I do love you, but I'm scared."

"Of what?"

"That you'll leave me."

Regret slammed into him. He'd been beyond selfish and didn't deserve a woman like Summer. "Being away taught me I'm nothing without you in my life. I won't do that to you again." While there was still disbelief in her eyes, there was also hope. And he'd hang on to that.

She rose on her tiptoes and kissed his cheek. He had the urge to turn his head and capture her lips, coax them apart and kiss her until they were both breathless. He also wanted to strip her naked and sink into her body. They had time for that. For now, he'd take the innocent peck and the opportunity to just be with her.

"Should we continue with our date?" she asked, and, still holding his hand, led him back into the kitchen.

"I was worried I'd ruined it."

"Nope." She used a napkin to wipe her face and nose. "I think this is the best conversation we've had in years. It felt good to point out your flaws," she said with a teasing smile.

Chuckling, he relaxed and the tension rolled off his shoulders. "I'm glad I can still show you a good time."

They spent the next half-hour cleaning up the crappy dinner

he'd made, then made grilled cheese and fried bologna sandwiches. As they cleaned, cooked and ate, they talked. He discovered Summer hated pecans and mustard—how had he not known that—along with her other likes and dislikes. It amazed him that they'd lived together for nearly seven years and there were still things he was learning about her.

After they'd polished off a couple cupcakes, which thankfully were good, they went into the living room. Once they were on the couch, she surprised him when she rested her head in his lap and stretched out her legs on the cushions. Instead of putting on the television, he spent the evening running his fingers through her hair, caressing her cheeks and doing most of the talking. Now that his mind was clear enough to see through his clouded past and into the future, he was able to truly open up to her. When she hadn't said anything in a while, he glanced down and smiled.

The light from the end table lamp touched along her high cheekbones, slightly parted lips and closed eyes. She looked so beautiful and peaceful, and reminded him that he'd wasted too much time being a selfish prick. Instead of being alone and miserable, he should have been here with her. He still believed leaving had been the right decision, though. He'd been spiraling down a destructive road, and taking her with him. He could've driven them so far apart, this moment wouldn't have been possible.

He remained on the couch thinking and loving having Summer near. After a while, his eyes began to burn with exhaustion. Needing to head back to the hotel, he carefully lifted her head from his lap, then bent and scooped her in his arms. As he carried her to the bedroom, she wrapped an arm around his neck.

"What are you doing?" she asked, her voice thick, tired. She raised her head. "I'm sorry. Did I fall asleep on you?"

"I don't mind," he said, lying her on the bed, then smoothing her hair from her face. "Since you're taking tomorrow off, do you want to spend the day together?"

She gave him a sleepy smile. "I'd like that."

He kissed her forehead. "I'll lock up on my way out and call you in the morning."

"You don't have to leave," she said, crawling under the covers.

Good. After spending time with Summer, he wasn't ready to go back to the quiet, lonely hotel room. "You're okay with me staying in the guest room?" he asked, not bothering to suggest he sleep in her bed. There would be time for that, too. He was happy with the prospect of waking up and seeing her first thing in the morning.

She curled onto her side and tucked her hand under the pillow. "As long as you make me breakfast."

"You got it," he said, then after turning off the light, he closed the door. Once he'd made sure the house was locked up, he went into the guest room, stripped down to his underwear, then climbed into bed and waited for sleep to claim him.

Summer couldn't keep her eyes closed. Chase was in the next room and probably half naked, which was one reason why she had trouble falling back asleep. The other was their argument. They'd hurt each other tonight, but it was a necessary hurt. If they were going to make their relationship work this time around, they needed to be upfront and honest with each other.

She could've done without some of his honest answers, and was pretty sure he could say the same about hers. When he'd confessed he wouldn't have moved to Cleveland, he had confirmed her suspicions. Not that it mattered now. She firmly believed Chase wasn't the same man he'd been then. The man she'd fallen in love with remained, but the coldness that had distanced them had thawed. It also hurt her to know how he thought of himself. He wasn't weak, and she hated that he'd called himself a broken loser. If anything, she thought he was mentally and emotionally stronger. Physically, too.

His arms and chest were bigger, thicker, harder. It'd been a while, but she knew what else was big, thick and hard. Before she pictured him naked again, she shot up and slung her legs over the edge of the bed. She was hot, anyway. After she stripped down to her panties, she went back under the covers. As she lay there, waiting for sleep to come, a little flutter moved within her womb. She quickly touched her stomach. The flutter came again, but not enough to feel against her palm, and not enough of an excuse to wake Chase.

Did she need an excuse? Of course not. But what would sex do to their relationship? What could go horribly wrong? He could leave. He could do that whether or not they became physical. It would still hurt, so why deny herself the pleasure of his body.

She curled onto her side and squeezed her eyes shut. No. She would not allow her hormones to overrule her common sense. They were starting afresh, as if they were a brand-new couple. She hadn't jumped into bed with him on their first date, so she shouldn't go there now.

An hour later, and sleep still eluding her, she slid out of bed and into her thick terry cloth bathrobe. As she made her way to the kitchen for a glass of water, she didn't even glance toward Chase's closed door. She'd already made up her mind that sex would wait. But on her way back from the kitchen, there he was standing in the doorway wearing just his boxer briefs.

"What are you doing up?" he asked, looking incredibly sexy with a case of bedhead. "Is everything okay?"

"I couldn't sleep. You?"

"Same. But that's not anything new."

She thought back to what he'd said about having a hard time sleeping. "Maybe we'd both fall asleep if our heads are next to each other," she suggested, ignoring the anticipation pulling at her belly and her hardening nipples.

A smile tugged at the corner of his mouth. "Maybe. Are you sure?"

She nodded.

"Should I put on a shirt?"

"I don't think that's necessary," she said, and continued to her room. Once there, she regretted leaving on the light. While she wanted to make love to Chase, she wasn't ready for him to see the changes to her body. "I'm only wearing underwear beneath my robe. Should I put on a shirt?"

His eyes darkened with desire as he took over his usual side of the bed. "I don't think that's necessary," he said, his voice husky.

"I have to warn you, my boobs are enormous, my belly isn't flat and I noticed dimples on my rear."

"I'm a boob man, you're carrying our baby, and if you have dimples, I'd love to kiss them."

Her sex throbbed. "Now?"

"Whenever you're ready."

He was leaving sex up to her, which was a mistake since that was all she'd been thinking about for the past hour. "Give me a second," she said, then went into the bathroom. She didn't have to go, but wanted to brush her teeth and make sure she smelled pretty. Once her teeth were cleaned, she gave her neck a little spritz of perfume, then finger-combed her hair. She took off the robe, caught her reflection and slipped right back into it. There was nothing good to see there, and he could rediscover her body in the dark with his hands and mouth.

Aroused and anxious to be with him, she left the bathroom, then stopped and shook her head. The lights were still on, but Chase was asleep. Though disappointed, it was okay. She'd missed sleeping next to him, and looked forward to waking up in his arms.

After turning off the light, she got rid of her robe, then carefully crawled into bed. She inched over until she met skin, rested her head near his and closed her eyes.

When she heard the shower running, she sat up and checked the alarm clock. It couldn't possibly be eight in the morning, not when she'd just gone to bed. She stretched and yawned. God, she hadn't slept that hard in a long time. Like Chase, she was used to waking up during the night, and was surprised that hadn't happened.

She yawned again, then stared at the bathroom door. Neither of them had to work today, so why hadn't he stayed in bed? They could have had lazy, satisfying morning sex. Maybe he didn't want to fool around and was avoiding her. Doubtful. Chase was the most sexual partner she'd ever had, and had always been ready and willing.

"Time to find out how willing," she murmured, and opened the door. Steam fogged the mirror and instantly clung to her skin. After she removed her panties, she drew in a steadying breath and walked over to the shower. The glass was also steamy, but not enough to hide Chase's sudsy back, or the way the soap carved a path to his tight butt.

"Aren't you getting in?" he asked without turning.

Ready to touch and be touched, she stepped inside the shower. "How'd you know I was in here? And why are you showering now? We don't have to be anywhere this morning."

"You let in cold air." He dipped his head under the spray, then faced her. His thick erection brushed against her stomach. When she looked down at it, he said, "And this is why I jumped in the shower. It was either take care of this in here or pound you into the wall. I'd prefer the latter, but didn't want to wake you."

"Pound me into the wall." She grinned and took his length in her hand. "It's been a while since you've done that."

He cupped her bottom and pulled her close enough that her nipples grazed his chest. "You wouldn't have complained?" He moved a hand to her breast and rolled her nipple between his fingertips.

She stroked him with one hand, pushed her other hand through his wet hair and drew his mouth closer to hers. "Only if you didn't make me come."

"Like that could ever happen," he said, then kissed her.

She parted her lips, slid her tongue along his and sank into the kiss. Rubbed his length and wished it was inside her, filling her, bringing her to orgasm. As they kissed, he nudged her backward until her legs hit the built-in tile bench. Chase loved the bench, loved bending her over it or sitting her on it and going down on her. While she'd love to have his lips and tongue licking and sucking her clit and labia, she wanted hard and fast. It had been too long and she needed instant gratification.

Instead of having her sit, he moved his hand over her hip, then between her thighs. She gladly opened them for him, and gasped when he pressed his fingers deep inside her sex. He fingered her. Dragged his mouth down her neck and chest until he captured a nipple, then sucked hard. She groaned, held his head there and rolled his testicles between her fingers the way he liked.

He released her nipple and moved her hand away from his groin. "Sit." He gently touched her shoulder. "I want to taste you. It's been too long."

"No. I—"

In a flash he was on his knees and pressing his mouth against her sex. His tongue slid between her lips, along her clit. Her knees weakened. She sat on the wet tile and spread her legs, welcoming his skillful fingers and tongue, ran her hand over his hair, then gripped his slippery shoulders. He was right. It had been too long and she'd missed him so damned much. His passion, his body and simply being with him. Lying next to him last night had been pure heaven. Feeling his skin against hers, the warmth of his strong body and the rise and fall of his chest had helped her to easily drift off to sleep. She didn't want him to ever leave her again. After the amount of time they'd been apart, she didn't even want him to go back to Chicago to give CORE his notice and pack his things. What if he returned for a few days and changed his mind about them? What if he'd been lying and he had a woman there? Why was she in her head instead of enjoying this moment?

Because she'd lost faith in them, had lost confidence in herself and was terrified of being hurt. Of being the pathetic fool who had waited on a man only to be dumped by him again.

Despite her thoughts, an orgasm neared, coiled deep inside and had her body humming. She gripped the edge of the bench and spread her legs wider, met his intense, hungry gaze, watched as he flicked his tongue over her clit, then she came. Her orgasm spread through her body, had her leaning against the wall for support and her breath coming in quick pants.

Before she could gather a thought, he pulled her into his arms and kissed her with so much passion he took her breath away. "I need to be inside you," he said between hot, sexy open-mouthed kisses. "Deep inside." He rubbed his large hands over her rear. "Turn around. That's it. Bend over for me."

She raised her bottom in the air and glanced behind her. His body blocked the shower spray. Water glistened along his skin, ran off his shoulders and arms as he held his hard length. Then he gripped her hip and, in one swift motion, entered her. They both groaned.

He stilled. "Am I hurting you?" he asked, his voice rough, strained. "Is this bad for the baby?"

"No, but it'll be bad for you if you stop."

"Yes, ma'am," he said, pulled out, then plunged in again.

Using the tile for support, she matched the rhythm of his hips and met each thrust.

"God, you feel so good." He stayed locked inside her and drew her up until her back was against his chest. "So good," he murmured, and kissed her shoulder, her neck. He cupped her breasts with both hands and toyed with her nipples. Drove her crazy with desire, with the need to orgasm again.

She reached around and grabbed his tight ass. "Make us come."

He nipped her earlobe. "Now?"

"Right now."

"Fuck, yeah," he said, then bent her forward.

Gripping both of her hips, he pounded into her until they were both groaning. Her orgasm hit hard and fast, tore through her and shattered her senses, while Chase stiffened and released a cross between a growl and grunt. Breathing hard, he slid from her body, then quickly turned her to face him. He hugged her and brought her under the spray. As water coated her hair, he touched her cheek and met her gaze. His eyes held satisfaction and love.

"I can't be without you again." He moved his hand to the slight swell of her belly. "I didn't think I would want a family because mine was so messed up, but…" He bent, kissed her belly, her breast, then her lips. "I want us to be a family. I want…I just want to love you."

Her tears mixed with the water dripping down her face. She hadn't wanted children, either. But from the minute she'd discovered she was pregnant, she'd planned on being a single mother. Now she had the chance of having a family of her own. "I want the same." She kissed him. "I love you, too."

He held her, and they stayed that way until the water started to cool. While he left the shower, promising her he would make breakfast, she had to quickly wash herself before she used up all the hot water. After she'd toweled off, then took care of her toiletries, she dressed in another pair of comfy leggings and a pale blue, button down shirt. As she headed for the kitchen, her cell phone rang from the charger in the bedroom. She reached the phone on the fourth ring and saw Dave's number on the screen.

Damn it. She did *not* want to go into work today. "Morning, Dave," she answered.

"Morning. We have a problem."

Crap. She tensed. "With?"

"Lauren checked Shultz's Bitcoin account this morning. A transaction was made last night at ten forty-two. All five hundred thousand dollars was moved."

Oh, my God. She slumped onto the edge of the bed. The phantom kidnapper was real.

Summer's House, Fairview Park, Ohio
Monday, January 23rd, 1:04 p.m. Eastern Standard Time

Chase stared at the laptop screen waiting for the video call to connect. He usually liked being right, but not today. Since a dead man couldn't have made the Bitcoin transaction, the FBI were now on the hunt for whoever had transferred the money, focusing on Matthew Shultz and who he'd been in contact with prior to the kidnapping.

Instead of conferencing with CORE, he and Summer should be doing something fun, either downtown or in her bed. It didn't matter where. He just wanted to be with her. He'd woken up this morning more refreshed than he'd been in years. He couldn't remember the last time he'd slept through the night, and had missed lying next to her soft, warm body, listening to her breathe. He'd also missed being inside her, her passion, her kisses and was glad she'd joined him in the shower. While he had wanted to make love to her last night, he had fallen asleep instead. He had no idea what had happened. The moment his head had hit the pillow, he'd closed his eyes, inhaled her scent lingering on the sheets and had drifted to sleep.

That wasn't going to happen tonight. Shower sex was hot, and he'd loved every minute of being with her this morning, but he wanted to take his time and rediscover her body without having to worry about slippery tile or running out of hot water.

Rachel Malcolm appeared on the screen, seated in CORE's evidence and evaluation room, which was similar to the FBI briefing room he and Summer had left an hour ago. "Hey, Chase. Are you ready to compare notes?"

"Yeah, but I'm waiting for Summer," he said, then explained her role with the FBI. Seconds later, Summer entered the living room. She sat next to him on the couch and handed him a can of Coke.

After he introduced the two women, Summer began telling Rachel what they knew about the Bitcoin transaction. "The money was transferred to a bank in Panama. The suspect went through a company called World Privacy. This company allows the end user to have a legit and anonymous bank account. They get a debit card and can make online transactions, just like with a regular bank."

Rachel gave them her profile as she tapped the keyboard of the laptop next to her. "Got it. Okay, so World Privacy makes the user an anonymous nominee shareholder, which allows said user to have the offshore bank account. Wow. No ID, utility bill, passport or references are required."

"That's right," Summer said. "For approximately eight grand, you too can have an anonymous offshore bank account."

Rachel frowned. "Not so anonymous. It says here that the client is assigned an attorney who will work on their behalf and keep their personal information in private files."

"Right. Even though the nominee shareholder isn't registered within whatever Central American company being used, or with any public offices, the attorney would have that information."

"Any luck finding the attorney?" Rachel asked.

"We're still working on it. The CEO of World Privacy said revealing the identity of their client goes against their policy, and they refused to cooperate. They're based in Poland, so we're working with U.S. counterparts there, hoping to lean on them and get that ID."

Rachel's fingers flew quickly over the keyboard. "All transactions are done online. Let me see if I can get into the company's server and...nope." Leaning back in the chair, she ran her fingers through her short red hair and let out a breath. "Hacking into their system is going to take time. I'll work on that after we're through. What else do you have for me?"

"Our agents have pulled together a list of Matthew Shultz's known associates. Chase is going to email it to you. We confiscated his work computer on the day of the kidnapping. Our forensic analysts have found nothing in his files, email or search history that indicate he planned the abduction, or that he was working with someone else who had. We believe his personal laptop or phone would have that info. Unfortunately, we haven't been able to locate either."

"I just had a thought," Rachel began, leaning forward. "Just like with regular online banking, you can schedule Bitcoin transactions. Isn't it possible Shultz scheduled the transfer *before* he died?"

Chase hadn't considered that. "They were using burner phones."

"Which were smart phones, correct? So he'd have the ability to download the Bitcoin app and use that to see or make transactions."

"Except CSI didn't find Shultz's phone."

Rachel frowned. "Interesting."

"What's interesting?" Sloan North asked as he stepped into the evidence and evaluation room, then gathered papers off the printer behind Rachel. Sloan was also a CORE agent and had been hired the same week as Chase. The six-foot-six, bearded, tattooed walking muscle was a former undercover cop who had worked Vice, and had infiltrated biker clubs and street gangs. His knowledge of street life had proven valuable a number of times for CORE.

"Chase is on the case and it's an interesting one," Rachel said, while Summer laughed.

"Why is that funny?" Chase asked.

"It's from a kid's cartoon, *PAW Patrol*," Summer said. "My sister's kids love the show. Chase is a puppy and...never mind."

Chase looked away from Summer to meet Rachel's innocent gaze. "You've been using that line on me since I started at CORE, and I figured it was because it rhymed."

"What can I say? I have kids and get stuck watching their shows. I have to amuse myself somehow."

"I'd be pissed at Red for that one." Sloan took a seat next to Rachel. "Well, hello there," he said, his gaze locked on Summer. "Sloan North. And you are?"

"With me," Chase said a little more harshly than he'd meant. He liked Sloan, but the womanizer needed to sniff elsewhere.

"Yeah, but do you think she wants a puppy or a wolf?" Sloan asked with a smile, then waved a hand. "Just messing with you, man. What are you working?"

"The bus kidnapping," Rachel answered for him.

"I thought you'd resolved that."

"We did, too," Summer said, then introduced herself. "From the start, Chase thought there were others involved, and he was right. The evidence we're compiling, and the lack thereof, also indicate there was more going on than we'd originally thought."

Chase nodded. "Shultz's missing phone and his cousin's murder have me convinced there was someone else at the park."

"How so?" Sloan asked. "I heard Rachel tell Ian that the kids said Shultz killed his cousin, along with four other people."

"That's what the kids *assumed*." Chase opened the Coke. "None of them saw him murder Joel, and I don't believe Shultz would've been stupid enough to kill his cousin, then leave a knife and rifle for the kids to find."

"But the kids claimed there were only *five* kidnappers," Summer countered. "And CSI found no evidence that anyone other than the boys and kidnappers were on the property."

Sloan shrugged. "Then it's got to be one of the boys."

Chase stared at the man, dread pooling in his stomach. He hadn't wanted to consider that option, even when it had crossed his mind. That meant a teenager had not only orchestrated the kidnapping of his friends and teammates, but he'd ordered Pembroke and Stokes' murders.

"The kids?" Summer shook her head. "No way. I met them and interviewed several myself. They all were scared and badly shaken up by what happened. I can't see any of them being capable of murder and kidnapping."

Sloan cracked his neck. "Back when I was with Vice, I was looking for a drug dealer who'd been selling bad cocaine. People thought they were getting coke, but instead they were pretty much snorting boric acid. Two people died and several others were hospitalized. When I found the dealer? Yeah, he was a twelve-year-old, and so were his two buddies. Don't let age fool you."

"Sloan's right," Rachel said. "And I find it interesting that the rest of the kidnappers ended up dead shortly after the deposit was made. Five hundred thousand dollars is a lot of money, especially for a kid."

"But we're dealing with wealthy families," Summer argued. "With the exception of one family, every one of those kids has it made. Why risk prison when Mom and Dad are buying cars, paying for school, and handing out big allowances?"

"What's wrong with the one family?" Sloan asked.

"Chad Everett's parents earn about one hundred and fifty thousand a year. The only reason their son is at the school is because his grandfather set up a trust so he could go there."

"Start with that kid first," Sloan suggested. "I'd hate to be surrounded by a bunch of rich kids who had it all, while I had nothing. His teammates could've hazed him for being poor, and he figured out a way to get revenge."

"He has a point," Chase said. "We should look into the kids' activities. Yes, they *were* scared and shaken, but for one of them it could've just been an act. I told you and Taggart I thought something wasn't right about Joel's murder. Why isn't it possible one of the boys killed the man?"

"Then wouldn't they all have to be involved?" Summer asked. "They were never allowed to be alone or left unsupervised."

"Ooo, I like that idea." Rachel cocked a brow. "The team hires the Shultz cousins and their buddies to kidnap them, but the kidnappers don't know this. When Shultz takes it too far and shoots Alex, that's when they sabotage things, ultimately bringing the ordeal to a close."

Sloan leaned forward and rested his forearms on the table. "But before they're rescued, they kill the cousin, then Shultz."

"That's nuts," Summer said, but with less conviction than before.

"Is it?" Chase asked. "The kids are all telling the same story, and yet the ending doesn't make sense. If they were all in on it together, they would cover for each other."

"What does the evidence tell you?" Sloan asked.

"The knife found in Shultz's chest was the same one used to

kill the cousin. Analysts found the cousins' blood, but no finger-prints." Chase lifted the Coke can. "What's interesting to me is Shultz also had the same knife on him. There wasn't a speck of blood on it, but it had Shultz's fingerprints all over the handle."

"Why is this interesting?" Rachel asked.

Summer tucked a lock of hair behind her ear. "I'm wondering the same. All that means is the knife might've been Joel's, not Shultz's. Joel was found wearing gloves. It's possible he never touched the knife with his bare fingers."

"Hang on a sec." Chase turned to Summer. "Remember our interview with Chris Demko? The part where he talked about how Shultz had used Tyler's pocketknife to cut the kid's face."

"What about it?" Her eyes widened and she gasped. "Oh, my God. I know where you're going with this." She looked to the screen. "Chris said Shultz made him and another boy, Tyler, go with him to the hotel. While they were there looking for two-way radios, tape and rope, Tyler used his pocketknife to stab Shultz in the rear. In turn, Shultz used Tyler as a punching bag. Chris said when they got back to the fun house, Shultz left to take a radio to Woody who was at the burger stand. When he returned, he pulled a knife out of his pocket and showed it to Joel."

"And Joel shook his head," Chase added. "Was it because he didn't want to keep it, or was he telling his cousin it wasn't his?"

Summer gripped his forearm. "We have to go back to the park. Remember the evidence report? CSI found an unused burner phone in the hotel, and Woody's was in the snow by the Ferris wheel. So let's say Woody loses his phone, which forces Shultz to go to the hotel for the radios. Why use the radios if there was a perfectly good burner phone at the hotel?"

Chase smiled as excitement rushed through him. "Because he didn't know it was there."

"This just got wicked good," Rachel said.

"Yeah, it did," Sloan agreed. "If someone planted the knife, and Shultz couldn't figure out who did it, the guy had to be paranoid. He probably started questioning how the ballroom blew up, too."

"No doubt." Summer took the Coke can from Chase. "Fire investigators confirmed gas was used in place of kerosene." She sipped the pop. "Woody and Randy stayed at the Motel 6 in Lodi Thursday night. The employee who'd waited on them said they had checked in at three forty and, except to step outside for a cigarette, they never left until the next morning at six fifty."

Rachel tapped her keyboard. "It takes one hour and thirty-three minutes to drive from Newhouse Academy to the amusement park. If one of the boys is behind this, he could have gotten there right after the two men checked into the hotel, planted the phone, the knife—"

"Switched out the fuel," Chase finished. "And be back in time for dinner. Rachel, can you take another look into the boys' activities? I'm especially interested in bank transactions. None of the kidnappers had money, and couldn't afford to buy the guns and supplies."

"Can do. How far back should I look?"

"Shultz bought the first gun in October, but I'd go back a few months prior."

"How about credit card activity?"

"It's one thing to hack into World Privacy," Summer began, "but I'd rather get a search warrant for banking and credit card information. If one of these boys was in on the kidnapping, we need to make sure we do this right. I don't want him to get a lesser sentence because of a technicality."

"Fair enough. But what about the school's video surveillance?" Rachel asked. "It's my understanding you've only requested video from the morning of the kidnapping. It'd be interesting to see which kid left the campus on Thursday."

"Good idea. I'll contact the headmaster."

"I need to run." Sloan stacked his papers and stood. "Lemme know how this ends."

After Sloan left, Rachel said, "If you contact the headmaster, he's going to want to know why." She tiptoed her fingers across the table. "Are you sure you want anyone outside of us and your agents to know?"

When Summer met his gaze, there was indecision in her eyes. "No one has to know but us," he said.

"You can access their security system?" she asked Rachel.

"I'm not sure, but I can try."

They talked with Rachel for a few more minutes, then ended the call. Summer leaned into the couch cushions. "I'm not comfortable knowing Rachel is hacking on our behalf."

"Again, we're the only ones who know." He stood, then took her hand and forced her to rise. "Put on some warm clothes. We need to take another look at the park."

13

Horizon Pointe Estates, Avon, Ohio
Monday, January 23rd, 1:36 p.m. Eastern Standard Time

"HEY, BUDDY. WHERE'VE you been?" his mom asked as she exited the office.

None of your fucking business. "Just driving around." He headed for the kitchen in search of something to eat.

"Are you doing okay, honey?"

Honey, Buddy, sweetie…God, he liked it better when she ignored him. The cute names bugged the crap out of him and sounded fake. "I'm fine." When he reached the kitchen, his mouth watered. "What's that smell?"

His mom went to the crockpot and lifted the lid. The aroma instantly grew stronger. "Pot roast with potatoes, onions and carrots, just the way you like it. I also thought I'd make green beans and bake beer bread."

"Are you going to add bacon and onion to the green beans?" he asked, and started making himself a ham sandwich.

"Of course." She smiled. "I know that's your favorite."

"So is beer bread."

She set the lid back on the pot. "I talked to Mr. Kavel about you leaving the academy. He said you aren't the only student not returning."

"Really? Who else?" he asked. He didn't care, but he'd rather talk about that than have her start questioning his *feelings* again. Yesterday's drive to Newhouse had been miserable. For two hours and ten minutes, he had to listen to her go on and on about how worried she'd been, how he needed to open up to her, how they needed to communicate. She'd also talked about Emma, and how she wanted him and his sister to join her in family counseling.

That'd be a big fucking no.

For one thing, she knew how he hated the idea of therapy. He didn't want anybody in his head. Secondly, she and Emma would be dead soon, so what was the point? Even if she bribed him with money he wouldn't go. He had five hundred thousand sitting in an offshore account.

"Dillon Patricks, Chris Demko and Evan Barry aren't returning to school," his mom replied.

The senator's grandson, the knife-wielding psycho and the Eagle Scout. Dillon and Chris didn't surprise him. The senator was a well-known figure and would probably want his grandson at a school that offered more security than Newhouse. He wouldn't be too shocked if Headmaster Kavel ended up getting fired over the kidnapping. The man should have personally taken care of Joel's background check. Because he hadn't, Shultz had been able to kill Stokes, bring in his own driver and had Joel to help him keep the team under control. As for Chris not returning... After the way the kid had snapped on Shultz, ramming the knife into the guy's chest, he pictured Chris dealing with years of therapy. Evan, on the other hand, did surprise him. He was a senior, one of the more levelheaded guys on the team, and he'd expected the kid to finish out the year and graduate from Newhouse.

"Hear anything else about Brennan and Alex?" he asked, and finished making his sandwich.

"Brennan is still the same. But Alex is awake," she said, her tone positive. "When he's up for visitors, you should go see him."

I can't. I'll be grieving over your and Emma's deaths. "Sure." He snagged a Mountain Dew from the fridge, then a bag of Doritos from the pantry. "I'm going to eat in my room."

Ignoring the disappointment on her face, he headed upstairs. Once in his room, he searched for the TV remote. As he looked on the dresser, he heard his sister's door close. Curious, and in the mood to fuck with her, he cracked open his door and spotted her red head as she rounded the corner to go downstairs. Though his stomach grumbled, he'd eat in a minute. For now, he wanted to see what the recluse was doing.

Since coming here Saturday night, he'd only seen her a couple of times, and she had yet to say a word to him. Her fear was a good thing, and would make his plans that much easier to accomplish. Even though his mom was a bitch for moving without telling him, he didn't want to personally kill her. He wasn't exactly sure why, because it wasn't as if he loved her. He loved her money and what it could do for him. Whatever the reason didn't matter. She still had to go, and Emma was going to do it for him.

He snuck out of his room and down the stairs. When he heard the front door close, he quietly raced back to his room then looked out of the window to where he'd parked his car in the driveway. Anger clouded his vision, had him shaking. What the fuck was his sister doing by his car?

She tried the doors, but they were locked. Then she looked inside. Hugging herself, she hurried back into the house.

Wanting to pounce on the bitch and teach her to mind her own business, he left his bedroom. As he neared the staircase, he told himself to be calm, and that he would soon get even. He still continued down the steps. When Mom and Emma began talking, he stopped on the bottom stair.

"Where did he go?" Emma asked.

"Up to his room."

"No, where was he this morning? He left at nine. What has he been doing for the past four and a half hours?"

His mom sighed and dishes clanked. "I don't know, Em. He said he went for a drive. So much has happened to him in such a short period of time. He needs to find ways to cope with the murders and kidnapping. I'm sure he's probably worried about starting at a new school, too. He doesn't know anyone around here. He doesn't even know much about his own home."

"He deserves everything that's happened to him," Emma said, her tone filled with hatred.

Metal thumped against a hard surface. "Really? Tell that to the two boys in ICU. Did they, or any of them, deserve what happened?" Mom sighed again. "We've been over this before, and I don't want to discuss it again. I'd like for the three of us to go to family counseling."

Emma laughed. "What a joke. He won't do it, but sure, I'll go. I'll tell the counselor what he did to me. Maybe *they'll* believe me. No one else has."

"No one else? Oh, God. Emma, did you tell your psychiatrist your brother made you cut yourself?"

"Yep. Don't worry. Your poor innocent baby boy is safe. My doctor was as bad as you, and didn't believe me."

"Em—"

"Did you notice when he left he had a backpack with him?" Emma asked.

Worried his mom would eventually grow suspicious if his sister kept planting dark seeds in her head, he took that last step and made sure his foot hit the hardwood floor with a thud. Emma stopped talking. Thank God. He *had* left with a backpack filled with the laptop and burner phones that he had wiped clean and smashed. He'd gone in search of a place where he could dump the evidence in Lake Erie. Since part of the lake was frozen, he'd had to drive quite a distance to find a thawed area. Now the backpack, weighed down with rocks, along with the evidence, was at the bottom of the lake.

"Emma," he said, entering the kitchen. "Where've you been hiding?"

Emma's face turned red and her gaze lit with terror and hatred. She looked to her mom, then rushed from the room. Good.

Problem solved.

"What's with her?" He took another pop from the fridge. "She acts as if *I'm* the bad guy."

"I know, and I'm sorry. She's...I don't know what to do with her." Mom dried her hands with a paper towel and stared at him with worry. "Where did you drive to this morning? You were gone a long time."

Shit. The dark seed had taken root. "I drove to Vermillion and parked by the cottage you and Dad used to take us to in the summer."

Her eyes softened as she approached him. "I didn't think you liked going there," she said, brushing his bangs off his forehead.

The hugging, the affection, was suffocating. Even as a little kid—for whatever reason—he hadn't liked being held. "I don't know," he said. "I guess, looking back, it wasn't that bad. And it was the last place we went to for a vacation with Dad. Maybe that's why I went there."

"When I'm feeling down, I often take myself back to happy times, too. I think we do this because our minds need to be reminded that it's not always bad, and if we work at it, tomorrow can be a good day."

He forced a grin. "I think you're right. I'm pretty down about Alex and Brennan. And I don't know what to do about Coach Pembroke's funeral. I...don't think I can go."

She wrapped an arm around him. "No one is forcing you. But it'd be nice if you sent a card to his wife. Maybe say something nice about Coach."

"Yeah, I can do that." He started for the stairs. "What time is dinner? I might go see a movie later."

"By yourself?"

"Unless that's a problem?"

"No, but why not stay here? We can put on a fire and watch something together. We haven't done that in so long."

He'd rather be back at the park freezing off his ass. But he supposed he could give her one movie night, and didn't see anything wrong with allowing her a tiny bit of happiness before the shit-storm hit. After all, she was going to be dead soon.

Ottawa Lake Amusement Park, Village of Ottawa, Ohio
Monday, January 23rd, 2:56 p.m. Eastern Standard Time

Summer shivered and pulled her thick scarf to cover her mouth and nose. The temperature hovered around twenty degrees, but with the wind chill it was closer to six and the icy air made it difficult to breathe. Fortunately, they didn't have to trudge through several feet of snow. Plows had come through yesterday in order to remove the bus and getaway car, and the areas not plowed were packed down from the number of investigators who'd walked over the snow.

"Looks like a war zone," Chase said as they stood in front of what had been the ballroom. Snow coated most of the charred wood. The trees that had surrounded the backside of the building had either burned down to stumps or were covered with black soot. She glanced to the right of the building where a small pocket of burnt trees remained.

"This must be where Shultz shot Alex and Clay," she said.

Chase nodded. "And where Shultz had the boys looking for the bus keys."

Nick Janson, the boy who'd taken the keys, had stated that he had placed the keys under one of the ballroom's floorboards. Investigators had recovered them once the fire had cooled, and had used them to drive the bus from the park.

She walked toward the left side of the decimated structure and to where the woods hugged the plowed path to the hotel. After looking over her shoulder to where the bus had been, she refocused on the woods. "The explosion happens. Brennan and Chris take Alex to the bus, and Brennan runs this way."

"Right. Which boy chased after him?"

"*If* Brennan was attacked. He could have fallen," she reminded him. She still didn't want to believe one of the boys could be responsible for setting up the kidnapping. But Chase had been right from the start. The evidence didn't match what the kids had told them. Couple that with the Bitcoin transaction, and she had no choice but to follow up on their suspicions.

"Every kid said they were busy helping move gear from the building." She imagined the chaos, the fear. "I think it would've been easy for one of the boys to sneak away, assault Brennan, then head back before anyone noticed that he'd left."

"I do, too. Let's go to the hotel."

When they reached the dilapidated building, there was nothing inside but old wooden planks. After they'd talked with Rachel, Summer had called Rich to ask him for more details about the burner phone's location. The unused phone had been telling. Again, why would Shultz give Woody a two-way radio when he had a phone? "Rich said the phone was found here." She pointed her flashlight to the corner of the room. "Behind planks, and covered with dead grass and leaves."

"There wasn't much snow here on Thursday. Our bad kid would've been able to gather the grass and leaves." His breath hung on the air as he also used a flashlight to look around the room. "The SUV was where we're standing. The kids who hauled out the kerosene said the cans were against the wall behind the vehicle. The phone was found to the right...and what is this?" He walked over to the left wall and moved a piece of wood aside. "Dead grass and leaves. Coincidence?"

Despite the gravity of what the evidence suggested, excitement worked through her. She'd been in a management role for nearly two years, and had missed working in the field, the hunt, the mystery. She shook her head. "I don't think so. Chris Demko didn't see Shultz with the knife until after they'd been in here. Same with a few other kids. It's possible the knife had been under the leaves and grass."

"Let's put ourselves in Shultz's position," Chase suggested as they left the building and walked toward the Ferris wheel. "The ballroom explodes. Shultz wonders how, but maybe chalks it up as an accident. But then he finds a knife that doesn't belong to any of his crew."

"Now he's paranoid. Would a paranoid man kill the only person he can trust? From everything we've gathered about the cousins, it's clear they were as close as brothers."

"Only if Joel tried to attack him. But I don't believe that happened. Most of the boys said Joel acted very nervous, and we know he has no history of violence."

They reached the fun house. When she'd been here in the dark, with two dead bodies laid outside it, the place had been eerie. In the light of day, with the stark white snow covering the worn building and faded lettering across the top, the fun house was downright creepy.

"I want to take a look inside," Chase said, making his way up the steps.

Since she'd viewed the photos of the interior—which had been dark, the walls covered with modern graffiti and faded drawings of disturbing clowns—she would rather not join him. But curiosity outweighed the creep factor, so she followed him. "Do you want to try to reenact what happened?"

"Even in the daylight, it's dark in here," Chase said, stepping inside. "It has be pitch black at night."

"The boys said a lantern was hanging off a nail outside the door. It wouldn't give them much light, but they would've been able to see Joel's shadow."

"It would depend on which direction Joel moved." Chase directed the flashlight around the room, touched on the graffiti and faded clowns, and on the blood stain Alex had left behind, then on the back of the room.

"Turn off the light," she said, gripping his arm as the thrill of the chase gripped her from the inside. "Look. In the corner. Outside light is coming through the wood."

He turned off the flashlight and walked toward what she thought might be an opening. "Light's coming through in a bunch of places. The building isn't insulated and the wood is separating in plenty of spots."

When they reached the corner, Chase knelt and turned on the flashlight again. Part of the floorboard had been removed, and the light revealed fresh cut marks. There were even a few black fibers attached to the jagged edges of the wood.

Chase moved the light along the wall, then ran his gloved hand over the wood planks. One piece moved. "Hold this." After handing her the flashlight and using both hands, he slid two planks to either side, creating an opening. "I couldn't fit through this, but someone smaller and thinner could."

Chase stood close to six-foot-three, and was around one hundred and ninety pounds with broad shoulders. There were several boys on the team that had a similar build and wouldn't be able to fit through this hole. But she could. Ready to act out how one of the boys had escaped to possibly kill Joel, she took off her scarf and unzipped her coat.

"What are you doing?" he asked.

"Reenacting."

"It's freezing. I don't want you to get sick, and I don't know what's beyond the opening."

"Then go outside and wait below. Take my coat and scarf with you."

"Summer."

She slid the plank. "Chase," she said, and put her boots through the opening. "Better hurry."

Chase swore and rushed from the fun house. While she waited for him to make it outside, she once again looked around the dark room. Bad Kid, as Chase now referred to their suspect, could have easily escaped without anyone noticing. The darkness would have cloaked him, and his teammates' fear, exhaustion and lack of sustenance would had them focusing on their circumstances, not what he was doing in the corner of the room.

Chase tapped her boot. "Ready when you are."

Freezing, and anxious to put on her coat, she slipped through the opening with ridiculous ease and quietly landed in the snow.

As she put on her coat, and Chase moved the wood back in place, she looked at the naked saplings, larger trees and bushes that were about one foot, maybe more, from the building, then to the ground. The snow wasn't smooth but lumpy, and reminded her of the photographs the forensic investigators had taken. "Remember the crime scene photos? There were footprints all along the back of the fun house, and at the sides."

He wrapped the scarf around her neck. "If Bad Kid did escape through the human doggy door, he'd have left prints in the snow. But those prints would've got mixed in with the ones the boys made when they walked around the back of the building."

"The kid is smart."

"Diabolical. But he's made mistakes, and we're going to catch him." He took her hand. "Come this way."

Holding Chase's hand was as natural as breathing. It amazed her how easily she could picture him in her future, when a week ago she'd worried over telling him about the baby, and possibly never hearing from him again. They still had work ahead of them, but yesterday had been a strong start. The line of communication was open and they both wanted to make their relationship work. While she still struggled with the idea that Chase might become a negotiator again, at least he now knew why she didn't want him working that job.

He stopped them at the corner of the building where the landing had rotted. "We found Joel here. What if Bad Kid came out of the hole, then walked over to here. Maybe Joel is by the door, the kid gets his attention, he comes over and *bam*. He gets his throat slit."

She took another step and stared at the fun house door. "If the lantern was on a nail, wouldn't the boys inside have seen Joel walk across the landing?"

"Not if he took the steps and walked in front of it."

"Good point." She studied the landing, the snowy ground, the side of the building. "Where did Bad Kid get the knife? And I'm thinking he had a phone. How else would Shultz have known we made the five-hundred-thousand-dollar deposit?"

"If Bad Kid left a burner phone and knife in the hotel, he must've planted a few more around the park."

As an idea occurred to her, she gripped his hand. "The explosion. Bad Kid switched the fuels hoping for an explosion. If the ballroom blew, Shultz would have been forced to move them and the fire would've given the kid a moment when eyes weren't on him."

"How much do you want to bet he had a phone stashed outside near the ballroom?" Chase asked, the eagerness in his eyes matching her own. "And with the ballroom gone, the fun house was the only building that would fit the team."

"A building he'd rigged for escape."

He released her and began walking toward the back of the building. As he did, he concentrated on the lower portion of the structure.

"What are you looking for?" she asked.

"Somewhere he could've used to store a knife. If he planted one at the hotel with the intent to arm himself, either he wasn't one of the kids who'd gone there, or he didn't have a chance to grab it." He used the toe of his boot to clear away snow. "And if he planted a couple of phones around the park, why wouldn't he do the same with knives? Why not have backups and—" He stopped and looked at her, a smile tilting his mouth.

"Hurry up and look," she urged him.

He quickly crouched and dusted off the snow with his glove until a small wooden box—big enough to hold the knife—was exposed. She stood behind him and held her breath as he opened it. Empty. Though disappointed, this was a huge find for them. The box was new and in no way matched the wood from the original building. Bad Kid had to have been the one to plant it here.

Chase stood. "Ready for my theory? Bad Kid is banking on the gas blowing up one of the heaters so that he can get out of the ballroom."

"But is he one of the boys who carried the gas back to the building?"

He half shrugged. "Doesn't matter. He planted the fuel. Whoever poured it was nothing but a casualty."

"Right. The kid wouldn't care. He just needed out of the ballroom."

"Exactly. So he gets his chance, sees Brennan run and wants to stop him."

This is where the investigation was fuzzy to her. "For what purpose? He had to know that once there was an explosion, the cops would come."

"True. But remember several of the boys said Brennan had overheard Shultz say he and Joel went to the farmhouse. There's a path by the hotel leading to the lake, and Brennan wasn't too far from there. Let's say the kid got to the farmhouse before the deputies and fire truck were dispatched."

Her mind worked quickly. "If Brennan had alerted the authorities, we would have told the county sheriff and fire department not to approach the park. Taggart would've had his men surround the place, then take the kidnappers by surprise. Bad Kid wasn't ready for the kidnapping to be over. *That's* why he tried to take out Brennan."

"God, we have great minds." Chase gave her a quick, unexpected kiss. "Bad Kid couldn't let the kidnapping be over too soon because he needed to make sure his crew was dead."

"Otherwise Shultz could have told us about the person who'd paid for the weapons and supplies."

Chase stepped backward and pointed toward the landing. "Bad Kid escapes, kills Joel with the knife he had stashed, leaves it for the others to find with the body and goes back inside. We know the kids realized Joel was quiet and decided to head out of the building. Bad Kid had to hope the boys didn't run, because he still needed to kill Shultz."

Good Lord, the boy was an evil genius. "Instead, he got the entire team to do it for him." The medical examiner wouldn't have his final report to them for a few weeks, but his preliminary findings indicated that Shultz had ultimately died of traumatic asphyxiation. He'd had six broken ribs, some of which had punctured both lungs and caused them to collapse. She was sure the three gunshot wounds to the thigh, stomach and shoulder hadn't helped, along with the stab wound to the chest.

"Then he took Shultz's phone and continued to give the performance of his life." He took her hand again and they started walking toward the gate. "We've been snowed by a greedy kid. But which one?"

"My team is working on financial records." She walked closer to him, hoping to steal some of his warmth. "Between them and Rachel, I'm hoping we can narrow down the list. We know for sure Alex and Brennan aren't involved, but that still leaves us with thirteen kids."

"We can narrow the list further thanks to the human doggy door. You're five-six and weigh—"

"None of your business."

He chuckled. "The point I was trying to make is that you slid out of there without a problem. I think anyone over five-ten and weighing more than one hundred and sixty pounds would have a hard time. That's a wild guess, and we'd have to test it."

"If Rachel can hack World Privacy and get us a name, we won't need to test anything." As they drew closer to the gate, she nudged him toward the burger stand, then stopped. "One thing still bothers me. Actually, two. The snowmobile and how Shultz planned to leave here once the ransom had been paid."

"We assumed Shultz knew nothing about the snowmobile."

They'd discovered that the snowmobile had been reported stolen last week from a farm in Marietta, Ohio, not far from where Randy had lived with Woody. From there, they'd concluded that the two men had hidden the snowmobile from Shultz and the others as a backup escape plan. "True. Then that would mean Bad Kid didn't know about it, either."

He looked at her. "What point are you trying to make?"

She shrugged and moved closer to him. "I'm not sure. But I keep coming back to *why* this was the chosen location. If Bad Kid set up the kidnapping, there had to be a reason why he picked this park. And I'd think Shultz and his men would've questioned the choice."

"Maybe the kid promised them a safe way out of here, knowing they wouldn't get the opportunity."

"Because he planned to find a way to kill them all," she said, hating the morbid thought. To think a teenager, a kid barely old enough to drive, could be so cold-blooded was not only scary, but sad. If they were right, the boy had orchestrated the kidnapping, had ordered the murders of his coach and the bus driver, assaulted Brennan and slit Joel's throat. What else could he do? What else *would* he do in the future?

"On that note..." Chase led her back to the car. "What do you want to do now?"

"Go home and get warm."

"I know how to heat you up," he said with a sly grin.

Her cold body instantly warmed. "You did a great job of it this morning."

He scrunched his brow in confusion. "I was going to suggest chicken noodle soup, but if sex is what you want, I'm game."

"You were not." She shook her head and grinned. She'd missed the teasing, fun Chase. "Now that you've mentioned soup, I'm craving some. I could go for broccoli cheese, though."

"I'll stop for takeout on our way home."

"And I'll call the office to see if they have any leads we can use."

Summer's House, Fairview Park, Ohio
Monday, January 23rd, 6:11 p.m. Eastern Standard Time

Chase brought over the soup and sandwiches he'd picked up for them, then set the food on the table. Since Summer's team was still researching the boys' finances, and he hadn't heard from

Rachel yet, he looked forward to simply hanging out with Summer tonight. They'd already agreed to not discuss the case, and to focus on themselves instead. He hoped that focus involved the two of them in bed later. After not having been with her in five months, a quick round of sex in the shower wasn't enough.

"Need anything else?" he asked her as she sat at the table looking warm and comfy in a pair of pajamas. After traipsing around in the cold for a couple hours, they'd both been chilled to the bone. The moment they'd arrived back home, he'd also exchanged jeans for a thick pair of sweats.

"No thanks. Would you please stop waiting on me and sit. You're making me feel bad." Steam rose from her broccoli cheddar soup as she stirred it. "If I want something, I'll get it."

"I like taking care of you." When he lifted the lid off his chicken noodle soup, his mouth watered. "I didn't do enough of that when we were together." Which was the truth. These past few days had him looking back on their relationship, past the shooting, and beyond his personal issues.

He hadn't always been selfish or controlling, and had certainly never meant to treat Summer in a way that had hurt her. Thinking about his time with CNU made him realize the job *had* changed him. He'd been consumed by moving up the ranks, worked too much, and had expected Summer to take care of everything else while he was gone. He couldn't recall how many nights he had come home late to discover his dinner on a plate in the fridge, a cute note from Summer attached to it. Or how many times he had returned from a negotiation that had taken him out of state for days or weeks to find out something major had happened at the house and Summer had to take care of it on her own.

Over the years, she'd fixed minor things around the house, painted, had learned to change light fixtures and had become a skilled landscaper. Their rental house hadn't had a big yard, but Summer would mow it, trim the hedges and plant flowers. He'd helped occasionally, but his job had made it difficult to participate in household chores. Instead of ever thanking her for holding down the fort when he'd been gone, he had taken her for granted. Just another regret to add to the list of his many fuck-ups when it came to Summer.

"You took care of me," she said, tearing off a piece of the baguette that accompanied her soup. "Who dealt with my car's oil changes, tires and whatever else? That'd be you. You worked around the yard, the house…"

"I might've helped with the car, but you did those other things." While the soup warmed him from the inside, his face heated with embarrassment. He was supposed to be the man. The guy who took care of his woman, and he'd dropped the ball. "I wasn't a good partner."

She stared at him for a moment, her gaze holding regret. "If you weren't, we wouldn't be having a baby. And when you were home, you did help around the house. I've never resented you because your job forced you to travel or work late, or that I had to learn how to be a handywoman. My dad still does everything for my mom. Changing a light bulb is probably the extent of her fixer skills. It's nice to know I can take care of myself." She dipped the spoon into the soup. "I resented how the job had changed you, but we've been over that."

Right. And she didn't need to say anything else about it. Except, if he decided to apply for a position with the Cuyahoga County Sheriff or the Cleveland PD, they would have to discuss the job move. He'd been fooling himself to think he could find employment outside of law enforcement. He had no other job skills except investigating and negotiating, and honestly no desire to do anything else but go after bad guys.

"I'm sorry," she said. "I shouldn't have thrown that last line out there. I'm not trying to make you feel bad or anything."

"You're reminding me why I shouldn't apply for a job here in Cleveland. I get it." He tore off a piece of bread. "I could be a stay-at-home dad. You go to work, and I'll take care of the baby and the house."

Her eyes unreadable, she used a napkin to wipe her mouth.

"That would require you to move back in with me."

"Correct. I can sleep on the pullout couch in the office, if that's what you want," he suggested, though there was no way that would happen. Not after sleeping with her last night. If he was going to live under the same roof as Summer, they were going to share a room, the bed, everything…even his last name.

She half-laughed and shook her head. "Sleeping in separate rooms lasted for about an hour last night, so I can't see that happening." She leaned back. "It'd be nice to have you here, helping with the baby."

"Is that the only reason?" he asked, hopeful, yet not wanting to push. They had history together, but hadn't been in a relationship for a year. He didn't want to bully his way back into her life.

"No. You did a great job on de-icing the walkway." She grinned. "And you're handy in the shower."

"Well, at least I'm good for something. Have you thought about any baby names?" he asked, ready to change the subject. He didn't want to think about his faults, or a past he couldn't change. He also wanted to get sex off his brain. If he had it his way, they wouldn't be eating. Instead, he would find other ways to warm their chilled bodies.

"A little." She picked at the baguette. "I like old school names like Betty or Alice for a girl, and maybe Henry or Albert for a boy. What do you think of those?"

He hid his dislike. "Would you nickname Henry Hank?"

"Why would I do such a thing? You hate the names, don't you?"

"Hate is a strong word, but I'm not a fan. What's wrong with Reagan for a girl?"

"It makes me think of Ronald Reagan, and the girl from *The Exorcist*."

Now he did, too. "Daphne?"

"Too Scooby-Doo."

True, damn it. "Brooke?"

"No way. I knew a girl in high school named Brooke. She was

a slut and bully. She used to pick on me, until I gave her a reason to stop." She smiled. "It was worth the suspension."

He chuckled as he remembered Summer telling him about the fight. "We have time to come up with a name, and we might as well wait until we know the sex before we get into a heated debate about it."

"Agreed. Same with the color of the baby's room. I'm leaning toward apple green for a boy and lilac for a girl." She frowned. "By the expression on your face, I can tell you don't like those ideas."

"I like lilac, but green is too boogery."

"You're comparing green paint to boogers? That's just gross."

"Sorry, I'm trying to make myself less attractive so we can get through dinner without you tearing off my clothes."

She laughed. "Is that what's happening? How did you know I was ready to ravage you on the kitchen table?"

God, he'd missed her laugh and smile. Thanks to him, she hadn't done enough of that during their last year together. "Just a hunch. You've got this hungry look in your eyes."

"Oh, that." She pointed to the counter behind him. "I was thinking about those chocolate cheesecake cupcakes you made."

"And how I could spread frosting on your body and lick it off?"

She laughed again. "Sounds messy. We'd require a shower, which, by the way, was how I think we made this baby. When you were in town last August, we used condoms all weekend, except the one time we showered together."

Summer had taken birth control pills during the years they'd been a couple. After he'd moved out, she had stopped taking the pill. That had been what she'd told him last summer, and why he had stocked up on condoms for the weekend. But he'd been so used to making love to her without having to worry about contraceptives, he hadn't worn a condom in the shower. Now they were having a baby.

He picked up half the turkey sandwich he'd ordered for them. "That's just another reason to love that shower," he said as the doorbell rang. "Are you expecting someone?"

Her brows furrowed. "No."

Chase reached the foyer the same time Summer peeked through the curtains hanging across the front windows. "There's a delivery truck backed into the driveway," she said. "Must be a mistake. I didn't order anything."

Damn. He'd forgotten to cancel the baby furniture.

"Aren't you going to answer?" she asked when the doorbell rang again.

He let out a sigh and braced himself for an argument. "Don't be mad."

She let go of the curtain. "About?"

"I ordered baby furniture." He held up his hands. "*Before* we talked about my control issues. I forgot to cancel. I'm sorry. It wasn't my place. I'll return everything."

Her gaze was more curious than angry as she moved past him and opened the door. She greeted the driver, then had him and his helpers follow her to the guest room. Two of the three boxes were huge, and Chase had to move the bed in order to make them fit. Once the delivery had been finished, Summer closed, then locked the door.

"You're mad," he said. Without a word, she went to the kitchen, returned with a pair of scissors, then headed for the guest room. "Again, I'm sorry. I was trying to help, not take the fun out of setting up the nursery."

She kept her back to him as she cut away the cardboard, then the protective wrap surrounding the five-drawer chest.

"I bought a three piece set," he continued. "I'll have to put the crib together, but it converts to a toddler bed, then eventually a full-sized bed. The seven-drawer dresser can be used as a changing table. And I figured the espresso color was good because it wouldn't show dirty fingerprints. I also thought that if we have a girl, we can change out the drawer handles and replace them with something more feminine, maybe crystal or whatever." He waited a moment and stared at her back. "Tell me I'm a dick, or that you love it. I don't care. Just say something."

She set the scissors on top of the longer box, then faced him. Tears shimmered in her eyes, along with…desire. What? Impossible. She should be angry, not hot for him.

"I have been looking at baby furniture for months, so have my mom and sisters. They've been making me crazy because they all hate every style I've found, and I haven't liked any of their suggestions. You have taken a huge burden off my shoulders."

"I have?" Relieved, he relaxed. "You like the set?"

"I love it." She walked toward him. "It's practical and the color is perfect. Your idea about knobs is a great one." When she reached him, she twined her arms around his neck. "Thank you."

"You're sure you're not mad?" he asked, still not certain what was happening here.

"Mad?" She slid a hand from behind his neck to his chest, then lower. "Total opposite." She cupped his groin. "The furniture makes me hot."

He glanced at the boxes and exposed chest, and wondered if he would ever truly understand women. "Now that I know that, I'll buy you a new desk tomorrow."

She chuckled as she stroked him through his sweats. "It's not the furniture, it's what you've done for me. You put thought into what would work for the baby now, and in the future. What's even hotter? You saved me from having to argue with my mother."

Although he loved Summer's mom, the woman could be incredibly nosey and bossy. "That was all part of my master plan," he said, running his fingers through her hair until he held her head.

She inched closer, darted her gaze from his eyes to his mouth. "A brilliant plan," she said, then kissed him, parted her lips and slid her tongue along his.

He tightened his hold on her head and deepened the kiss. Though he loved having her hand on his erection, this morning was the first time he'd had sex in five months. If she kept it up, he wouldn't last long, and he wanted to last. Wanted to taste her, touch her, fill her body and make her come.

She gasped against his lips when he lifted her, then immediately wrapped her legs around his back. "I'm too heavy for you to carry me," she said, moving her fingers through the back of his hair and pressing soft kisses along his jaw.

"Here I was just thinking I needed to feed you more. You're too light for a pregnant woman."

"You already won me over with the furniture, so you don't have to try to make me feel good about my body."

After entering the bedroom, he placed her on the bed and began tugging off her slippers and socks. "Do you think I'd lie about how you look to me? Do you think the extra pounds are going to make me stop wanting you?" He took her hand and forced her to stand, then pulled her pajama top over her head. After he pushed the bottoms over her hips, leaving her in only her panties and bra, he touched the slight swell of her belly. "You're carrying our baby, and sacrificing your body and health for me and our child. I've been in love with you almost from the moment we met. I love you more now than ever, and I didn't think that was possible." He let her remove his shirt, then went back to touching her stomach. "I will always regret leaving you."

"Stop." She went to her tiptoes and kissed him. "I don't want to hear about regrets or receive any more apologies. We can't redo the last year, but we can learn from it." Her hands slid under the waistband of his sweats as she turned him until his back faced the bed. "If you don't mind, I'd like to do a little less talking and a lot more touching."

"Can I talk dirty?" he joked, even though the regret was still there. But she was right. He couldn't undo his actions, he could only learn from them. And with the way she inched down his sweats, he didn't want to think about the past, he wanted to focus on this moment.

Her mouth tilted into a sexy smile and desire darkened her eyes. "You might not be able to talk at all." She yanked his sweats and underwear to his ankles, then gave him a shove, which, because she was so small in comparison to him, did little to move him. But anxious to see what she had in mind for them, he climbed on the bed and scooted to the center of the mattress.

"Why won't I be able to talk?" he asked as she stepped out of her panties. When she unhooked her bra and her full breasts spilled forward, he gripped his aching dick. "You're beautiful." He rolled over to take her hand. As she got onto the bed, instead of curling next to him or lying on her back, she straddled him. She curved her fingers through his and kissed him, hot and open-mouthed, then trailed her lips along his chest. Releasing his hand, she moved lower. Her silky hair fell over his skin as she drifted closer to his erection. After tossing her hair away from her face, she took his length in her hand and looked up at him.

"This is why," she said, and drew him deep in her mouth.

As she sucked and licked him, stroked his erection and cupped his balls, he couldn't form a coherent thought. He ran his fingers through her hair and followed the rhythm of her head, urging her to take him deeper. When she did, her warm, wet mouth, her hands and fingers...the intense pleasure was almost too much. Wanting the moment to last, but needing to make sure she came first, he held her head in place. She looked up at him. Damn, she looked so fucking sexy with her lips wrapped around the tip of his erection.

"Come here," he somehow managed, and forced her to slide back up his body. When they were chest to breast, he urged her to keep moving until her sex hovered above his mouth. "Sit."

She shook her head. "I...this is—"

Determined to have his way, he gripped her hips, forced her down, then kissed her labia. He used two fingers to part her swollen lips and slid his tongue along her. When he reached her clit, he gave the flesh a gentle suck. She gasped, leaned forward and used the top of the headboard for support. From between her thighs, he watched the rise and fall of her breasts, the pleasure crossing her face and flicked his tongue over her clit.

"Oh, my...like that," she murmured, and cupped one breast.

"More."

Even without touching himself or being touched, there was a good possibility he could come if he didn't stop. Her desire, her satisfaction was all that mattered to him. Holding her rear in place, he worked his tongue on her clit. When he slipped two fingers inside her heat, she released a throaty moan. Her soft pants and groans had him painfully hard. He could easily roll her onto her back and fill her, give himself and her what they needed. But he wanted her to come against his tongue, taste her passion.

Seconds later, her thighs trembled and she gripped the headboard with both hands. He knew Summer's body well, knew the signs and that she was about to climax. He pumped his fingers and darted his tongue along her clit until she tensed and tossed her head back with a low groan. Normally he might've let her catch her breath and enjoy the orgasmic buzz, but not today. He lifted her off him, moved her until her damp sex brushed his length, then reached between their bodies and held the base of his erection.

He met her gaze and pressed the head of his arousal against her heat. They both let out a satisfying sigh when she sat down on him.

"You want control?" he asked, and captured a tempting nipple. "Ride me. Set the pace."

She pressed her hands against his chest, then straddled him. "Gladly," she said, and bounced her sweet ass. God, how he'd missed her. This morning, in the shower, had been fantastic. But shower sex had made it difficult for them to be face to face. And he'd wanted to see her face, read her reaction, make sure she was enjoying herself.

She gripped his pecks. He looked from her parted lips to her eyes. She was staring at him with more love than he deserved and it humbled him. He'd put her through hell, yet she'd stuck with him. She hadn't changed the locks because she had wanted him to come home. She had stood by him during his darkest moments and he had still left. Which made him a piece of shit who had been given a second chance to redeem himself and appreciate this woman. Love her, care for her, be there for her...be the man she needed to stand by her side, raise their children... Children? Did he want more?

He gripped her hips and pumped his own. Hell, yes. He wanted the family he'd never truly had. And he wanted it with Summer.

"I want more," he said, driving deep inside her.

"I...yes," she hissed, and closed her eyes as her sex clenched around his length.

"I want more babies, more years with you." He drew her head down until their mouths were so close her breath fanned across his lips. "I want till death do us part."

She fell on top of him, kissed him and he took over, rocking his hips, and bringing them both to climax. As his orgasm ripped through him, he saw her crying tears of joy as she lay on a hospital bed looking down at their baby, a beach wedding, where they were surrounded by her family and friends, more babies...he saw their future. He wrapped his arms around her and cherished the moment. Cherished her.

While she lay limp along his body, he ran a hand down her back. "Thank you."

"For riding you?" she asked, her voice sleepy, satisfied.

He kissed the top of her head and grinned. "For not giving up on me."

She moved just enough to meet his gaze and cupped his jaw. "I loved you."

"Past tense?"

A slow smile curved her pretty mouth. "No." She rested her arm on his chest and her head in her hand. "Did you mean what you said about more babies and marriage?"

"I love you, I need you and want to spend the rest of my life with you. I didn't appreciate what we had until it was gone. And I don't want to lose another day with you." When she didn't respond, he asked, "Too soon?"

Tears filled her eyes. "Not at all," she said, and kissed him.

"Good." Physically and emotionally sated, he slid out of her and rolled her until she was curled against his chest. "I'm ready for bed."

She lifted her head and looked at the clock. "It's not even eight."

"Sorry," he said, fighting a yawn. "I've spent too many days apart from you. I swear, you're better than any sleep drug out there. Trust me. I know."

She rested her head against his chest, and also yawned. "I love you. Present tense."

He smiled and held her close. Then drifted off to sleep.

14

Summer's House, Fairview Park, Ohio
Tuesday, January 24ᵗʰ, 6:54 a.m. Eastern Standard Time

SUMMER FINISHED DRYING her hair. Instead of using the flat iron to straighten it, she decided to leave the natural waves to do their own thing. Which she preferred. Last October, after she hadn't heard from Chase in two months, and the day after she'd discovered she was pregnant, she'd had five inches lopped off her hair. The cut had been impulsive. She'd needed to be in control of something in her life. Plus, she'd wanted to retaliate against Chase, who had loved her hair long. But he'd gone AWOL again, and hadn't been around to look at her head. She'd sure showed him.

With a sigh, she continued on with her toiletries. What was she going to do about the man sleeping in her bed? They loved each other. Check. They were both excited and committed to having the baby. Check. The sex was better than ever. Triple check. They lived in separate states and his job was in Chicago. Double X. Chase could move in with her, so that problem was easy to solve. Finding a job wouldn't be an issue for him, either. With his references, he could work at one of the Cleveland area law enforcement agencies. Except she didn't like that idea. She wouldn't tell him what to do, but she refused to live with him again if he started to change back to the old Chase.

After glancing at her phone's screen and noting the time, she let out another sigh. She wasn't in the mood to head to the office. There were reports to be read, case files to look over, agents to manage, and she'd do all of this from behind her desk or sitting at the table in the briefing room. Yesterday had been fun. She'd loved brainstorming with Chase and his CORE people, then walking through the park and trying to make sense of the evidence.

When she had been a special agent, she'd enjoyed the investigation aspect of her job, but she'd wanted to move up and be boss. The pay was better and she hoped to one day run her own field office. And while she was good at managing her team, the position carried plenty of stress with it. She usually didn't work weekends or holidays, but she was almost always at the office by seven a.m. and tended to put in twelve-hour days. Once the baby came, and their child was in daycare, she wouldn't want to put in those long hours. If she did, she'd see her baby for only a few hours a day.

Her sisters were stay-at-home moms, and their mother had been, too. The idea of being at home, all day, every day, didn't appeal to her, though. She loved working, loved being challenged and loved the income. Too bad she couldn't work part-time, and find a happy medium to the whole work-life balance thing.

She let go of those thoughts and considered the day ahead of her. Since Chase was still here, she had seeing him after work to look forward to. Hopefully, between her team and CORE, they could narrow down their list of suspects and begin interviewing some of the kids and their families. Chase would probably like to take part in those interviews, which she wouldn't mind. She enjoyed working with him. They hadn't always agreed on aspects of this investigation, but they were both open-minded enough to compromise and take each other's theories into consideration. When he'd been with the FBI Cleveland Division, he hadn't worked for her team, so she had never had the opportunity to watch him in action. Now that she had, she'd love to work with him on other cases. Not as a boss, but a partner.

Partner. Till death do us part.

Chase wanted more babies. More years. She wanted the same, but she also didn't want to have to choose between career and a family. She didn't want to spend her days in an office while someone else raised her babies.

She finished her makeup, shut off the bathroom light and went back into the bedroom to change. Careful not to wake Chase, she quietly opened the closet door and searched for one of her suits in the dark.

The light from the nightstand brightened the room. She turned. Chase was on his back, a couple of pillows propped behind his head, the sheet and comforter covering his lower half but leaving his muscular chest exposed. When he gave her a sleepy smile, she had the urge to crawl back in bed with him and pick up where they'd left off last night.

"Morning," he said.

"Morning." Now that she could see inside her closet, she pulled out one of her many black suits. She couldn't allow his body or sex to distract her. The sooner she went to the office, the sooner she could make it back home. "How'd you sleep?"

"Great. That's two nights in a row where I didn't wake up in the middle of the night."

She set the clothes on the bed. "Must be my mattress."

He chuckled. "Or the woman on it. Take off that robe and come back to bed." He pulled the sheet and comforter aside and revealed his erection straining against his cotton boxer briefs.

She quickly looked away. "Don't tempt me. I have to get to work. But you can save that for later."

"It'll be waiting for you," he said, covering himself.

She finished buttoning her blouse, then stepped into her pants. "What are your plans for today?"

"I'll check in with CORE and follow up on any leads Rachel has found for us. If I have time, I'll put the crib together. What do you want to do with the guest bed?"

"I'm not sure. This is when I wish we had a bigger house. My parents are going to want to come visit after the baby is born. My sisters, too. We're going to need a place for them, and I don't want them to have to use the pullout bed in the office."

"Then let's get a bigger place. Or, we can make a section of the basement your office. How often do you use it anyway?"

The basement had been finished, and wasn't one of those dark, creepy, spider-filled spaces. "That's a good idea."

"I'll ask Tony to come over this weekend and help me move the office furniture. Maybe he and his wife can stay for dinner. It's been a long time since we've done that." He started to stretch, then stopped. "Never mind. You're supposed to go to Florida."

And miss out on spending time with Chase? "I think I'm going to postpone the trip."

"You hate this weather. Go see your folks and get some sun before seasonal depression catches up with you."

He knew her too well, and that she hated the gray skies constantly hanging over the Cleveland area. "Why don't you come with me? My parents would love to see you. We can fly down in a couple weeks."

"I'd like that," he said with a grin. "Are you still going to wear a bikini and show off your baby bump?"

"Uh, no." She half-laughed. "I'll leave that to pregnant celebrities." She finished adjusting the waist expander on her pants, then put on her suit coat. "Do you think it's weird we're having this conversation?"

"About bikinis and baby bumps?"

She sat next to him and gave his arm a light pinch. "You know what I mean."

He took her hand. "We've known each other for eight years, lived together for almost seven. I don't think it's weird that we're able to move past the bad and fall back into a familiar routine. If anything, it shows we have a strong relationship." He kissed her knuckles. "One worth fighting for, don't you think?"

She nodded. "The problem is I think too much."

"What's on your mind? Let's talk it out."

She glanced to the clock. Explaining her concerns about both of their careers would take too long. "Later, over dinner. Who's cooking tonight?"

"I'm determined to wow you with my culinary skills, so I've got dinner. And I promise no pecans or mustard will touch your food."

She grinned, then kissed him. "I'll call you after I meet with my team. Fingers crossed we have some leads."

"I'll do the same," he said, then pulled her in for another kiss. This one wasn't quick, but slow, sensual and lingering. When he cupped her breast, then grazed her nipple with his thumb, she pulled away with reluctance.

"You're making it hard for me to leave you."

"Good." He kissed her again. "Because I don't ever want you to leave me," he said, his gaze serious, intense.

"Do you think I'd welcome you home only to leave out of spite?" she asked, knowing he wasn't talking about work. "If so, you need to get over it. That's not how I operate. If I were going to seek revenge, I'd shave your eyebrows."

He grinned. "You're pure evil."

"I know," she said, then, after one more kiss, left for work.

Forty minutes later and irritated she'd spent half the drive stuck in traffic, she entered her office. Before she had her coat off, Dave called her to ask if they had the boys' financial records. She liked working for Dave, but the man could be a pain in the butt. When he wanted something from her, he wanted it then and there, and didn't understand that her magic wand was broken.

She explained she'd just arrived, but would have a meeting with her team within the hour. After ending the call, she then contacted the agents working on the financials and asked them to head to the briefing room in fifteen minutes. Once she'd answered a few emails and skimmed through her daily To Do list, she gathered her notebook and left the office.

Dave caught up with her in the hallway. "I want to sit in on this." When they reached the briefing room, and everyone was seated, he said, "Before we begin, I want to make it clear that none of what we're doing can be leaked. If the media catches a whiff of this, it won't look good for us. We just rescued fifteen kids who went through a horrible ordeal, and there will be people who will think *we're* the bad guys for suspecting one of those boys is a murderer and kidnapper."

Lauren cocked a brow, while Tony and Rich looked offended.

"Other than Chase, no one outside of this room knows about our suspicions," Summer said, leaving out that Rachel and Sloan were aware. Dave was a by-the-book kind of guy, and wouldn't appreciate that she hadn't discouraged Rachel from hacking into World Privacy's server, or Newhouse Academy's security system. "Lauren, any luck with World Privacy?"

Lauren shook her head. "None, but our U.S. counterparts in Poland are still working on it."

"What about the list of boys you took?" Summer asked. She had given each agent a list of names, and had asked them to not only look at the boys' records, but their parents. They didn't believe a parent was involved, but wanted to be sure their suspect hadn't used a parent's credit card to pay for the weapons, supplies and offshore account.

"My list included Simon Thorpe, Hunter Perry, Chad Everett and Logan Huneck. Of the three, Hunter Perry had questionable transactions." Lauren stared at her laptop screen. "Last June, July and August, he made five different ATM transactions where he took out a cash advance using his credit card. Interestingly, he paid back the debt, which totaled twelve grand, in September. He receives a one thousand dollar monthly allowance, and during those summer months, he'd drained just under three grand from the account. But, by the end of September, he not only replaced the money, he deposited an additional five thousand. I was able to view his bank deposit slips, and they were all cash. Not one single check."

"Does he have a job?" Summer asked. "Maybe he gets paid under the table."

"No legal job," Lauren said, a small smile playing on her lips. "I got a search warrant for his cell phone records. I still need to go through them, but I'm suspecting he's dealing drugs."

"Okay," Dave began, "so he uses the credit card to get cash to buy the drugs, turns around and sells it for a profit."

Lauren nodded. "That's what I'm thinking. But, I do feel he should remain a person of interest. Just because he made hefty deposits and paid off his credit card debt doesn't mean he didn't keep additional cash to pay for the weapons and offshore account. He could have easily gone through the post office to send an anonymous money order to World Privacy."

Summer would definitely suggest to Dave that Lauren should take over for her while she was on maternity leave. The woman was smart, well-organized, knew the team well, and was an excellent investigator. Plus, she was Summer's closest friend in Cleveland. She needed to tell her about the baby, about Chase. Though Lauren was very pragmatic and offered excellent advice when needed, Summer wasn't looking for guidance. She was looking to maintain their friendship.

"Thanks, Lauren," she said, noting Hunter Perry's name. She vaguely remembered what he looked like, and wanted to find out his height and weight. If he was too big to fit through the opening at the fun house, he wasn't their Bad Kid. "Tony, what about your boys?"

Dave held up a hand. "There was nothing on Chad Everett? He's the kid whose parents make one hundred and fifty a year."

Lauren glanced to her screen. "Chad earned four grand last summer running a landscaping business with his brother, and it looks like he used that money to buy a car just before the school year started. He doesn't have a credit card. His parents have two, and both have low balances."

Summer understood why Dave had questioned the Everett boy. The kid's family made peanuts compared to the other boys' parents, and jealousy would have been great motivation for the kidnapping.

"Thank you, Lauren," Dave said. "Go ahead, Tony."

Tony also had a laptop in front of him. "My boys were Tyler Ziss, Evan Barry, Dillon Patricks and Mitch Connelly. Nothing in any of the boys' or their parents' financial records drew red flags. The Connelly family is experiencing financial troubles, though, so I did dig deeper into their accounts. I still came up with nothing."

"This doesn't mean they weren't involved," Summer said. "But after interviewing or reading these kids' statements, I have my doubts."

"I don't know." Lauren looked up from her laptop. "Tyler Ziss could have planned this. His dad told us it was Tyler's idea to give the team a ski weekend, and his grandparents used to own one of the cottages along Ottawa Lake."

That Summer hadn't known about.

Tony shook his head. "Not buying it. He stabbed Shultz in the rear with a pocketknife."

"Don't forget we have video of Shultz cutting the kid," Rich reminded them.

"Shultz threatened to *hurt* a kid, not kill him, if he didn't get his money," Summer said, thinking back to yesterday's conversation with Chase. "Tyler could have stabbed Shultz in the hope that he'd be the next kid hurt. Why would we think he was involved after his kidnapper cruelly cut him? Let's not forget he shot Shultz three times." She released a breath. "Chase and I interviewed him though, and while I'd like to pounce on this theory, I just don't feel it in my gut. Plus, I think he's too big to fit through the opening we found at the fun house."

"Speaking of which," Tony began, "forensics went to the park yesterday and brought back the leaves and grass from the hotel. They want to compare what you discovered to what they found covering the burner phone. They also brought the wood box back, and searched near the ballroom for any others. Near the back of the building, buried in the snow was another box. It was empty, and the top had been slightly burned, but they believe the boxes are from the same manufacturer, and were probably purchased from a craft store."

"Were there any labels or a manufacturing stamp on the boxes?" Summer asked.

He shook his head. "There was a small amount of adhesive on the bottom of the one found by the ballroom, leading them to believe there'd once been a label there. The suspect didn't leave behind any fingerprints on either box."

"Has CSI been able to determine whether the fun house opening was recently made?" Dave asked.

"Yes, the cut marks are fresh and indicative of a reciprocating saw."

"Anything else?" Summer asked Tony. When he shook his head, she looked to Rich. "What do you have for us?"

Rich slipped on a pair of reading glasses. "Okay, on my list I had Chris Demko, Riley Gallaher, Zach Strauss, Nicholas Janson, and Kyle Dodson. I found nothing on Chris or Zach, but Nicholas and Kyle both liked to hit the ATM. Between June and October, Kyle took out forty-seven hundred dollars. Nicholas wasn't far behind him at forty-two hundred."

"What do these kids buy?" Lauren asked with a shake of her head. "When I was in high school, I was lucky to be able to afford to put gas in my car or rent a video tape."

"But you didn't have parents worth millions," Rich said.

Tony grinned. "And you've just dated yourself. I bet our suspects have probably never even seen a video tape."

Lauren narrowed her eyes. "If Dave wasn't in the room, I'd give you the finger."

"Be my guest," Dave said. "The smartass deserves it."

Summer hadn't realized there'd been tension in the room until Tony and Lauren's light exchange. But she could understand why. No one wanted to consider one of these young boys guilty.

When Lauren chose to maintain professionalism and not flip Tony the bird, Rich said, "Kyle and Nicholas never used a debit card for purchases, just cash withdrawals. I found that Kyle does have a credit card, mostly for online purchases, clothes, and apps for his phone or tablet. Nicholas doesn't have a credit card. I also got a search warrant for Kyle and Nicholas's phone records, looking for activity from unknown callers starting in September, since Shultz made his first gun purchase in October. There was nothing there."

"Because our suspect used a burner phone," Summer said, disappointed the financial records showed so little.

"Where do Kyle, Nicholas and Hunter live?" Dave asked.

"All three are local," Lauren replied.

"Interviewing them would be a good idea," Summer said. "My concern is that once we do that, the boys and their parents will know we haven't closed the investigation. Right now, one of those boys thinks he's gotten away with the perfect crime."

Dave turned toward her. "We need to see if the headmaster will give us access to the school's video surveillance from Thursday."

Yesterday, during the drive home from the park, Summer had not only told Dave about what they'd discovered there, but their theory of how Bad Kid had been able to plant the phones, knives, gas, and cut the wood. At that time, he'd suggested the school's video surveillance, but she'd asked to hold off, explaining she had worried the headmaster would leak this information to the boys' parents or the media. "I thought we agreed to wait until we've reviewed their financial history."

"Which we just did."

"I think Summer is right," Lauren said. "If our suspect knows we're looking for him, he has five hundred grand at his disposal."

Tony shrugged. "Five hundred thousand is a lot of money, but it wouldn't get him far. Plus, if he runs, we'll know for sure who the kid is, and can plaster his picture over every media outlet."

Rich took off his glasses. "Or the kid could snap and kill again. He slit a man's throat, and that's damned cold-blooded."

Dave rubbed the base of his neck and looked to her again. "Is Hunter Perry small enough to fit through the fun house opening?"

Tony hit a few keys on his laptop. "He's five-ten and one hundred and fifty-three pounds. Kyle is almost five-eleven, but is only four pounds heavier, and Nicholas is just five-nine and one hundred and forty-two pounds. CSI ran a few experiments, and they believe a kid who's as tall as six feet could fit through the hole, so long as he has a slighter frame."

"Any of these boys would be able to fit." Dave nodded. "Okay, then let's keep our focus on them. Summer, I think it would be worthwhile to have a conversation with the boys' parents. You don't have to mention anything about finances, or what we're suspecting."

"Sure, I can do that. I'll tell them we're following up on a few things. I'd like to talk with the boys again, too. They've had a few days to relax and digest what happened. It'd be interesting to see their body language, or if their stories have changed." She looked to the others. "Rich, take Hunter from Lauren's list, along with the two boys on yours, and dig deeper into what we already know. Tony and Lauren, I need you two to help Greg with the Blackman investigation."

While the agents left the room, Dave remained. "Is there something else?" she asked.

"CORE had information about the Shultz cousins that we didn't. How do you suppose they managed that?"

"I think you and I both know," she answered honestly. Dave wasn't a stupid man, and hadn't landed his position for being blind to the world around him.

He stood and started for the door. "I'm worried about our suspect finding out that we're investigating the team, but I would love to see what's on those surveillance videos."

"Yes, it would be good to have them." She also rose, then walked over to the closed door. "I don't want to assume or misinterpret this conversation. Are you asking me to get the videos any way I can?"

Outrage lit his eyes. "The men and women of this division, patrol officers, deputies…you know how many people put their life on the line to save those boys. We've got a boy in a coma, another still in critical condition. It really pisses me off to know that one of those kids had no problem putting his friends' and teammates' lives in jeopardy, or ordering the murders of two men. Rich is right. Anyone who could slit a person's throat *is* cold blooded. And if he gets away with this, he can do it again. I want this kid, so make it happen without Kavel knowing."

He opened the door, and left her standing in the briefing room. In the eighteen months she'd been working for Dave, she'd never seen him this angry. When she'd been in the field, there'd been many times when she had taken an investigation personally. If Chase hadn't been in town, and they hadn't been dealing with their relationship, she might have had more invested in this case. She didn't. While it interested her, and she wanted it solved and Bad Kid caught, the investigation was more of a distraction. If she'd had it her way, she would have taken the week off, asked Chase to do the same, then spent time focusing on him, on them and their future.

Thankfully Dave gave her the go ahead to use Rachel and her hacking skills. Agreeing to Rachel going into the academy's security system made her uncomfortable, same with World Privacy's server. If the powers that be learned she'd approved of an outside agency hacking on her behalf, she could lose her position, and possibly her job.

As she walked down the hallway to her office, she ran into Lauren, who held a fresh, steaming cup of coffee. "Got a sec?" Summer asked, deciding she'd call Chase about the boys in a few. She didn't want to lose Lauren's trust or friendship, and needed to take a moment to talk to her.

"Sure." Lauren followed her into Summer's office. "What's up?"

Summer closed the door. "There's something I need to tell you."

"About one of our cases? Or is this personal? I've been wanting to ask you how things went with Chase."

"He's still in town, and staying with me."

Lauren looked away for a second. When she met Summer's gaze, there was concern in her friend's eyes. "Is that a good thing? He hurt you. Badly."

"He hurt himself even worse." She leaned against the desk. "I'm pregnant."

Lauren's eyes widened. "What? How far along? Oh, my God. Who's the father?"

"Five months, and Chase."

Lauren sat in the chair in front of the desk. "Holy...wow. Why didn't you tell me?"

"I don't know. At first I wasn't sure how to deal with it. Once I accepted that I was going to have a baby, I had to worry about what to tell Chase. He found out on Friday."

"And?"

"He's excited," she said, then explained how the baby, and having been back in a negotiator role, had shocked him back to reality. "I swear, the change in him has been amazing. It's only been days, but I know Chase. And I believe in him. We're going to be a family and raise this baby together." She smiled. "Who knows? Maybe we'll have more kids."

Lauren stood and hugged her. "I'm happy for you, but scared, too. I don't want to watch you get your heart broken again."

"I won't," she said, leaning back. "I'm sorry I didn't tell you sooner. I haven't told Dave, either. When I do, I'm going to recommend he uses you as my replacement while I'm on maternity leave."

Lauren grinned. "Really? Thank you." She picked up her coffee from the desk and glanced to Summer's waist. "Now I know why you haven't been draining the coffee pot. You can't tell you're preggers. When's the baby due? Oh, and you better believe I'm throwing you a shower."

They talked for a while longer. After her friend had left,

Summer wondered why she'd waited to tell Lauren. Instead of keeping the pregnancy a secret, she should have leaned on her for support. Now that Lauren knew, she needed to tell Dave, which she'd do another time. With the mood he'd been in after this morning's meeting, she'd rather wait until they resolved the kidnapping investigation, or at least came close to it.

Anxious to call Chase and let him know about the three boys they were targeting, she sat at her desk and picked up her cell phone. With any luck, maybe today would be the day they found Bad Kid.

Summer's House, Fairview Park, Ohio
Tuesday, January 24th, 10:11 a.m. Eastern Standard Time

Chase sipped a cup of coffee and kept his gaze locked on the laptop's screen. Rachel had sent over the surveillance video about fifteen minutes ago. Last night, after she'd put her kids to bed, she'd stayed up late embedding code to hack into the school security system and World Privacy's server. The code cracked the security system this morning, but she was still working out the kinks for the other server, and hoped to have something later this afternoon.

She hadn't had the chance to go through the security video, which was fine. He had pictures of the kids spread out on the coffee table and had the time to compare whoever showed up on the video to the photos. Plus, he'd rather she concentrate on World Privacy. All they needed was a name, and Bad Kid was cooked.

When the phone rang and Summer's number popped up on the screen, he forgot about the video and his mind immediately went back to last night and this morning. He was a lucky man to have a woman as patient, honest and loving as Summer. And he would never take her for granted again. "Hey, how's it going?" he asked after answering.

"Not too bad. We have three boys we're investigating," she

said, then told him that Dave had suggested CORE hack into the school's surveillance. Knowing the hack had bothered her, he was glad to hear the heat would fall on Dave, rather than Summer, should there be an issue.

He paused the video. "I'm staring at the surveillance video now. Who are the boys?"

"Hunter Perry, Nicholas Janson and Kyle Dodson. You and I interviewed Kyle after we talked to Tyler Ziss."

"I remember. What do you have on them?" he asked, and shuffled the photos around until he lined the three boys in a row on the table.

She told him about their financial activity, then what CSI had to say about the boxes and human doggy door. "Any one of those boys could fit through the opening. I have Rich digging deeper into the boys' activities, and I'm going to reach out to their parents."

"For? We don't want them to know their sons are possible suspects."

"They won't have a clue. I'm going to play it off as a follow-up interview, that we want to see if they remember anything else, and find out how they're doing."

"Do you plan on meeting with the kids?"

"I'm hoping I can. I'd love to read their body language, but…I don't know." She sighed. "Since taking the ASAC job, I haven't spent a lot of time in the field or interrogating suspects. I usually watch from a distance or from behind a two-way mirror."

"Do you think you're rusty?" He shook his head. "Come on, Summer. You didn't get to where you are because you can tell a joke."

"I can't tell a joke."

"Exactly."

She laughed. "That has nothing to do with anything, but it lightened my mood and I get where you're heading."

"You should. During the last crisis negotiation I worked, two people ended up dead. Don't be insecure about being back in the field and interviewing possible suspects."

"Thank you. I needed to hear that. So how far along are you into the video?"

"The timestamp says it's about one fifteen in the afternoon. According to the school's schedule, the boys were in class until three. But some of them had study hall as their last period or two. If Bad Kid is one of those boys, he could've left at around one thirty, gotten to the Ottawa Lake area by three, and hung out until he saw Woody and Randy leave."

"I kind of envy what you're doing. I miss those days."

"I'm realizing I do, too," he admitted. "Working this case has been a nice blend of investigative work and negotiation. Since I've been with CORE, I've taken whatever case Ian has given me, but I've never pushed for anything that might challenge me. I need a challenge. And you can't say being ASAC isn't a challenge."

"I'm a manager who carries a gun and hears about the mystery of an investigation as it unravels."

Surprised, he leaned back into the couch cushions. "You don't like your job."

"I never said that. At all. It boils down to the whole grass is always greener thing. When I was in the field, I wanted to be boss. Now that I'm in charge of a team, I sometimes don't want the responsibility and just want to enjoy the hunt. Make sense?"

"Yeah, I struggled with the same when I switched over to crisis negotiating. That was a different kind of hunt. I already knew who the bad guy was, I just had to convince him to turn himself in or let people go."

"Why didn't you tell me?"

"I don't know why I didn't tell you a lot of things. I suppose I didn't want you to think I wasn't manly, or something along those lines."

"Right. God forbid if you share your emotions," she said, her tone teasing. "I have to get back to work. Let me know if you find anything or hear back from Rachel. If I don't talk to you, I'll call before I leave."

"Sounds good. Love you," he said, the words floating naturally from his mouth.

"Love you, too."

After the call ended, he stared at the still frame of the school parking lot. There was a part of him that said something was going to happen that would sabotage their shot at happiness. The other part told him to stay out of his head and roll with his good fortune. Deciding to listen to the positive side of his brain, he started the video.

Ninety minutes later, he paused it again, then went to the kitchen for a Coke. When he returned to the living room, he glanced at his notes. So far, only one kid—Chad Everett—had left the premises, but he'd returned within twenty minutes, carrying a Chipotle bag. The timestamp was only at three, though, so he expected more activity soon.

He settled on the couch again, and hit PLAY. Ten minutes passed, and Brennan Williams left. The father, Kevin, told State Highway Patrol that Brennan had spent the night at home, and that Kevin and his wife had dropped him off Friday morning to catch the bus. After a few minutes, Riley Gallaher and Zach Strauss left. Chase noted the time and the make and model of the car they drove off in together. Alex McGuire also left, but was alone.

Chase fast-forwarded, then paused the video at three thirty-five. Hunter Perry, Nick Janson and Mitch Connelly walked out of the school together, toward Nick's car. The three climbed in, then drove out of camera range. He once again marked down the time, but wasn't sure if what he'd viewed meant anything or everything. Hunter and Nick's finances had come into question. Was it possible those two were the moneymen and maybe Mitch was the person with the plan? Could the three of them have pulled off the kidnapping, or were they simply heading for dinner?

By one fifteen, the timestamp read five-ten. Since the three boys had left, several others had, too. Logan Huneck, Chris Demko and Simon Thorpe had taken off at four forty-five, Simon driving separately, and Kyle Dodson had gotten in his car moments ago. Twelve of the fifteen boys had left at some point, and thus far, only one had returned with food.

He once again fast-forwarded the video, pausing when first Alex, then Simon returned. At six p.m., Logan and Chris also came back to the campus. Riley and Zach showed up fifteen minutes later. Anxious to discover the time when the other four boys returned, he moved the video along, then slowed it when the parking lot lampposts touched along Nick's car. Chase read the time: seven forty-eight. What had the boys been doing for the past four hours? And where was Kyle?

Chase watched as the three boys stepped out of the car. Nick was the only one carrying a bag, but he couldn't read the store label. Maybe the boys had gone to the mall. They could have seen a movie, had dinner and Nick had bought something. He would have Rachel take a look at this portion of the video, and hopefully enhance the image of the bag. If they knew what store Nick had gone to, they could verify whether they'd gone to the mall, and possibly trace their steps. Or, Nick could have made a quick purchase to serve as an alibi, then driven them to the park.

Wanting to know about Kyle, the last of the boys who'd gone off campus, Chase jumped ahead, then paused the video when the kid returned at eight-forty. He also carried a few bags. The only one Chase recognized was from Smith's Sporting Goods, which made sense. The boys were leaving the next day for a ski weekend, and Kyle might've needed cold weather gear.

Newhouse Academy had a strict nine o'clock weekday curfew. The weekends were extended to eleven. Rachel had learned that the academy's doors were locked for the night, and couldn't be opened except by one of the security guards stationed in the foyer of the dormitory. Unless Bad Kid had a security guard on the payroll, he wouldn't be able to leave after nine. Then again, the kid, or kids, had concocted a brilliant kidnapping plan, and had coerced grown men into helping, so anything was possible.

He kept the video going, just in case someone left during the night, and called Rachel. "I need you to enhance a couple of parts of the video." After telling her which, he heard tapping from her keyboard in the background.

"Okay," she began, "Nick is carrying a bag from Hollister."

Chase paused the video, opened up the Internet browser, then typed *nearest mall to newhouse academy*. There were two: Tuttle Crossing and Polaris. While she enhanced the still shot of Kyle's bags, he checked the time it would take to drive to the malls from the school. Eight minutes to Tuttle Crossing and seventeen to Polaris. Tuttle Crossing had a movie theater, both malls had the store, Hollister, but only Polaris had Smith's.

"You were correct about Kyle carrying a Smith's Sporting Goods bag," Rachel said. "The other two are from American Eagle and Buckle."

Chase read through the lists of stores located at both malls. "Polaris has a Buckle store, but Tuttle Crossing doesn't."

"Sorry, who has what?"

He told her the names of the malls, what he'd watched, and about the boys' financial records. "Hunter, Mitch and Nick left at approximately three forty-five, and were gone for about four hours. If it's an eight-minute drive to Tuttle Crossing, they could have gone there, one of them gone inside, made a quick purchase, then they went on their way to the amusement park."

"Does the mall have a movie theater? They could have seen a movie, eaten and shopped."

"I thought of that, but it's too coincidental that the FBI not only flagged Hunter and Nick for their finances, but that they were gone for four hours the night before the bus was hijacked."

"Are you dismissing Kyle as a suspect?"

"No. Except two of the bags Kyle carried aren't from stores located in Tuttle Crossing, meaning he had to have gone to Polaris or another Columbus area mall. Polaris is a seventeen-minute drive from the academy. Kyle was gone for three and a half hours. We know it's a three hour round trip from Dublin to the park. Could he have staged the park in thirty minutes? Possibly. Could he have bought the items from the mall days earlier, then carried them Thursday night to establish an alibi should someone be watching? Absolutely. But there's no way he could have gone to the mall *and* the park in that timeframe."

"I can get you surveillance video from earlier in the week, but talk about a time suck." Rachel released a breath. "You said Kyle, Nick and Hunter only have ATM transactions, and didn't use a debit or credit card for purchases, right?"

"Summer said Kyle used a credit card, mostly for online purchases. I can run this by her and have her check to see if Kyle used his credit card Thursday evening. If he did, I think they would have noted that, though."

"I'd think so, too. If the kids paid cash, it'll be harder to track them down to the specific stores. But malls and many stores also have surveillance videos. I'm still waiting to get into World Privacy's server. Let me see if I can access the two malls' security systems."

For half a second, he considered checking with Summer first, then dismissed the idea. Dave wanted Bad Kid. The FBI would need a warrant which would take time, and possibly alert Bad Kid that they were on to him.

"Go for it," he said, then asked her to email him copies of the enhanced still shots. After hanging up, he called Summer and told her about the surveillance video, and what Rachel was working on now.

"This is great news. I'll let Dave know, and I'll also contact the Columbus Field Office," she said, a smile in her voice. "They can send a couple agents to the malls and stores, flash the boys' pictures to mall security and the stores' employees. I'll also check with Rich about Kyle's credit card activity."

"And I'll let you know when Rachel sends me the new videos." He looked at his email, clicked on the one Rachel had sent him seconds ago, then forwarded it to Summer. "Check your inbox. I emailed you the still shots from the academy."

"I will. What are you going to work on next?" she asked.

He glanced to the clock on the laptop screen, and couldn't believe it was shortly after three. Rachel was right. Viewing the videos was a time suck. "Until I hear from Rachel, there's nothing more I can do from my end."

"I envy you. I'm so behind. I could probably work throughout the night and still not be caught up on everything."

"Does that mean you'll be late?" he asked, and hoped his disappointment didn't come through. He might need Summer in his life, but he didn't want to *sound* needy.

"Nope. The paperwork will still be here in the morning."

"Good, because I'm going to attempt to make meatloaf."

"With mashed potatoes and gravy, and no ketchup on the meat?"

"You got it."

"I haven't had that in years, and will definitely be walking out of here by five."

"Looking forward to seeing you," he said. "In the meantime, I have a crib to put together."

15

Horizon Pointe Estates, Avon, Ohio
Tuesday, January 24ᵗʰ, 3:16 p.m. Eastern Standard Time

PATSY SET THE Target bags on the washing machine, as Emma came in behind her through the door to the garage. "Em, can you take the bags to my room for me?" she asked, removing her coat. Since Emma had yet to speak to her brother, she wouldn't have her deliver the toiletries Patsy had bought for him.

Emma crinkled her nose. "What's that smell?"

Patsy had also caught a huge whiff of a musty odor when they'd entered the laundry room. She glanced to the utility sink where her son's clothes were clustered together, bent forward and sniffed. "Buddy's clothes from the…from the weekend. I forgot to deal with them." She let out a sigh. "Just take up the bags. I'll get rid of these, then start dinner. I'm making lasagna."

"Oh, joy. Another one of your precious baby's favorites." Emma rolled her eyes. "Whatever. I'll make myself a bologna sandwich."

"Damn it, Em, you'll do no such thing." Last evening, Patsy had made pot roast. Emma had eaten it, but only after Buddy had cleaned his plate and was in his room. Later, when she'd suggested the kids watch a movie with her, her son had surprised her by agreeing. Of course Emma had once again refused to be anywhere near him. "This has to stop. I can't deal with the way you keep acting toward your brother." She pulled a large black garbage bag from the box in the cabinet above the dryer. "If you don't want to eat lasagna, then don't. Eat a sandwich. But you *will* eat at the same table as us."

"Make him leave and I'll eat every meal with *you*."

"That's not happening."

Emma tossed her auburn hair over her shoulder, then placed a hand on her hip. "So you're choosing him over me."

"Jesus, that is not what I'm doing." What would it take to get through to her daughter? "I'm trying to piece my family back together."

"When he was the one who tore it apart?" Tears filled Emma's eyes. "Did you ask him about his backpack? I'm telling you. He took it with him when he left yesterday, but didn't bring it back."

"I did ask him, and he said he never took one with him. Since I didn't see him carry it out of the house, how can I not believe him?"

"Because he's a liar. How can he go from hating us to suddenly wanting to be a family again?"

Patsy snapped open the plastic bag. "I already explained this. Being apart from us, and then the kidnapping…it changed him. It made him realize family comes first."

Emma rolled her watery eyes. "I guarantee those are your words, not his." She stepped closer. "I've never lied to you. *Ever.* But you'll take the prodigal son's word over mine. He wanted me dead, and probably still does. Do you ever think about how Shawn and Dad died?"

She turned away from Emma. "Every single day. I don't want to do this right now."

"No, you don't want to admit the truth to yourself."

Before Patsy picked up the soiled clothes, she faced her daughter. "What truth? That God hates me? He gave me a wonderful husband and three beautiful children, then punished me by taking your dad and Shawn away. *That's* the only truth I know."

Emma rubbed Patsy's arm. "I'm sorry, Mom," she said, her voice shaky as tears worked down her face. "I'm so sorry you think God hates you. I don't believe that. I think the only one who truly hates you is—"

"I was wondering when you'd be home." Her son leaned against the doorjamb. "Did you get me deodorant and shampoo?"

Emma kept her back to her brother. The fear and hatred in her daughter's eyes set Patsy on edge. Before she allowed her daughter to project her fears onto her, she picked up one of the Target bags, then glanced through it. "I did," she said handing it to him. "I also didn't know what else you might need, so I bought you soap, shaving cream, a new razor, toothbrush and tooth paste." She picked up another bag and gave it to him. "This has hand soap and air freshener. Can you take this, and a package of toilet paper to the hall bath?"

"Sure. What's for dinner?"

She smiled. "You're bottomless. I'm making lasagna."

"Awesome," he said, then left with the bags.

"You can move now." Patsy retrieved the garbage bag. "He's gone."

"I wish he was," Emma said, gathering the bags that belonged to her. "Forever."

With sadness and worry surrounding her heart, Patsy watched her daughter go. She had no idea how to mend their broken family. After she'd taken care of the dirty clothes, she would head into the office and make a few calls. They needed counseling, and they needed it now.

She lifted up her son's heavy winter coat, which she gave him this past Christmas. Not her personally. No, the mail carrier had delivered the packages. Before she allowed guilt to settle on her shoulders, she examined the coat. He'd only had it for a month, and she'd paid four hundred dollars for it. She might be wealthy, but she couldn't shake the frugality her parents had instilled in her at a young age. Even if her son no longer wanted the coat, she could wash it, then donate it to a shelter.

After taking the spot treatment detergent from the cabinet, she began hitting various areas along the charcoal gray coat. There was a small amount of what looked like soot along the sleeves, dirt on the back near the hem, as if he'd sat on the ground, and that was it. As she sprayed those areas, she noticed a tear in the lining. Deciding she would have to mend it before giving it away, she then tossed the coat in the washer. She reached into the utility sink, and lifted up the heavy black sweater he'd been wearing. A thermal shirt was stuck inside. She freed it, tossed the sweater in with the coat, then gave the black shirt a quick inspection. After placing it in the washer, she picked up the jeans. They were coated with dirt around the knees and ankles, and there were many brownish spots and smears along the thighs. She treated those stains, then did the same for his filthy gloves.

As she put the unused garbage bag back in the cabinet, she noticed a knit hat that had fallen between the sink and washer, and plucked it free. She had also bought the hat as a Christmas present, and it was the same color as the coat. It, too, had several brownish stains. They were tiny dots, as if someone had misted iodine at his head. Once again, she wondered what exactly had happened while the boys were at the park.

She placed the hat in the washer, then started it. After she cleaned her hands, she grabbed her purse, and headed for her office. Had those brown stains been blood? Her son had said he'd watched Shultz shoot Coach Pembroke. My God, had he been sitting that close to his coach when he'd been murdered? Close enough he'd gotten blood on his hat? Or maybe the blood belonged to Alex. Buddy had said he'd been one of the kids who'd tried to help the poor boy when his body had first been dragged into the ballroom. She wanted to ask him, but wouldn't. Now that she thought about it, she should have disposed of the clothes because they might serve as a painful reminder of what had happened to him and the others.

When she reached her office, she checked her voicemail and found she had three messages. One from her editor, the next from her agent, and the last from a telemarketer. She pulled her cell phone from her purse and discovered she'd missed several calls on that, too. Last night, while they'd been watching a movie, she'd placed her phone on silent, but had forgotten to change it back. One of the missed calls had been from her son. The other was from a number she didn't recognize.

She listened to the message: "Hi Patsy, this is Special Agent Summer Raines. Now that a few days have passed, we're reaching out to the victims' families. I was hoping you and your son would give me a few minutes of your time. I want to see how he's doing, if there was anything else he's remembered from the days when he was held, and to talk to you about an organization that helps victims of violent crimes—and their families—to learn to cope with their ordeal. Several of the boys are taking advantage of this. I won't take up much of your time, so if you could please give me a call back, I'd appreciate it."

Patsy relaxed into the leather office chair. She'd spoken to the agent a couple times while her son had been missing, then met her briefly when she had picked him up outside the park. The pretty blonde had been very helpful and empathetic. And Patsy particularly liked the idea of a group that helped victims of violent crimes. Her son had been adamant about not meeting with a therapist, but maybe he would seek counseling through this organization. Especially once he found out several of his friends were doing the same.

Emma snuck past the office door, then raced up the stairs carrying a Diet Coke and a bag of pretzel rods. Patsy rubbed her temple where her head had begun to throb. She couldn't continue to have her daughter living in fear and slinking around the house to avoid her brother. Maybe this organization could recommend a group for Emma. Her daughter's three hundred dollar an hour therapist certainly wasn't helping.

She dialed the agent's number, talked with her briefly, and

anxious to help her son, she set up their interview for four-thirty that afternoon. The timing would be perfect. She and Buddy would meet with Agent Raines, then discuss the group counseling over dinner. Hopefully, Emma would join them.

A door on the second floor slammed, followed by another. Worried her children were finally communicating, but in a way that wasn't good, she left the office and climbed the steps.

"Stay away from me," Emma said, her voice laced with terror. "I hate you."

"But Mom wants us to be a family again. C'mon, sis. It'll be fun living together again."

Before Patsy reached the second floor landing, she peered around the corner. Her son stood in Emma's doorway, keeping it open with his shoulder.

"She's going to figure out what you are." Emma, who shared Patsy's petite, five foot two inch frame, pushed on the door. "When she does, she'll kick you out again."

"I heard you tell her I was the reason why you slit your wrists. She didn't believe you. No one believes you. They all think you're crazy. Guess what? They're right. That's why you have no friends. It's why you can't keep a boyfriend...why you're not at Ohio State. It's why you're a fucking loser. You should just do it again. Take the razor and end it." He cocked his head. "You know, I still have those pictures of you. Would you like to see them again, or maybe I should put them up on social media for the world to see."

Patsy's heart raced as dread pooled deep within her. She had no idea what he was talking about, but she didn't like it. Hated it, and herself. Had Emma been telling the truth? Had he done something so incredibly awful she'd wanted to end her life?

"Go ahead," Emma said, and for the first time since the suicide attempt, there was strength in her voice. "I don't care anymore. I'll show Mom what you've done. I'll go to the police."

Her son's profile changed, morphed into an ugly, angry creature's that she didn't know.

"Do it, and I'll cut your wrists like I should have in August.

One of the best days of my life was talking you into killing yourself, then watching the blood drain from your body."

Patsy quickly covered her mouth. Her vision blurred with tears. He'd been there? He'd tried to talk Emma into committing suicide? Terrified of what she'd let back into her house, she quietly walked down the steps. When she reached the bottom, she cleared her throat. "Emma," she called, and hoped her son wouldn't hear the fear in her voice. "Can you come here?"

She needed to take Emma out of the house. She needed time to think about how she should proceed. Guilt crashed down on her. Emma had tried to tell her the truth behind the suicide attempt and she hadn't believed her, she hadn't *wanted* to believe that her son could do such a horrible thing.

"Em?" She squeezed her eyes shut and fought back the tears. "I need you to run to the store for me."

"Emma's not going anywhere."

Patsy looked up the staircase. Her son stood at the top of the steps holding a gun to her daughter's head.

"I didn't plan on doing this so soon," he said as he forced Emma to walk in front of him. "But my sister is a bitch, and I'm sick of living in this shitty house. Really, Mom. Why would you think moving from a ten thousand square foot mansion to this shit box was a good idea?"

"I…" She blinked the tears from her eyes. "Where did you get the gun?"

"Your closet."

Tim's gun. Her husband had taught her how to fire it, and while she hated guns, she'd kept it for protection. Now she wished she'd gotten rid of it.

"Honey," she began, "please—"

"Shut up, Mom. I can't stand when you call me honey or Buddy. And I'm sick of all the fucking hugging. It's fake. You don't love me. If you did, you wouldn't have moved without telling me."

"I apologized and explained myself," Patsy said, backing away from the steps. "Please. You're angry with me. Emma had nothing to do with my decision to move."

"I don't care if she did. She's in my way." When he and Emma reached the foyer, he waved the gun toward the office. "Get inside."

"Please," Patsy begged. "Let us go. We won't tell anyone. Is it money you want? I'll give it to you. Just—"

"Shut the fuck up, *Mom*, and get in the office."

Patsy hugged Emma to her side, and together they walked backward into the office. "What are you going to do?" she asked, and prayed the FBI agent would be able to help them.

He stepped inside, ripped the phone and Internet cords from the wall, then took her cell phone from the desk and pocketed it. "What I've been wanting to do for years. Watch you both die."

Summer's House, Fairview Park, Ohio
Tuesday, January 24ᵗʰ, 4:01 p.m. Eastern Standard Time

Chase pulled the pot of peeled and cut potatoes from the stovetop, then drained them. When he set it back on an unused burner, he glanced at the clock. The meatloaf would take an hour. The potatoes would be fine if he mashed them now, but since it was barely four, and he didn't anticipate Summer to be home until closer to five-thirty or six, he decided to wait another half-hour, maybe even forty-five minutes, before putting it in the oven. She'd need time to change and relax when she came home. Plus, this would give him a chance to figure out how to put the damned crib together.

He'd started that project after he'd gotten off the phone with Summer, then had given up fifteen minutes later to check if there was a video tutorial anywhere online. He was usually good at putting things together, so the crib, the rocket science instructions, and the ridiculous amount of nuts, bolt and screws were pissing him off to no end. Which had been why he'd started dinner earlier than necessary.

When his cell rang, he stepped away from the stove and pulled it off the charger on the counter. Rachel's name showed on the screen, and he hoped she was calling to say she had more video for him to view. He'd rather go back to that tedious task than try to tackle the crib again.

"Hey, Rachel," he greeted her.

"Hi, I have more video for you."

Thank God. "Both malls?"

"Yes, but not the individual stores. I'm still working on that."

"Great. Did you email the links?"

"Already done. If I have any luck getting into the stores' security, I'll call you back."

He thanked Rachel, then opened up his email. She'd sent him nearly two dozen links, likely because there were that many entry points into the malls. Yep. This would be a total time suck. Chances were he'd be watching these videos until late tonight. But at least he had a general timeframe to work with and could narrow down the search to a specific window.

He clicked on the first link, which instantly displayed Tuttle Crossing's main entrance. Since the three boys had left the academy at three forty-five, and it took eight minutes to drive to the mall, he forwarded the feed to three fifty. He watched the screen for fifteen minutes. When he saw no sign of the boys, he went back to the Internet browser and opened the mall's website to search for the location of Hollister. If the kids were looking to get in and out of the mall quickly, they might've avoided the main entrance, and opted for one that had less traffic. After finding that surveillance link, he opened it and once again cued it to the three fifty timeframe.

Four minutes later, Nick's blue Honda rolled to a stop outside the entrance. Mitch and Hunter exited, then started for the doors while Nick drove into the parking lot.

His cell rang. Rachel's name was on the screen again and he answered the call.

"Got him!"

"What?" Excitement rushed through him. The hunt was almost over. He paused the video. "How?" he asked as his phone beeped, indicating he had another call coming through. He quickly glanced at the screen, saw it was Summer and decided to let the call go into voicemail. Summer wouldn't care if he could deliver the name of Bad Kid.

"I finally got into World Privacy's server. I'll have to say it was probably one of the most secure sites I've encountered. These people know their stuff and—"

"The name," he said to keep her focused.

"Sorry. I got a little carried away. Ready? Nicholas Adam Janson opened an account with World Privacy last November 13th. And guess how much money is in the account?"

"Five hundred thousand dollars." He grinned. "You are brilliant."

"I know. You can talk to me about my brilliance when you're back in Chicago. Actually, since my husband didn't appreciate that I spent all last night working on this, you can take us to dinner."

"Done." After he thanked Rachel, he hit PLAY, then watched Nick Janson's car drive out of the parking lot. "Gotcha," he said, then picked up his phone and called Summer.

Horizon Pointe Estates, Avon, Ohio
Tuesday, January 24th, 4:28 p.m. Eastern Standard Time

Summer's phone rang as she pressed on Patsy Janson's doorbell. Since she'd opted to leave her winter coat in the car, she dug the phone out of her suit coat, saw Chase's name, then slipped it back inside. The interview shouldn't take more than twenty or thirty minutes, and she'd rather not be on the phone when Patsy came to the door. The goal behind the meeting was to get in front of the son. Before she'd left the office, Dave had suggested she take another agent with her, but she'd declined. Between the voicemail she'd left Patsy, and their brief conversation, she'd hoped to put the woman at ease. She wanted to come across as one of the good guys who was there to help her son. If she'd brought another agent with her, Patsy and her son might become intimidated, limit the conversation, or, even worse, hire an attorney and not talk with them at all.

There wasn't enough evidence to accuse any of the boys they were targeting. Even if CORE came through with additional video surveillance, the evidence was still circumstantial and not enough to make an arrest. Prosecutors and jurors liked DNA, and they had nothing.

A woman with auburn hair, cut in a bob, opened the door slightly. "Agent Raines?" she asked, her voice tired, strained.

When she'd had a break today, Summer had read about the woman. Patsy's story was interesting and heartbreaking. After her youngest son had died of SIDs six years ago, she and her husband, Tim, had taken their grief and turned it into something positive. They'd written two books together, had hit the bestseller lists, become motivational speakers and had made a small fortune. Tragically, Tim had accidentally drowned, then, four years later their daughter had attempted suicide. Summer hadn't read any of their books, or the ones Patsy had written on her own, but she considered the woman a survivor. Who could bear so much loss, so much tragedy, yet still find the strength to motivate others?

Looking at the stress etching Patsy's face, the worry in her eyes, Summer wondered if the kidnapping, the thought of losing yet another loved one, might've taken the positive, motivational speaker down a few notches.

Summer planted on a smile. "Yes, I'm Agent Raines," she said, flashing her badge. Patsy didn't move, didn't invite her inside. "Is this no longer a good time?"

Patsy gave her a tight smile. "I'm sorry. I've come down with a migraine. Can we reschedule?"

The woman had been fine forty minutes ago. If anything, she'd sounded enthusiastic, relieved, and had expressed interest in the Victims of Violent Crime program. While the program did exist, in order to put mother and son at ease, Summer had told a white lie about the other boys taking part in it.

"Are you sure you can't take a moment to talk to me? I won't stay long. I want to see how Nick is doing, and give you the information about—"

"He's fine." Patsy gave her another smile. "Great, actually. We're getting along okay. I do want to talk to you about the victims' program. Maybe we can do that tomorrow," she said, then mouthed the word *help*, just as someone screamed.

Alarmed, Summer reached for her weapon, then froze when the door opened wider, revealing Nick Janson holding a gun to a young woman's head. Summer's heart hammered. "Dozens of people, *federal agents*, know I'm here."

Nick pressed the muzzle of the gun against the woman's temple. "Get inside, or I'll blow her brains all over you and my mom."

Patsy's veneer cracked. Her face crumpled and tears filled her eyes. "Run!"

"Do you really want to be coated with Emma's brain and blood? Because that's what will happen. I know. I've seen it." He narrowed his gaze at Summer. "Get inside. Now."

Dave, Lauren, even Tony knew she was here. So did Chase. She'd told Chase in her voicemail that she'd be home around five-thirty. If she wasn't home by six, or not answering his calls, he'd become worried, and hopefully look for her.

Except she didn't want to go inside. She didn't just have herself to consider, but the baby she carried in her womb.

Summer slowly moved her hand from her holster. "I'm going to walk away. Get in my car and leave. You don't want to do this. I'm a federal agent. You shoot me, you shoot anyone in front of me, and I promise you the outcome won't be good."

He stepped behind Emma, who Summer remembered was his sister, then placed the gun in the girl's hand. As Emma cried, he wrapped his own hand around his sister's.

"No shit," he said, then fired.

16

Summer's House, Fairview Park, Ohio
Tuesday, January 24ᵗʰ, 4:36 p.m. Eastern Standard Time

CHASE CALLED DAVE as he ran out the door to the rental car. The moment he'd heard where Summer had gone, his knees had weakened and his heart had nearly stopped. If he hadn't taken a couple minutes to turn off the oven, don his vest and arm himself, he would have already been on the road.

Fucking Nick Janson. He and Summer hadn't interviewed the kid, but Chase remembered seeing him the night the team had escaped and reading over his statement. He'd been distraught, shaken and his story had matched the other boys'. With the exception of Alex and Brennan, Chase hadn't dismissed any of the kids from their list of suspects. But until Summer had told him Nick had been flagged for his financial activity, he'd thought the boy might be innocent because he'd been the one who had attacked Randy the night Clay and Alex were shot. And, according to Simon and Tyler, Nick had also discussed an escape plan with Brennan.

The kid had played them all. He was also extremely dangerous.

As he drove toward the freeway, the call to Dave finally went through. "Chase, sorry to keep you waiting."

"You need to send agents to Nicholas Janson's house in Avon," he said, then quickly explained how Rachel had hacked into World Privacy and ID'd Nick.

"Summer went there," Dave said, his tone low, angry.

"I know. I'm driving to the house now. I'll be there in fifteen minutes."

In the background, Dave yelled for Tony to assemble the SWAT team and have the Avon police dispatched to the Janson address. "I'm on my way," he said when he returned to the line. "Do not engage until you have backup."

Screw that. "If I have an opportunity to get inside, I'm going to take it."

"No, damn it. We'll have units surround the house—"

"So the kid knows? If you surround the place, then try to establish communication you'll turn this into a hostage situation. Summer didn't go there to accuse him of anything, just to talk, correct?"

"Yes. But… I should've had another agent go with her. I should have—"

"Stop," Chase said, needing the man to stay with him. "Let me try to get inside the house before you have officers and SWAT make their presence known. We don't want Nick to panic and do something that will endanger Summer or anyone."

"How do you plan to get inside?" he asked, commotion in the background, likely from other agents scrambling to leave.

Good question. He could knock on the front door and pretend he was selling something. Or, he could pose as another agent who needed to talk to Summer. Better yet, he could bust through a window or door and put a gun to the kid's head. "I'll assess the situation once I'm there."

"I'm walking out of the building. Call me when you get there."

Chase ended the call. "Maybe," he said, weaving through traffic. As he barreled down the freeway, he couldn't stop thinking about Summer and their baby. When Summer had taken the ASAC position, he'd been happy for her. Not only because she'd earned the promotion, but because she wouldn't be in the field that often. When she'd been a special agent for the Baltimore Field Office, there'd been a few cases she'd worked where her life had been put in danger. Bullets had flown, and people had been shot. He would have never told her to leave the Bureau, to find a safe office job, but there'd been many times over the years when he'd wanted to make the suggestion. Even then he'd needed her in his life, but had been too stubborn to admit it to himself.

Now she and their baby were in danger.

He slowed the car when he neared the Avon exit. Maybe he was panicking for nothing. She wouldn't answer his call if she were already in the house talking to Patsy Janson and her son. The unanswered call could mean she was busy doing her thing. His phone might ring at any second, and Summer would be telling him she was on the way home. If not, they still had the element of surprise on their side.

Once Nick had made sure the kidnappers were dead, and the FBI had given a press conference where Dave stated the investigation had been closed, Nick had probably thought he'd gotten away with the perfect crime. He wouldn't suspect Summer had come to his home to fish for information. Meaning Summer might not be in danger.

His voice of reason did little to calm his nerves. Summer's interview would come off as innocent, but the boy wasn't. He was a killer. A devious, greedy little prick.

The GPS told him he was close. After making a turn, the ornate sign for Horizon Pointe Estates came into view. His stomach twisted with nervous energy, while dread climbed up his spine. In less than five hundred feet he would arrive.

Four hundred.

Three hundred.

Two hundred.

One hundred…

"You have arrived," the GPS informed him.

Summer's car was in the driveway, parked behind Nick's blue Honda. Instead of pulling in next to her car, he drove past the house, then parked a few doors down from it. The Janson home was a typical, cookie cutter McMansion, with a large yard and long driveway. SWAT and the Avon PD could easily surround the place, hide in the mature evergreen bushes, or bust through a number of lower level windows. But was it necessary? Fuck, he wished he knew what was going on inside the house.

Deciding he was making this too complicated, he dialed Summer's number again. When the call immediately rolled into voicemail, he went with his gut and turned around the rental and drove back to the house. As he parked behind Summer's car, Dave called him.

"Just talked to Avon PD. They received a call from a resident in Horizon Pointe Estates, who claimed she'd heard a loud bang at approximately four-thirty, but couldn't be sure if the noise had come from a neighboring house, or from the development on the next street."

Chase opened the car door, noticed a woman two doors down peeking through the curtains of a second story window. He listened for sirens. "Where are the police then?"

"Without an address, they didn't know where to go."

He looked away from the woman, and walked toward the front door. "What's your ETA?"

"We're following SWAT, and should be there in less than ten. Do not engage. If the shots were fired from the Janson home—"

"Then we already have a hostage situation." He walked toward the front door. "If you don't hear from me by the time you get here, send in SWAT."

"Damn it, Chase. How do you plan to get inside?"

"Through the front door."

The agent should be dead. If Emma hadn't fought him for control of the gun, the bullet wouldn't have grazed the fleshy part of her upper left arm, it would be lodged in her chest. And why the fuck was the agent here? Had Brennan woken from his coma?

"Please, Nick. Don't do this," Mom pleaded from where he'd forced her and the agent to sit in front of the office's wall-to-wall built-in bookshelves.

The doorbell rang. He froze and stared at the FBI lady. "Your partner?"

"Yes, and if you don't answer, this place will be surrounded by SWAT within minutes."

He didn't believe her. If she'd had someone with her, they and a dozen other agents would have busted into the house the moment they'd heard the gunshot.

He glanced to the gun he'd had the agent place on the desk next to her cell phone, which had rung several times since she'd arrived, two of the calls from the same number. Keeping his father's pistol aimed at Emma, who stood a few feet from him near the desk, he put the agent's gun in his pocket, then stepped over to the window. He moved the blinds slightly. A man he recognized from the amusement park left the porch, then took the walkway to his car.

Shit. Not good. He'd have to come up with a way to make it look as if he were once again the innocent victim.

"Please, Nick," his mother repeated.

"Shut up!"

Damn it, he needed to think. If SWAT or other agents weren't already here, they'd be soon.

He considered the FBI lady's gun. What if he killed Emma with the agent's weapon, then shot Mom and the agent with his dad's gun? Emma should already have gunpowder residue on her hand. The agent wouldn't, but he could resolve that by placing her weapon in her hand and firing another round or two. All three would be dead, so no witnesses would be left behind to say things hadn't gone down as he would present them, and he'd be on his way to live with Grandma. Wealthy and free to do what he wanted.

Yeah, that plan would work. It would have to, since he was getting nowhere with Emma. He'd tried the same tactics he'd used on her back in August when he'd talked her into cutting her wrists. Unfortunately, her hatred for him had made her stronger than he'd anticipated. Since he didn't have much time, he'd have to make this fast. Kill Emma, then Mom and the agent.

Except...he wanted his sister to suffer. The bitch had brought this on herself. "From the moment I knew how to, I've hated you. Hated how Mom and Dad would treat you differently."

"We never did any such thing," Mom said. "We loved you equally."

"Give me a break." He snorted. "You guys were always nicer to her. If Emma wanted something, she got it. Remember my seventh birthday? I wanted a piñata for my party. You said that it was too messy. Two months later, Emma asked to have one at her party and you bought it for her."

"I was worried about seven-year-olds swinging a bat blindfolded. Honey, please believe me. We *never* favored your sister."

"Liar! And look at how you acted after Shawn was born. It was all about *the baby*. I had to be quiet because *the baby* was sleeping. I couldn't have friends over because *the baby* might catch cold or whatever the hell from them. We couldn't go on vacation because *the baby* was too little. Fuck *the baby*."

His mother gasped. Tears rolled down her cheeks. "How could you be so cruel? Shawn's death was tragic, and your father and I loved you. We loved all of our children."

"What's cruel is a mother who abandons her son. But I can top that," he said, needing her to hurt. Had she given him what he'd wanted without making him have to work for it, this might not be happening. For years he'd looked at Emma as his enemy, the one person who'd stood in the way of his parents' money, their affection—not that he wanted them touching him—their attention. He'd wanted their focus to be on him. But it wasn't Emma's fault she'd been born first, or a girl. No, it boiled down to bad parenting skills.

"There's no need to top anything," the agent said.

He looked at the blonde. "What's your name?"

"Special Agent Summer Raines."

"Well, Agent Raines, I certainly can, and I will." He looked to his pathetic mother. "Shawn didn't die of SIDs. I smothered him."

When his mom started to rise, Agent Raines took her hand. Mom shook the woman off her. "I don't believe you."

"Because you're stupid. I overheard what you said to Emma in the laundry room. You know, about God hating you. If there is a God, that might be true. After all, He gave you me. And *I* took away your baby and husband." He smiled as his mother and sister wept. "Poor little Shawny. I suffocated him, then just when I thought he was about to die, I let him breathe." He shrugged. "I think I did that about three or four times before I finally killed him."

Mom shook her head. "No. No! You were only ten. Ten!"

"So? I was a ten-year-old who saw an obstacle in my way and did something about it. You should be proud. Isn't that one of the lines of bullshit you give the idiots who pay to hear you speak?"

Mom sobbed. Tears and snot dripped from her red face. He'd gone this far, and figured he'd twist the knife a little deeper.

"I thought Dad would be harder to kill. But he trusted me. When I pushed him off the boat, I laughed about it. He did, too, thinking I was joking around. He stopped laughing when I hit him over the head."

Mom wiped her tear-soaked face. "The medical examiner said his head injury was consistent with him hitting the bottom of the boat," she said, her voice rising, almost manic. She glanced to the agent. "Police said Tim must have hit his head when he tried to surface, then he drowned. Why wouldn't I believe that?" She faced him. "Why are you telling these lies?"

"Mom," Emma cried. "Stop it! Open your eyes. You heard what he said to me. You know what he's capable of. Stop denying what's right in front of your face."

"For once, I agree with Emma. You're so pathetic. You want your family together so badly, you refuse to believe me, even when I'm finally telling you the truth." He turned the gun on his mother. "How about this for proof?" he asked, and pulled the trigger.

Emma screamed. His mother fell against the bookshelves, clutching her chest where blood oozed onto her pale yellow sweater, and, with the help of Agent Raines, she slowly slid to the floor.

"Don't touch her." He aimed the gun at the agent. When he caught Emma moving in his peripheral vision, he swung the weapon toward her. "Stay."

The agent's phone rang, displaying the same caller who'd already phoned her twice. "Someone is looking for you. Probably the guy outside, so I better make this quick." He aimed his dad's gun at her, just as his phone rang from his back pocket.

"Nick," Agent Raines began, "I guarantee that's my partner. Answer the call. Talk to him. We need to get your mom help. Turn yourself in before anyone else gets hurt. You're only sixteen. I know what you went through at the park. I know it was a very traumatic and life-altering experience. People will understand that this isn't the *real* you."

She didn't know? Oh, my God, the FBI didn't know, and she hadn't come here to arrest him. "Or, I could kill you all, blame my sister and not do one day in prison. That's a better plan," he said with confidence. He still had this. Yeah, the agent out front was a problem. But if he took the call and let the man inside, he could kill him, too, and still blame Emma. Except, what if the guy outside had heard the gunshot and called in for backup. It wouldn't take long for the police or FBI to surround the house. Damn it, he'd planned everything perfectly, and these two agents were fucking it up for him.

Furious, determined to have his way, he pulled the phone from his pocket, saw that it was the same number that kept showing up on Agent Raines's phone. "Not a word," he said to the three women, then answered.

"Nick," a man said. "I'm Chase Sawyer. I heard a gunshot, and I need to know if everyone is okay."

Nick looked to his mother. Blood had spread across her chest, making her sweater look as if a large, red rose had been knitted into it. "No," he said, infusing panic into his voice. "My sister...she's crazy." He winked at Emma. "She...she just shot my mom. I'm so scared. I...I think she might shoot Agent Raines."

"Where are you?"

"I managed to get away from her," he said, moving the pistol between the agent and Emma to keep them scared and quiet. "I'm hiding in my bedroom closet. You need to get inside. I'll give you the code for the garage. The door to the laundry room is always unlocked."

Chase rubbed a hand along his jaw to keep from punching the car. Indecision and outrage tore through him. He knew Nick was lying, and had caught him looking between the lower level blinds. He needed to go in there and diffuse the situation, yet worried he would lose control of his emotions. He was also concerned Nick was setting a trap. In all the years he had worked as a crisis negotiator, he'd never had a hostage taker invite him inside this quickly.

"Give me the code," Chase said. "Stay where you are. I'm coming to help you." He ended the call after the boy gave him the number, then immediately dialed Dave's phone. "ETA?"

"Seven minutes."

"Good," he said, then explained the situation as he went to the garage and punched in the code.

"Don't go in there, Chase. Let SWAT handle it."

"If I'm right, Nick is holding his mother, sister and Summer at gunpoint. And if you send in SWAT, he might start shooting. I know for sure he's fired once, and I wouldn't be surprised if the gunshot the neighbor heard came from this house." He entered the garage, walked past an Audi, then reached the door. "I have to get Summer out of here."

"You have no legal authority to—"

"She's pregnant with my child. Fuck legal authority," he said, and hung up on him. Fighting for control of his emotions, his anger, the utter terror moving through him, he drew in a deep breath at the same time he drew his weapon. This would be the negotiation of his life, and it *would* be successful.

Chase entered the house. The laundry room was dark, but lights from other rooms cast shadows over the walls and furniture. Since he'd last spotted Nick at the front of the house, he exited the laundry room with caution, and quietly moved in that direction. When he reached the foyer, he pressed his back against the wall. From a room to the right, light spilled onto the hardwood floor and staircase. An office? Didn't matter. With his gun raised, he edged around the corner and tensed.

"Hello, Chase." Nick stood in front of the desk, his pistol aimed at the office door way. *At him.* "Glad you joined the party."

Chase took another step, and looked inside. A middle-aged woman with auburn hair leaned against bookshelves, blood soaking her yellow sweater. Summer sat next to her, her gaze filled with a combination of fear, worry and the same anger that rolled through him. Near the desk was a younger version of the injured woman, the sister, he assumed.

"Thanks for the invite," Chase said, his insides twisting with dread. This couldn't be happening. He and Summer were expecting a baby, were planning a future, and if this kid thought he could fuck it up, he'd thought wrong. He took a cautious step. "It looks like you were able to wrestle the gun from you sister."

Nick grinned. "Got that right," he said, and fired.

Summer's ears rang. Chase's gun slid across the floor. Her skin prickled with horror as she stared out the doorway at the love of her life, the father of her unborn child. Stunned, heartbroken, she prayed to God Chase was wearing a vest and that the bullet hadn't hit any vital organs. Her chest and throat tightened. She couldn't lose him, didn't want to spend her life without him. Tears clouded her vision. She loved him so much. After the hell they'd been through the past two years, they deserved happiness, not more pain.

She blinked back the tears. Focused on the slow rise and fall of his chest. From the angle where Chase lay, she couldn't see how badly he'd been wounded, but knowing he was still alive gave her hope. Shivering, trying desperately to keep calm, and find a way get Chase help, she slowly shifted her gaze to Nick.

He yelled at his screaming sister, but his voice and hers were muffled, distant. She glanced to Patsy, whose face was alarmingly pale. Tears fell from the woman's heavy-lidded eyes and she winced with each breath she took.

"Shut up," Nick shouted, his words becoming distinct as the ringing slowly abated. He waved the gun at Emma. "Not another word."

"You just shot a federal agent," Summer said, her words thick, her mouth dry. She swallowed and tried to keep from crying. "You should have turned yourself in the moment I arrived. At that point, your prison sentence wouldn't have been so bad. And like I told you, prosecutors would have taken into consideration the fact that you were the victim of a kidnapping."

A complete lie. For what he'd done, chances were Nick would be tried as an adult, and spend decades or even life in prison. Since he'd murdered a baby, his own father, tortured his sister and shot his mother, he deserved the maximum sentencing. She considered the .357 Magnum tucked in the ankle glove holster strapped around her boot and hidden by her pants. For shooting Chase, Nick deserved death.

"But," she continued, "then you shot your mom and Chase. If

they die, it's going to be worse for you. Do the right thing. Turn yourself in so we can get them to the hospital and save their lives."

He pointed his gun at her. "Yeah, that's not going to happen."

"Wait!" Heart in her throat, she pressed against the bookshelves until the wood dug into her back, and the wound along her left upper arm burned and throbbed. She drew her knees to her chest to protect her abdomen and gain better access of the Magnum should she have an opportunity to use it. "Just wait. I need to know something," she said, hoping to keep him talking. Chase wouldn't have come here unless he'd discovered Nick was Bad Kid. If he had, then listened to her voice message, he would have then called Dave. Reinforcements had to be on the way. She hoped.

"That'd be what?"

Nick could have killed her, Patsy and Emma before Chase had rung the doorbell. He'd hesitated, not because he had suddenly struggled with his conscience—she didn't believe he had one—but to brag. Nick had wanted his mom to know that he had killed his father and brother, and had tried to coerce Emma into committing suicide. If he were Bad Kid, would he want to brag about it? Could she get him talking and stall for time?

"The amusement park," she said. "In all the years I've been an agent, I've never witnessed anything like it. I believe it was the most elaborate, diabolical and idiotic kidnapping ever attempted."

His face reddened and his eyes filled with irritation. "Are you finished, or can I shoot you now?"

"The mastermind behind the kidnapping was a fool to think he could get away with it," she said, counting on his adolescent arrogance to crack. She didn't need for him to admit his involvement because at this point it didn't matter. She needed to buy time. "But I will give him some credit. He almost pulled off the perfect crime."

"What do you mean *almost*? Shultz is dead and didn't get the five hundred thousand dollars. So I'd say the crime was far from perfect."

The FBI had never shared the paid ransom amount with the media, or the boys. The only one who would know the exact dollar amount was one of the kidnappers, agents and the senator who'd paid the ransom. "True, but he still made mistakes. Holding you kids at the amusement park was stupid. Murdering Joel, then leaving his cousin's knife and rifle behind was a horrible mistake. It's almost as if he *wanted* to get caught...or someone set him up for failure."

His mouth tilted in a condescending smile. "Who would do that?"

"I know *who*, I'm wondering why."

Next to her, Patsy let out a wheezy gasp. "Please, no. Don't let it be true."

"Shut up, Mom, and just die already." He narrowed his eyes at Summer. "Is Brennan out of the coma?"

She shook her head. "Unfortunately, no. Why did you try to kill him? Did he figure out that you'd hired Shultz to execute the kidnapping?"

He frowned. "I don't know what you're talking about. If you're trying to accuse me of kidnapping and murder, then I guess your line about prosecutors considering me a victim was a bunch of bullshit."

Summer hunched her shoulders, smashing her breasts against her thighs, and wrapped her hand around each calf, until her left palm settled over the concealed Magnum. "It's interesting that you had no problem admitting what you'd done to your dad, brother and sister, yet you don't want to brag about the kidnapping. Honestly, I was lying about the plan being idiotic. It *was* almost the perfect crime. If you hadn't been greedy, we would never have suspected there was someone other than Shultz and his crew involved. The human doggy door you made at the fun house was brilliant, same with planting the knives, the burner phones and switching the fuels. I bet Shultz was freaking out wondering what was happening."

He straightened and tossed his bangs to the side. The gesture was confident, cocky. He took several backward steps. When he peeked through the blinds again, revealing darkness had fallen, Summer was tempted to raise her pant leg and free the weapon from the ankle holster. She undid the holster's thumb snap instead. If she wasn't quick on the draw, she could end up with a bullet in her head. But with the thumb snap released, and once the right opportunity presented itself, she could have the Magnum pointed at him within seconds.

"Who knows?" he asked, walking back toward her.

"That *you* were the mastermind? Everyone will soon. Killing me won't help you. Even if you get out of this house before SWAT arrives, you won't get far. We know about World Privacy, and that you have an offshore account. Sorry, bud, but it's now frozen. You can no longer access the money," she said, another lie. She still wasn't one hundred percent sure Rachel had hacked into the company, and that had been how Chase knew to come here.

Chase...

She refused to look at him, refused to do anything but talk her way out of this house. She needed to survive, needed to bring their baby into the world. "So just tell me...why'd you do it? Your mom is wealthy, and I know you have a trust fund and get a nice monthly allowance. Was it really for the thirty million dollars?"

"Nope. It was to get to my mom and sister."

"Not following," she said, not understanding what he'd meant.

"I planned the kidnapping to get to them and do this." He waved the gun at his mom and sister. "Imagine what it's like to drive to the house where you were raised, only to find that it's been sold and someone else is living there. I don't have to imagine it, because that's what happened to me. The great Patsy Janson, motivational speaker extraordinaire, moved herself and her daughter without telling her son." He shook his head, and narrowed his gaze at his mother. "She abandoned me, and wouldn't give me her new address. And if I don't have an address," he said his voice rising with outrage, "I can't get in her face and threaten her to give me more money."

Summer forced a laugh. "Seven people died, fourteen others were injured and terrorized because *you* couldn't get Mommy to increase your allowance?" She sobered. "And you called your mom pathetic."

"Pathetic? Fuck you!" He aimed for her head. "I'll show you pathetic."

Another gunshot thundered from the foyer. Emma rushed to her mother's side as Nick gripped his thigh and staggered against the desk.

Summer gripped her pant leg with both hands, grabbed the Magnum, then pointed it at one seriously bad kid. "Drop it!"

"Now," Chase shouted.

Summer didn't dare look away from Nick to check on Chase. He was talking and shooting, and, for now, that was good enough for her. "You heard us," she warned Nick.

His face covered with a sheen of sweat, his eyes wild with pain, panic, he shook his head and refused to lower his weapon. Instead, he shifted his gaze to Emma. The malice, the utter hatred in his eyes, was unlike anything Summer had ever witnessed. This kid hated his sister, had planned to kill her and Patsy, and take the inheritance he'd considered rightfully his. If he went to prison, he'd lose it all. If he were ever released, he would find and kill Emma. Of that, she had no doubt.

The corner of Nick's mouth turned up in a mocking smile. "Fuck it," he said, and swung the gun toward his sister.

Summer squeezed the trigger, rapidly releasing two shots and hitting Nick in the throat and gut. He dropped his weapon and, clutching his neck where blood poured from the wound, fell to his knees. Keeping her gun trained on Nick, Summer rushed over, then kicked his pistol away from him.

Rather than stop her, Nick inched toward his mother. Tears streamed down his face as he parted his lips, mouthed *Mom* and reached for Patsy.

Patsy held Emma's hand tight, and shook her head. When

Nick's bloody fingertips touched his mother's shoe, she wheezed and coughed, but managed to kick his hand away. "Go die over there," she said between short pants. "You're dead to me."

Wood splintered and frantic voices came from the foyer. Nick curled onto his side and cried, bleeding all over the office's beige carpet. Agents dressed in SWAT tactical gear rushed in. Summer immediately spotted Kipp Taggart. "The woman was shot in the chest. She needs immediate medical attention."

She sidestepped Nick's still body and the agents hovering over him, and hurried to Chase's side. Wincing and gripping his chest, he pushed himself to a seated position with Dave's assistance and held out his hand to her. She knelt beside him and hugged him. When he grunted, she tried to pull away.

"Don't go," he said. "Not yet. Are you okay?"

"But you're hurt." She leaned back and ran her hand along his chest, and when her fingers connected with the bulletproof vest she let out the breath she hadn't realized she'd been holding. "Thank God."

His gaze moved over her face, chest and stomach, then touched on the bloody tear along her upper arm. "*You're* hurt. Summer—"

"I'm fine." She looked up at Dave. "Patsy Janson isn't." She swallowed around the lump in her throat. "Neither is her son." She'd likely killed a sixteen-year-old boy. He might've been a psychopathic serial killer, but he was still a kid. And she didn't know what to do with any of that.

EMTs hurried through the front door, wheeling gurneys. Within minutes, Patsy was being transported from the office, Emma by her side. As they moved past her and Chase, Patsy rolled her head toward Summer. She'd seen people die before and knew in her heart this woman wouldn't make it. Patsy met her gaze and the look in her eyes, the pain, the defeat, the overwhelming sadness would likely haunt Summer for a lifetime. Soon, she would be a mother. She already loved the baby she carried and couldn't imagine coming to hate her child.

She quickly rose to her feet and took Patsy's hand. "I'm so sorry," she said, choking back the tears. This woman had already lost so much, and she'd probably killed her son. "You didn't deserve any of this. He's not your fault."

A tear slipped into Patsy's hair.

"We've gotta go," the EMT said with urgency.

"Wait," Patsy whispered, and tightened her hold on Summer's hand. "Thank you. I can die knowing he can't hurt my Emma."

"You're not going to die." Emma wiped her eyes, then nose. "It's just me and you. You're all I have." She released a heart-wrenching sob. "How can I go on without you?"

Summer covered her hand over her mouth to stop herself from crying. It didn't work. Tears blurred her vision as she watched the medics rush Patsy from the house. When an EMT tried to look at Summer's arm, she shook her head. "Him first," she said, referring to Chase, then she walked to the staircase, sat on the second step and held her head in her hands.

God, what have I done?

A hand pressed against her shoulder. She looked up and met Chase's worried gaze. "I...ah..."

He shook his head. "Not here. Keep it together until we get you out of here." With a wince, he helped her rise. "Please, let the medic look at your arm."

She stared at the hole where the bullet had gone through his sweatshirt. "You're good?"

"I'm sure I'll have a bruise, but it'll heal." He caught a tear with his thumb. "I'm more worried about your wounds."

"I only have one, and the bullet grazed my arm. I doubt it'll need stitches."

He caressed her cheek. "I'm talking about the wounds here." He touched her head. "And here," he said, placing his index finger in the middle of her chest.

She nodded and cleared her throat. "I'll be okay. I...I have to talk to Dave." When she approached the office, Dave stood next to Kipp and Tony, and they all stared down at Nick's unmoving, bloodied body.

Dave glanced back at her. "Give Tony an account of what happened. Make sure you let medics look at your arm."

Knowing the drill, she went with Tony into the kitchen, while Rich took Chase's statement. Two hours later, emotionally drained and exhausted, she stood under the shower spray and tried to wash away everything that had transpired today. She'd maintained strength and composure when she'd had to tell Tony what had happened, had tried to maintain patience when the EMT cleaned the small wound on her arm, then had gone home with Chase. She hadn't been able to talk to him during the drive, and she loved him for not forcing her to talk. But maybe she should have said something. Her killing a teenager had to have hit home for him. Brody had only been a year younger than Nick.

Before she started thinking about him, about Patsy and Emma, and all the pain and misery the family had suffered, she shut off the faucet, then toweled off her body. After applying lotion and deodorant, she brushed her hair, then slipped into panties and a T-shirt. All she wanted was to crawl into bed next to Chase and let sleep consume her.

When she exited the bathroom, Chase was sitting on the edge of the mattress. His hair was wet and he wore nothing but his underwear.

"You didn't need to use the guest bath," she said, then went to the nightstand where her phone was on the charger.

He stood, took the phone from her, then set it back down. "No one has called, and you don't need to set an alarm. Dave told you to take a few days off, and that's exactly what you are going to do."

A few days? After being held at gunpoint and killing a kid, she wasn't sure if a few days were enough. Right now, she wasn't sure of anything when it came to her job. She wasn't even sure about Chase. Yes, she loved him with all her heart, but he'd only been in town for five days.

Five days.

So much had happened since Friday, it was too overwhelming to accept, digest, comprehend… God, her thoughts were so scattered, and she couldn't pull them together. Couldn't make sense of anything.

His strong hands wrapped around her wrists, sending a zing of pain to where she'd been grazed by the bullet. She met his gaze, wanted to weep over the understanding in his eyes and the concern etched on his face. He, of all people, knew what she was going through, which added to the sadness, the regret surrounding her. She didn't want him to compare her killing Nick to the Wakefield case. There was no comparison. Shooting Brody Wakefield had been accidental. Nick? She let out a breath.

"I need to go to bed," she said.

"Me, too."

"It's okay if you want to stay up for a while." She broke away from him to crawl onto the mattress. "Can you turn the light out on your way?"

"Are you dismissing me?" he asked, and the hurt in his eyes had her turning to her other side.

"No, I'm just tired," she said, her throat tightening with tears. She didn't want to talk about the Jansons anymore. She wanted to forget.

The light went off, then Chase climbed into bed. "I'm tired, too." He rested his head on the pillow next to hers, then scooted over until their foreheads touched. "Turn over so I can hold you. This can't be comfortable for your arm."

No, it wasn't. But she didn't want to lose the connection. She needed to feel his breath fan across her face, to know he was safe and alive. "When he shot you—"

"Baby, don't." He wrapped an arm around her and pulled her closer. "I don't want to relive what I saw when I reached the office. You were…I was so damned scared. Knowing what he was capable of, seeing what he'd done to his mother." He kissed her. "I love you. You're everything to me."

Tears welled in her eyes. "I love you, too. And I didn't know whether you'd worn a vest, didn't know where he'd hit you…I tried to be strong. For you, for Patsy and Emma, and I worried if he shot me I'd survive, but lose the baby. And if I lost the baby, then maybe I'd lose you."

He quickly rolled her onto her back and pinned her to the mattress. "Do you think that's the only reason I want to be with you? Honestly?" He pressed his forehead along hers again. "When I said you mean everything to me, I meant it, even if I haven't shown it for long time. You're my best friend, my partner, the first person I think about when I wake up, and the last person I think about when I try to go to sleep. Our child is a bonus, something I never thought I'd want or have in my life. But I *need* you. I'm here now because I love you." He moved his hand to her stomach. "This baby was created out of love, even if we—I—was in a dark place at the time. What do I have to say or do to prove that to you?"

She ran her hands along his jaw and let the tears fall. The prospect of being a father had shocked sense into him, made Chase realize there was more to life than regret. She understood this, and they'd already discussed it. And while she did believe he loved her and wanted to be with her, the thought that she'd lose him had briefly crossed her mind. But she had faith in him, in them. Fate and a bad kid had brought them back together, given them a second chance, and she wouldn't allow insecurity to tear them apart.

"You don't have to say or do anything," she said.

"Maybe I do. It kills me to know you'd think I'd leave if there were no baby. I want to marry you because I love and need you in my life, not to make babies."

She tensed, stared up at him, but it was too dark to see his face and eyes. "Can you turn on the light?"

"I don't need it to see you." He brushed his lips across hers. "I just need to feel you against me."

She hugged him. When the rapid rhythm of his heart lightly drummed against her chest, she squeezed tighter. Blocked out the image of him crashing to the floor after the bullet had hit his vest, and needed to feel his body against hers, too. She never wanted to come that close to losing him, but they were in law enforcement and there would always be a risk. Which was why she needed to cherish each moment and enjoy life rather than spend her days questioning her or Chase's choices, or worrying about being hurt again. She had to trust her heart, instinct and Chase.

"I want to be your wife," she said, then kissed his shoulder.

He lifted slightly. "Yeah?"

She traced her fingertips along his spine. "Yeah."

"When you're not expecting it, I'll surprise you with a proper proposal and ring. I'll need to ask your dad if he'll let me marry his daughter. And—"

"Chase?"

"Yes."

"Stop talking and kiss me."

Without another word, he kissed her, softly, gently, leisurely. He removed her T-shirt and panties. Let his fingers, hands and mouth explore her body. As he entered her, rocked his hips and pressed himself deep, the connection, the oneness was unlike anything she'd ever experienced. Chase was her other half. Without him, her life wouldn't be complete. Instead of telling him this, she showed him through touch and passionate kisses. And when they climaxed together, she clung to his shoulders and thanked God Chase had found his way back to her.

He brushed her hair from her face. "I love you. Don't ever give up on us."

"I won't. I love you too much," she said, then kissed him again. Later, her body sated, her heart filled with relief, with love, she rested her head next to his. She closed her eyes, and as she listened to him breathe, she drifted off to sleep. She dreamed of Chase smiling down at a swaddled newborn baby, then looking at her with more love than she probably deserved. When he brought the baby over to her and placed the child in her arms, she moved the blanket aside...and stared at the bitter, hate-filled face of Nick Janson. And screamed...

17

Summer's House, Fairview Park, Ohio
Wednesday, January 25ᵗʰ, 9:24 a.m. Eastern Standard Time

CHASED SHIFTED HIS gaze from the crib parts he'd lain on the floor to the directions, which might as well had been written in Chinese. When he'd still been in his teens, he'd worked plenty of odd jobs to earn money. Aside from being employed by a restaurant, he'd also taken up with the local handyman and had learned how to change electrical outlets, install windows, toilets and sinks, and even build walls. He should be able to put the damned crib together with his eyes closed. But every time he tried to read the directions, his mind drifted to Summer, to her waking in the middle of the night screaming and shaking.

He understood. He'd had his share of nightmares over the past two years, and worried she would have a hard time dealing with the life she'd taken—even if it hadn't been a good one.

"Need any help?"

He turned. Summer stood in the doorway wearing a baggy sweatshirt, leggings and a pair of boot-like slippers. She'd let her hair dry in natural waves and wore no makeup. Her face was etched with exhaustion, and he didn't like the worry in her eyes.

"What's wrong?" he asked.

"Patsy died." A tear slipped down her cheek as she looked away and hugged herself. "I prayed she'd make it. That maybe with Nick gone she could find some happiness. Poor Emma." She wiped her cheek with her shoulder. "My heart goes out to her. She's lost so much."

But at least the girl wouldn't have to go through life knowing her brother was still out there, plotting and planning her murder. Chase would keep that thought to himself, though. He suspected Summer was dealing with the guilt of taking a life, and didn't want to bring up Nick's death unless she wanted to discuss it.

"I didn't have to kill him," she said, then walked over to where the crib parts lie. "I could've hit him in the shoulder, shot the gun out of his hand."

He knew this, and had spent many hours at the gun range with her. She was a dead shot, especially with her .357 or Glock.

"You know I've only fired in the line of duty a half dozen times. Four were warning shots, the other two I purposefully aimed to wound and successfully hit my target." She sat on the floor and crossed her legs. "Now I've taken a life. A boy's life. I had no right."

When she looked up at him, he couldn't stomach the regret in her eyes. "Nick Janson started killing when he was ten. By the time he was sixteen, he'd killed—either directly or indirectly—nine people. Ten, now that Patsy's gone. You did the world a favor, and you gave Emma justice."

She began rearranging the crib parts. "The court would have done it, too."

He sat next to her. "What if he got out in thirty or forty years? Do you think he would've found Jesus in prison and turned over a new leaf? Or do you believe he would have gone after his sister?"

"He could have gotten the death penalty. I would've been good with having someone else kill him."

He rested his hand on her knee. "What are you doing to yourself?"

"I don't know." She shrugged. "I guess truly understanding

what you went through after Brody and Larry died. Except you killed Brody by accident."

From the moment he'd watched her fire the Magnum, he wondered if her aim had been off out of stress and fear, or if she'd purposefully killed the kid. Either way wouldn't have mattered to him, and now that he knew the truth, it still didn't matter. No, it wasn't her right to have decided his fate. But after what he'd done, and how many lives he'd affected and destroyed, he hadn't deserved to breathe.

"You're not commenting," she said, taking a look at the directions. "I don't know how to take that."

"What do you want me to say that hasn't already been said? Are you worried I'll think less of you?" He leaned forward. "Baby, look at me."

When she did, her eyes were filled with tears. "You stood by my side, and never gave up on me. Our shootings are different. Brody was innocent, Nick wasn't. He is not worth your time or energy, so don't waste it grieving or regretting. He shot you, and if he hadn't taken the time to boast about all the bad he'd done, he would've shot you again." He took her hand. "When I fired at him, I wasn't aiming for his leg."

"Stop. You're a better shot than me."

"Well, I've never fired a weapon while lying on the floor, either," he said, and tucked a lock of hair behind her ear. "My point is that I didn't care if Nick lived or died. I wanted him away from you. Did you tell Tony any of this last night?"

She shook her head. "You're the only one who will ever know the truth."

"Good. But don't be surprised if you're questioned about it once you're back at work."

"I…I'm not going back." Her gaze was probing, anxious. "I can't."

"Don't be like me. You're stronger than that, and you've worked too hard to quit."

She released a shaky breath. "Chase, I'm going to be a mom.

Who knows? Maybe we'll even have more kids. Regardless, I want to be around and watch our baby grow. I can't do that dead."

Though relieved she would no longer be potentially placed in a dangerous situation, he also didn't want her to quit a job she loved. "You said yourself that you're a manger who carries a gun. What happened at the Janson house was unusual, and I doubt you'll find yourself pointing a weapon at a suspect again."

"I get that, but there's more to my decision. I don't want to work twelve hour days, but I also don't want to not work at all." She sent him a wry grin. "I don't know what I want."

"Me." He rubbed her arm. "The baby. Happiness. Health. Me."

Her smile broadened. "You said yourself twice."

"Did I?" He leaned in and kissed her. "If you don't want to work for the Bureau any longer, then quit. Take the time to enjoy the pregnancy and prepare for the baby. Worry about finding a new job once the baby is older."

"I'd like that, but my quitting changes everything. You wouldn't need to move here, unless you have your mind set on getting a crisis negotiating position with the Cleveland PD or Cuyahoga County Sheriff."

"No, I'm good."

She chuckled. "I take it you don't need time to think about it."

"I made up my mind last night when I was getting ready to enter the Janson house. I couldn't keep my emotions in check. I know yesterday was different, that it was personal, but I'm not sure I'm qualified to work crisis negotiation on a regular basis. And I had fun investigating this case. I think I'd rather hunt down a suspect than talk him out of doing harm to himself or others."

"Does this mean you'd like to stay with CORE?"

"I...yes. But if you have your heart set on living in Cleveland, then that's what we'll do."

"I have my heart set on living with you. I don't care which city. If it's Chicago, I was thinking... Rachel has kids, right?"

"Except for me and Sloan, every CORE agent is married and has kids. Why?"

"How's the work-life balance there?"

He stilled and wondered where she was going with this. "Good, I guess. I've never heard anyone complain."

"And how would you feel if *I* worked for CORE? I'm thinking part-time, and that I'd come in as more of a consultant than investigator, although I would enjoy researching criminal activity and suspects' backgrounds. Similar to what Rachel currently does for CORE, minus the hacking."

When he'd been with the FBI, he and Summer had never worked an investigation together, not even when he'd been with the Cleveland Division. He'd enjoyed partnering with her on the kidnapping case. They'd meshed just as well on the job as they did at home. "I'm all for it, except I heard Ian gets all sorts of resumes and has never hired anyone that way. He seeks out his agents."

She frowned. "He approached you?"

He nodded. "Based on the other agents' backgrounds, I think he prefers to hire damaged goods."

"There's a first time for everything." She picked up the crib instructions again. "I'll just have to wow Ian."

"Of that, I have no doubt." Excited Summer was willing to come to Chicago, and that he could keep his job with CORE, he gave her another kiss. "My condo is a tiny two-bedroom. We're going to have to start looking for a house immediately. I heard it's a seller's market, so we'll have to be ready when we find the right place for us."

"You want to *buy* a home? Are you sure you don't want to wait?"

"I'm tired of waiting and holding out for whatever it is I thought I wanted, when what I need is right in front of me."

She dropped the instructions, then straddled his lap. "If I'm not going to be living here much longer, I don't see the point in putting together the crib." She twined her arms around his neck. "We should save it for when we move into the new house."

"I planned on spending the morning working on it. Now that I don't have to, is there something you'd like to do?"

She let go of him, leaned back, then pulled her shirt over her head. "Yeah, I have something in mind," she said, unhooking her bra. "Does this work for you?"

Everything about Summer worked for him. He pulled her close. "Absolutely," he said, then kissed her.

One week later…
FBI Cleveland Division, Cleveland, Ohio
Wednesday, February 1st, 11:43 a.m. Eastern Standard Time

"Are you sure this is what you want?" Dave asked when he entered Summer's office. "I hate losing you."

While Summer loved the compliment, and knowing she'd be missed, she was more than ready to start a new adventure in Chicago. Even if Ian didn't hire her, she'd eventually find something part-time. For now, her focus would be on house hunting and preparing for the baby's arrival.

"I've loved working for you and with my team. This position has been challenging, and an excellent experience."

Dave rolled his eyes and sat in the chair near her desk. "Come on, Summer, don't say what you think I want to hear."

"It's true. I did love working here." She rested her rear against the edge of the desk. "But I admit there were times I missed being in the field, the hours were too long and managing the team was an added stress I hadn't expected when I applied for the promotion. That being said, I needed this position, and to be in Cleveland. My job, you and my coworkers…none of you would know it, but in some capacity you've all helped me through a tough period."

"Chase."

She nodded. "I'm sorry I didn't tell you about the pregnancy sooner. I'm glad you took my suggestion into consideration and pushed to have Lauren take over as ASAC. I think the job is perfect for her."

"Agreed. She'll do well. Speaking of which, I wish you luck with getting a position at CORE. Check your inbox. I emailed your letter of recommendation. Hopefully, it'll help get your foot in the door there."

"Thanks. If not, I'm sure I'll eventually find something to keep me busy."

Dave grinned. "I have two kids. Trust me. You'll be busy with one." He sighed. "Patsy Janson's funeral was three days ago."

She knew, but hadn't attended. Though tempted to go and pay her respects, she'd worried how Emma would react if she saw her. "I heard. Tony told me Emma refused to claim her brother's body."

"That's right. He's in a wooden box and buried in an un-marked grave." His brows pulled together. "My youngest son is almost sixteen. It's hard to believe a kid that young could…" He shook his head. "It's over. Emma wants it to be over, too. She doesn't want investigators looking into her father or baby brother's death, and doesn't see the point in it since their killer was dead."

"I agree with her. Hopefully, she'll find closure knowing Nick can't hurt her or anyone else ever again."

He nodded. "Her house is up for sale, and she left town im-mediately after the funeral. Which was smart. The media has been relentless."

Fortunately, Summer and Chase's names had been kept from the press, and neither had had to deal with reporters stalking them, or shoving cameras and microphones in their faces. She placed the last of her personal belongings in a box and smiled. "I also heard Brennan Williams is doing well."

Brennan had come out of his coma four days ago. The first word out of his mouth was *Nick*. Later, he told his parents, then agents, how Nick had smashed his head against the tree. He'd said he hadn't expected Nick to harm him, but to escape. After all, they'd had a plan. They would never know what had been going through Nick's head at the time, but Summer believed the kid had worried that if Brennan had managed to leave the park and go to the authorities, this wouldn't have allowed Nick the opportunity to kill off the men he'd hired.

"Yes, Brennan should make a full recovery. His doctors plan to release him once he's stronger."

"I'm so happy to hear," she said, warmth spreading throughout her body. All was good and right. Alex McGuire had gone home the day before Brennan had woken, and was also going to be just fine. And, come Friday, she would call Chicago home...with Chase.

"Let me help you with that." Dave picked up the box, but didn't head for the door. "Can I say something? Off record."

"Sure."

"The evening at the Jansons. You did the right thing."

Lauren, Rich and Tony entered her office carrying a bouquet of flowers, stopping Dave from saying anything more. Which was fine by her. There wasn't anything else to say, discuss or regret. The way Nick had turned out hadn't been due to his upbringing. In her opinion, Nick Janson had been born bad, and no amount of therapy would have changed that. Had he gotten away with murdering her, Patsy and Emma, she believed he would have eventually killed anyone else who stood in his way. Had she the right to play judge, jury and executioner? No. Would she make the same choice if she'd been given the opportunity to do it all over again?

She'd never know.

Ten weeks later...
CORE Offices, Chicago, Illinois
Wednesday, April 12th, 4:47 p.m., Central Standard Time

"Thank you for meeting with me," Summer said as she took a seat across from CORE's owner, Ian Scott.

"Anytime." Ian smiled. "Congratulations on the engagement and baby. Chase said you're having a girl."

When she rested her hand on her large, hard belly, the baby gave her a big kick. "Thanks. We're excited."

"Have you moved into the new house yet?"

She and Chase had purchased a brick colonial located in the Chicago community of Beverly. One of the other agents, Dante Russo, lived a few streets over with his wife, Jessica, and their two children. Summer had met them, along with several of the other agents, their wives and children when the Russos had hosted a party two weeks ago. Everyone was friendly and she could see herself getting along with the agents, and settling into CORE nicely. First, she needed to land the job.

"Yes, just last week. We still have boxes to unpack, but each day the stack gets smaller." Done with the small talk, she reached over and handed him her résumé. "This is why I asked for you to meet with me."

He glanced from her to the résumé, then set the papers on his desk. "I don't need to read about your education or experience."

"I understand that you don't usually entertain unsolicited résumés," she began, disappointed, but not deterred, "and that you hand pick your agents. I think you'll find that I would be a valuable asset to CORE."

Ian held up a hand, and gave her a small smile. "Summer Raines is an interesting name. Do you know why your parents chose to call you Summer?"

Though surprised he'd asked her about her name, not her experience, she enjoyed telling people how her parents had come up with it. "There was a blizzard the night I was born. The roads were so bad the ambulance went off the berm and ended up stuck in the snow. My dad had to drive my mom to the hospital, but apparently I was ready to see the world and couldn't wait for a doctor." She grinned. "My dad delivered me in the backseat of his Ford. According to him, my mom looked down at me and said I was a warm ray of sunshine in the middle of a winter storm, then decided to call me Summer. This was after he made her promise they would leave Massachusetts and move south."

"She got her way, didn't she?" he asked with a smile. "You grew up in Bradenton, Florida, and your parents are still living in the house where you were raised."

Well, this just got a little weird. "Why would you know this?"

He casually half-shrugged, but his blue eyes remained sharp. "You're right, I do hand pick my agents, and when I'm interested in recruiting someone, I find out everything I can about them. Chase had been with you for seven years before joining CORE. I wanted to know why he walked away, and if I should be concerned his past relationship with you would take him away from my agency. While I was mildly concerned about that and how he was still coping with the Wakefield investigation, I liked the idea of having a former crisis negotiator on my team."

She was beginning to think Ian Scott had a bit of a God complex. "If you were worried about our past interfering with his job, why would you send Chase to Cleveland? Not once, but twice."

He drew in a deep breath. "Last August was a test. Of course, I expected him to do his job, which he did, but I assumed he would see you." He glanced to her stomach and smiled. "Which he clearly also did." When their gazes met again, his eyes held no apology. "I was hoping he would either get you out of his system, or quit CORE and stay in Cleveland. You see, I like Chase. I liked his background. When he was a special agent for the Baltimore Division, he did great things and was an excellent investigator. I had hoped he'd perform the same way for CORE. Instead, he didn't want to be challenged, did the bare minimum, and gave me the impression that he looked at CORE as *just a paycheck*, not a career."

Since she knew that had been how Chase felt about CORE, she couldn't argue with Ian. "Why didn't you let him go?"

"Because he came back to Chicago after seeing you in August. At that point I thought, 'this is good, he's got her out of his system.' But his work ethic hadn't changed. If anything, he'd become more withdrawn."

"You assigned him the kidnapping case because of me," she said, deciding the man did indeed have a serious God complex.

"I sent him because I was concerned it would result in a hostage situation. And...he needed to know he was going to be a father."

Furious, Summer stood and took the résumé from the desk. "I don't know who you *think* you are, but you had no right to interfere with our lives."

"Summer, please sit down."

"No." This conversation was over and she no longer wanted to be in the same room as the arrogant ass. "You didn't have to tell me any of this, but you're no better than..." She stopped herself from saying Nick Janson's name and drew in a deep breath to control her temper. Ian was still Chase's boss. Between the new house and baby, they couldn't afford for him to lose his job with CORE. "All you had to do was tell me you weren't hiring." She started for the door. "I will not be telling Chase about this conversation."

"I'm no better than who? Nick Janson?"

She stopped and faced him. My God, was the man a mind reader? "I never said that."

"You were going to, though." He stood and came around the desk. "Dave let me read your statement. You mentioned how Nick liked to brag about murdering his brother and father. I'm not bragging. I'm being honest."

She disagreed, but kept her mouth shut. Again, for now, Chase needed his job.

"Did you know I have a daughter?" he asked.

"Yes, she's married to one of your agents, John Kain."

"Her mother didn't tell me about her, and I never met Celeste until she was an adult. I've always been a driven workaholic, but there are many times when I look back at my life and wonder how different things might have been had I been given the opportunity to be a real father to Celeste."

"I planned on telling Chase."

"I have no doubt. You have too much integrity." He stepped closer. "I like Chase," he repeated. "Even as a boy, he knew there was only one direction he could go, and that was up. I like hard workers and survivors. Knowing what he was capable of was the reason why I kept him with CORE when other employers would have let him go. I couldn't predict what would happen if he went to Cleveland either time, but I wanted to force him to face the demons haunting him. If that meant I'd lose him to you, I wouldn't have been happy about having to find a replacement, but I would have been happy for him." He gave her a wry smile that was almost smug. "Not only did I get to keep my agent, who's performing better than I'd hoped, but I have the opportunity to hire his future bride."

Summer had no idea what to make of this conversation or Ian. While he'd had his own agenda, the man, in his strange, manipulative way, had also tried to help Chase. "Then you're interested in employing me?"

"I had planned to approach you after the baby was born. I have a soft spot for former FBI agents, and with your background, I do think you'll be a valuable asset to CORE."

"I...thank you," she said, confused. Instead of telling her about his reasons for sending Chase, why hadn't he made the offer at the beginning of the conversation? Maybe it boiled down to him wanting to show that he was not just the owner of CORE, but an all-knowing, omnipotent jerk. Either way, she didn't care. As she'd learned more about CORE, their resources and investigations, she wanted to work for the agency. This way she could, in some capacity, work within law enforcement and do so with a healthy dose of work-life balance.

He offered his hand. "I look forward to working with you, even on a part-time basis. When you're ready for more hours, take them. I'll send you the official offer detailing salary, benefits, etcetera."

After shaking his hand, and thanking him again, she left the office. Chase was leaning against the wall in the hallway. He pushed himself off the wall, then approached her. "How'd it go?"

"Are you sure you're okay with us working together?"

He grinned. "You got the job." When she nodded, he pulled

her into his arms. "Congratulations." He leaned back. "I'm finished for the day. We have so much to celebrate, let's go home and get wild."

"Sounds good." She hooked her arm through his as they began walking down the hallway. "I'll break out the water bottles, while you carry over the boxes we need to unpack. It'll be epically wild."

Ian stepped away from the door and went to his desk. Summer and Chase were a good couple. Had he been bragging about his hand in getting them back together? Absolutely not. He wasn't a damned matchmaker, and had hoped Chase would return from Cleveland still single but missing his demons. He'd recruited Chase because the man could round out his team with his investigating and negotiating skills. But Chase had been a disappointment Ian hadn't been willing to give up on, not without trying to gain a return on the investment he'd made in him.

In the end, by manipulating the situation, he'd not only gotten the agent he had hoped for in Chase, but a former ASAC who had more balls than most men. When she'd been sitting across from him, he'd had to refrain himself from asking about Nicholas Janson. In a way, he almost wished she hadn't ended the boy's life. Nick had been an interesting individual, and he'd wanted to know what had made him so damned bad. Had it been psychological? Trauma as a child? Or had he been born carrying the Devil within him? He'd also wanted to ask her why she had chosen to kill Nick. Any of Summer's peers who'd been aware of her shooting skills had to wonder why her aim had been off that evening. Stress? Concern over her injured boyfriend? Worry about the baby she carried? Maybe one or all of the above.

He supposed it didn't matter why she'd decided to end his life. What mattered was that Emma was now safe.

The phone rang. He glanced at the time and admired Sloan's

punctuality. "Everything go as planned?" Ian asked after greeting the former undercover cop.

When he'd learned Summer had killed Nick, and that Patsy Janson had also died, he'd made the mistake of telling his fiancée, Cami, and his daughter, Celeste, about what had happened. Both women hadn't just urged him to help Emma, they had nagged him to the point where he'd wanted to drive ice picks through his ears. He understood their concern. Emma was young, wealthy, grieving and now alone. Given the chance, the media would eat her alive. Patsy hadn't been a household name, but she'd been well known. The fact that her son had not only devised the kidnapping, but had turned out to be a serial killer had made the story of Patsy and Nick's lives and deaths that much juicier.

While Ian donated to charities and such, he didn't usually help people unless there was something in it for him. The only thing he'd gain from assisting Emma would be a pat on the back from Cami. And he liked her pats. Being constantly around his fiancée, daughter and grandkids must have made him soft. Because after less than a day of consideration, he'd contacted Emma, and had made her an offer he knew she wouldn't refuse.

To protect the young woman from a media circus, he'd sent Sloan to Cleveland. From there, Sloan had used Ian's private jet to fly Emma to Chicago, where she'd stayed with Ian's friend, Maxine Morehouse. Maxine was also wealthy, a bit eccentric and completely trustworthy. She'd taken the girl in, had kept her whereabouts from the public, and had kept her safe. But Emma couldn't stay with Maxine forever. Once the media had moved on to other juicy news stories, Emma had decided it was time to leave and figure out what to do with the rest of her life.

"We've landed and I escorted Emma to the new truck," Sloan said. "What do you want me to do from here?"

"Nothing. She knows where to go. Come home. I have an assignment for you."

"I hope it's more exciting than delivering a package. Emma's a nice kid, but..."

Ian grinned. "How do you feel about going undercover again?"

"Beats flying an eighteen year old across the country. I'm getting back on the jet. I'll see you tomorrow."

Ian ended the call, then dialed another number. "It's Ian," he said. "She's there and heading your way."

"Got it. I'll keep an eye on her."

"Thanks, Sheriff. Call if you need anything." After Ian hung up the phone, he reached out to Cami.

"Well?" she asked. "Is Emma okay?"

"She's fine." He closed the file he had on the girl, stacked it with the one he'd created for Summer before he'd hired Chase, then slipped them into his briefcase. "Everything is going to be just fine."

Newhouse Academy, Dublin, Ohio
Wednesday, April 12th, 5:25 p.m. Eastern Standard Time

Brennan Williams gathered Newhouse Academy's varsity lacrosse players into a circle. Butterflies infused his stomach as he looked to his teammates who had elected him their captain. For support, he glanced to Alex, who'd dressed in a jersey but would sit out the season—doctor's orders.

Alex clapped. "You've got this," he shouted, rallying the others.

When the team whooped and hollered, Brennan regained his confidence. This was the first game of the season and it meant a lot to each of them. And not because of the team they were playing against.

"Lead your team." Their new head coach slung an arm around Alex's shoulders. "Who is this win for?"

Brennan met the eyes of each player. Every kid who'd been on the bus—with the exception of Nick the Dick—was there. Even Dillon Patricks had talked his parents, and senator grandpa, into letting him return. What did that say about them?

"We are survivors," he began, his original speech forgotten as he met Simon's encouraging gaze. The goalie lifted his lacrosse stick and released another shout. The guys laughed and joined him. Brennan waved his gloved hand to calm them. "This win is for us. For Coach Pembroke and Frank Stokes. For the FBI agent who killed Nick."

When the team cheered, Coach silenced them. "Brennan, you shouldn't go there."

"You can say that because you weren't with us. You didn't see men being murdered, you didn't watch your friend get shot, your other friends be beaten and terrorized while guns were pointed at your head. You don't understand the fear, the hatred or the betrayal." Brennan looked away from Coach and to the team. There was pride in their eyes and anger on their faces. "We've already faced our toughest competition. Before some of us were pulled out of the game early, we scored a few points and let our opponents know this wouldn't be an easy win for them." Tyler rested his gloved hand on Brennan's shoulder pad, while Chris nudged Alex with his elbow.

"The rest of you stayed in the game," Brennan continued, "and with guts and determination, you led us to victory." He raised his lacrosse stick. "Are we going to let anyone try to beat us down again?"

"No," the team shouted in unison as they all lifted their sticks to form a pyramid.

"Will we accept defeat?"

"No!"

"Then let's get out there and show the world we're survivors. Let's get out there and kick some ass!"

Brennan and his teammates rushed on the field, cheering and wearing their game faces. They went on to win the game, then the next and the next, until they finished the season with a perfect 15-0 record.

And none of them ever rode on a bus again...

****

Kristine will raffle off one $50 gift card among all subscribers of her newsletter each month. To sign up for Kristine's email newsletter please go to www.kristinemason.net.

**Look for Sloan's story in Sinful Vows
(Book 3 Sinful C.O.R.E.)
Fall 2017...**

Other Books by Kristine Mason

C.O.R.E. Shadow Trilogy

Shadow of Danger (Book 1)
Shadow of Perception (Book 2)
Shadow of Vengeance (Book 3)

Ultimate C.O.R.E. Trilogy

Ultimate Kill (Book 1)
Ultimate Fear (Book 2)
Ultimate Prey (Book 3)

C.O.R.E. Above the Law

Perfectly Twisted (Book 1)
Perfectly Toxic (Book 2)
Perfectly Tortured (Book 3)

Sinful C.O.R.E.

Sinful Deeds (Book 1)
Sinful Sacrifices (Book 2)

Psychic C.O.R.E.

Celeste Files: Unlocked (Book 1)
Celeste Files: Unjust (Book 2)
Celeste Files: Unforgotten (Book 3)
Celeste Files: Poisoned (Book 4)
Celeste Files: Possessed (Book 5)
Celeste Files: Primal (Book 6)

About Kristine Mason

Kristine Mason is the bestselling author of the popular romantic suspense trilogies, C.O.R.E. Shadow, Ultimate C.O.R.E. and C.O.R.E. Above the Law. She is currently working on her next C.O.R.E. series, along with more Psychic C.O.R.E. novels.

Although Kristine has published a few contemporary romance novels, she focuses most of her energy on her romantic suspense stories, which she loves for their blend of dark mystery/suspense and sexy romance. She is fascinated with what makes people afraid, and is famous for her depraved villains whose crimes present massive obstacles for her heroes and heroines to overcome.

Kristine has a degree in journalism from The Ohio State University and lives in Northeast Ohio with her husband, four kids, and adorable mutt. If she's not writing, she's chauffeuring kids, gardening, or collecting gnomes. Oh, and she makes a mean chocolate chip cookie, too!

Connect with Kristine on Facebook facebook.com/ kristinemasonauthor, Twitter @KristineMason7 or email her at authorkristinemason@gmail.com. You can also find out more about Kristine's books at www.kristinemason.net.